AUG 1 3 2016

MAHOMET PUBLIC LIBRARY DISTRICT

3 3031 00157 0270

COTTON

D1407695

COTTON

A NOVEL

PAUL J. HEALD

YUCCA

Mahomet Public Library District
1702 E. Oak Street
Mahomet, IL 61853-8526

Copyright © 2016 by Paul J. Heald

All rights reserved. No part of this book may be reproduced in any manner
without the express written consent of the publisher, except in the case of brief
excerpts in critical reviews or articles. All inquiries should be addressed to
Yucca Publishing, 307 West 36th Street, 11th Floor, New York, NY 10018.

Yucca Publishing books may be purchased in bulk at special discounts for
sales promotion, corporate gifts, fund-raising, or educational purposes. Special
editions can also be created to specifications. For details, contact the Special
Sales Department, Yucca Publishing, 307 West 36th Street, 11th Floor, New
York, NY 10018 or yucca@skyhorsepublishing.com.

Yucca Publishing® is an imprint of Skyhorse Publishing, Inc.®, a Delaware
corporation.

Visit our website at www.yuccapub.com.

10 9 8 7 6 5 4 3 2 1

Library of Congress Cataloging-in-Publication Data is available on file.

Cover design by Slobodan Cedic at KPSG
Cover photo credit: Bigstock/Bonish Photo

Print ISBN: 978-1-63158-086-4
Ebook ISBN: 978-1-63158-093-2

Printed in the United States of America

For Jill

COTTON

I.

GHOSTS: 2013

James Murphy made a deal with himself, and it worked for a while. During the increasingly long periods of time when his wife rebuffed his attempts at intimacy, he permitted himself to peruse lingerie shows on YouTube or surf through the PG-13 submissions on Mygirlfriendsbikini.com, just so long as he did not dip his toe into the cesspool of hardcore porn. He rigorously kept this promise, but as a volunteer deacon in the First Baptist Church of Clarkeston, Georgia, he was not supposed to indulge lustful impulses under any circumstances, so each click to a teasing bikini girlfriend came with a tug of guilt. Nonetheless, he carried on, regret never quite managing to divert his eyes from the computer monitor nor his hand from his manipulable mouse.

James sat in his study on a quiet Sunday afternoon, ignoring that morning's sermon on the tenth commandment and working his way through the week's newest swimsuit posts. Sondra was out shopping, and he clicked idly for almost a half hour before an unexpected image froze his restless finger and his hand fell to his side. He shook his head slowly and murmured an obscenity, unable to take his eyes from the familiar face smiling from the high-definition screen. He had never met her, but their relationship was truly intimate. Her eyes called out to him and his whole body went limp, initial shock giving way to failure and impotence. He had let her down, and now she was back and he was shaking.

The images on the monitor belonged to Diana Cavendish, a twenty-year-old dance major who had disappeared five years earlier, presumably abducted by her boyfriend from a blood-spattered apartment in downtown Clarkeston. James, an investigative reporter with the *Clarkeston Chronicle,* had covered the sensational story until—and well after—the authorities finally gave up on the case. And now Diana was suddenly back in his life, one hand on her hip and another touching a strand of hair teasingly close to pouting lips, languid body outlined distinctly in front of a white bedsheet. He had spent hours combing over every known photo of her, and he had never seen any of the pictures staring at him from the computer. Nor did he recognize the floral swimsuit she was wearing.

He gave his temples a hard rub, grimaced, and opened up an Excel spreadsheet stored in a file folder containing everything he had collected on the disappearance of Diana Cavendish. He confirmed that the official police inventory of her possessions listed no swimsuit, but that did not necessarily mean anything. The photos could have been taken long before the girl ever came to school at Clarkeston College. But there was something strange about the pictures, wholly apart from the fact that they had unexpectedly appeared in the "This Week's Babes" section of the website. Her expression in the photos was inviting . . . enigmatic. What had she been thinking as the shutter clicked?

He stood up and forced himself to look away. A cat was stalking squirrels in the backyard, its shoulders high and bobbing, slinking through the monkey grass like a miniature tiger. The tabby's prey scattered as soon as it leapt, but the unfazed feline hopped nonchalantly up on the birdbath, ignoring the angry chatter coming from above. James closed his eyes and pictured Diana in his mind, remembering the photo he published of her the day after her apartment had been forced open by the police. He held fast to that image, sat down again in front of the computer, and studied the series of pictures dispassionately.

Her hair. The bikini-clad beauty had short hair, clipped just to the edge of her ears, a thick wedge of meticulously groomed auburn locks. In every other photo he had seen, Diana sported luxuriously long tresses, falling well past her shoulders, obscuring her face in shots taken from the side. James knew every step she had taken during the week before the crime, every place she went, every person she talked to and what they talked about. Two days before her disappearance she went to her favorite salon and got her hair cut short for the first time in anyone's memory. Her longtime hairdresser was surprised by the request but did a beautiful job, or so her friends said. Only her boyfriend, a photographer for the newspaper named Jacob Granville, did not like the new look. It was one of several things they argued about that week.

He studied the face one more time, checking for any signs of aging that would indicate the photo was somehow of recent vintage. What a wonderful thought: Diana resting peacefully, on vacation. He wished with all his heart that he could give her that peace. Then he noticed that the sheet hanging behind her did not completely hide the corner of a bookshelf. He recognized it from her apartment and shivered involuntarily. Within two days of the haircut and the taking of these pictures, she had disappeared, perhaps killed by the person holding the camera.

He almost bookmarked the page, but the paranoia he had developed during his investigation of Diana's disappearance resurfaced and instead he wrote down the URL and slipped it into his pocket. Then he deleted all temporary Internet files and search history, logged off the computer, and left the house, looking for a place to carefully consider what to do with the potential story of a lifetime.

Clarkeston, Georgia, was experiencing a particularly colorful spring, but James barely noticed the blossoming fruit trees lining the residential streets on his way downtown. He briefly considered driving west and out into the countryside, but the winding roads and kudzu-covered fields were not conducive to meditation, unless one wanted to run into a ditch. Besides, he did not crave loneliness and green vistas. He needed to be closer to the epicenter of the disaster, nurse a hot coffee, and figure out what the hell to do next.

As he turned away from an avenue of gracious older homes and onto the edge of downtown, he spotted an angled parking slot a half block from Clarkeston's best café. The meter needed no feeding on Sunday, and soon he was working his way around the racks of dresses on the sidewalk in front of the vintage clothing store that shared space with the coffee shop in an old remodeled bank. He pushed open the polished brass door, placed his order, and took a quick look around while a tattooed hipster in a stiff plaid hat frothed his latte. On a sunny afternoon in May, the interior of the place was almost empty, the student clientele preferring to squeeze themselves around the tiny tile-covered tables that sat outside.

He absentmindedly loaded up his drink with artificial sweetener and cinnamon and walked out into dazzling sunshine. The air was mild and carried no hint of the oppressive summer weather that waited just around the corner. Having grown up in the breezy mountains of western North Carolina, James had never made his peace with Clarkeston in July and August, but early May was a different beast altogether and the antebellum brick warehouses that dotted the business district were glowing gently in the late afternoon sun. He treasured every feature of the town as if it were an old friend. He often wrote as though the town were alive, both a reader and a character in his news stories.

As he rounded the corner and passed the courthouse, he approached Diana Cavendish's old apartment. Someone had spray-painted *remember* on the bricks next to the front door several years earlier; repeated scrubbings and pounding rain had failed to erase its urgent whisper.

According to her friends, Diana had been both a free spirit, caring little what the mainstream thought about her, and a community-minded volunteer who spent much of her free time helping children in various public dance programs around the county. The Clarkeston Park District had been about to give her its big yearly service award when she disappeared. She had grown up in a wealthy suburb of Atlanta but eschewed the ubiquitous sorority scene at Clarkeston College. Her friends, mostly other dancers, described her as loyal and passionate about anything that interested her. Unfortunately, this included several boyfriends who had failed to charm her inner circle. She was *so* original, a fellow dancer had explained, but such a cliché when it came to men. The edgier the man, the more she was intrigued. James resented this side of her. Were he twenty years younger, maybe things would have turned out differently.

He turned away from Diana's building and headed toward the Episcopal church that occupied a nearby corner of Main Street, right across from the obelisk commemorating the town's fallen in the Civil War. The memorial sat in the middle of a small grassy square, and James crossed the street and slumped down on a green bench facing the church. The neo-Gothic structure had been built at the same time as the college campus on the far side of the river that paralleled Main Street, and it managed to pay homage to the past without committing historical parody. The limestone and granite chosen by the architect blended easily with the older downtown buildings. James had always envied the Episcopalians the elegance of their house of worship compared with the clunky plantation-style pillars of his own First Baptist complex.

Unfortunately, the dignified old building had almost certainly watched the murderer of Diana Cavendish grow up in its congregation, and a former priest may well have conspired with the sheriff and the district attorney to keep her boyfriend from justice. James' sources suggested that Jacob Granville still had influential friends in the incestuous world of town and temple, and James could not discharge his duty to Diana simply by making a call to the local authorities alerting them to the new online photos, nor did he want to unnecessarily risk his own neck by doing so.

He took a sip of coffee, flicked a ladybug off of his pants leg, and then took another sip and sighed. The proper course of action was really pretty obvious. What did one do in the South when one caught a whiff of local political corruption? Go to the feds, of course, and that meant driving to Atlanta and talking to a bunch of transplanted midwesterners who would probably do nothing more than nod condescendingly at his tale. He did not look forward to dealing with the US attorney's office, nor did he relish the time-sucking drive to Georgia's sprawling capital, but he owed it to the victim and to himself. He had worked as hard as the detectives on the case and run into the same brick walls. He had failed her, but maybe now the feds could track down the source of the swimsuit photos and finally crack the case of the young student's bloody disappearance and presumed death.

As he stood up and tossed his cup into the garbage bin, he wondered whether he might find some way to help spur the feds into action or maybe even track down the perpetrator himself. Who knew what sort of reactions he might be able to get by flashing a new picture of Diana at folks who had not thought about her for years? Maybe the passage of time had loosened some tongues. There was no reason why his own queries might not reveal as much as the authorities'.

James ran his hand through his hair and rubbed the back of his neck as a gust of wind rustled the litter collecting at the base of the obelisk. A quick look up reminded him that many of the same surnames etched on the granite memorial still populated the St. James church rolls. Yeah, Atlanta was the best place to start his journey, and after he returned, he needed to make two more visits, one to his wife and one to his pastor. Secrets did not stay undiscovered for long in Clarkeston, and if the pictures reopened the investigation, then the whole town would soon know that its star reporter and volunteer deacon had been spending time at Mygirlfriendsbikini.com. Thank god, it wasn't outright porn, just titillating poolside photos sent in by persuasive boyfriends. The possibility of a more malevolent photographic intent had not occurred to him until he saw Diana offered up as the website's "treat of the week."

II.

IDYLLS

First assistant US attorney Melanie Wilkerson was too young for a mid-life crisis. Still in her early forties and fresh off her ninth marathon, she carried herself with a bounce and confidence that betrayed no regrets about the past and no doubts about the future. So, why did she feel like moving to Atlanta had been a mistake? She tapped her fingers on the windowsill of her spacious office and looked out over the asphalt parking lot next to the federal building. Springtime in Georgia and not a single dogwood or azalea in sight. She wondered if newly appointed federal prosecutors had any jurisdiction over the gardening around the massive office complex. Probably not. She could help hunt down serial killers and shut down meth labs all over the Southeast, but putting some barrels of pansies in the parking lot probably required more power than she was allowed to wield.

She spun back in her chair and checked the agenda that her assistant had laid next to her computer. The first meeting of the day was with a newspaper reporter from Clarkeston. Now that was a city with no shortage of flowers. Twenty years earlier, she had spent a year in the pretty college town clerking for a federal judge and developing a taste for criminal prosecution that earned her dizzying success in Washington, DC, and a move back south to head up a team of crack federal prosecutors (or, as she sometimes called them, federal *crack* prosecutors). She had grown up in Atlanta, but had returned to Georgia only once in the ten years before taking the new job. That lone trip was for her judge's funeral on an appropriately grim and rainy day, but she never forgot the tidal wave of color during her one spring in Clarkeston. Of course, young stupid love tends to make flowers more vibrant.

But she had not come to Atlanta for the flowers, nor was she merely fleeing a tattered relationship with a commitment-phobic FBI agent. Ambition and opportunity had brought her home, but the first six months on the job had yet to offer anything interesting to justify the move back, and a hint of that old southern lassitude had begun to seep into her bones.

"Mr. Murphy to see you, ma'am," a bright voice popped over the phone, and before she could hang up, a middle-aged man stuck his head in and knocked on her door frame.

"Come on in." She waved him to a chair facing her desk. He was slim, with a thick shock of graying hair pushed back over his forehead and an anxious look on his face. She recognized the type. If she put him on the lie-detector machine and asked him if he killed JFK, his nervous denial would register a lie even if he'd never been to Texas.

She introduced herself and offered her hand over the desk. "What can we do for you, Mr. Murphy? You were a little vague with my assistant."

His voice was not what she expected. It was strong, with a dry hint of a drawl, his manner straightforward and self-assured. "I'm not usually so paranoid, but I'd like to keep what I have to say between you and me for now." He took out a battered black notebook, much like the ones her FBI investigators sometimes used, and flipped it open.

"About five years ago—to be precise, four years, ten months, and six days ago—a young woman named Diana Cavendish disappeared—presumed murdered—in Clarkeston. I covered the story for the local newspaper and in between flower shows and pet-rescue stories spent around three months investigating the case." He looked up and tapped his swollen notebook as if to emphasize that there was a lot more that he could say. "To summarize: The police found a large amount of blood and a bullet in her apartment, but her body was never found. The last person seen with her was her boyfriend, a part-time photographer for the newspaper who also disappeared at the same time. Most people assume that he killed her, hid her body, and fled, but he was the son of the district attorney in town and the investigation may have been . . . well, flawed."

The tale was interesting, but Melanie failed to see the immediate connection to any sort of federal crime. "Was there evidence that she was taken across state lines? Was the FBI alerted that the boyfriend had fled the state?"

"The FBI was not informed until three days after the disappearance." He spoke in a tone that suggested the delay was intentional. "As far as I know, the feds never found any evidence of where her boyfriend went." Murphy put his notepad on his lap and continued. "I'm not really here to complain about the local cops." A brief smile suggested, however, that he would be happy to do so on a moment's notice. "I'm here to talk about what I saw Saturday on my computer." He paused and a slight flush infused his face.

"And that was . . . ?"

He sighed, took off his glasses, and polished them while he spoke. "I was surfing a website called Mygirlfriendsbikini.com. It's sort of like YouTube, but guys post pictures of their girlfriends in swimsuits—nothing racier than that," he emphasized before daring to put his glasses back on and glance up at her. "Anyway, I clicked on one of the photo series and up pops Diana Cavendish. She's wearing a floral bikini and posing for the camera."

"Five years is quite a while for someone to wait to post a picture." Melanie thought back to a child-pornography case she had prosecuted in Maryland. It was amazing how quickly a single set of photos could find its way around the world. "Maybe it was posted years ago; a lot of this trash gets recycled from site to site."

"Maybe." He looked relieved that she was focusing on the mystery and not his taste for swimwear. "But there's two more things." He reached into his breast pocket and handed her a printout of one of the pictures. "First, her hair. She got it cut short for the first time in years the week before she was killed."

Even in black-and-white print, on regular computer paper, the prosecutor could see that Diana Cavendish had been beautiful. She had a lovely round face with high cheekbones and a stunning figure.

"Second," the reporter continued, "that swimsuit is not described in the inventory of her possessions taken after the murder." He pulled another paper out of his pocket and handed it to her. "I think she may have been shot in it."

She studied the spreadsheet of items found in the Cavendish apartment. This sort of information was not typically shared with the public, especially not with reporters. She handed it back to him. "How did you get this?"

"I helped make it." He shrugged and explained. "Some of the police were dragging their feet in the investigation. My friend on the force was not. We entered Diana's apartment without the permission of the lead detective and looked around."

The guy clearly had some big ones if he was willing to stick his nose so deep into a potentially corrupt murder investigation. He might be slightly younger than she first thought, about her age probably, early forties or so. Vaguely handsome, too, in a Liam Neeson sort of way, despite the concern creasing his brow. "Do you have anything else?"

"No, just the pictures. I've written the website URL on the back of the printout I gave you." He blushed again. "I'm sorry to admit that I know the postings are new on the site. I called you as soon as I saw them."

She smiled and was briefly tempted to pry into his web-surfing habits, but making him squirm would be poor sport. "Like I said before, this is very interesting for its own sake, but exactly what would you like us to do? We need some sort of basis to assert federal jurisdiction. I mean, the website shows use of interstate instrumentalities, but you're just guessing that there's a connection to the crime."

"It's a good guess, though, isn't it?"

She tilted her head doubtfully in response.

"I was hoping that you could track down the person who uploaded the photos. Whoever took the photos was probably either the perpetrator or one of the last people to see her." His eyes brightened. "How about interstate distribution of stolen evidence?"

"If the killer took the photos and uploaded them, then they're not stolen."

"Interstate obstruction of evidence?"

"I don't see how posting something for the world to see is obstruction."

"Well," Murphy persisted, "he hid vital evidence for years."

"That's usually not a crime unless the government first asks you to hand it over and you don't." She smiled. "And besides, the crime is hiding it, and that was not necessarily done across state lines." The reporter was starting to grow on her. Instead of yelling about First Amendment rights and justice, he seemed to understand that at the federal level, the jurisdiction game needed to be played first.

"But if your tech people discovered that the photos were uploaded from another state, then you'd have evidence that the suspect, or at least a prime witness, had fled and crossed state lines." He leaned forward in his chair, poised to launch his next riposte.

"Fair enough," she replied, as she turned her attention to her computer and rapidly tapped and clicked her way to a confidential FBI database, "but still awfully thin." She stared at the screen for a moment and entered some more information. "Didn't you say that the FBI was alerted three days after the crime?"

"That's what I was told when I asked the detective how the manhunt for Jacob Granville was going." He slipped his notebook back into his jacket pocket. "Granville was the boyfriend."

She entered the names of the suspect photographer and the victim into the database and gave a little hum of curiosity. "There's no request here for help finding either Jacob Granville or Diana Cavendish," she said, with a brief frown at the confidential notation she saw next to Granville's name, "nothing that indicates fugitive status." She turned toward Murphy. "That's pretty unusual, given the suspicion of abduction and flight." She paused. "You're only . . . what . . . fifty miles or so from the South Carolina border?"

"More or less. And less than a hundred from North Carolina and Tennessee."

"Tell me more about the investigation." She smiled again, welcoming the distraction from the endless parade of drug cases coming through her office. There were hundreds of interesting federal crimes on the books, yet ninety percent of her time was spent on a single one: Possession of Narcotics with Intent to Distribute. Her career had started with a juicy murder case but she had not had another one since. "We've been known to intervene upon evidence of a conspiracy to deny someone her civil rights."

"I can't give you any definite evidence of a conspiracy." He offered her his first smile of the day. "I'd have a Pulitzer on my desk if I could prove anything for sure." She reached for a yellow pad and took notes while he spoke, backtracking and adding information from the beginning of the interview whenever he paused.

"Diana Cavendish was a dance major at Clarkeston College and had been dating Jacob Granville off and on for almost a year when she went missing. By all accounts they were a mercurial couple but didn't seem to have an abusive relationship. They were last seen together at a bar on a Friday night. She didn't show up for work on Monday morning, but no one got suspicious until a neighbor complained of her dog barking incessantly. On Monday evening, the landlord went to investigate and found Diana's dog had tracked her blood all over the apartment."

He popped a mint into his mouth and continued. "The investigation was screwed up from the get-go. To start off with, neither of the city's detectives could be found and way too many regular cops went in and out of the crime scene before it was secured. The dog didn't make matters any better either. It had spent the weekend ripping the place up and smearing blood everywhere. When the detectives finally got on the case, they put everything on total lockdown." He paused. "Jacob Granville was not only a part-time colleague of mine, but he was the son of a prominent family. He had grown up in Clarkeston and everyone important in town knew him. The sheriff had taught him how to throw a football, for chrissakes."

A look of disgust crossed his face. "You or I would have called in the state police immediately to take over, but that didn't happen. Everything was done in-house and not very transparently. Jacob was never found and no one was ever charged. Suffice it to say that many people in Clarkeston have their doubts about how hard the cops were looking for him."

"How well did you know him?"

"Not well. He had been with the newspaper a year or so when he disappeared." The reporter thought for a moment. "He was a good-looking guy and very ambitious. He clearly saw his job in Clarkeston as just a stepping stone to bigger things elsewhere. He was a little hard to read, quite frankly."

"You said that Granville never turned up." Melanie stopped writing for a moment and pushed a strand of blond hair behind her ear. "Cavendish was never found either, right?"

"No, ma'am. There were rumors that someone saw his car driving out of town early on Saturday morning, but I could never get the cops to admit it."

"Did they find the car?"

"No. The Georgia Bureau of Investigation eventually got involved, but it never found anything either. A source of mine there claimed that the local cops were not very cooperative, but he wouldn't elaborate."

"Well, the weirdest thing to me is that the FBI didn't swoop in." She got up and looked out the window. Nine out of ten people at the US attorney's office would thank James Murphy for the information and politely send him on his way. The FBI was not going to be very interested in an old domestic-violence case, even if there were some promise of unearthing a little local corruption. On the other hand, she had solved one cold case in Clarkeston already, and it would be nice to have an excuse to get out of Atlanta and see some flowers.

She sat back down at her desk. "Thank you so much for coming by. We'll definitely be in touch." The reporter got up and reached his hand in the breast pocket of his jacket. With an apologetic shrug, he handed her his business card.

"Please don't hesitate to contact me." At the door, he turned. "I never met Diana Cavendish, but after so many years of studying her, I've come to know her pretty well." He paused and his eyes flashed. "She was a caring person who helped a whole lot of kids in Clarkeston. She did not deserve to die, and whoever did this does not deserve to get away with it."

After he left, Melanie looked at the web address scrawled on the back of the photo of the murdered girl. She flipped the paper over and studied the young student's face. The FBI database said nothing about the abduction or any formal investigation, but a note and phone number next to Granville's name stated that any inquiries about him should be reported. Maybe a little digging by the computer staff on the source of the pictures wouldn't be a bad idea. Something was a little whiffy about the case, and sometimes one scratch at the surface was enough to uncover all sorts of interesting social rot.

III.

NOTHINGNESS

A man in a pale windbreaker trudged up the side of Mt. Baldy and took a moment to stare down on the eastern edge of Los Angeles. He kept hoping that the view would improve as he approached the ten-thousand-foot summit, but instead the chlorine-yellow air over the city mushroomed more densely with every step. A climber's website had claimed that the ocean was visible on a clear day, and he paused at a rocky outcrop and peered to the west. The horizon was so indistinct that he could only guess where the coastline lay. Turning his back on the city, he sat down, pulled out a Nalgene container, and took a long drink of water. The view to the east was clearer, and he could trace where the trail had emerged from the tree line and wound its way through a dozen switchbacks to his feet.

He took another sip and continued his climb. Late spring meant remnants of winter snow, but he had wagered that his well-worn pair of hiking boots would be sufficient, given that the climb was supposedly entirely nontechnical. A pair of gaiters would have been nice, though, to keep the ice crystals from slipping past his ankles. The top of the snow was glazed and crusted, but his boots broke through to rock with every step and he sensed no danger of slipping and sliding down the steep ravine on his right.

By the time he crossed the last patch of snow, his socks were soaked, but the sun was shining and it was fifty degrees, perfect weather to be at altitude, even if the air below was so bad that

LA was just a brown smudge in the distance. When he found the brass elevation plate marking the top, he sat down and took out a sandwich and bag of chips that he had bought at the Vons back down in Claremont. He ate slowly, started on his second bottle of water, and pushed the detritus of his picnic deep into his backpack. When he was through, he took out a candy bar and cursed when he saw that he had mistakenly bought one laden with nuts. He broke off a piece, sucked away the chocolate from around a large almond, and spit it onto the rocks at his feet. He continued until the chocolate bar was consumed and the small pile of nuts had attracted two curious blackbirds. Then he zipped up his pack, took one last look over the city he had come to hate, put his head in his hands, and began to cry.

★ ★ ★

Stanley Hopkins had lived a Southern California dream for almost two years. He had come to LA as a sociology professor hoping to complete the first serious academic study of women working in the porn industry. Although his scholarly mission had failed and his work was rejected by his home institution in the Midwest, his videotaped interviews had been used as the backbone of a successful documentary. A private liberal arts college in Claremont with less squeamish sensibilities than his former public employer asked him to join its faculty, and soon he became the go-to expert on the sleazy world of adult media for both the talk-show circuit and the LAPD. Between his salary, some film royalties, and appearance and consulting fees, he quickly amassed a surprising amount of savings. He and his wife bought a small home on the plain beneath Mt. Baldy and awaited the arrival of their first child, conceived in the turbulence of his fateful visit to California.

Their daughter was eighteen months old when his wife merged onto I-10 heading west and was pinned between a semi-trailer and a large SUV whose impatient driver had tried to squeeze illegally past her on the right. Both the trucker and the other driver suffered minor injuries, but Angela and Carrie were killed instantly when their car disappeared underneath the semi. He had been relaxing on their back deck when the phone rang with news of the accident. He refused to bury them in the state that he blamed for taking them away, and he ignored the wishes of his inlaws that they be buried thousands of miles away in an Atlanta suburb. So they were cremated and still sat in the laundry room, where he set them after the memorial service. He originally planned to scatter them from the peak of Mt. Baldy, but once he got to the summit, the gesture felt wrong. Hiking was his thing, not hers. She had never really appreciated the barren beauty above the tree line.

Inertia kept Stanley in Los Angeles, and his classes at Belle Meade College provided the best weapon against the morbid thoughts and depression that plagued him when he had too much free time to think. The college was only a twenty-minute bike ride from his house, and his students provided some distraction. They seemed to have a more genuine interest in his courses than his former students in Illinois. This might be explained by the fact that Belle Meade wanted him to teach upper-level electives like the Sociology of Media, whereas he had previously been stuck teaching required classes like Introduction to Sociology to hundreds of bored freshmen.

In his media course, he assigned the students an alternating diet of reality television and traditional texts, while lecturing about the interaction of human subjects within groups, the distorting effects of observation, and the creation of norms of judgment and leadership. He had no opinion about the aesthetics of the shows or whether reality television constituted a legitimate art form, but he was convinced that he could teach almost all of undergraduate sociology by observing social interaction in *Survivor, America's Next Top Model, Project Runway, Flavor of Love, Charm School,* and *Top Chef.* He felt especially vindicated on days when the students dove into the textbook and illustrated their understanding of traditional doctrines of group formation by reference to Tim Gunn and Heidi Klum.

His other course, provocatively entitled Social Exploitation of Women was even livelier and often kept him after class, arguing with those willing to defend pornography in one form or another and with their counterparts who thought he was too open minded. True to his early training as a lawyer, he found his teaching method becoming more and more Socratic, with the result being a more rewarding engagement with his students. But at the end of the day, he still had to go home, pass through the laundry room into the kitchen, and cook a meal for one.

The day after his mountain hike, the young professor sat in his office watching a couple of students toss a Frisbee around the small quadrangle that fronted the student union. He had no plans for the summer. When invitations for conferences were issued around the time of the accident, he tossed them away or hit the delete button without even reading them. Belle Meade taught almost no summer-school classes, preferring instead to encourage its students to study abroad, which left Stanley with a three-month vacation looming before him, a terrifying state of affairs that earned little sympathy from anyone he knew with a nine-to-five job.

As he got up from his chair and reached for his coffee mug, the phone rang, and he greeted the LAPD detective on the other end of the line. Stanley had been helping out the vice squad on a complex human-trafficking investigation. The case involved the forced immigration and prostitution of Eastern European women, and the police were trying to find a link to a major player in the American porn industry. His prior research had introduced him to a number of producers and directors. He had been happy to sit in on strategy sessions with the detectives as a pro bono consultant, and they were grateful for his suggestions on who would be worth interviewing.

The detective explained that the case was heating up again and wanted to know if he had some free time. Sure, Stanley answered without deliberation. Spending the summer with sleaze and crime just about fit his mood. After he hung up, he grabbed his coffee mug and tried to decide whether he wanted to make the walk across the quad to the campus Starbucks. He stared at the mug for a moment and then slid it back across his desk. There was really nothing that he wanted to pour into it.

IV.

KINGDOMS

"Father Thor, what were you thinking when you suggested these hymns for Sunday?" A stout woman swathed in gray tweed stood in front of the priest's desk, quivering with indignation. "They are totally inappropriate!"

The priest had a perfectly good theological explanation for why he had selected several traditional Epiphany hymns for the fourth Sunday after Easter, but he knew better than to argue with Shelly Woodall, longtime choir director and organist of St. James Episcopal Church in Clarkeston, Georgia. She not only looked like Margaret Thatcher, she took the same defiant and combative approach to every issue, from the proper length of the choir robes to the font style of the numbers posted on the hymn board. The last time he had crossed her, the entire alto section of the choir shunned him for a week.

"Could you suggest some alternatives?" He responded weakly, hoping to maneuver her out of his office. She chided him for not asking for advice earlier and then left in a scuffle of worsted wool.

Thorsten V. Carter had been in charge of St. James for only two years. He preferred Thor as a nickname, with its racy pagan connotations, instead of Thorsten, the name of his father's favorite economist. Many in his stiff and old-fashioned congregation chose to call him Father Carter, when they referred to him by name at all. Although St. James was a prime parish, located in a pretty college town full of wealthy professionals that made stewardship campaigns a breeze, the congregation had a horrible reputation for troubling its priests soon after they arrived. Since priests in the Episcopal Church were technically employees of the diocese and not the parish, the church had been fighting with the bishop for years and had gotten the reputation of being a snake pit. Only a handful of candidates had applied for what in other circumstances would have been a plum job, and the parish committee recommended young Thorsten (certainly not one of the two female candidates!), who at the time was only three years out of seminary. His first job in a small mission parish in rural Illinois had in no way prepared him for the parade of self-righteous congregants who frowned in disapproval as they shook his hand after the Sunday service.

By all accounts, the last popular priest in the parish had been Ernest Rodgers, who had served during all of the 1970s and 1980s and most of the 1990s. After he retired, he lurked around the parish for years, contrary to diocesan policy, and had only passed away six months earlier. A stack of his boxes still sat in the choir-room closet, guarded jealously by Woodall, whose loyalty to Rodgers's memory bordered on fanatical. A bronze plaque bearing his name and profile graced a prominent position in the foyer of the church.

Thor checked his computer for his next appointment and put his feet up on his desk when he saw that he had another hour before the altar guild arrived and presented him with their yearly flower and linen budget. His office had been remodeled by Father Rodgers, and the massive cherry desk provided plenty of space for a footrest. Dark walnut bookcases towered behind him and lined the wall facing the window. An eighteenth-century print of Canterbury Cathedral took up most of the space on the wall next to the doorway. Through the door lay the vestibule where the church secretary had her desk and photocopy machine. Heavy velvet curtains hung next to the windows, but the young priest had tied them back to maximize the amount of sunlight in the dark office. He wished he were bold enough to put up a poster of his favorite English folk-rock band, James, but a parish that sometimes referred to him as Doogie Howser, MDiv, was not ready for any such unconventional move.

Were it not for the windows looking out onto the shady parking lot and playground beyond, he would have felt completely suffocated in the space. So, he spent a lot of time resting his eyes on the greenery and watching visitors approach the church. He had developed a sixth sense for trouble as it came up the sidewalk and had become adept at preparing for it by rehearsing a quick speech or darting into the bathroom down the hall.

Thirty minutes before the arrival of the altar guild, Thor saw a middle-aged man in a blue seersucker suit park his car and head toward the church. He looked vaguely familiar, and the priest hoped that he was not a parishioner whose name he really should remember.

The man introduced himself as a newspaper reporter and a Baptist deacon, and the young priest thought that he recognized the name on the business card he was handed. He seldom looked at bylines, but he remembered a very even-handed story by James Murphy about several Muslim families, mostly associated with Clarkeston College, who had established a tiny mosque in a storefront in a failed strip mall. The article emphasized the mosque's charitable works in the community and was accompanied by a large photo of smiling children. The story had made the transplanted midwesterner less apprehensive about his new home and rather ashamed of his presumption that a story about Muslims in a small-town Georgia newspaper would have to be negative. He mentioned his appreciation of the article to his visitor and asked Murphy what he wanted.

"I'm doing a story on a murder that took place before you came to Clarkeston." The reporter gave an outline of the disappearance of a community-minded student named Diana Cavendish. As the fifth anniversary of the murder approached, the newspaper was planning on running a retrospective, complete with pictures of the girl and appeals from the authorities for those with information to come forward. "St. James," he added as he cleared his throat, "was sort of at the heart of the initial investigation."

Thor was not surprised that he had heard nothing about the matter from his congregation. After all, it had taken the vestry three months to inform him that the absent junior warden had resigned and was not just on vacation.

"The prime suspect in the killing grew up in this church. His name is Jacob Granville." The name meant nothing to the young priest. "His parents moved shortly after the investigation was concluded, but I believe the sheriff at the time is still a member here."

Thor nodded. Sheriff Porter Johnson was a regular attendee, a large, bluff fellow who had told Thor on several occasions that he had been raised Baptist and suffered St. James because his wife was a cradle Episcopalian who could not forsake her favorite Anglican hymns and the "bells and smells" of feast days.

"The sheriff and Jacob Granville's father worked closely together for years. The older Granville was the prosecuting attorney for the county at the time of the murder." The reporter spoke cautiously and watched Thor closely, as if gauging his reaction to the news, with a peek over the top of his glasses. "He claimed that he stayed away from the investigation, but few people believed him."

Thor wondered what all this had to do with him, but he continued nodding his head and encouraged Murphy to keep talking. The church was full of secrets that he was not deemed worthy of knowing. Sometimes he felt like the nerdy high school student who was never told the location of the big party until after it was over. The reporter was passionate about the death of Cavendish, and, without being too blatant, had successfully communicated that someone or something in the tight-knit southern community may have thwarted justice. He had experienced enough impediments in his own ministry to be sympathetic to the journalist's mission.

"In the middle of all this mess was Ernest Rodgers, your predecessor here. No matter how much evidence stacked up against Jacob Granville, he'd tell anyone who would listen that the kid could not possibly be the murderer." Murphy motioned to a small portrait of the priest hanging on the wall. "He must have written a dozen letters to the editor. Heck, he even preached it from the pulpit."

The reporter explained how the Cavendish murder had marked the end of an era in Clarkeston. As in many southern towns, the power elite had long congregated at the downtown Episcopal church, but even before the death of Diana Cavendish, its influence had begun to dissipate. Politics at all levels had become dominated by evangelical Bible-thumpers, not adherents to the Book of Common Prayer. Despite the fact that Jefferson Davis and his vice president had both been good Episcopalians, the church was not nearly conservative enough anymore to attract the new breed of politicians and businessmen determined to bring their born-again theology into all walks of public life. The people who wielded the real power in Clarkeston were some flavor of Baptist or Pentecostal or attended one of the new nondenominational megachurches that kept springing up along the ring road circling Clarkeston. The murder and perceived cover-up were the final blow to St. James's dominance. Power flowed elsewhere now.

"Thanks for the history lesson, Mr. Murphy," Thor replied, with a genuine appreciation of a fresh perspective on his church and his flock. Much of Clarkeston, Georgia, was still a mystery. "But I'm not sure what any of this has to do with me."

"Nothing, really," the reporter said. He sat back in his chair and cast a glance out the window before he spoke further. "I just came here to ask you a favor." He smiled and polished his spectacles while he continued. "I was hoping that you might let me have a look at Father Rodgers's papers. I've been told that they're still around here somewhere, and no one has ever poked through them to see if they might shed some light on the whole story."

Despite the reporter's inoffensive demeanor, alarm bells started going off in the young priest's head. What good could come of letting an outsider poke through his predecessor's boxes?

Just because Thor didn't like Father Rodgers's decorating tastes did not mean that his privacy was forfeit. Although the congregation's devotion to the departed priest grated at times, Rodgers himself had always been very civil. In fact, as he lay terminally ill in the hospital, he let it be known that he wanted Thor to conduct his funeral. This gesture generated some temporary goodwill, but not enough to prevent the vestry from inviting a bishop from North Carolina to lead the service.

"I'm not sure that I can let you see his private papers, Mr. Murphy."

"Call me James."

"The papers aren't mine," the priest reasoned aloud, "and they're technically not the church's either. They probably belong to Mrs. Rodgers."

"Then," the reporter said gravely and with evident sincerity, "I have an even bigger favor to ask you: could you ask her permission to share them?"

Thor tried to explain how difficult talking to her would be but quickly realized that the reporter already understood. Murphy had a baleful expression on his face and the posture of a knowing supplicant. The widow Rodgers was one of the thorniest people the transplanted midwesterner had ever met. She was a native of Clarkeston, and he had no doubt that her fierce reputation was as well known as it was well earned. On the other hand, he had not seen her since the funeral and had been putting off making a visit to inquire why she seemed to have abandoned St. James. And the vestry had pointed out in their last meeting that she was an elderly and wealthy woman who needed to be approached about leaving part of her estate to her husband's parish. "Exactly what would you want me to do?"

"Well," his visitor could not help but grin, "don't tell her that I want to poke through his stuff. She can't stand me." He stood up and moved toward the desk. "Just ask her if she wants it. My guess is that she doesn't care, or she'd have picked it up already. If she says no, then it's abandoned and you can do whatever you want." He reached out his right hand and laid the palm flat on the priest's desk. "And you can count on me not to reveal my sources. If I find any useful information in there, no one will ever know where it came from."

Thor nodded, his mind already contemplating what approach to take with the formidable old widow. The problem of the boxes actually gave him a nice excuse to pay her a visit. It would provide a neutral topic to justify their conversation and maybe even help him move deftly to the question of a bequest for the church. He thanked the reporter for stopping by and made a mental note to see Mrs. Rodgers the following day.

V.

EXITS

James Murphy shut the door to his car and decided to make a stop on the way home from St. James. He had a hunch that something was going to explode with the Cavendish story. A niggling itch behind his right ear told him that somehow, for better or for worse, all hell was going to break loose. The feds might trace the pictures back to a mountain cabin containing Jacob Granville, or Ernest Rodgers's old boxes might yield a scrawled confession. Something was going to happen if he kept pushing, and when he finally broke through the last barrier, a Pulitzer Prize for investigative reporting stood sparkling within his grasp, and peace and closure would finally come to the family of Diana Cavendish.

The cause of the breakthrough, of course, would be clear to anyone reading his as-yet-unwritten award-winning story. Without the serendipitous discovery of the racy photos of the victim, the mystery would have remained unsolved, and that meant questions would be asked about the source of the discovery. And that meant lying to avoid embarrassment or confessing at some point that he sometimes surfed the net looking at photos of bikini-clad young women. He could dissemble and say that he received a tip from a confidential source. That might elicit some snickers at the Pulitzer press conference, but no one would be able to prove that the resolution of the mystery had begun with his own failings. Murphy saw the out that was available, but he hesitated to take it. He had the strong intuition that if he paid no personal price for the story, it would never materialize in the first place.

In the South, superstition and guilt get tangled in spectacular ways, and the middle-aged deacon was susceptible to seeing the fortunate and unfortunate events in his life as related to sins successfully resisted or those slavishly indulged. One never heard the word *karma* at the First Baptist Church of Clarkeston, Georgia, but the notion was alive and well in various doctrines associated with blessing and retribution. James was not merely chagrined by his inability to stay away from the sleazy side of the Internet, he felt guilty about his weakness. Lusting in one's heart was a sin and there was no denying that his gazes were lustful. And the fact that he evoked those alluring images in his head on the increasingly rare occasions when his wife wanted to have sex affirmed the sinfulness of his surfing habits. So he had two reasons to visit Pastor Johnson at his home church, a genuine sense of shame and the superstition that he needed to come clean or the Diana Cavendish murder would never be solved. There was a price to be paid and he needed to pay it.

The middle-aged penitent pulled into the parking lot of the massive church and sat for a moment contemplating the white Doric columns supporting the roof of the old sanctuary. The nineteenth-century space that used to house the entire congregation had been relegated to children's activities after a new addition was built in the early 1980s. The church now took up most of a city block, with its two thousand members struggling to find parking space downtown on Sunday mornings. He would have preferred to attend the small Methodist church near his home, but his wife had grown up at First Baptist and he stood no chance of moving her away from her power base.

He got out of the car and walked over to the side entrance to the church office. The church had six different ministers now, and he wondered who would be on pastoral duty on a Wednesday afternoon. As a member of the board of deacons, he rated private time with Curt Johnson, the senior minister, but James doubted that the head of the whole operation would be available. He had an empire to run and delegated all mundane matters, other than fund-raising, to his associate pastors. The journalist entered, took off his hat, and asked the church secretary if anyone was around.

He was sent down a plushly carpeted hallway to see Neville Armstrong, associate pastor and slugging first baseman for the church's league-winning softball team.

"James," the burly minister exclaimed as he greeted his former teammate, "what brings you by?" Murphy had played sparingly as a left fielder until a series of heel injuries ended a mediocre career. Whenever he looked at Armstrong, he imagined him screwing up his meaty face before taking a swipe at a looping pitch. The minister got up from the desk and pulled a chair around so that they could both be seated in the corner of his office.

"Not too much," the reporter replied, "do you mind if I shut the door?" Even though he had not yet confessed, he was already feeling better. He remembered the relief he felt years ago when he finally told his mother that he was going to college in Clarkeston. She needed him to stay at home, to earn some money for the family and serve as buffer between herself and his drunk of a father, and yet she understood. Thinking about the rare hug she had given him and the simple *good luck* she had spoken still had power to bring tears to his eyes.

He sat down in the offered chair and realized that he had not thought through the connection between his Internet surfing habits and the renewed murder investigation. Omitting the context of his behavior might make his confession a little awkward, but dragging city politics and the memory of Diana Cavendish into the room seemed risky and pointless.

He cleared his throat and spoke haltingly for a while before getting to the point, "Uh, Nev, this is kind of an uncomfortable conversation to have, but something's been bothering me and I just need to talk to someone."

"That's why I'm here, Brother James," said Armstrong, beaming the same look he gave a sixteen-inch softball as it approached the plate. For his part, James hated being called brother. He considered it an affectation borrowed from the Pentecostalists. "What kind of a burden are you carrying today?"

"That's the word for it . . . a burden." He looked out the window and saw the church secretary leave the building and walk to her car. Although her skirt was conservatively long, there was no hiding the pleasant swish and sway of her derriere as she bent down to put a bag in the trunk. "It's lust," he said to himself.

"You've been cheating on Sondra?" A storm cloud passed the brow of the minister as he leaned forward to hear better.

"No!" The reporter exclaimed. "Not that!" The mere thought was appalling. His relationship with his wife was in a rut, but he loved her deeply. Her beauty still made him shake his head at his good fortune. "No, it's the Internet. I haven't done anything with anybody."

"Ah," the minister said knowingly, "we see Internet porn addiction all the time. Sometimes I wish the damn thing had never been invented." He shook his head and then said thoughtfully, "Or at least the porn part of it."

James drew a deep breath. "I don't know if you'd call it porn exactly." But it was porn. When a man looks at porn, he has lustful thoughts in his head. That's the whole point of pornography and that's why it's sinful. Why should his bikini website be preferable to hard-core porn just because the women are wearing swimsuits rather than nothing at all? If a man fantasizes about having sex with a woman in a picture, does it really matter what she's wearing? "We're talking about sexy swimsuit pictures." He sighed. "Still, I'm not proud of myself."

Armstrong seemed disappointed that the reporter's revelation wasn't more lurid. He shifted in his chair and took up the Bible that rested on the round table separating them. "No triple-X-rated orgy sites?"

"Not yet, at any rate."

The pastor looked let down. He did not seem to understand that sin was in the heart and not on the page. Armstrong scratched his head and suddenly looked like he had an idea. "How old are the girls in the pictures?"

The deacon thought for a moment. It never really said anywhere on the website how old the bikini girlfriends were. Most of them looked like college students, but he had met the occasional fifteen- or sixteen-year-old who looked much older. A wave of disgust flooded over him. What if he had been regularly fantasizing about sophomores in high school? "I don't know," he admitted as his face began to redden, "most of them look like they're eighteen or twenty, something like that."

Now he had the pastor's full attention. "You mean that some of them could be younger?"

"I suppose so. It's boyfriends sending in pictures of their girlfriends in swimsuits." He shrugged his shoulders. "There's no way to tell how old anyone is." He watched warily as Armstrong opened up the Bible. "It's not little kids, if that's what you're thinking."

"No, of course not," nodded the minister, who thumbed through a book in the New Testament while he added, "but some of them could be thirteen or fourteen, I suspect. There are girls who ripen pretty early."

James had no immediate response to this observation, and he doubted that the fruit analogy was even appropriate. Maybe the pastor was trying to evoke Garden of Eden imagery, but unless Eve's body were the forbidden fruit, then his choice of words was just creepy. There was no way, however, to refute the charge. Some of the girls could be under eighteen. He had never thought about it. He sat still in the chair and watched the pastor search unsuccessfully for whatever snippet of scripture was eluding him.

"This is pretty serious," Armstrong finally concluded as he shut the book. "I'll have to talk to Brother Johnson, but I'm pretty sure that for liability reasons he's going to want to keep you away from the kids' Sunday school classes and the youth groups." He nodded, becoming more and more sure of himself as he spoke. "You may have to step down as deacon, too. There's something in the bylaws about deacons being able to 'participate fully in the life of the church,' and if we need to keep you away from the kids, then that'll be a problem." He frowned and suddenly stood up.

James joined him upright in panic. His confession was spinning out of control, and it was rapidly becoming too late to protest. "Isn't that a bit excessive? I'm not a child molester, for heaven's sake! I mean, shouldn't I just be praying about this and offering my sin up to God?"

The pastor smiled indulgently. "Of course." He reached out and grabbed the reporter's hands. As he bowed his head, James could feel their sweaty palms slide away from each other slightly as the other man started to pray aloud. "Dear Lord, please hear us as we call upon you for your tender mercies. Feel the shame of this sinner as he seeks to find a way out of the darkness where sin has cast him. Guide him to a place where his compulsions do not control him, where your love can shield him from the wickedness of his desires. In your Son's name, let your healing power come upon this sinner." James felt a squeeze of his hands. "Amen."

"Amen," the reporter repeated, with doubt in his voice that he knew should not be there. He felt like he had just been run over by a truck. As he moved slowly toward the door, he turned around and saw that Armstrong stood rooted in the same spot where he had prayed, traces of ecstasy still lingering on his face. "There's no need for anyone else to know about this, is there?"

The pastor looked at him as if he were having trouble processing the question, and James imagined a memo being passed around stating that he was not to be allowed around any innocent Baptist teenagers. How could they police him if no one but Armstrong and Johnson knew about his supposed pedophile tendencies? He saw only one way out, and he took it before the minister had a chance to reply.

"Neville, don't worry about me." He took a step forward and held up his hand, trying to salvage the situation by sheer force of will. He would give the big man no excuse to ruin him. "I'll hand in my resignation as deacon tomorrow, and you won't see me here again at First Baptist. I swear." He fought the urge to run through the door, but he forced himself to stop and look the confused minister once more in the eyes. "You don't even need to talk to Pastor Johnson. I'll keep up my monthly pledge, but I'll go worship someplace else. Okay?"

As soon as he saw Armstrong nod, he turned and bolted down the hall.

★ ★ ★

Sondra Murphy, the ex-deacon's wife, was a petite redhead who had succeeded in keeping a trim figure at thirty-nine despite the challenge of measuring barely five feet two inches tall. She had been one of the most eligible girls in Clarkeston until she met a handsome young journalism major at the college. She herself had stopped at a high school diploma, preferring to help her mother manage a small interior-design business, but she met James when he came over to do a story on a local charity that her mother was involved in. He was attractive and well spoken, more sophisticated than the local boys, and unlike the other college boys, who both despised and chased after the townie girls. They had two children and were married only three years before she realized how little ambition he had.

When they met, he talked about going to New York or Los Angeles and working for one of the big papers, but he fell in love with Clarkeston. He was blissfully content with life in the little college town. Even the smallest story captured his imagination, but the town was big enough that stories of murder and political corruption occasionally came his way. Sometimes his stories were picked up by the national wire services and a job offer would materialize. Just last year he turned down a job at the *Chicago Tribune*. Chicago! What a perfect chance to get out of this podunk burg! He turned it down without even consulting her.

The Chicago job would have been much better money too. When she went back to work after the kids were in preschool, her income quickly surpassed his, and she had been supporting the family for more than ten years now. If they had to survive on his salary alone, they'd be living in a trailer somewhere in a kudzu field on the edge of town.

As she stood at the kitchen sink washing some lettuce for a salad, she watched her husband park his car next to hers in the driveway and trudge up the sidewalk to the front door. He was a gardener, and this time of year the garage was filled with seedlings, tools, and other gardening junk, and she'd been caught in a downpour that afternoon because there was no room to park a car inside. A moment later, James came in and slumped down at the kitchen table without a word. Sometimes work put him in a dark mood when he realized (surprise! surprise!) that he could not solve all the problems that he wrote about in his articles. The back of her collar was still damp from the rain and she was in no mood to listen to his musings.

"Hey, hon," he murmured as he got up and pulled a beer from the refrigerator, "what's for dinner?"

She glared at the bottle in his hand. Every time her friends came over to play bridge someone remarked on the beer in the fridge or the bottles in the recycling bin. Baptist deacons were supposed to be role models, not beer-guzzling targets for the pastor's sermons. "Nothing much," she sniffed. "I made some chicken salad from last night's leftovers."

He did not reply. She looked at him carefully as he sucked on the Budweiser tit. Something was bothering him, but she decided to let it simmer. When he finished his drink and started worrying the label with his fingernails, he finally broke the silence.

"I stepped down as deacon today."

"You did what?" She was momentarily caught off guard but managed to raise her voice to a shout by the third syllable she spit out.

"I told Pastor Armstrong that I was resigning." He looked up at her briefly before he began tearing the label off the bottle with an obviously feigned nonchalance. "And I told him I was quitting the church altogether."

She opened her mouth, but nothing came out. She looked down for any sign that he was joking, but he ignored her and continued deliberately stripping off the red paper. She was about to really let him have it, to blast him away with the righteous venom of a teetotaling, industrious Christian woman who was sick to death of living with a hedonistic, left-leaning, penniless journalist, but the vitriol caught in her throat. She had said it all before and no doubt he was waiting for the inevitable blowup, cooldown, and gradual return to normal, or at least as normal as things ever got around their house since the kids had left. He did not seem to realize that this was different. How the hell could she explain why her husband was staying at home on Sunday mornings?

"Can I ask why you're considering doing this?" Her voice was pure steel, her politeness precarious.

"I'm not just considering it." He pinched the label into a tight ball and pushed it into the bottle. "I already did it."

"Are you crazy?!"

His voice was irritatingly calm. "I may give St. James Episcopal a try. The new preacher over there seems like a nice guy."

That was it. He may as well have said he was signing on with Satan himself. She yanked the beer bottle from his hand and flung it across the room at the recycle bin. The neck hit the wall with such force that it popped into the sheet rock and stuck for a second before plopping down into the container.

She looked around for something else to throw, but paused when her hand touched a glass vase of fresh-picked flowers. Her husband was looking at her with curiosity, not fear or respect. A sudden wave of coldness stayed her hand and she pushed the vase aside. She marched through the kitchen door and into the bedroom to pack. "I'll be staying with my sister."

VI.

CLUES

Melanie stared at the phone in her hand before slamming it back into the cradle. Leave it to the FBI, where arrogance was a job requirement and acting like a dick was essential for promotion, to find the rudest person in Arkansas to answer its phone. When she had decided to pursue James Murphy's inquiry, she had briefly debated whether or not to call the number she had found in the FBI database next to the name of Jacob Granville. It was an odd notation. There was no case file associated with him, nor had any official investigation been undertaken, but there sat the name, listed with no data other than a contact number with an Arkansas area code in case anyone made an inquiry about him. She had no obligation to call the number before she followed up on Murphy's story, but a professional survival instinct told her to call and cover her ass.

She dialed the number, assuming that it belonged to a bureau agent stationed in Arkansas, but the responding voice on the other end of the line did not state her name or her department; she just repeated the phone number back to Melanie by way of greeting. Melanie identified herself vaguely as an assistant US attorney and asked to whom she was speaking, but she was ignored and in turn was asked abruptly why she was calling. She bit back a remark about people from Arkansas usually being more polite and then reluctantly explained the notation that had popped up when Granville's name was entered into the FBI database.

"And who initiated the query that you're reporting?"

Melanie hesitated for a moment. The woman's voice was nasal, not southern at all, and it set her teeth on edge. Ten years earlier, she might have hung up, but with advances in phone technology, the person on the other end of the line was undoubtedly staring at Melanie's office number on some display. If she hung up now, she'd likely get a visit from a local bureau agent repeating the question in person. Bloody-minded bastards. The number made her easy to track down. She decided to tell the truth and then ask some hard questions about what the FBI knew about the Cavendish-Granville case.

"A newspaper reporter from Clarkeston, Georgia, by the name of Murphy," she answered grudgingly. "And now maybe you can tell me who you are?"

In response, she heard only the rapid tapping on a keyboard. "James Murphy? The *Clarkeston Chronicle*? You need to tell me why he came to you." No *please*, just a command with more than a whiff of urgency to it.

"Look, Miss Whatever-The-Hell-Your-Name-Is, I'm not answering any more questions until you answer some of mine—"

The phone line went dead, and Melanie strangled the handset as if she could reach through the fiber-optic cables all the way to the throat of the rude bitch three states away. She stared out the window and emitted a barely perceptible growl. She'd ratted out Murphy and gotten nothing in return to help him. And, for the first time, she wondered whether she'd been talking to the FBI at all. She would track down the Arkansas number later, and in the meantime she felt a renewed commitment to follow up on Murphy's tip.

The best place to begin was the courthouse's IT department. In theory, the cybercrime techies would be best at tracking down the source of something posted on the web, like Murphy's bikini photos, but they were so busy laying traps for pedophiles and tracing laundered drug money that she knew from experience they would have little time to answer her questions. Instead, she walked down to see Hans Peterson, the

IT guru who fixed her computer whenever it wouldn't print and who removed the annoying viruses that splattered pop-up ads selling anti-pop-up software on her computer screen. Hans and his bespectacled minions were not investigators—their only official job was to keep the computer network running—but they loved getting questions related to real cases and, unlike the snooty cybercrime crowd, they didn't take three weeks to return phone calls.

She took the elevator down to the basement and asked if Hans was around. The bottom floor was the coolest part of the building on a hot day, but even an East German architect would have found its aesthetics challenging. Yellow cinderblock walls and brown-flecked linoleum gave it the air of a church basement circa 1950 or so. The oldest furniture in the building found its way down whenever replacements arrived on the upper floors, and the hallway lobby in front of the elevator was crammed with gutted CPUs sitting on chipped wooden desks. Melanie leaned around a filing cabinet and spotted a woman behind a huge monitor, who said that the IT head was in his office. She picked her way past the techno junkyard and into the sanctum of its cannibalizer-in-chief.

Hans was a lean bike racer who kept his graying hair out of his face with a neat ponytail. Melanie had been in Atlanta for only six months, but it had not taken her long to figure out that Hans was a key person to have on her side. In the old days, the conventional wisdom said not to piss off the person looking after your horse; nowadays the same held true for the person taking care of your computer.

"Everything all right, Ms. Melanie?" Being back in the South was a mixed blessing, but it was kind of nice to be Ms. Melanie again. His eyes tracked back to the screen in front of him and he quickly typed in a command before looking back up at her.

"Everything's great, Hans," she replied brightly, "I can't thank you enough for working out the IP address issue with the Wi-Fi at my apartment." He nodded, glanced briefly back down at his keyboard, and shot off a couple of rapid key strokes before pushing back from his desk.

"What's up?"

"I've got a question about a case I'm working on." She was gratified to see his left eyebrow rise slightly. "Basically, I need to track down some photos that are posted on the web." She handed him a piece of paper with the link to the pictures of Diana Cavendish, and he leaned forward to enter the URL into his browser.

"Nice!" he exclaimed when he got to the website.

"Calm down, Hans. She disappeared five years ago, probably dead."

"Sorry," he looked up and shook his head. "That's a shame."

"What can you tell me about the photos?" She walked around his desk so that she could look over his shoulder. "Is there any way to track down the source?"

"Well," he said as he downloaded one of the images and clicked on Properties, "it's a standard JPEG file. Sometimes there's a date stamp or some comments entered by the person who uploaded it, but the only date you can see is from last week, which is probably the date it was posted and not when the picture was taken." He looked over his shoulder at her. "You said she's been dead five years, right?"

"Yeah." She put her hand on the top of his chair and leaned down to take a closer look.

"You can see where one could add information to the file, but it's all blank."

"What about the website? Can you find out anything about who runs it?"

"That's easy," he replied, shooing her back a bit with a flick of his right hand. "In order to get an Internet domain address, you have to register as owner of the address and provide contact information." He opened up another window on his browser and showed her a database called Whois. "It's basically a directory of who owns what domain names on the web. So, we just type *mygirlfriendsbikini* into the box, hit Enter, and voilà!" He copied the information that appeared, pasted it into an email to Melanie, and fired it off. "Now you know who claims to be the registrant and owner of your little website."

"Thanks, Hans!" She rapped a knuckle on his desk and turned to leave the room. When she reached the door, the funny tone she had heard in his voice registered with her. "Claims?"

"Sorry, Ms. Melanie," he replied as he settled back in his work station, "but no one polices the truthfulness of any of the data in Whois. With reputable firms, the information is pretty reliable, but people who run sketchy websites frequently try to hide who they really are. Don't be too disappointed if the names and number I sent you are bogus."

She nodded and headed back down the hall to the elevator, anxious to see whether she could track down the owner of the website and ask about the source of the pictures of Diana Cavendish. Unfortunately, Hans's instincts turned out to be correct. When she opened her email and called the phone number provided by James C. Smith, the agent for the registrant, Sweaty Palm Productions, she got the reservations number for a Marriott Hotel in Los Angeles. When she googled the street address provided for Sweaty Palm, it turned out to be for the same hotel. "Shit," she said under her breath.

She googled *Sweaty Palm Productions*. The first item listed in the search result indicated that the company existed; at least it had a rudimentary website, which touted its provision of "top flight soft-core content." The one-page site provided no physical address or phone number for the firm. It included an email address, swp69@gmail.com, for sales queries, but listed no names of anyone associated with the business. She sent a brief message to the address from her personal email account, politely requesting a content list and pricing information. Then she sent the email address to Hans and asked him how easily it could be traced.

While she waited for Hans's reply, she clicked her way through the other results that had come back for Sweaty Palm Productions. There were not many, but clearly the business was not wholly fictitious. It was mentioned several times in various porn blogs as a good source for soft-core content, and a couple of adult sites thanked SWP for help in setting up their web pages, but nowhere did anyone mention any names or addresses associated with the business. Moreover, no one had mentioned it in several years. The last reference was a question in an adult-business forum that asked, "Who bought Sweaty Palm?" The empty thread indicated that the question had gone unanswered.

As Melanie tapped her fingers on her desk, wondering what to try next, she got a phone call from Hans. "Do you want to know how to trace an email address?"

"Please!"

"Okay, go to your inbox in Outlook and right-click on any message there and then click on Message Options." He paused for a moment. "Do you see the header that appears at the bottom with all the information? Unless the sender has engaged in some deliberate cloaking, you should be able to study that information and see who the Internet service provider is and probably the city of origin."

"Does it give you the physical address of the sender?"

"Nope, just the IP address of the computer, and the computer could be anywhere in the city."

She thought for a moment. "So, I'm going to have to wait until I get a response from Sweaty Palm before I can right-click on it and learn something?" If SWP had not been heard from in years, she doubted that she'd be getting an answer to her query.

"Not really," Hans replied. "I can tell you right now all you need to know about that particular address. Unfortunately for you, it's a Gmail account, so if these guys answer, all you're gonna learn is that Google is the Internet service provider."

"We know that already."

"And you also probably know that you'll need a court order to get Gmail to provide further details about the holder of the email address, and that response probably won't include any sort of physical address."

She flicked a styrofoam coffee cup off of her desk into a wastebasket, put her feet up, and leaned back in her chair. "So just having the email address doesn't get me anywhere."

"Not in and of itself, no, but you might do some spade work out in Los Angeles on the company. I poked around a little and it appears to have been a real business at one time, so someone might have heard of it."

She thanked him and tried to remember the name of anyone in Los Angeles who might be willing informally to track down the operators of James Murphy's bikini website without officially initiating an investigation. In the meantime, she was stymied. There would be no quick answer to the mystery of who had posted the photos.

She rested her head against the back of her chair and closed her eyes, trying to decide what to do next. She could just give up. She'd expended no significant time on Murphy's request, and for all the reasons she had given him already, the federal connection to the case was pretty minimal. Or she could go full-out, get the FBI involved, and request that office resources be devoted to a fresh investigation. Neither option seemed very attractive. Murphy had dropped an interesting problem in her lap; she did not want to let it go and return to the endless string of dope prosecutions. On the other hand, she really did not want to convince her superiors that pushing hard on the case was the best use of departmental resources. Better to keep things low-key, call in a few favors, and do a little legwork on her own under the radar. She could always request help later, if concrete evidence justified involving others.

And besides, even Murphy was unaware of the biggest questions his visit had posed: Why hadn't the local police notified the FBI of Diana Cavendish's disappearance and why had they lied about doing so to the news reporter? And why did some snippy bitch in Arkansas care about Murphy's inquiry? If Melanie got in her car now, she could beat the traffic and get to Clarkeston well before six o'clock, a perfectly appropriate time to pop in on the sheriff and hear what explanations he had to offer.

Melanie opened her eyes, swung her legs down from her desk, and studied the pile of motions that needed to be argued the following morning. They were all straightforward, and she was sitting second chair in order to give the department's newest hire a bit of experience. There was no reason why she shouldn't temporarily break away from Atlanta's orbit and make the seventy-five-minute drive to Clarkeston. Maybe she'd even see some flowers.

★ ★ ★

When Melanie turned north on the I-75/I-85 connector, she popped on her sunglasses and weaved the BMW Z4 convertible in and out of traffic until she was safely past the perimeter road and out into the countryside, or at least what passed for countryside past the outlet stores that lined both sides of the highway. She searched in vain for a radio station that played something other than oldies or country music and finally popped in a CD of Broadway show tunes that her oldest niece had mixed for her birthday. Although she never mentioned the subject at work or to her friends, or to anyone, for that matter, her family was keenly aware of her history as a pageant contestant that had culminated with a runner-up finish in the Miss Georgia Pageant more than twenty years earlier. Although her niece had not even been born at the time, she knew that Auntie's talent had been singing a medley of showstoppers, and the adoring twelve-year-old had spent hours asking about her favorites in order to mix a CD.

To Melanie's surprise, the recordings were pretty good, many from shows she had seen on Broadway, and she found herself adding to the music on her own. Even after twenty years, she was still intensely embarrassed by her checkered antifeminist, rhinestone-encrusted teenage past, but she could not deny the guilty pleasure of singing along with something from *Evita* as she slowly left the suburbs behind.

Clarkeston was only seventy miles from Atlanta, but somehow it fell outside the gravitational pull of the sprawlingest city in the South. Even though the city's suburbs reached halfway there, grasping and swallowing more and more green space and another clutch of sleepy towns every year, Clarkeston remained out of its reach, protected by a large state park and sheltered by a wall of dense kudzu climbing the trees at its border. About twenty-five miles from the little college town, Melanie left the interstate and took a two-lane road that would eventually turn into Main Street. She glided through hay fields and pine plantations, delighting in the tight steering of the car as she accelerated through each turn, until she felt the leaden yoke of her job loosen a bit and found it replaced by a sweet melancholy she had not felt for a long time.

She had pushed herself relentlessly in Washington to build a reputation as one of the toughest prosecutors in her department, and although she had complained about the unavailability of her ex-boyfriend as he was sent around the country by the FBI, she had been only slightly less obsessed with her job. After her last promotion, her workload had eased a bit, but she had had no clue what to do with the hard-won respect and the extra bits of free time. When the opportunity arose to impress a new set of attorneys and judges, back in the state that had known her only as Miss Georgia Runner-Up, she jumped at the assignment. The smart thing would have been first to spend a couple of months meditating in a Buddhist monastery or seeing a really good therapist, but instead, she packed up her bags, rented a townhouse in Buckhead, and dived headfirst into a new challenge.

But it wasn't really a new challenge. It was the same sorts of cases and the same sorts of people as before, and now she was stuck in a town loaded with crummy high school memories and filled with as many box stores and strip malls as the DC suburbs, but with no National Mall or Old Town Alexandria or Adams Morgan or Rock Creek Park to soften the assault on her aesthetic sense. Worst of all, she had known this before she moved back. She had been self-aware, knowing precisely what she was getting into, and yet unable to say no.

In less than an hour, the outskirts of Clarkeston suddenly appeared below her as the car parted a field of sorghum like the Red Sea and crested a steep hill west of the town. She smiled and turned off the stereo. It was tempting to think about what life in a small college town might be like. Her co-clerk still lived in town, having turned down a prestigious job with the Office of Legal Counsel in Washington to teach history at Clarkeston College and stay with the beguiling widow he had met there. His life offered the road not taken: spouse, children, golden retriever, and plenty of time to play, think, walk the dog, whatever.

After she passed through the ugly thicket of Hardee's and Dollar Generals that ringed the edge of town, she hit a string of green lights and soon found herself in the middle of downtown Clarkeston, fast approaching the federal courthouse where she used to work. She drove two blocks past it and found a parking place on the street a short walk from the police substation located in the county courthouse. She almost hoped she would not find the sheriff in his office there. She had asked her assistant to find his home address, and confronting him there might throw him off his guard. There was nothing like the feds showing up at dinnertime to unsettle a small-town cop.

She walked to the back of the county building and followed a string of police cruisers to a glass door almost hidden by a pair of potted crepe myrtles. The station lobby was empty, so she walked up to a battered wooden counter and studied the city map taped to its top while she waited for the sergeant to return. When he did, he looked like he had just shot himself up with steroids in the back room. His biceps and shoulders were massive, barely contained by a khaki short-sleeved shirt. His identity badge, naming him as Officer E. LeQuire, looked like it was pinned directly into his chest, but his unblinking eyes and pinpoint pupils suggested that pain was just a minor inconvenience. A polite request to see the sheriff was initially met with resistance, but her business card got the officer's attention, and after a couple of minutes of waiting, the walking tree stump was leading her down a dingy hallway to his boss's office.

"Ms. Wilkerson," the sheriff said graciously, glancing at her card and waving her into a wooden chair across from his desk, "what can we do for you?"

Melanie knew a little bit about the man in front of her. He sat back informally, with his fingers laced behind his head, but she knew better than to underestimate him. Her assistant had told her that Sheriff Porter Johnson was a former football player at the University of Georgia who had gone to the state police academy when a knee injury ended his playing career. He was not a dumb jock, however. He had made the dean's list all five of his semesters at Georgia, and despite the fifties-style buzz cut, distended paunch, and down-home country mannerisms, his piercing brown eyes looked anything but stupid.

"Sheriff Johnson," she said with a smile and the sweet flattened vowels that she seldom dared to use in Washington, "thank you so much for making the time to see me." She reached into her purse and pulled out a copy of one of the pictures of Diana Cavendish that James Murphy had found on the Internet. "I've had a bit of something cross my desk and, quite frankly, I thought you would be the best person to ask about it." She handed the picture to him.

He raised his eyebrows at the racy photo, but he offered no sign that he recognized the beautiful woman. "Should I know her?"

He was now watching her as carefully as she had been watching him. She blinked innocently and offered him the same smile she had used to edge out Miss Fulton County for Miss Congeniality at the Atlanta teen pageant. "Her name is apparently Diana Cavendish." She looked down at the picture as if to make sure she had given him the proper photo. "I was told that she was kidnapped, presumed murdered, here about five years ago. The Clarkeston police conducted the investigation." She reached over and pushed the photocopy back toward him. "Are you sure you don't recognize her?"

He reluctantly picked the paper back up, squinted, and cocked his head to the side. "Yeah," he replied with a practiced thoughtfulness, "the hair threw me off. This does look a lot like Cavendish." He pushed the picture back toward her and offered his own attempt at a disarming smile. "Where did you get this? Has someone found her?"

Despite his attempt to appear disinterested, she clearly had his attention. "No, not yet. Someone in Clarkeston sent us the picture, and before we took any action, we wanted to confirm her identity." She took the photocopy, folded it carefully, and put it back in her purse. "I thought you might be the best person to talk to."

"Now, Ms. Melanie," he said, managing to mix equal parts condescension and steel in his voice, "the college could have done that for you."

"I know," she lied, "but I have another question that only the Clarkeston police can answer."

"And what's that?" His cell phone rang, and after looking at the number, he slid a finger across the screen and put it back in his pocket. "I'll be happy to tell you anything you need to know, but please tell me what's really brought you over from Atlanta. I don't understand why anybody in the US attorney's office would have an interest in an old local case."

It was a good question and an inevitable one. She had given it some thought on the drive. Admitting she was purely on a fishing expedition was not a feasible option, so she had decided to go with a tinted version of the truth. "The person who uncovered this picture asked us to reopen the FBI investigation into Cavendish's disappearance. When I contacted the FBI for details of the kidnapping, they told me that they had no record of any involvement. There never was an FBI investigation, even though kidnapping is a federal crime. So that sort of becomes the question: why was the FBI never contacted in this case?"

She expected him to bristle. After all, it was essentially either an accusation of incompetence or a suggestion of some sort of deliberate malfeasance, but instead of getting defensive, he knitted his eyebrows and shook his head slowly.

"I don't know where you're getting your information, but we informed the FBI three days after the disappearance." While Melanie struggled to process the claim made by the sheriff, he rolled his chair backward across the space behind his desk and pulled a file out of a gray metal cabinet. He flipped through the first couple of pages and then nodded his head. "Yup, exactly three days after." He slipped the file back into the cabinet. "Not that they were much use."

After years of questioning witnesses, Melanie had a good feel for when people were lying, and Sheriff Johnson sounded like he might be telling the truth, especially since he must have known that she had the ability to double-check his statement with the bureau. But it was damn convenient that he remembered the precise moment when he called the FBI and just happened to have a five-year-old file so handy. He was staring hard at her, his expression straddling the border between curiosity and annoyance. She'd wait to process the implications of his claim, and she pressed the only advantage that she had.

"Isn't three days a long time to wait to call the FBI when a kidnapping has clearly occurred?" The sweet edge to her voice had faded, and for the first time in the interview, Johnson responded with irritation.

"We don't need to justify our investigation to you, ma'am. As you know, being a lawyer and all, we have no obligation to report a kidnapping to the FBI, especially when there's no evidence of any interstate transportation." He stood up and walked past the desk to the door. "Now, I'm sure you need to be getting back to Atlanta before it gets too late. Rest assured that we can handle our own cold cases."

She was tempted to respond with something cute: *Is it really a cold case if you know Jacob Granville is the murderer?* But she bit her tongue. She had only James Murphy's word that Johnson had stonewalled the investigation in order to aid Granville's flight. She reminded herself she was just on a fishing trip and stood up to shake the sheriff's hand. "Thank you for your time, Sheriff Johnson. We'll be in touch if we have any more questions."

"Well," he pushed open the door and held it long enough for her to slide out into the hallway, "now you know where to find me." It shut behind her almost immediately and she was left with an unsettled feeling. Why hadn't he been more curious about a new source of information in one of his murder cases? Why did the specter of a federal investigation not intimidate him? He should have been way more upset by the suggestion that the FBI should have been called in sooner, but he had barely blinked.

Melanie drove through the streets of Clarkeston aimlessly, trying to figure out whether she was smelling a rat or just being paranoid. Not every small-town southern cop was corrupt, after all. Mostly, she was annoyed at her inability to engage with Johnson and drag any information out of him. She had been disarmed by the good ol' boy, but he did make one interesting statement. He stuck by the story that the FBI had been asked to help in the Diana Cavendish case. That conflict with her own brief research was worth checking out from the federal end of things.

VII.

WILLS

Father Thorsten Carter sat in his car outside the home of Caroline Rodgers, the widow of his predecessor and a potential blockbuster donor to St. James Episcopal Church. Her large two-story brick house stood out on a street consisting mainly of older Victorian homes and the occasional shotgun bungalow. Despite the family money that she and her deceased husband had purportedly inherited, the home looked a bit run down. Rusted steel awnings cantilevered gloomily over the windows, suggesting correctly that no major renovations had taken place since the 1950s. The short front porch was made of poured concrete, and over the years it had cracked and caused the black wrought-iron railing to pull away from the frame of the front door. The driveway, however, hinted that the rumors of wealth might well be true. A gleaming Mercedes convertible was parked under a large tulip poplar and a young man with a chamois was carefully buffing every inch of the car until he could see the pores of his face in the reflective surface.

After a silent rehearsal of his speech, Thor got out of his battered Corolla and walked up to the house. He did not enjoy asking parishioners for donations, nor did he relish the task of approaching a notoriously difficult lady for any kind of favor, but her absence from the congregation provided him with a good excuse to drop by, and her husband's death gave him a reason to talk about her estate planning. He took a deep breath and pushed the yellowed button to the right of the door. A large bicycle bell seemed to jangle within the house and a few moments later Caroline Rodgers appeared at the door in a dark blue dress, reading glasses pushed up into her steely gray hair, piercing green eyes registering both recognition and disdain.

"What are you doing here?" she asked in a clear, high voice that could have belonged to a much younger woman. He shifted his weight forward but she made no move to let him in.

"Just a courtesy call, Ms. Rodgers." He adjusted his dog collar with a nervous tug. "We haven't seen you over at St. James for a while, so I thought I'd stop by and see how you're doing."

"I'm doing just fine," she replied impatiently. She opened her mouth as if to say something more, but instead she stepped back to shut the door and end the brief interview. Just as it began to close, a young woman in a bright sundress appeared and blocked its movement with her hand.

The attractive woman, who looked to be in her early thirties, outmuscled the taciturn widow and smiled brightly at Thor. "You must be Father Carter! Please come in and we'll get you some tea." She stared at her mother until the septuagenarian grudgingly moved aside to let the young priest in.

"I'm sorry," he replied to the blond angel, "have we met?" Certainly, he would have remembered such a face.

"No, no," she laughed brightly.

"Then how—?"

"Black suit, white collar, and a little deduction. I'm Miriam." She took the priest's hand and guided him to a sitting room crowded with overstuffed furniture covered in a faded floral brocade.

"Goddamn blackbirds," the older woman scowled and shook her head as they passed by her in the hallway.

"Momma! Be polite!" Thor took a quick look back through the screen door.

"No, Father," Miriam continued, "not real blackbirds." She cast a sour look at her surviving parent. "She means priests. Since Papa died, my mother has revealed quite a horrifying attitude toward all clergy. She doesn't mean anything personal."

To this, the older woman offered an audible "harumph" and stalked into the kitchen. "She'll bring us some tea," the daughter continued.

"But will it be safe to drink?" Thor managed a smile at Miriam, intending a joke, but not entirely sure that the sniping senior was completely harmless. He was rewarded with a laugh and he extended his hand to her. "Call me Thor. I haven't gotten used to Father Carter yet."

She pressed it warmly in return and smiled, "I used to call my dad 'Father Father' when I was a kid. He was pretty terrifying from the pulpit, but at home he was a sweetheart." She pointed to a family picture on the mantle, displaying the familiar face of Ernest Rodgers in the midst of three beaming children and a stony-faced wife. "Those are my brothers Eli and Joseph. I'm the youngest . . . we all still miss Papa horribly."

"I didn't get to know him well." Thor searched for the right word to describe the imperious old cleric. "But he certainly was an impressive guy." At this point, the widow emerged from the kitchen with a platter that contained three glasses of iced tea and a tiny plate of peppermints. She set the items down on the round table that separated Thor's chair from Miriam's and sat herself down on the sofa facing them. Thor thanked her and took a glass.

By way of misdirection, he spoke once again to the daughter, hoping to prompt a more civil response from the mother. "I just stopped by to check on your mom and ask what she wanted done with your father's papers. We haven't seen her at church for a while and everyone is wondering if she's okay."

"And you're not going to be seeing me," the widow responded authoritatively and then paused, waiting until the priest turned to her. "The only reason I ever went was to support Miriam's father," she explained. "With him gone, there's no reason for me to spend any more of my time with that pack of hypocrites at St. James." She picked up a peppermint and popped it in her mouth. "Besides, I'm an atheist."

"Momma!"

"Always have been, darlin'." She sucked on the candy and brought it briefly to her lips. "You know that. I just never let the congregation catch on."

"Momma," Miriam stated firmly, accustomed to her mother's irreverent outbursts, "I don't think that we need to discuss theology with Father Thor."

"Well," she snorted, "who else should I discuss theology with if not a priest?" Thor watched Miriam roll her sparkling blue eyes. "And as far as your father's papers go, this young man can burn them if he wants. The church secretary told me that they're just a bunch of old sermons and *Anglican Monthly* magazines."

"Thank you, ma'am," replied Thor, thrilled to make a positive response to anything the woman was saying. "I'll go through the boxes carefully and save anything that you might want to keep."

The widow shrugged her shoulders and popped another peppermint. For a moment, Thor could see where Miriam got her distinctive and pleasing looks. She shared intelligent eyes and an aristocratic nose with her mother, and they both had the same slender neck and full lips. Miriam was taller and curvier. Her mother's rigorously slim figure must have been the envy of the stolid matrons at St. James.

"That leaves just one more thing . . ." Thor almost abandoned his plan to broach the subject of money, but he had sworn that he would not chicken out. Fund-raising was the most painful part of his job, but it was important to the parish, and if he did not carry through with his duty, then he might lose his nerve permanently. Of course, he had never had to schmooze a clergy-baiting atheist before. "Ms. Rodgers, your husband's passing might have gotten you thinking about your own mortality. His ministry left a lasting legacy at St. James, and I was just wondering whether you might want to leave your own mark with a testamentary gift of some sort."

"My God," the widow said, grinning broadly and turning to her daughter, "I do believe he's asking me for money!" She was positively gleeful at the audacity of her guest.

"Given ... uh ... what you've said," stammered the priest, "you may not want to maintain a monthly pledge." He knew for a fact that she had not kept up her husband's tithe nor any part of it. "But you might want to look to the future and make some sort of commitment."

He prepared for a blast of vitriol, but instead of cursing him or laughing him out of the house, the old woman uttered a single word in a decisive voice.

"Bells."

"Bells?"

"Bells! Mr. Carter," she explained impatiently. "The only thing that I ever enjoyed at St. James was playing in the handbell choir, and I would be happy to make a bequest large enough to buy a new set of bells and to endow a permanent director just for a bell choir." Her voice began to raise in pitch, "The current music director, that—"

"Mother!"

"—trollop," she compromised reluctantly, "hates handbell music and convinced the vestry to sell the bells. It would please me tremendously to think of them ringing again at St. James."

"That's very generous, ma'am." Thor did the math quickly in his head and determined that such a bequest, if she really meant to endow a salary, would have to be in the neighborhood of $250,000. "That's very generous indeed!" He stood up and took her hand. She remained seated, but nodded her head slightly.

"Good luck over there, young man," she dismissed him with a wave. "You're going to need it."

He thanked her again and walked to the door with Miriam, who could barely stifle her amusement at the negotiation she had just witnessed. She followed him down the concrete steps onto the lawn and took his arm before he reached his car.

"I know my mother said that you could burn my father's papers, but I'd like to have a look at them before you get rid of them." She shrugged her shoulders and smiled. "I'm curious."

"No problem." He felt a sudden impulse to ask her out to dinner. While he gathered himself for the effort, she made a quick survey of her mother's yard and plucked a couple of dandelions that were growing in the crack between the lawn and the driveway. "Momma's got plenty of money to keep this place up." She shook her head and gestured to her childhood home. "But she's got this old-fashioned shabby-chic attitude about the house. You see how smartly she dresses. She'd never let her personal appearance slide like this."

Instead of agreeing that her former residence could use an update, Thor returned to the subject of the papers, "Would you like to come over to the church next week and look in your father's boxes? Maybe you'd let me take you out to eat beforehand?" He was aiming for nonchalant but was not sure that he had hit the mark until she accepted his proposal without batting an eye. They agreed to meet on the following Tuesday and parted with an awkward handshake initiated by Thor that seemed to amuse the young woman.

As he pulled away, he decided to let James Murphy look at Ernest Rodgers's papers over the weekend before he turned the boxes over to Miriam. Rodgers's widow clearly had no interest in them so there seemed no reason not to help the journalist out. Nonetheless, vague concerns troubled him while he drove back to St. James. What if the reporter did find something that implicated Rodgers in the cover-up of Diana Cavendish's murder? The thought was ludicrous, but neither Miriam nor her mother would appreciate his ruining the priest's reputation. He pulled into his parking space in front of the church and decided to go through the papers himself before showing them to anyone else, just to see if there was anything as extraordinary as a signed confession from Jacob Granville among the sermons or a pile of gay porn slipped inside an *Anglican Monthly*.

★ ★ ★

He greeted Shelly Woodall, the church music director, as he entered the building and asked her for the key to the closet in the choir rehearsal room.

"But that's where Father Rodgers stores his papers." Her expression dared him to question her use of the present tense. "I'm not supposed to let anyone in there."

Woodall had been Rodgers's organist and choir director for years before his retirement, and she still revered his memory. Several parishioners had recommended that Thor hire a replacement, as was his prerogative as the new priest, but he kept her on. When she was not reminiscing about her former boss, she was an excellent keyboardist and managed to coax a nice full sound out of the small parish choir. He was used to her defending Rodgers's turf, so he patiently explained that permission had been granted by the widow and emphasized the need to finally make space for the boxes of old hymnals currently stacked in one of the Christian Education rooms.

She reluctantly handed over the keys but could not resist taking a shot at the woman who had authorized the trespass. "Caroline Rodgers doesn't care a bit about what's in those boxes," she sniffed. "And I don't think she cared about him either! I used to make him coffee whenever he came in. Bitter, he said it was, always too bitter back at home."

She hovered over him disapprovingly as he opened the door, and a pleasant piney smell seeped into the air. Thor stuck his head in the closet and saw that it was lined in cedar, a common means of coping with mildew in the days before air conditioning transformed the South. Three boxes were stacked in the far corner of the space, almost covered by a pair of musty surplices and several choir robes in a style that the church no longer used.

"Ah," remarked the priest with a wicked grin back at Woodall, "so that's where we keep the surplus surplices!" His wit earned him only a puzzled look, so he reached back into the closet with a sigh, pulled out a box and carried it to the desk in his office. Woodall carried in the others, and soon he was ready to plunge into the dusty remains of his predecessor's presence at St. James. She stood close by as he opened the first box. It took a long stare and a request for a cup of coffee to get her to leave him alone with the jumbled papers.

As he had been told, the boxes were primarily filled with typed sermons, many of them bearing extensive notes in the margin, along with various church-related publications and printed programs from conferences Rodgers had attended. He had been a delegate to the national Episcopal convention several times, and one whole box was devoted to agenda items and position papers drafted on issues such as the ordination of women and church policies toward confirmation.

After an hour of sorting through the papers, he felt certain that the boxes contained nothing unusual, so he called Murphy and left a message. He looked out the window and saw that it had started to rain, a slow drizzle that promised to last the rest of the day. A glance at his watch and calendar revealed that he had an afternoon in front of him with no meetings or commitments of any kind. He sighed. Unable to think of an excuse not to write the sermon for the following Sunday, he flipped on his computer and scrolled through his email before finally opening up his word processor.

Normally, sermon writing was a pleasant task, but the readings assigned by the lectionary all related to the observance of Trinity Sunday, and wading into the theological quagmire of the triune God was a notoriously daunting clerical task. Thor sat for fifteen minutes, drafting and redrafting a single sentence before finally deleting it and then getting up to go to the bathroom. As he reentered his office, he remembered that the box of sermons had been ordered according to the rhythm of the church year, and it took only a couple of minutes to locate three sermons on the subject of Trinitarianism. The paltry number of pages suggested that his predecessor had preached off topic on most years or conveniently gone on vacation, as many clergy did on the first Sunday after Pentecost, in order to cast the preaching burden onto a visiting priest.

Thor skimmed the sermons and saw that they were essentially regurgitations of each other. Although they showed some sophistication and erudition in tackling the notion that one God manifested himself in three ways, the quotations from Aquinas and St. Augustine did little to make Trinitarian doctrine seem anything more than a holy mishmash of theological truisms. The young priest longed to tell the truth to parishioners and expose his whole flock as the rampant polytheists they undoubtedly were. He fantasized about telling the congregation that if they envisioned two beings in heaven, a father and son, sitting side by side as two distinct rulers, they should not call themselves monotheists. Had they noticed anything amiss at the Academy Awards several weeks earlier when an evangelical winner thanked both God and Jesus for helping him become a better actor? To make matters even more confrontational, he could troll through Paul's letters and identify the source of the heresy, and then accuse Christians of being polytheists from the very beginning. He would finish by admitting that he only mouthed the words in the Nicene Creed that proclaimed Jesus was "seated at the right hand of the father," because he considered the phrase to be absolute blasphemy.

Although he lacked the boldness to rail so directly at his congregation, he saw the potential for a toned-down version of his fantasy and sat down to write the sermon. The words quickly tumbled out and he was proofreading the first draft when the phone rang and James Murphy announced he was coming over to pick up the boxes.

VIII.

SUMMONS

S tanley Hopkins was chewing on a candy bar and staring at a stack of exams in his office at Belle Meade College in Los Angeles when the phone rang and a sweetly lilting southern voice brought him back to full consciousness. The woman's request was of a sort that had been coming with greater frequency in recent months. After helping the LAPD track down the location of a gonzo pornographer shooting a series of *Girls Gone Wild*–style videos with high school sophomores in the San Fernando Valley, his name had been passed along to the FBI as a possible resource for an ongoing investigation of interactive websites featuring the coerced performances of Eastern European women. His academic expertise in the labor and economics of the sex trade, not to mention his willingness to work for little more than the reimbursement of his expenses, had led to a series of calls from law-enforcement officials seeking his advice. To many of them, he had nothing to offer, as when a police chief in Oklahoma asked what he knew (absolutely nothing) about organized gangs of porn-for-meth dealers, but sometimes a query fit nicely, and he was happy to tell the well-spoken US attorney from Georgia that he might be able to help her.

"What's the name of the company again?" he asked, after she introduced herself and explained how exhaustive Google searches had produced nothing but dead ends in her search for the real owner of a soft-core website named Mygirlfriendsbikini.com.

"Sweaty Palm Productions," she repeated. "I'll send you the URL of the pictures that we're trying to track down and a brief reference we found to the company online."

"And what do you need, exactly?"

"Well," her tongue lingered on the liquid consonant and Stanley decided that she had a second career as a narrator of romance novels if the Justice Department ever let her go. Her accent was light and subtle, a flick of golden-brown hair in a summer breeze. "In order to figure out who posted the photos of our victim—a student named Diana Cavendish—we need to find the owner of the website where they were posted. The website owner may have contact information for the photographer. The Whois database lists Sweaty Palm—with a false address—as the owner, but Google suggests that a firm by that name did exist in the Los Angeles area. Maybe it still does."

"How did you get my name?"

"I called the FBI office in Los Angeles yesterday and asked for some help, but they've got more urgent things to spend their time on. They gave me your name as someone with expertise in the area." He could hear her tapping on a keyboard. "There. I've just sent you the URL. If you click on the link, you'll see the victim. Definitely kidnapped, probably murdered. We don't know if there's a connection for sure between the crime and the pictures, but I'm intrigued enough to want to track down the lead."

His email was already open, so he clicked on the high-lighted web address in the new message and saw the intriguing smile of Diana Cavendish. For a perverse moment, he imagined the voice from Atlanta belonging to the disappeared woman. He merged the lovely face and the lovely voice as he considered the attorney's request. Classes were over, and once grading was done, there was no reason not to divert himself by tracking down an obscure soft-core pornographer.

Stanley asked the young woman to repeat her name and contact information. He was surprised that she was a Melanie, a name he strongly associated with Scarlett O'Hara's simpering friend in *Gone with the Wind*. Despite the Georgia connection, he suspected that the US attorney was nothing like the passive wife of good old Ashley Wilkes. As soon as their conversation was concluded, he searched her out on the Internet, but *Melanie Wilkerson* generated too many results on a Google image search to be helpful, although a beauty pageant contestant by the same name was worth a lingering glance.

★ ★ ★

The exams could not grade themselves, so the sociology professor postponed his search for Sweaty Palm Productions until he finished a marathon ten-hour session with his red pen flying, fueled by two pots of strong coffee and almost a dozen doughnuts. He arrived home, buzzing and bloated, unable to sleep and curious as to whether he could find more on the Internet about the shadowy website than had his new acquaintance in Atlanta, so he sat down on the reclining chair in his living room and surfed from his laptop until exhaustion hit around two in the morning.

He found nothing more than the Atlanta attorney had when he did a general search of the web, just the same traces of a commercial presence and then the hint of a buyout by another company. He went to the California secretary of state's website and searched for Sweaty Palm, but it had never incorporated or filed a d/b/a registration. A search of online yellow pages and white pages revealed nothing more interesting than a medical clinic in Arizona advertising a cure for the glandular condition that caused sweaty palms. In his academic work on industrial sociology, he had used several fee-paid services to search the corporate structure of the firms that he was studying. A year-long subscription paid for by the college was still in force, so he checked the Dun & Bradstreet and Hoover's databases for any sign of the company but came up empty.

He sat in the chair and tapped the frame of his computer with the ring finger of his left hand. The moon was rising and the mountains that seemed to begin at the edge of his backyard were bathed in a soft yellow light. A coyote howled in the distance and it was hard to believe that he was sitting in Los Angeles County and not some rural town in New Mexico. Sleep was finally slipping upon him, but he needed to check two more sources before he went to bed.

Sweaty Palm had neither incorporated nor registered as a partnership in California, but it might have wanted to protect its intellectual property. He ran a search on the US Patent and Trademark Office website and was not surprised to discover that the company name had been registered as a service mark. The address, however, was the same fictitious listing he had found in the Whois database of Internet domain-name owners. Stanley muttered and scrolled down the complete record. The filing date was from seven years earlier, well before the possible buyout of the firm. At the bottom of the page, he was gratified to see the name of the attorney who had prosecuted the trademark application: Xavier Quintana. No address was given, but the Martindale-Hubbell database of lawyers in the United States quickly revealed two attorneys of that name, one of whom was a trademark specialist in Burbank with an address out by the Bob Hope Airport.

"Bingo," he said as he snapped down the top of his computer and laid it on the carpet next to his chair. A quick trip to the attorney's office the next day might solve the little mystery.

★ ★ ★

The next morning all calls to Xavier Quintana went directly to the attorney's voice mail, so Stanley decided to drive to Burbank and track him down in person. He grabbed a breakfast burrito, a cinnamon roll, and a mammoth cup of coffee from a doughnut shop and took US 210 along the mountains toward Pasadena just as the sun was breaking through the late-morning haze. The

Los Angeles National Forest beckoned off on his right, traces of snow still whitening the highest elevations, and he wondered whether he should drive up the winding road to Falling Springs and take a little hike on the way back home. When he had arrived in Southern California for the first time, fresh off a plane from Chicago, he held nothing but movie stereotypes in his head: beach and smog, freeways and sprawl. He had no clue about the mountains, but they had spoken to him since his first drive west from the airport. Whenever he saw the rugged terrain, he felt his spirit lift, only to be reminded in the next instant that resisting its allure and staying in the Midwest might have preserved the lives of his wife and daughter.

I need to find the ugliest place in the world, he had once told a friend after too many beers. *Some industrial slag heap of a town in the old East Germany is where I need to go. Someplace with nothing to remind me of beauty.*

He turned on the radio, rolled down the window of the car, and tried to blast the memories from his head. With nothing but golden oldies, country music, and talk radio occupying the bandwidth, it was easy to avoid the tunes that formed the musical soundtrack of his life with Angela. Their special songs were college-radio favorites from alternative bands in the nineties that he couldn't find on the FM dial even if he tried. He finally settled on a public radio station just beginning to play a long Mahler symphony. Perfect, he thought. Mahler was a kindred spirit. The composer's wife had been upset by his plan to set a series of depressing poems about childhood death to music and warned him against it. Mahler ignored her and completed his poignant *Kindertotenlieder*, but shortly afterward their eight-year-old daughter died of scarlet fever and his wife never forgave him. Angela had been similarly unsuccessful in convincing him not to take them to Southern California.

The radio was not playing the *Kindertotenlieder*, but rather Mahler's mammoth Second Symphony, so Stanley stayed on the 210 through Pasadena and looped to the east of the Verdugo Hills that loom more than two thousand feet above Burbank.

He exited on La Tuna Canyon Road and spent almost an hour making his way down the back way into the city. He watched the planes landing and taking off from the airport and speculated that escape via Southwest Airlines, rather than Mahler, would be a more effective cure for his mood.

By the time he arrived at the attorney's address in a small, two-story professional building, it was well past lunchtime. His stomach was grumbling, but he went to check on the lawyer before eating. Stanley pressed the buzzer underneath the name of Xavier Quintana, Esq., and while he waited for a response, looked for any information on the tenant list that would help him locate the attorney in case he was not in. A business card with an email address tacked to the lobby's bulletin board would have been nice, but only a neighboring dentist had posted any listing of hours and contact information.

To the professor's surprise, a high-pitched male voice, completely devoid of any Spanish accent, responded from a small speaker next to the door.

"Bilski?"

"No," Stanley answered, "my name is Hopkins. I've got a trademark matter that I'd like to discuss with you." There was no immediate reply, but after a moment a loud buzz and a metallic click sounded and the professor headed up the stairs.

The large man he found standing in the office foyer looked to be about fifty, with a shaved head and wearing a lightweight poplin suit that had probably fit him better twenty years earlier. His eyes were intelligent, and he was barking directions over the phone in an authoritative manner. Eventually, he agreed to file the document that was the subject of the conversation, hung up the phone with a dissatisfied shake of his head, and turned his attention to his visitor.

"What can I do for you?" He reached out and shook Stanley's hand with a forcefulness that matched his bulk. "You need a trademark registered?"

"Well," the professor replied, "I wanted to ask you about a trademark that you registered seven years ago for a video-production company called Sweaty Palm. I want to talk to the owners, but the address listed in the registration is inaccurate." He could see the attorney's eyes narrow. "The company may have gone out of business."

"Why do you need to contact them?" He sat down behind the reception desk and motioned Stanley toward a chair in the near corner of the room. "I don't divulge the names and addresses of my clients without a court order." He offered an obsequious smile. "Nothing personal, Mr. Hopkins, it's just good business."

"Of course, it is." Although the sociology professor had never used his law degree, he was prepared for Quintana's predictable posturing. "I'm here on behalf of Milton Barkley," he dissembled, invoking the name of a sleazy porn-studio mogul with whom he had clashed in the past. "Chimera Productions is interested in purchasing the Sweaty Palm trademark from whoever owns it." He gave the attorney a disarming smile. "I'm sure there would be some sort of a negotiation fee involved."

"Sure," the attorney replied, all traces of suspicion disappearing from his face, "I've done plenty of transfers and licenses before." He ducked from the small reception area into his office with the evident expectation that his visitor would follow. The space was small, but surprisingly neatly appointed. The desk, chairs, and cabinets looked like they came from the same section of Ikea, maybe one of the slightly pricier corners of the megastore. Quintana sat down in his chair and rolled over to a wooden filing cabinet.

"I remember doing the registration—it's a pretty memorable name," he explained as he plucked out a file and began to flip through it, "but I don't remember the client." He continued to talk while he read. "Sometimes I never meet 'em at all. Some clients send me all their info by email—you submit trademarks and specimens to the trademark office in JPEG files now." He paused and then flipped to the last page. "Looks like that's what happened here." He read off a name and address. The information matched the Whois and trademark filing data exactly.

"That's what I already have," sighed Stanley. "It's an address and phone number of a hotel in Beverly Hills. Sweaty Palm was a porn-production company, as far as I can tell. Maybe the principals didn't want to be identifiable."

The attorney frowned as if he had already collected and spent his license fee in his head. He closed his left eye and squinted at the file. "I wonder how they paid me," he asked himself after a minute's pause. "A personal check might have a different address on it."

"Any way to find out after seven years?"

"Maybe." He nodded optimistically. "I'll ask my accountant to look."

The professor almost handed the lawyer his business card before he realized that it would not mesh with his story. Instead, he wrote down his name and cell number on a sticky note and passed it over the desk. Quintana promised to be back in touch if he heard anything. When the lawyer's phone suddenly rang, Stanley motioned for him to take the call and headed downstairs in search of a savory plate of loaded meganachos.

★ ★ ★

Burbank was only a couple of suburbs to the east of the porn epicenter of the United States, in Van Nuys and Canoga Park, so after lunch Stanley decided to visit one of his contacts in the industry and ask whether he had ever heard of Sweaty Palm Productions. During his first trip to Los Angeles, he had met with the heads of several major porn studios to get permission to interview their employees for an academic book he was writing. He had stayed in contact with several who had provided his entrée into the sordid world of adult entertainment.

After thirty minutes on busy commercial streets, he pulled into the parking lot of the former bowling alley that housed Janus Studio. He sat in his car for a moment and stared at the front door of the studio, resisting maudlin memories of his first trip to the place. With a shake of his head, he sprang out of the car, slammed the door shut, and strode briskly to the blacked-out storefront. Ten minutes later, Herb Matteson invited him into his office and listened carefully to his story.

Matteson was a rangy fellow, at least six feet two, and possessed an expressive but not handsome face. A thick mop of reddish hair crowned his head, and when he got excited it quivered slightly, like a willowy wall of Jell-O shaking in an earthquake. The walls of his office featured adult-film awards that he had won over the years, and the space also contained a generous sprinkling of DVD and video-box covers featuring various stars in the Janus stable of talent. Stanley had never been a fan of pornographic movies, especially after seeing one being filmed, but he found the promotional materials to be rather eye-catching. Lingerie, swimsuits, and suggestive poses did more for his imagination than the graphic close-ups that seemed more appropriate for an anatomy textbook than a sexy film.

"The name doesn't ring a bell," the director admitted, knitting his woolly brows together in consternation. "If it was a studio making videos, I'd know about them for sure—it's just not that big a world around here—but I don't keep track of every kid who's set up a website with some snaps of his ex-girlfriend."

"It's a bigger operation than that," Stanley explained. He told the director to wake up his computer and check out Mygirlfriendsbikini.com. It was an extensive website with thousands of pictures of hundreds of different girls, organized into different categories based on poses from "dancers" to "yoga girls" to "tramp-olines." Matteson clicked through a dozen pictures or so and nodded his head.

"Yeah, you're right." He turned and shrugged his shoulders. "Not too bad. You've got to have a decent viewership to justify that many uploads." He gave Stanley a sleazy little smirk. "I may have to troll through it again for some new talent."

"But no clue who might be behind it?"

"Nah." He thought for a moment. "What you want is to find out who's selling content to the site or who the guy running it might sell to. Find some other soft-core sites where at most you might see some cleavage or a bit of camel toe." He shook his head as if he did not understand humanity. "Some guys feel guilty about watching hard-core stuff, so they're waxing the dolphin at these swimsuit sites instead." He flipped down his laptop. "Anyway, find some similar sites and ask them if they know the competition."

"But how am I going to find out who owns those sites?" The professor despaired of conducting dozens of fruitless searches for website owners. He doubted any of them told the truth in their Whois disclosures.

"Not everybody is hiding." A thoughtful look passed over Matteson's face. "Some of the muscle magazines post this kind of stuff, but with super juiced-up chicks. Playboy even has a girls-next-door section on its site. I might be able to get you an intro over there."

Stanley considered his options and saw that the director had a valid point. Sweaty Palm would be best known within its own corner of the trade. He stood up and thanked Matteson for his help. Despite the director's lack of moral scruple, Stanley shook his hand and offered him a smile of genuine gratefulness. As he turned and walked out of the room, the director stopped him and flipped his computer back open.

"Hang on just a second!" He typed and tapped. "I'm just thinking that the site has to have advertisers. You could ask them who they write their checks to." He stared at the screen for a moment and laughed. "Yup, they've got two sponsors: somebody selling stay-hard pills and another selling herbal penis enhancement. It might be worth trying to track the advertisers down."

Stanley nodded, thanked his informant again, and soon was on his way back to Claremont. He eschewed the hiking expedition he had proposed on the drive to Burbank in order to dive more quickly into his research. As much as he loved the mountains, the distraction of work was more therapeutic than quiet contemplation in the wilderness.

IX.

GENEVA, 2007

Six years before Stanley went to California or Melanie moved back to Georgia or James discovered pictures of a dead student on the Internet and before Diana Cavendish had even disappeared, Elisa van der Vaart was sitting in a tavern in Geneva, Switzerland, wondering why her friend Brenda had all the luck with men. The young English woman had just marched into their favorite brewpub with a handsome young American who had been fortunate enough to be studying his map on the sidewalk in front of the train station when Brenda walked by. She gave him directions to the City Hostel Geneva but invited him to first have a beer or two with her friend. A few minutes later, she was showing off her prize to Elisa at their usual Friday afternoon haunt.

Elisa decided that intrinsic good looks had nothing to do with Brenda's success. The Dutch girl reckoned that she was somewhat slimmer than the busty English girl, a little less curvy, to be sure, but in the Eurozone an aggressive bit of cleavage was hardly the gold standard—the French girls proved that. She was surely in better physical shape than the Londoner, who was always ready to substitute a trip to the pub for a trip to the gym. Elisa jogged almost every day in the summer and skated whenever she could in the winter. Brenda's hair was a little darker and fuller, but when Elisa pulled her uninspiring locks back in a tight ponytail, her cheekbones leapt out nicely and her smile revealed a straighter and whiter set of teeth. No. It was Brenda's personality that attracted guys the way a politician attracts lobbyists. She wasn't slutty—although she did have more men stay the night than her roommate; she was simply open and friendly and possessed the sort of natural initiative that led her to scoop handsome young Americans off the street with no thought for the consequences.

Brenda had befriended Elisa their very first day at the World Trade Organization. She had sidled over with a cup of tea during the morning orientation session for new employees and by lunchtime had convinced her new friend that they should share an apartment together in Annemasse, just over the border in France, where they could save money on living expenses. Brenda was not the tidiest roommate, but she did her share of the cooking and included Elisa in every social event on her calendar. She just knew how to draw people out. Many was the night when Elisa was dragged away from a boring pile of documents to a museum opening or a party by the irrepressible Londoner.

Thankfully, Brenda's newest young man was polite and did not spend too much time staring at her sweater. He was over six feet in height, with long brown hair drooping down into an intelligent face. When he set his large backpack on the floor, she sensed a wiry strength in his lean frame. He was wearing shorts and hiking boots, and his calves were tense and muscled as if he had spent more time walking around Europe than riding trains. He seemed genuinely interested in what each girl was doing in Geneva and was surprised to learn that they were not students, but rather professionals at the WTO. Unlike most Americans, he knew more about the organization than just its acronym, and his eyes sparkled when he posed a teasing question about their plans to establish a one-world government and rule the world from Geneva.

"Not us!" Brenda exclaimed as she leaned to the side and bumped his shoulder. "That's the bloody Freemasons. They're over at the United Nations in that cute little pyramid building." She laughed and tipped her glass at a table of Asian men. "It's them you've got to worry about. If the Chinese government ever gets sorted, they'll be running everything."

Elisa rolled her eyes while the young man laughed. Brenda was already reeling him in. She did it so effortlessly. Elisa felt self-conscious and socially paralyzed whenever she set her sights on some handsome guy. That's why she preferred to wait for Mr.

Right to magically arrive all wrapped up and tidy, no fuss, no mess, no bother. The American across the table, however, had her second-guessing her strategy.

"I'm from a small town in Georgia called Clarkeston," he revealed when finally asked. Elisa had been impressed that he did not plunge into his life story as soon as he sat down, preferring instead to learn about the young women first. Americans were usually insistent on talking about themselves early and often. "You remember the 1996 Olympics in Atlanta? I live about seventy miles from there."

"Was your family originally French?" Elisa asked, a second beer jolting her mouth into gear. "Granville is a French name, isn't it?"

He nodded his head and continued. He looked at-home in the cozy bar, rumpled shirt and hiking boots meshing harmoniously with the dark scuffed wood of the tables and booths. Elisa wondered how he would fit in with the rest of Geneva, the starched and tidy world of bureaucrats and bankers who dominated life away from the train station.

"My grandfather was from Quebec. He and my grandmother met during the war and she dragged him back to Georgia." He laughed, a pleasant rumble that started low in his chest. "I remember asking my mom why he talked so funny."

"And let me guess what you're doing here, Monsieur Granville," Brenda interjected with a sloppy French accent. "Taking a gap year and traveling around Europe." How did she flirt so easily? There was nothing untoward about her approach, no thigh-rubbing or lip-licking, just good old-fashioned eye contact. How hard could that be?

"I wish I had a year," he sighed, "I've just got the summer before I start work at the local newspaper. I studied photojournalism in college." He mentioned the career in an offhand way, as if it were devoid of glamour. "And you can just call me Jacob."

★ ★ ★

Jacob Granville stayed in the women's apartment in Annemasse for almost a week during the summer of 2008, sleeping on the sofa and demonstrating some thoughtfulness by waiting until they had left for work in the morning to use their only bathroom. By the time they came home in the evening, he had usually straightened up the small living room and washed the dishes. He even cooked for them twice. Although Brenda clearly claimed him, he did not sleep in her bedroom, perhaps because they did not want to make Elisa feel uncomfortable. Nonetheless, he was not a monk. Or gay. One weekday, Elisa came home at lunchtime to fetch a book and found that Brenda had beaten her home. She never saw her roommate, but the enthusiastic cries coming from her bedroom left no doubt that the English girl was home and sharing a midday tryst with the handsome American.

Elisa had never heard Brenda be so vocal before. On other occasions, she must have been muffling her passion to avoid shocking her roommate. The embarrassed Dutch girl half expected the door of the bedroom to burst open and the two lovers to come spilling out into the living room biting and clawing each other like a pair of wet house cats. She paused a moment at the front door, but when the furor showed no signs of subsiding, she crept over to the living room table, picked up her book, and slipped out of the apartment. She had planned on making an egg sandwich in the kitchen but made do with a cheap crepe from a sidewalk cart. Meeting the couple right after their noisy lovemaking would have been too weird.

Later that day, after cooking a passable spaghetti dinner, Granville proposed leading a long walk on a path he had discovered in the Bois des Côtes, the biggest green space in their suburb of Annemasse. Brenda had turned an ankle in her heels on the way home from her office and encouraged Elisa to go with him. When Brenda pulled a stack of files out of her briefcase and waved her hand, it was clearly up to Elisa to entertain their guest for the evening. He put his right arm akimbo in a gesture that invited her to link up with him, and soon they were strolling out into the lengthening shadows of a warm summer evening.

Elisa was surprised that he kept hold of her for several blocks before finally disengaging in response to a group of teenagers blocking the sidewalk in front of them. When they met again on the far side of the pack, he turned to her and smiled. "You're certainly quiet today." She realized that she had not spoken a word since they had left the apartment. "Tough day at the office?"

The toughest thing about her day had been the cheese-and-mushroom crepe she had bought for lunch, but she had no wish to mention what had prompted the unfortunate purchase. "No, not at all. It was actually a pretty interesting day."

"What did you work on?"

"Do you really want to know?" She looked up at him with doubting eyes. He had been a considerate temporary roommate, but she still did not entirely trust him. His politeness seemed insincere and his southern American accent sounded strangely contrived to someone who had polished her English skills by listening to BBC One.

"Absolutely!" His enthusiasm sounded genuine. "It's not often that I get a peek at the inner workings of the World Trade Organization."

"Well, to start off with, it's not quite the place you might think it is. When I finished my PhD, I came here to be a lit-tle liberal mouse—mole?—in this big organization dedicated to evil globalization, but my first assignment was to help plug a loophole in compulsory licensing regulations for AIDS drugs that made it difficult for poor countries to get cheap pharma-ceuticals. Have you ever heard of the Doha Declaration?"

He shook his head as they rounded a corner and headed toward a large green space several blocks distant.

"I helped draft it, and I was so surprised when we—the WTO—declared that Indian and Brazilian generic manufac-turers should be allowed to import cheap drugs to South Africa, Botswana, and Zimbabwe without the permission of American and EU pharmaceutical companies. I still watch out for the big corporate boogeyman, but mostly I get to do really productive stuff like counsel developing countries how to creatively adapt to all these confusing intellectual property treaties."

"You sound a lot like Brenda." He laughed. "She gets really defensive if I kid her about the WTO and corporations running the world."

"I can imagine." She turned to him and explained while they waited at a stoplight. "She works in the section on Subsidies and Countervailing Duties, which sounds pretty boring, but basically her job is to help police countries that subsidize their goods at the expense of outside competition. She's been trying to convince the EU to drop some of the agriculture subsidies that make it so hard for farmers in developing countries to sell their products here. Imagine you're some poor orange farmer in Tunisia and you want to sell your crop in Europe, but the prices here are artificially low because the EU pays millions to Spanish orange growers. Sixty percent of the EU budget goes to agriculture subsidies! Brenda is fighting to open the EU market to the poorest of the poor farmers, so she really resents people trashing the WTO."

They crossed the last street in front of them and approached a wooded area. Granville led them fifty yards to its edge before ducking into a large bush. She found the narrow gap, pushed a branch out of her hair, and then cautiously followed him into the undergrowth. He was waiting a few yards ahead, proudly tracing the course of a footpath with a sweep of his arm.

"I found this yesterday," he said. "It goes up the hill to the other side of the city." He put his arm on a low tree branch and leaned against it. "We'll have to catch the bus home, but it's a nice walk over if you're up for it."

The trail looked well worn and safe, but the woods were gloomy and it would be dark in less than two hours. She looked up at him doubtfully, but his smile brimmed with confidence and he started to pad up the trail without waiting for her to answer. When she followed, he picked up the conversation where it had left off.

"So, if the EU won't budge, what happens? Do jackbooted thugs from Geneva invade Brussels?" She pulled even with him on a broad section of the trail and puzzled out the meaning of *jackbooted thugs*.

"No," she explained, "the WTO cannot force any country to change its laws, but it can require that compensation be paid by a country that doesn't comply with the rules, or it could authorize trade sanctions, like a new tariff or something like that. Brenda's trying to figure out how to change the rules to make more countries lower their subsidies."

Elisa looked down the path into the dark corridor of foliage ahead and saw the track extended for fifty meters or so before it bent uphill and sharply to the right. The woods were already plunging into dusk and she felt an involuntary shiver as they left the comforting hum of traffic behind them.

She cast a quick glance at her companion. He was beaming and a bit too close, eager to drag her along on his big adventure. Granville was friendly and physically attractive, but what did she really know about him? If he were Italian, she would fear nothing worse than an attempted kiss or a possible squeeze of her backside, with a rebuff ending in nothing worse than a shrug of the shoulders and a return to the status quo. A Frenchman might be just as forward but would be more likely to storm off in a huff when rejected. She had never dealt with an American— not that she thought it likely Jacob was interested—and she found it difficult to put aside her prejudices. Americans were different. Whether the news was about Ted Bundy or Jeffrey Dahmer, the Dutch people had long concluded that there was some sickness deep in American society. Most Americans were good-hearted and generous, but for some reason their country seemed to breed a special class of dangerous men. Even when things went wrong in Europe, like the Dunblane school massacre, the comparisons were inevitably to atrocities that had occurred first in the US.

As if he could read her mind, he moved away from her with another smile and struck off down the trail. She stood for a moment, shook off her paranoia, and followed the athletic figure in the stained leather boots. He must have heard her steps for he spoke without turning around. "It will take us about twenty minutes to get to the ridge, where we'll finally get a view."

He walked steadily, long strides eating up the terrain. She kept up without difficulty, grateful that her jogging routine and resistance to Brenda's offers of after-dinner cigarettes kept her in good shape. As the path started to level out and they approached the ridge, the trees thinned and she could see the sprawling suburb of Annemasse below them. It did not compare with the view down on Paris from Sacré Coeur, but it was satisfying to see the streets of her adopted home spread out before her. She took the last few steps to the crest and then saw Geneva, framed by a ring of rolling hills.

As she looked to the northwest, over Lac Leman, she felt her hiking partner come up behind her and put his hands on her shoulders. He spun her slowly ninety degrees, rotating his body behind hers. She stiffened but did not fight the firm sinew of his grip.

"See the little park and the red-brick building on the corner?" He spoke softly, his lips just inches from her right ear. "We live in the apartment block right next door. You can barely make out the building—you see the antennas on the roof?"

She found it impossible to concentrate on the view. Her eyes darted from place to place, and she was keenly aware of Granville's fingers resting on the edge of her collarbone. She turned suddenly and he released her. He was much taller and they stood so close that her gaze matched his Adam's apple. She looked up and his eyes narrowed.

"Are you afraid of me?" His usually smooth voice sounded dry and clinical.

"Of course not!" she exclaimed, involuntarily taking a step back. "I mean, why should I be? We're friends, aren't we?"

He looked at her hard before relaxing, and she noticed his shoulders drop slightly, as if some tension in his back had been released. "I hope so! I mean, Brenda is really special, but you're awesome too. If you all ever came to Georgia, I could show you some real southern hospitality."

Elisa relaxed, too, and chided herself for being so jumpy. This is why I never have a boyfriend, she thought, I always think the worst of people. She turned away, looked out over Annemasse, and resolved to be more open with him. "I would love to go to the States sometime. It's been great having you here."

"I'm so glad." His voice was behind her again, not as close as before, but she knew that if she reached backward with her hand, she would touch him. "I thought that you might be mad about Brenda this afternoon."

She kept her gaze straight ahead, scrambling to figure out how he could know that she had overhead the bumping and thrashing in her roommate's bedroom. "Huh?"

"Oh, come on." He leaned against her shoulder as they looked out over the city. "I put my cup of coffee on your book this morning, and when I got up, uh, afterward, it was gone . . . You don't have to be Sherlock Holmes."

His voice sounded neither sinister nor humorous; yet still, it was provocative, as if he hoped she would be scandalized or might comment favorably on the extraordinary noises he had elicited from his girlfriend. She had no idea what to say. A witty response and a quick start down the path to the bus was the best plan, but nothing clever came to mind.

As she stood for a long moment, avoiding his eyes by pretending to survey the city, he strode purposefully away from her side. "Let's go," he said, tossing the words over his shoulder. "I could use a cold beer after this climb."

She turned and watched him slide underneath the crest of the ridge. She shook her head, both as a gesture of incomprehension and to clear the cobwebs, before she followed his hungry stride down the hill and back to the reassuring confluence of cars, scooters, buildings, and streetlamps.

A week later, Jacob announced his departure after a breakfast of warm croissants he had fetched from the small bakery around the corner from the apartment. After he shouldered his backpack, he gave Elisa a hug while Brenda looked on, arms crossed over her chest, red-rimmed eyes cast downward, farewells having been said earlier that morning behind closed doors.

★ ★ ★

Late in the evening on her way to bed, Elisa tapped on Brenda's door and found her friend sitting in bed with her back against the wall, reading a book. She was less distressed than she had been that morning, but her face was pale and she looked exhausted. Elisa felt immediately drawn to her. She sat down on the bed and asked how she was doing, and Brenda held up the book in response.

"Jacob gave me this as a present before he left: *Midnight in the Garden of Good and Evil*. It takes place in Georgia." She laid the book down in her lap with a sigh. "I'm sorry I'm being so antisocial. I'm usually not this silly about a guy."

"Maybe you should visit him there on your next vacation?" She looked at the cover of the paperback. The book looked depressing, with a stone angel looming like a vulture over a decaying cemetery. Brenda's fingers traced the embossed edge of the book cover.

"Maybe," she replied in a weak and unconvincing voice. She sat in a pair of men's boxer shorts and a T-shirt, a diminished version of her normally commanding self. Elisa made a short speech about what a special guy Jacob was, but her attempt at comfort failed and eventually she put a hand briefly on her friend's shoulder and left. Fourteen months later Elisa would find her friend in the same bedroom, dead from an apparent drug overdose that the police suspected had been staged to look like an accident.

X.

HIEROGLYPHICS (2013)

"I'm home!" James failed to catch himself and muttered a quick *Shit* as he entered the house. His wife had been absent for three days, but this was the first time that he forgot to suppress the greeting he usually offered as he arrived home. Sondra hated being startled, so he had developed the habit of announcing himself rather than risking the charge that he was creeping up and spying on her. She was still gone, and he could only speculate how long it would take before she tired of her sister's vegetarian cooking and returned.

The first time she left, after he had announced he was turning down a better job at an Atlanta paper ten years earlier, he was crushed and then panicked at the thought their marriage might be over. But after a week of silence and despair, he saw her reappear without explanation, and he was so grateful that it took him days to press her as to where she had been. This was the fourth or fifth time that she had stormed angrily out of his life, and he was now resigned to her refusal to return his phone calls.

He did not understand why life had to be so complicated. Sondra thought he lacked ambition just because he wanted to stay in Clarkeston. She could not understand that interesting news happened everywhere, even in small-town Georgia. And Clarkeston really wasn't even that small. In a town of sixty thousand people, there was plenty of crime and corruption, heroes and half-wits, to dig your teeth into. If he kept honing his craft, he stood just as good a chance of winning a major journalism prize as some reporter for *The New York Times*, and without having to live in New York City. He was privileged to work amid the oak-canopied splendor of Clarkeston College and along the broad avenues of the historic downtown, and even when he ventured out into the squalid trailer parks off the bypass, he could always retreat back to his quiet street with the thoughtful neighbors who would collect his newspaper without being asked when he went out of town for a couple of days. If he had ever taken her up to the North Carolina mountains to see his childhood home, Sondra might have understood his contentment with Clarkeston better, but he just couldn't bring himself to do it.

But for once, he was grateful for her absence, at least for the afternoon. He planned to dive deeply into Father Ernest Rodgers's papers, and he was happy not to suffer snide comments about chasing phantoms in the dead priest's junk boxes.

He propped open the side door of the house, carried the cargo directly from his station wagon into the study, and then made a cup of tea. Rain was pouring down, but the double-paned glass and floor-to-ceiling bookshelves in the library kept him snug and warm. Several months earlier, he had bought a worn leather chair and matching stool at a garage sale and squeezed them in between his computer desk and the picture window looking out into the backyard. The little nook had become his favorite reading spot, even after Sondra had "accidentally" spilled nail-polish remover on the garish orange recliner in an attempt to get it out of her house.

Deciding to tackle the pile of sermons last, he sifted through conference programs and miscellaneous communications from the diocese of Atlanta, which provided insight into Episcopal church politics but little hint of Rodgers's impassioned defense of Jacob Granville. Toward the bottom of the box, he ran across a clipping describing the Clarkeston police's discovery of the bloody apartment of Diana Cavendish. To his surprise, he noticed that the story, slipped inside a brochure for a spiritual retreat, came from a small north Georgia newspaper rather than the *Clarkeston Chronicle*. The retreat had taken place at a conference center in the Appalachian foothills, so it appeared that Rodgers had been out of town at the time of the murder.

He read the clipping, but it contained no unfamiliar information. In fact, most of the language had been lifted straight from the first story he himself had filed with the AP wire service. Nonetheless, he laid it on his desk before he returned the rest of the papers to the cardboard container. When he put the box back on the floor and moved the next one to his desktop, he took a long sip from his mug of tea and contemplated the enjoyment he took from digging into other people's stuff. He suspected that no momentous discovery would be found in Rodgers's old papers, but there was something thrilling about drilling down into the most mundane details of someone else's life. The microscope focused on the most insignificant detritus sometimes revealed more than the most powerful telescope pointed out into space.

At a minimum, the reporter learned a good bit about the job of being an Episcopal priest. James's parents had taken him as a child to the whitewashed Primitive Baptist church down the dirt road from their house. The pastor had a small Christmas-tree farm close by and had no formal training for what was clearly a one-man, part-time operation. For Pastor Silas, saving souls meant a lot of yelling, and James started to find excuses to miss Sunday services once he was in high school. The hierarchy and formal structure of the Episcopal Church was far removed from his childhood experience. Nonetheless, Rodgers had one thing in common with Pastor Silas: his willingness to startle folks from the pulpit, such as his notorious excommunication of a parishioner for muttering a racial slur during Communion or his famous sermon on the persecution of Jacob Granville.

It was the Granville sermon that James especially wanted to find, but as he sifted through the typed sheets of marked-up text, he realized that the homilies were ordered by their place in the church calendar, and not in chronological order from year to year. He was not sure whether the sermon had been preached during Lent or Holy Week or Pentecost, so he went through the pages one at a time, constantly distracted by the content of Rodgers's talks as well as by the violent scribbles in the margin where he argued with himself or suggested impromptu points of departure from the written version of his message.

Before the reporter knew it, night had fallen and a deep rumble in his stomach reminded him that he had not eaten all day. A cursory glance in the refrigerator confirmed his suspicion that all possible leftovers had been consumed or gone bad. Too impatient to cook, he ordered a pizza from his favorite (and Sondra's least favorite) carryout joint and went back into his study to enjoy the sermons the old-fashioned way: beer in hand, feet propped up, pizza on belly.

Three hours later, an empty cardboard box lay on the floor next to a stack of discarded papers, and four brown bottles were creating an overflow problem in James's small wastebasket. He was nearing the bottom of the first box of sermons, with another box still unopened and destined for the next day's sleuthing.

After he pulled out the last four or five texts, he finally saw a reference to Jacob Granville, not by name, but in connection with "the mysterious disappearance of a young student here in Clarkeston." Rodgers had waited to lash out at the public's assumption that Jacob Granville had murdered Diana Cavendish until the Bible lectionary gave Psalm 35 as an optional reading. Verse 20 was his starting point: "They do not speak peaceably, but devise false accusations against those who live quietly in the land." Without ever mentioning Granville or Cavendish by name, he launched a rhetorical offensive against local gossip and declared his firm belief that the longtime member of his flock was innocent of any wrongdoing. He offered no alternative explanations for what the police had found in Cavendish's apartment, beyond hinting that a limited amount of blood had been found on the scene, not nearly enough to prove anyone had died there. The primary focus was his close relationship with the accused, and he made several references to long-suffering biblical characters to build his case.

The sermon was both wildly over the top and rather subtly done. Such personal subject matter was probably inappropriate for a mainstream church, but Rodgers had been very clever in how he made his point, by referring to events and characters from scripture. Unfortunately, the margins of the text were mostly devoid of notes, perhaps because it had been more carefully crafted than his normal sermon. The text conveyed a great deal about the attitude and personality of its writer, but little about its subject. The only hint of a clue was found on the final page, where the priest quoted from the first book of Peter: "Don't repay evil for evil. Don't retaliate with insults when people insult you. Instead, pay them back with a blessing. That is what God has called you to do, and he will bless you for it." Next to the quote, he had written in small letters, "Miriam."

James paused for a moment and then reread the final paragraph of the sermon, which concluded with a list of occasions when God had withheld judgment on his chosen people. He revisited the comment in the margin. Miriam was the name of Rodgers's daughter, but she was also the sister of Moses, a biblical prophetess in her own right. When Moses delegated important responsibilities to various elders during the long march through Sinai, she was snubbed by her brother and began a whispering campaign against him. To teach her a lesson, God turned her into a leper, then changed her punishment to one week's exile outside of the camp after Moses intervened on her behalf and she repented of her envy and slander. Was the marginal note a reminder to ask his daughter a question about Granville? Or was it a suggestion to add an impromptu reference to the biblical story of Miriam during the spoken sermon? Or perhaps *Miriam* was just shorthand for some unidentified Clarkestonian who had gossiped and slandered Jacob Granville.

The reporter put the sermon on top of the newspaper clipping about the murder and quickly flipped through the remaining papers. He found nothing of interest, and when the Pica typeface on the yellowing sheets of paper started to swim before his eyes, he pushed himself up from the worn armchair and went off to bed.

He had a series of interviews to conduct with candidates for the local school board election the following morning, but he would have time in the late afternoon to go through the last box before he took them all back to Thorsten Carter. After he crawled into bed, he called Sondra's cell phone, but it went immediately to voice mail and he turned off the light with a sigh, trying to think of an appropriate message he might text her. He considered firing off a biblical quote about dutiful wives, but there was no quicker way to infuriate a headstrong Baptist woman than to wield scripture, or worse yet, sarcasm, against her. He briefly considered paying a consoling visit to Mygirlfriendsbikini.com, but concluded sourly that the price of reconciling with his wife surely included foregoing the very sin that had led to the rift in the first place. Eventually, he drifted off to sleep, only to be awoken several hours later by the neighbor's German shepherd barking like crazy next door.

He got up, walked to his back window, and noticed that his motion-detector lights were on. Raccoons and opossums often set off the lights, and so did the neighbor's dog, for that matter. Once the dog stopped barking, he opened the window a crack and listened for noises coming from the backyard, but he heard nothing. After a trip to the bathroom, he lay down and turned off the cell phone he kept on the table beside his bed. One rude awakening per night was enough.

* * *

By the next morning, the rain had stopped and the air was warm but without the stickiness that came with precipitation later in summer. James decided to walk downtown to City Hall, where the school board candidates were filing their applications to be on the ballot. He had reserved a small conference room there, and six out of the eight hopefuls had agreed to be interviewed about their opinions on everything from the wisdom of having

Coke machines in school cafeterias to the county's decision to adopt an abstinence-based sex-education program. The interviews took all morning and by the end he despaired for the future of the county's children. If he could get away with it, the headline in the paper would read, "Inarticulate Morons Advocate Lobotomizing Local Children." At the end of the interview he summed up each candidate:

#1 Evolution and Dinosaur Bones = Conspiracy
#2 School Uniforms Will Solve All Problems
#3 Illegal Immigrants Are Bad
#4 Brain Dead
#5 Organic Lunch Food Will Solve All Problems
#6 Profoundly Brain Dead

He was so depressed that he treated himself to his favorite comfort food, even though the restaurant was five blocks away from the courthouse in the wrong direction from home. Williams Soul Food had occupied a bright yellow cinderblock building on the corner of Oak and Plaza for as long as he could remember. Once a month he chanced the massive amounts of cholesterol imbued in each mouthwatering piece of fried chicken, fried catfish, chicken-fried steak, Cajun fries, fried okra with bacon, or greens with pork belly. Even the drinks were bad for you: the sweet tea was the major cause of diabetes in the three-county area. Going to Williams was like going home, but minus the guilt and attitude.

As he contentedly popped a piece of Mama Williams's (God rest her soul) perfectly crunchy chicken skin into his mouth, he nodded to the server for more tea and decided that he wanted whipped cream with his blackberry cobbler. He reveled in the clatter of cheap plastic plates on ancient Formica countertops and the constant buzz of the servers, who doled out a "sweetie" or "honey" with every refill of tea to the lawyers and laborers who sat shoulder to shoulder at the lunch counter. There was no more diverse place in Clarkeston, and the journalist had long ago concluded that if all banks, corporate boards, and legislatures looked like Williams Soul Food at lunch, the country would be a far better place.

Murphy's editor did not want the story on the school board candidates until later in the week, so the reporter took his time with his cobbler and coffee and a day-old copy of the *Atlanta Journal Constitution*. He envisioned his name on the front-page byline of a story resolving the mysterious disappearance of Diana Cavendish, even better if he could reveal a cover-up that would take the story national. He folded the paper in half, stuck it under his left arm, and finished his coffee with new resolve. Once he finished working through Ernest Rodgers's boxes, he would expand his search. Neither the victim's parents nor Jacob Granville's had been willing to talk to him five years earlier. Maybe they would be now.

The twenty-minute walk back home helped him shrug off the lethargic legacy of his lunch. The vivid colors of spring had faded, but the dense green of summer had not yet overwhelmed the town. Leaves on trees and bushes were nearly fully formed and played with the late-spring sunlight, twinkling a maze of cool mint and light velvet hues. Here and there, plots of red, yellow, and purple pansies signaled that Clarkeston would still enjoy a bit of time before July and August made comparisons with the Amazon jungle seem not only appropriate, but quite possibly favorable to Brazil.

As James ducked under the bushy crepe myrtle that hung over the corner of his driveway, he was trying to decide whether sparkling water or more coffee would be the best accompaniment to his final plunge into Ernest Rodgers's papers, but all thoughts of beverages evaporated when he saw that the door from the garage into his house was ajar. He was sure that he had locked it firmly behind him earlier that morning. He had fumbled with his keys on the way out, dropping them to the garage floor and scraping his shoulder against the door frame when he reached clumsily down to pick them up. Sondra might have come by to pick up something during his absence, but writing about crime for a living had made him more cautious than the typical home owner. Before he went inside, he picked up a pitching wedge from his wife's bag of golf clubs and pushed open the door with his foot. He yelled into the house, telling whoever was there that he was coming in and warning any burglars to run before the police arrived. He listened carefully for any noise and, hearing nothing, he stepped into the kitchen, eyes surveying the room for any sign of disturbance.

He went through the downstairs rooms one at a time, slowly peering around each corner, pitching wedge cocked over his shoulder, ready to chop down any hostile intruder. He was relieved to see the new flat-screen television was still in the living room. Some books had been flicked from their shelves and drawers had been opened, but his wife's jewelry in the spare bedroom looked untouched. He was ready to conclude that Sondra must have come home in a pissy mood to pick up some clothes, when he arrived at the far end of the house and entered his study.

The room looked like a hurricane had struck. Every drawer had been ripped out of his desk and tossed on the floor. The file folders and papers inside them were all missing, leaving only a littered chaos of pencils, pens, scissors, rubber bands, paper clips, and a three-hole punch on the floor and chair. His new laptop had also been taken, and he groaned at the thought of having to migrate all of the files from his computer at work to its replacement. His voice-activated tape recorder was also gone, as were several notepads and a folder full of newspaper clippings that he had collected over the years.

Certain that the thief had left, he dropped the golf club, plopped down heavily in his armchair, and stared at the mess for several minutes, before pulling out his cell phone and calling the police. As he dialed, he scanned the room one more time and then swore aloud. Rodgers's boxes were gone too. Everything that Thorsten Carter had given him was missing. After he finished talking to the dispatcher, he contemplated everything that had been taken and made another call, this one to Melanie

Wilkerson in the US attorney's office in Atlanta. The journalist did not believe in coincidences, and he wondered why the thieves had targeted only items related to his job and left all personal valuables in their place. He could think of no story that he was working on, apart from the disappearance of Diana Cavendish, that might possibly interest someone daring enough to pillage his study in broad daylight. He had just reopened the case, and even if the break-in was unconnected, it provided an opportunity to prod the attorney into action.

XI.

BACKROADS

Melanie was sitting behind a worn wooden table in a federal courtroom when her phone began to vibrate quietly in the pocket of her jacket. Although the judge was notorious for scolding attorneys who dared check their messages in his presence, she slipped the device out carefully and held it under the table where he could not see. He was not paying attention to her anyway. She had accompanied one of her newest hires to make sure that the rookie knew how to properly conduct a plea hearing. A dozen defendants were making formal guilty pleas that afternoon and it was up to Amy to justify a proposed deal if the judge had any questions about the appropriateness of the agreement. Amy had done arraignments and some grand-jury work, but she had never worked the tail end of the process, and Melanie was there to make sure that she could jump through the relevant hoops and make the proper recitations to satisfy the procedural requirements of the court.

As the young woman explained to a dubious judge that a suspended sentence and diversion to an alcohol-treatment facility was an appropriate fate for a drunk driver caught on the local air force base, Melanie swiped her finger over the face of her phone and saw that James Murphy had called. A moment later a text came through asking for her to call as soon as possible. She tapped a perfectly manicured nail on the side of the phone and contemplated the three exclamation points that followed the request. The reporter had not struck her as the hysterical type.

She looked up. The judge was nodding and seemed satisfied with what he was hearing. As her subordinate returned from the bench with a confident wink, Melanie nodded, pointed to the phone cupped carefully in her hand, and went out into the hallway to make a call to Clarkeston.

She leaned against the wall outside the courtroom and listened to Murphy's story. The reporter had obtained the personal records of a priest he suspected had shielded the murderer of Diana Cavendish, only to have them and his computer stolen from his house the following day. She asked him where the papers came from and who knew he had them, but he insisted that no one who knew had any motive to break into his house. Before Murphy could say anything more, the police arrived and he hung up abruptly to talk with Sheriff Johnson, leaving Melanie staring at her phone. None of it made a whole lot of sense.

First of all, who would have any interest in a bunch of boxes stored in a church closet for years? And why would the sheriff come out to the house for an ordinary burglary? It could just be a random crime, but Murphy said nothing else had been taken. His wife's jewelry collection was still intact and their new fifty-two-inch HD television was still sitting in the living room. She cracked open the door to the courtroom. The young attorney seemed comfortable sitting alone at the table, shuffling papers in response to a new round of questions by the judge. Melanie shut the door carefully. No one had held her hand during her first plea proceeding. Satisfied that her help was not needed, she walked briskly over the marble floor to a bank of elevators, which took her up to the twentieth floor.

She nodded absentmindedly at a colleague, who stepped in as she exited, and walked down the hall to her office. Although the message light on her landline was blinking, she ignored it, walked over to the window, and scowled at the parking lot. An unsettled feeling had begun roiling in her stomach as soon as she got Murphy's text, and hearing his brief synopsis of events in Clarkeston had intensified the sensation. She was proud of her hard-headed approach to investigations and prosecutions, but she had also come to trust her instincts. And right now something was tickling her Spidey-sense.

All journalists had enemies, but a daylight burglary was an unusual operation. Could it have been prompted by Murphy's renewed investigation of a five-year-old murder? As unlikely as it seemed, the connection could not be dismissed. She texted the reporter and asked him to call her back as soon as the cops left. Three exclamation points. In the meantime, she called and left a message for Professor Stanley Hopkins in Los Angeles to get an update on his search for Sweaty Palm Productions, the registered owner of Mygirlfriendsbikini.com.

She fidgeted in her chair, trying to decide what to do next. The draft of an appellate brief in a search-and-seizure case sat on her desk waiting to be proofread, but it was not due to be filed for another week, and the attorney she was supervising on the case was a good writer. She gave the first couple of pages a quick scan. She had tried the case herself two years earlier, an anonymous tip and a questionable wiretap leading to a huge drug bust. Now the defendants were challenging the FBI investigation that led to their convictions. She stopped in the middle of the recitation of facts at the beginning of the brief and impulsively checked her email. Nothing of interest. Back to the brief. She was so distracted that she found her own distractibility annoying.

She kicked back from the desk and stared out the window, dying to ask James Murphy exactly who knew that he had taken the boxes home from his church. She forced herself back to the FBI drug appeal and was scribbling a comment in the margin of the brief when the phone finally rang.

"So, who knew that you had the boxes?" She slid over a yellow pad and doodled to make sure her pen was working.

"No one except the priest and the church choir director," he explained. "Father Carter helped me carry them to my car." He paused for a moment. "I've been thinking about this. Carter had permission to open the boxes from Mrs. Rodgers—that's the widow—but she wouldn't have known that I had them. I don't even know if Carter told her about me at all—I rather doubt it."

"What about your wife? She must have known." The question was met with dead air. "Are you still there?"

"Yeah," he sighed, "I'm still here, but she's not. She's staying at her sister's for a while."

"All right," she replied, ignoring the family drama. "Anyone else? Cleaning lady? Coworker you talked to?"

"No one." His voice evidenced his frustration. "This must have something to do with the murder and cover-up, but I don't have a clue who could have known I had the freakin' papers."

"How did Sheriff Johnson behave when he came over?" She changed directions, curious about the cop who had given her the brush-off during her brief visit to Clarkeston the week before.

"I don't know. Porter's always been a little self-important."

"Did you tell him what was in the boxes?"

"No." He paused. "Not that he asked. I told the first cop who arrived that the boxes just contained a bunch of personal papers. Maybe he told the sheriff. Oh, and one of my neighbors came over when she saw the cruisers in the driveway and told the cops that she'd seen a UPS truck parked in front of my house while I was gone. I figure that's who did it, unless UPS dropped off a package and the guy who broke in stole it too."

She advised the reporter to install a burglar alarm in his house and to continue to think about who might have an interest in the stolen papers. When they hung up, she reached over her desk and grabbed her cell phone.

Whoever took the papers and Murphy's computer had probably waited until the reporter went to work and then broken in. Was it just random or had he been targeted deliberately? She slapped a palm down on her desk and cursed. She had alerted the anonymous woman in Arkansas. That bitch knew Murphy had been asking questions, because Melanie herself had ratted him out.

She sat down, opened up the FBI database on her computer, and dialed the Arkansas number. This time she would be asking the questions, starting with the answerer's name, location, the name of her superior, and whether she knew anything about a UPS truck picking up boxes without permission in Clarkeston, Georgia. Maybe the number was connected to an FBI office, maybe not. Just because the FBI database indicated that all inquiries about Jacob Granville be directed to a particular number did not mean that the bureau was directly involved. It could be a number at the Justice Department, another US attorney's office, a state law-enforcement office, or even a private contractor. But whoever answered had some explaining to do. After three rings, a recorded voice announced that the number had been disconnected. Swearing aloud, she called it again and got the same metallic voice on the end of the line.

She stared at the phone for a second and then slammed it back down in its cradle. Really? Did people really think it was that easy to evade a US attorney? Did they not know that she was a fuckin' Mountie? She always got her man, or woman as the case may be. Of course, the anonymous voice on the end of the Arkansas phone line might be utterly unconnected to the break-in. The woman had certainly not killed Diana Cavendish, but Melanie didn't care. No one was going to treat her like a school-yard snitch and then presume to magically vanish. Not when there were questions to be answered.

Melanie was not a conspiracy theorist. Usually she reveled in ripping conspiracy theories to shreds. She loved prosecuting paranoid tax objectors for the IRS. All of them had some sort of theory why the government, or possibly the Trilateral Commission, was out to get them, but in the end they all turned out to be drug dealers, child pornographers, slumlords, or dog fighters trying to hide their earnings. But even a conspiracy skeptic would find it hard to ignore the possibility that her prior contact with the Arkansas number was related to the break-in at Murphy's house.

In any event, she was not just going to forget and let go of Murphy's little mystery. She picked up her cell phone and placed a call to Clarkeston. "We've got to talk," she said, interrupting the reporter's greeting. "Could I come down on Saturday?"

He hesitated for a moment. "I was planning on visiting Jacob Granville's parents in Vidalia."

"I'll come with you," she volunteered impulsively. "We can talk in the car." They solidified the time and place of their rendezvous and soon she was back on the phone with another man, someone she had not spoken to for six months.

Samuel "Slammin' Sammy" Goodson III had been her lover and off-and-on fiancé for almost five years, but the two had never really been friends. Even so, she knew that he would pick up when she called. She had been the one to end their relationship, but he would probably be amenable to doing a little snooping on her behalf. As the head of a large FBI field office in Minnesota, he had access to databases and information that she did not. If anyone could quickly uncover the people behind the disconnected Arkansas number, he could.

"Baby!" He exclaimed with genuine enthusiasm when he heard her voice. "Long time, no hear! How's everything in Hotlanta?" His enthusiasm sounded genuine despite the fact that in their last conversation, she had not sugarcoated the conclusion that she had wasted almost half a decade on a handsome, charming, intelligent, insincere, self-absorbed man-whore who was incapable of truly caring for anyone or anything other than his obsessively waxed '67 Corvette. The length of their relationship had been a testament to how seventy-hour workweeks, frequent travel, and pent-up sex drive could keep even the most doomed couple together.

"It's fine, Sammy," she replied. "Still too many drug cases, but we did have an interesting human-smuggling case last month." She cut the small talk and got right to the point of her call. "Speaking of interesting cases, I was hoping that you could help me with a bit of research. I was looking into an old kidnapping that happened about five years ago and when I ran the victim's name through the general FBI database, all I got was a notation to call a phone number with an Arkansas area code. I talked to a woman there, but when I called back today to get more information, the phone was disconnected." Her voice was as nonchalant as she could make it. If he sensed that she was desperate, he might want something in return. "Is there any way you could track down the origin of the number for me?"

"Can't you just get a court order?" Despite her efforts to sound breezy, he was already on guard.

"Not yet." She scrambled for an explanation. "It's really early stages, and we don't have any probable cause. In fact, it may even be an FBI number, in which case we don't want to waste our time."

He hummed into the phone for a moment. "I'll tell you what. I'm coming to Atlanta in two weeks to do some recruitment interviews." She knew what was coming even before he spoke. "When you have dinner with me, I'll tell you what I've found."

She failed to stifle a groan.

"For chrissakes, Mel, I'm not fucking Hitler or something. It's just dinner."

"Yeah, yeah," she mumbled into the phone. "You're right. We're grown-ups. We should be able to have a meal together."

"Excellent!" he said. "It's a date!"

No, it was not a date, Melanie told herself, but Sammy could think whatever the hell he wanted to.

"Great," she said, "and let me know when you've got something on that number." When she hung up, she felt vaguely slimy, as if a mucilaginous tentacle had reached out across space and time to caress her. The worst thing wasn't the memory of him, but rather the incomprehensible span of years when she had lacked the will to walk away, like the gormless meth-head who can't figure out that leaving the trailer lab is the right move.

★ ★ ★

The Saturday morning traffic leaving Atlanta was blissfully clear, and Melanie cruised at eighty miles per hour into the Georgia countryside, sipping a double latte and rocking to the soundtrack to *Legally Blonde: The Musical*. Early summer was still touching the landscape with a light hand. She had the air conditioning on, but only because the sky was cloudless and the interstate was bathed in sunlight. In the shade it was still spring, and the hay fields and pine plantations she passed on the way to Clarkeston were swathed in shades of living green.

She arrived in Clarkeston twenty minutes early and decided to gas up at a crusty old station not too far from the historic center of downtown. Twenty years earlier, her co-clerk, Arthur Hughes, had introduced her to this wreck of a business, which sat on a prime corner, surrounded by upscale modern buildings. The station itself was brick, with a swooping roofline that made it look like a house. A battered green dinosaur on a sign out front declared it to be a Sinclair station, even though the brand had been defunct in Georgia since the late sixties.

Arthur had the widest nostalgia streak of any young man that she had ever met, and he refused to gas up anywhere else during their time together in Clarkeston. She had been less charmed by the place, but occasionally she had stopped by for a childhood treat that Arthur had discovered in the far corner of the station, an old-fashioned red soda machine shaped like a small freezer and filled with ice-cold bottles of orange and grape Nehi. After she paid the attendant for her gas—there were no self-serve pumps—she went in and found the machine still humming quietly next to a rack of Little Debbie treats. She slid a bottle of grape soda from the rack and cracked off the top against an opener screwed to the side. The cap dropped down into a metal box with a satisfying clink, and she stepped out into the sunshine to savor her fizzy madeleine.

What if she, like Arthur, had never left Clarkeston? Could she have been happy prosecuting smaller cases and maybe teaching criminal law at the college? She took a sip and coughed when the carbonation tickled its way up her nose. It was a stupid question. Arthur had married Suzanne, and hanging around would have been an act of self-flagellation. Leaving had been the right thing to do, but that didn't mean that she was immune to the charm of a quieter life amid the warm red brick and spreading trees of Clarkeston.

She looked at her watch. If she wanted, she had time to drive past Arthur's house and say hello. She turned onto Oak Street and slowed as she approached the familiar old house. Why was her heart suddenly pounding? She saw a beautiful young woman water the plants on the spacious porch that wrapped around two sides of a two-story Queen Anne. For a moment, she thought it was Arthur's wife, but that was impossible. The girl bore a strong resemblance to her, but she looked barely in her twenties, younger even than Suzanne had been eighteen years earlier. It must be her daughter, Arthur's step-daughter, who had been just a sweet little kid during the year she and he clerked together in Clarkeston.

Shit, I'm old, she thought, and the grim conclusion was confirmed when she saw Arthur pull into the driveway and trudge up the steps, bearing a touch of gray in his hair that had not been present at the judge's funeral five years before. She watched him embrace his daughter and walk with her into the house, leaving the watering can underneath a hanging planter of pansies swaying in the breeze. She stayed in the car, watching the flowers and contemplating a breath-stealing parade of might-have-beens.

James Murphy's house was also close to downtown, and she arrived five minutes early. She found him outside on his front porch, reading a newspaper and sipping a cup of coffee. He did not live in the grand older neighborhood where Arthur lived, but rather in the pre-WWII subdivision that lay just to the north. Nonetheless, he had a pleasant outside nook with a small swing under the eaves of his little brick bungalow. She pulled up behind his battered Civic and sketched a wave as she got out of the car and walked up the sidewalk.

Mahomet Public Library District
1702 E. Oak Street
Mahomet, IL 61853-8526

She cast a glance back at his vehicle. "Do you mind if we take my car? I just gassed it up."

He agreed with a smile and nodded at the bottle in her hand. "So you know about Cecil's secret stash, I see."

She laughed. "I used to clerk for the Judge, remember."

"No." He frowned and shook his head. "You never mentioned that before. I would have remembered." She noted with satisfaction that she did not need to mention her former boss's name. During the civil rights era, the Judge had run much of the state of Georgia out of his Clarkeston courtroom. He had not only been the best-known federal judge in the state, but the most famous judge in the country not sitting on the Supreme Court.

"What year did you clerk?"

"1988 to '89."

The reporter nodded his head in the unspoken understanding that she had missed out on the juiciest civil-rights cases. If he had had a deeper sense of judicial history, he would have understood that those years were the high-water mark of the federal policing of state death-penalty appeals. She had watched in dismay as those cases ate up both of her co-clerks.

"Oh," Murphy replied, "then you might know Arthur Hughes? I'm pretty sure he would have clerked around then. We sing together in a community choir."

Although Clarkeston was a town of almost sixty thousand people, she was not surprised that the reporter and her former colleague were acquainted. The professional class in the town was pretty small, and after twenty years they were bound to run into each other.

"We clerked the same year," she replied, "but I haven't seen him since the Judge's funeral. Say hi next time you bump into him."

The journalist set his cup and saucer down on the concrete floor of his porch, flicked a crumb off his pants as he stood up, and then locked the door to his house. He was taller than she remembered and more athletic. He moved gracefully off the porch and waited for her to walk to the car. He really was a rather handsome guy. Too bad he was married, but whether they learned anything in Vidalia or not, it would be pleasant to spend a day in his company. Maybe there was just something intrinsically attractive about a man without a law degree.

XII.

QUESTIONS

James eased down into the soft leather of the sports car's seat and Melanie pulled out of the driveway. He had no macho need to be the driver. He was perfectly happy to be chauffeured around by a beautiful woman, especially when it saved him gas and wear and tear on his aging Honda. "How long have you had the car?"

"About three years."

"Wow," he exclaimed, "I never would have guessed. It looks brand new."

She shot him an ironic smile. "Your side, maybe." She pointed to a large stain on the carpet underneath her feet. "I don't have many passengers."

He doubted such a glamorous woman ever lacked for company. Maybe this was her oblique way of telling him she was divorced or between boyfriends. God, if he were single, would he have the balls to ask her out?

"So, what's the strategy for questioning Jacob Granville's parents?" She pushed a lock of thick golden hair behind her right ear and glanced at him. "Talking to an ex-prosecutor like Granville's father is kind of a delicate thing, isn't it? What was he like on the phone?" She spoke again before he could answer. "You did call them and let them know we were coming, right? Tell me we're not driving a hundred miles there on just a hope?"

"Phillip Granville was a little cagey," he assured her, "but he said that they were willing to talk. He and his wife always claimed that Jacob was innocent and maybe a victim, too, so I implied that he would get more sympathetic treatment in the press this time around."

"Tricksy, tricksy," she laughed. "Do you really think that Granville might be innocent, or were you just blowing smoke?"

"I don't see any way that he didn't kill her." He shook his head. His gut had always told him that Jacob killed Diana in a fit of anger and was forced to flee to avoid the Georgia electric chair. "I mean, he disappeared on the same night she did, and his car was spotted driving away from town. The blood in the apartment was hers, not his. Not to mention that the two of them had been fighting that week."

"Did the car ever turn up?"

"Nope."

"But what about the photos?" She reached up and flipped a pair of sunglasses down from a small compartment in front of the rearview mirror. She slid them on and glanced at him, a perfect advertisement for the elegance of Ray-Bans. "Jacob and Diana couldn't have been having too bad a week if she was doing a little bikini modeling for him."

"Maybe." He paused for a moment, distracted when she suddenly took off the glasses, licked the right lens and polished it high on her blouse without slowing down the car. "But if he didn't kill her, then why did the police cover for him? And I'm not the only one who smelled a rat. My friends on the force were told not to talk to certain potential witnesses and not to contact the FBI. They said it was like working with one hand tied behind their back." He looked at his own glasses and noticed a smudge, which he eliminated with his handkerchief. "Why cover up for someone who hasn't committed a crime?"

"Hmm . . ." She pursed her lips and frowned. "Wouldn't you push even harder on behalf of someone you thought was innocent? I'm just playing devil's advocate, but maybe the cops thought that he didn't do it."

"Well, if they had exculpatory evidence, then why didn't they produce it when half the town's old money at St. James, not to mention the sheriff and the prosecuting attorney, wanted to see the kid exonerated?" He frowned. "His being innocent just doesn't make any sense."

Suspicion was one thing, but learning the details of Diana's disappearance and proving Jacob's guilt were quite another. And who was secondarily guilty for covering up the trail? He told Melanie about the reference to Miriam that he had found in Rodgers's sermon on the persecution of Jacob Granville and wondered aloud whether the parents might have some clue as to what the priest was thinking when he drafted the famous public defense of their son.

For a while, they were quiet and he watched the countryside roll by. Georgia had been one giant cotton field until the 1910s, when the boll weevil and increasingly bad soil conditions had made the crop unprofitable. The state had been left an ecological disaster, but pine trees and peanuts thrived in the nitrogen-depleted soil and slowly the region greened again. Nonetheless, they drove through no proper hardwood forests in the miles to Vidalia. The stands of oaks and poplars they encountered stood within the borders of small towns, islands surrounded by a sea of hay and pine. Cotton had come and gone, but its mark was still indelibly etched in the central Georgia landscape. If one went far enough north into the southernmost reaches of the Appalachians or down to the Okefenokee Swamp, close to the Florida border, one could imagine the wilderness that General Oglethorpe found with his first group of exiles in 1733. But for the two hundred fifty miles in between, the land had long been tamed, and its charm lay in the farmer casting a line into his fish pond or the secretary taking her lunch break on a park bench in front of the county courthouse.

Eventually, his attention migrated from the countryside back to the driver of the car, and his gaze lingered too long on the athletic legs working the clutch and accelerator of the six-speed roadster whizzing them through the countryside. She caught him staring and turned with a mischievous glint in her eye. "So," she asked as they slalomed between a creek and a farmhouse, "when did your wife fly the coop?"

"Huh? What . . . ?" He panicked but then remembered his allusion to Sondra's absence in their phone call. "Oh, she's just visiting her sister."

"I'm sorry. I shouldn't make assumptions." She smiled. "Where does her sister live?"

"Uh . . . in Clarkeston."

She waited for him to elaborate.

He needed a glib explanation but one was not readily at hand. He was not about to admit to a beautiful woman that he could not always keep his wife happy.

"If you really want to know," he hoped his explanation might head off a follow-up question, "I'm leaving her church and she's a little upset about it."

"Which church?"

"Which church? What does that have to do with it?"

"No Methodist or Presbyterian would care enough about that to *go visit her sister.*" Was that a smirk? "She's gotta be Roman Catholic or Baptist . . . Pentecostals and Mormons are too sure of themselves to freak out that bad."

"Baptist," he conceded defeat. "It's the same church she grew up in—she's pretty pissed."

The next moment, she threw him off guard again. "Did she ask why you're quitting?"

How the hell could she cut so quickly to the heart of the matter? He looked hard at her for a minute, trying to discern whether any animus lurked beneath her perfectly composed face. She turned her head and dipped it just enough to peer over her sunglasses. She must have learned that trick from the Judge, he thought. The old codger's eyes were famous for unraveling lawyers who approached the bench.

"No," he admitted, "she didn't."

"What a bitch!" He started to protest, but she cut him off. "Hey, I should know," she said with a wicked grin. "I'm the biggest bitch you'll ever meet."

"She's not so bad." He let out a guilty sigh. "Could we change the subject?" The former deacon was a loyal husband. He supported his wife's career and had never once cheated on her, but this did not make Sondra a warm person. In fact, she often showed more annoyance with him than affection, so his loyalty had become rather existential. Good husbands did not complain about their wives; therefore, he never complained about Sondra, viewing it as his duty to behave properly regardless of her strengths and weaknesses. He still loved her deeply, but he sometimes wished he could disconnect his heart from his head.

"How far is it to the Granvilles' house from here?" She shifted gears smoothly as the outskirts of Vidalia approached.

He pulled out a sheet of paper. "They're on the edge of town past the country club. Go ahead and take the next right."

In a few minutes, they entered a wealthy neighborhood of large plantation-style homes with expansive lawns. Every house seemed to have a swimming pool, and luxury SUVs dotted the long circular drives. The Granvilles' home was slightly more modest than its neighbors, a two-story brick Cape Cod lacking a pool but framed by exquisite landscaping. When the two travelers got out of the car and walked to the house, they saw the flick of a curtain next to the entryway, and the front door opened almost immediately after they knocked.

Jessica Granville was a cherubic brunet in her mid-fifties, gray touched up a bit too aggressively, sporting a pair of capri pants and short-sleeved knit top. Her husband stood behind her, a tall, lean figure looming protectively over her, casting a penetrating look at James that suggested he knew the reporter considered his son a murderer.

James introduced himself and when asked about Melanie described her as a "friend from the Justice Department" who had taken an interest in the case. Mrs. Granville replied with an offer of drinks, and a few moments later the four were sitting in a large screened porch at the back of the house. On the pebbled glass top of a wrought-iron table lay a manila envelope covered with pictures of Jacob Granville.

"We didn't know what you wanted to see," Jessica explained as she spread out the pictures with a surprisingly elegant hand.

"There's some nice photos of Jake on the high school football team." She pointed with pride at her son striking the Heisman pose in front of a pair of white goalposts. "He was too small to play in college, but he started at Clarkeston High."

"Darned good wide receiver," Phillip Granville said. He was standing away from the table, unable to glance at the photos for more than a brief moment.

"He did some drama, too," the proud mother added, singling out a picture of Jacob dressed as a cowboy and spinning a girl around on a stage. "It wasn't the best production of *Oklahoma* ever, but the singing was pretty good." She pursed her lips and furrowed her brow. "We probably have a CD around here somewhere."

"That's okay," James jumped in, "the pictures alone are very helpful."

He had been uncomfortable hinting that he wanted to help the Granvilles clear their son's name, but he could not argue with the results of his disingenuousness. Jessica, at least, was ready to talk about her son, and the photographs provided a useful collage of his life, a good starting point for conversation. He pointed at a picture showing an awkward high schooler in a tuxedo posing woodenly with his arm around an equally awkward girl. "Who's she?"

"I think that's Peggy Winthrop." She squinted and held the print in her hand. "Yup, that's Peggy. Maybe you know George Winthrop? He runs the Toyota dealership out by the Mall of Clarkeston."

Melanie reached out and picked up a picture that had come uncovered at the bottom of the pile. "Is this Jacob with Diana Cavendish?"

Mrs. Granville's face darkened, but she confirmed the guess. "Yes, that's them. Wasting the afternoon at Six Flags, it looks like."

Melanie looked at the photo again and made a sound that suggested she, too, disapproved of the girl. James was impressed at how quickly she read the situation.

"You've never seen a picture of her in a floral bathing suit, have you?" she asked.

"A floral suit?" Mrs. Granville shook her head slowly. "No. I don't believe so."

Melanie shrugged and held up a print where Jacob's face could be seen in the reflection on the back side of a metal spoon. "This one is really interesting!"

His mother's face brightened. "Jake was a journalism major, so he took several photography courses. This was from a series of self-studies that he was required to do." She pulled aside a picture of an intense and brooding young man staring into the camera. "I think this one was too." Her son's green eyes seemed to pop out of an image that was more Hollywood head shot than truly artful. Melanie murmured an exclamation of appreciation, nodding her approval of the sex appeal on display. As Mrs. Granville expounded on her son's photographic skills, James noticed another picture of Jacob with a very attractive young woman.

"She looks familiar," James interrupted. The girl in the print hung adoringly on the young man. The picture was full of vitality, telling a more intimate story than the artsier photos in the pile.

"That's Miriam Rodgers, the priest's girl from St. James." Her sigh told a tale of opportunity lost. "That's who Jake should have ended up with. What an utterly lovely girl . . . I'll never understand why Jake dumped her for Diana."

Mr. Granville walked quickly over and steered his wife onto safer ground. "Now, Diana was a perfectly lovely girl. Why things went off the rails is no one's business." Phillip Granville struck James as someone who would do or say anything to protect his son. Was he trying to suggest Diana as a suspect? Or was there something in their relationship that put Jacob in a bad light? The expression on the father's face did not invite further inquiry into what he labeled "no one's business." Time for a new tack.

"You know," James gestured at the pictures now spread all over the table, "I would have loved to know all this five years ago.

I'm sure that my stories in the *Chronicle* at the time did not seem very sympathetic."

Mr. Granville responded with a snort. "Well, you didn't ask, did you? Not that it mattered. We weren't supposed to talk to the press, so Jake's side of the story never came out."

"And what was Jake's side of the story?"

"That he's innocent, of course." Granville's look dared anyone to disagree with him.

James was about to plow ahead, but Melanie cut in and laid a hand gently on the arm of the woman next to her. "You've talked a lot about Jacob, stuff that never made its way into the newspaper, but were there also things about the disappearance that you weren't able to share?"

Mrs. Granville looked anxiously at her husband, whose mouth opened and then shut soundlessly. James shifted uneasily, but an imperceptible shake of Melanie's head silenced his impulse to fill the dead air. The eyes of the married couple met, and the husband nodded at his wife.

"Wait a moment," she said, before she left the room. "There's something more that I want to show you."

James and Melanie directed their attention back to the photos while Granville walked over to the screen door and stood tensely surveying his backyard. After an awkward minute, his wife returned with a sheaf of papers in her hand. She peeled off the first three sheets and handed them to James with an air of solemnity.

"We got the first email a couple of days after they disappeared."

James could feel his partner sidle up next to him. Her shoulder pressed against his and he felt a warm hand on his back. He held the pages out so that she could see more easily. Each piece of paper contained a single email message sent by Jacob Granville. The first was dated March 31, 2009, three days after Diana Cavendish's apartment was found spattered in blood. *Don't worry. We are fine.* A week later, another email from the same address. *Finally safe. Will explain all later.* Six months after that, a longer message. *I know we have a lot to explain. We are okay. Please be patient.*

"That was the last one we got," Mrs. Granville said. "I check my email every day, but there's never anything more."

James looked over and saw Melanie looking at him, her eyes alive and full of interest. She took the sheets from his hand and looked at them briefly once more before posing a question. "Who have you shown these to?"

The woman smiled with relief. She seemed grateful that someone was taking her troubles so seriously. "Well, we went straight to the police, of course, but they told us not to mention them to anyone else. You and Mr. Murphy are the first to see them since then."

James heard Mr. Granville clear his throat behind them. "That's not quite true, is it, Jessie?" He stepped up next to his wife and wrapped his arm tightly around her shoulder. "We showed them to a private investigator, but he had no luck tracking down the email address, except to say that it came from somewhere in Mexico."

Melanie pointed at the top of the first page. "Was this your son's regular email address?"

"No," the father replied, "but the investigator said that if Jake was running from something, he might have felt safer opening up a new Gmail account that no one knew about."

James studied the elder Granville. Did he really believe his son was innocent? He looked like an unassuming country gentleman, but he had been an aggressive and effective criminal prosecutor in Clarkeston at the time that his son was investigated. And the sheriff would have kept no secrets from such a close friend and colleague.

"Mr. Granville—" the journalist started a question and then interrupted himself. "Can I call you Phil?" The older man assented with a curt nod. "Phil, you worked for the city when all this was going on. Were you happy with the way the police conducted the investigation?"

The attorney shrugged in response. "The sheriff took me aside at the beginning and asked me to stay out of it. He said he'd give me a call when they had a suspect in custody and there was a case to be brought. Until then, he said, it would be best for me to stay away from the investigation."

For an attorney, he was a terrible liar. "Surely you must have been curious?"

"Of course, I was, but the police were treating Jake as a suspect." He shook his head in irritation. "We were passing on information, but it was a one-way street."

Mrs. Granville then handed over the remaining papers to James. "We also found these in Jake's room after he disappeared."

James and Melanie looked at the documents. The first two pages were printouts of YouTube pages, each showing the face of a distressed individual. One was labeled "Hopeless in Africa," and the other, "Hell Just Across the Border." The uploader was identified as j-gville. Each of the following dozen pages was topped by the name and picture of a US senator or representative from the state of Arkansas above a summary of campaign contributions, voting records, committee assignments, and tax disclosures.

"It's all stuff from stories Jake was working on, I suppose." Mrs. Granville shrugged. "I didn't even notice it until I went through his room after he disappeared."

Her husband looked as if he wanted to add something to her explanation, but instead reached into his pocket for his cell phone. He looked at it and took a step toward the door. "Sorry, but I need to take this."

Murphy looked at Mrs. Granville, hoping that she would amplify her remarks, but Melanie spoke first.

"It must have been hard on you, too, Mrs. Granville, to be shut out from an investigation involving your own son."

"Oh," she clasped her hands together, "it was horrible! Porter—he's the sheriff—and Phil were best friends, on the vestry together at St. James and all that, and suddenly Jake's gone and the officers are asking all kinds of questions, and I didn't know where Jake was or what had happened to him. Phil was gone all the time and not talking much when he was around." She sighed and her shoulders slumped. "I still don't understand any of it."

At that moment, Granville returned to the screen porch and abruptly took the papers from the hands of James and Melanie. "I'm afraid that I'm going to have to ask you two to go." He forced a smile and gestured at the door with his hand. "We have a prior commitment."

"What commitment?" Jessica Granville asked.

"They need to leave now, sweetheart." His eyes flashed the expectation that they make a prompt exit. Melanie cast a quick glance at her companion as they made their way to the front door. James blinked his noncomprehension, took out his business card, and handed it to Mrs. Granville as they exited.

"If you can think of anything more," he said, as the door was shut in their faces, "please let me—"

He looked over at Melanie to see if she, too, was struck by the abrupt behavior of their hosts.

"Oh," she beamed and nodded, "this is getting interesting."

XIII.

DATES

Thorsten Carter decided to tell Miriam Rodgers about the theft of her father's boxes during dinner, despite the risk that the news might ruin his first date of the year. Not surprisingly, the love life of the young priest had taken a nose dive after his move to Clarkeston. Dating someone in the congregation was out of the question, and his social life did not extend much further than to those he met at church or in committee meetings. The gym where he worked out was full of lovely young ladies, but they were mostly undergraduates at Clarkeston College and not interested in a thirty-year-old cleric. He attended a weekly Bible study/gripe session with a number of other ministers in town, but the only attractive woman in the group, the new head of the Unitarian church, had a partner and three children.

Dinner with Miriam presented a rare opportunity to spend time with a woman his own age who already knew the ins and outs of his profession. Of course, with opportunity came pressure, and his romantic moves, to the extent he ever had any, were seriously out of practice. His last relationship, commenced while he was still in seminary, had ended two years earlier, after months of post-graduation phone calls and emails finally petered into silence. In the end, neither of them cared enough to do much more than "like" the occasional Facebook posting. When his parents asked about her, he was at a loss to explain what had happened, but since his brief meeting with Miriam, he had a theory. Never during his entire time with Karen had he felt a jolt of electricity as when Miriam consented to dine with him. Never before had he spent a whole day meditating on a woman's perfect nose or the way a shock of her lustrous hair framed the curve of her delicate throat. A single chance encounter with Miriam had already been worth a month of dinners and movies with Karen.

When he returned home on Tuesday afternoon, he shaved for the second time that day and spent five minutes with his trimmer tidying up his sideburns and beating back a tuft of ear hair. He found a checked shirt in his closet and slipped on a new pair of blue jeans. A glance in the mirror, however, produced nothing but disappointment. He looked like he had just walked out of a Soviet-era men's fashion catalog. Styles from the seventies might be coming back, but not the Steve Martin "wild and crazy guys" vibe. He went back to his closet in search of something hipper, but realized with chagrin that he had not bought a new article of clothing for several years. Thirty years old, he thought to himself, and still relying on Christmas presents to provide his wardrobe.

He decided to keep the jeans, match them with one of the plain white shirts that he often wore to work, and complete the ensemble with a serviceable cream jacket and a skinny green tie. If he was going retro, the early eighties was the better move. He really didn't look too bad. He still weighed the same as he had in college and a daily elliptical regime had kept him pretty fit. Although an unruly shock of ginger hair topped his head, his face was friendly, his jaw strong, and his brown eyes warm and understanding. There was a chance, he thought, that Miriam would not storm out when she heard the bad news about her father's papers.

They had arranged to meet at a local dive called the Wild Boar. She had been a student at Clarkeston College and claimed that he could not call himself a true Clarkestonian until he had drunk at least one pint there. He arrived first and found the place was not nearly so low brow as she had described. The long bar, made from slats of maple reclaimed from a bowling alley, displayed a number of Thor's favorite microbrews, and the windows that looked onto the street had been pushed open to let in the warm early-summer air. He took a seat by one of them and looked contentedly onto the southernmost part of the college campus.

A few minutes later, he saw Miriam park a new Prius across the street and walk toward the door of the bar. He was relieved to see that they would not be too mismatched at dinner. She wore a pair of tastefully cut designer jeans and a short-sleeved silk blouse that pressed against her as a breeze wisped down the road. He absolved himself of an impure thought and reminded himself that treating her with respect was more important than keeping on her clothes in his imagination.

She entered with a smile and waved him over as she walked to the bar. "No table service, I'm afraid," she said as she got herself a gin and tonic. "Part of the charm."

He ordered an IPA brewed in Atlanta. "It's nice. You made the place sound like I should get a tetanus shot before coming in." The bartender shot him a queer look but brightened when Thor pushed a couple of dollars into the stein that served as a tip jar. They went back to his window seat.

She took a sip and looked around. "When I was an undergraduate here, the Boar was a lot shabbier. You could go across the river on a nice date downtown with the frat boys or come here and hang out with the bad boys."

She did not look like someone who had ever hung out with a crowd much racier than the St. James youth group, but her eyes flashed dangerously over her drink, and he wondered whether she might have been the typical clergyman's child: rebellious, out of control, resentful of authority. He imagined a girl in a leather miniskirt and chain-laden boots, smoking a joint smeared with black lipstick. Then she smiled and suddenly looked more like Gwyneth Paltrow than *La Femme Nikita*.

"What did you study at the college?"

"History," she said. "I thought that I wanted to go to law school."

He realized that he had no idea what she did for a living. "I take it you're not a lawyer now?"

"No," she looked wistful. "I work in the state insurance commissioner's office doing public-affairs stuff, planning the next Don't Play with Matches campaign, that sort of thing. I still read history books though. I've been toying with the idea of writing a history of Clarkeston. There hasn't been a new one for almost fifty years, and that was mostly the story of a few leading families. I'd love to do the job right someday."

He watched her closely. She had a lovely way of tucking her hair behind her ear before she reached for her drink, and the left corner of her mouth came up slightly higher than the right whenever she smiled. She had a real passion for local history, and when he pushed her a little about her job, it became clear that she enjoyed running the media side of the commissioner's office and relished pushing the state's tolerance for humor in the commercials she made.

When she paused, he just wanted her to keep talking. "What's the most interesting thing that you could tell me about the town?"

She gestured out the window to the lush campus. "Well, a hundred years ago the only trees you would have seen for miles around would be a few on the quad and some in the original antebellum settlement to the west of downtown." She nodded over her shoulder. "Everyplace else was planted in cotton, all the way up into people's front yards. The demand was so high that people would cut down their favorite shade tree in order to get in one more quarter acre. It's hard to imagine how bare the land must have been or how bright it must have looked when the cotton popped white in the late summer. Now it's all green again."

"What happened?" As a Missouri native, Thor knew a little about corn and soybeans, but nothing about cotton.

"Boll weevil and tired land." She waved at the bartender in the hope of getting another drink, and despite the purported lack of table service, he complied with a discreet bow. "The boll weevil was a menace for decades until the government got it under control, but cotton never came back because the soil had been destroyed. The alluvial sediment in a river delta is really the only sustainable place to grow cotton in the US, and even then you need an amazing amount of pesticide and fertilizer." She twisted her plastic stirrer into a knot and flicked it onto the floor. "In my imaginary book I'd put old pictures side by side with new ones taken from exactly the same angle so that people could really get a sense of how much things have changed and how quickly."

The young priest was ready for another beer, but the bartender was uninterested in his signaling. When Thor got back to the table, he tried to get his companion going once again. "I suppose St. James has a pretty interesting history too."

She laughed. "It's too bad you can't talk to Daddy about that. He loved poking around in the church archives. He once told me that Alexander Stephens, the vice president of the Confederacy, worshipped there. I don't know why. His family plantation was in Crawfordville, which is pretty far away. Anyway, as a native of Clarkeston, my father was both fascinated and appalled that so many of the rich planter class used to call St. James their home." She leaned back in her chair. "It's the dilemma of being an educated Georgian: you can't help but love a gorgeous place like Clarkeston, but you never quite know how to deal with the baggage. You could say that cotton pretty much built St. James, but it sure wasn't the plantation owners doing all that work."

"So," she took a sip of her drink and then grinned mischievously, "what do you think of the old pile of stone, anyway?"

"It's fine." He dared not say anything critical. He had her father's old job, after all, and she probably knew more about St. James than he did, so he offered up some fluff. "It has its challenges."

"Like dealing with the congregation from hell?" Her eyes challenged him to be truthful. "My mom doesn't go anymore because she's an atheist. I stopped because the people are just plain mean."

"I've met some nice people there," he said weakly.

"Of course there are some," she leaned over the table closer to him and he caught a flash of tan cleavage, "but they don't run the show. I've got a lot of great friends still at St. James, but they'll never serve on the vestry or the nominating committee for the next priest."

"So, I'm a lame duck already?" He expected her to laugh, but instead she raised her eyebrows and shook her head knowingly.

"They'll figure out some way to drive you off." She shrugged and, when a tire squealed in the street nearby, looked momentarily away.

"How come your father survived so long?"

"Because he was a fire-breathing son of a bitch, that's why!" She laughed and launched into a series of stories, the moral of which was that only a ruthlessly efficient autocrat with a love of confrontation could hope to beat back the forces of venality at St. James Episcopal Church. "When he started getting crap from the congregation about switching from the old 1928 prayer book to the 1979 revision, we spent a month worshipping with the original 1549 Anglican Book of Common Prayer! He said that if the traditionalists wanted the 'original' language read in church, he'd give them the real thing. I don't think anyone understood anything he said during those services. He even managed to find some old English Reformation sermons to read from the pulpit. After a week or two, the congregation was crying for mercy!"

Son of a bitch or not, he had her adoration, and she reveled in the tales of his blustery bulldozing of the congregation. It was hard not to be fascinated by her, and his admiration began edging toward infatuation. He pushed the black cloud of the disappearance of her father's papers to the back of his mind.

"Now," she said with a smile and look of genuine interest, "tell me what it's *really* like to take on St. James."

Thor confessed his frustrations, and she proved adept at keeping him rambling on about his job. The conversation flowed seamlessly through a third round of drinks and the walk to the restaurant. It was a balmy evening and the college was quiet as they made their way through campus and toward the bridge that led over the river to downtown. Final spring-semester exams had already been given, but summer school had not yet started, so only a single wandering professor prevented the leafy campus from being their private nature preserve. Since the college had been constructed first along the river and then southward in the direction of the former farmland where the Wild Boar now stood, each step took them deeper into history as they entered the original quadrangle, a series of red-brick buildings that all dated from before the Civil War.

As they stood in the middle of the space, a shaggy black dog raced toward them, skidding to a stop next to Miriam. When she stepped back and raised her hands out of reach of the dog's tongue, the canine reversed course in the general direction of a middle-aged man calling "Abigail" in a commanding but ineffective voice. The dog ignored him, veered to a garbage can, and began rooting around in the grass next to it. Miriam and Thor talked about their childhood pets as they crossed over the pedestrian bridge that dropped them onto the north side of the river, just a block away from the Italian restaurant that Miriam had suggested.

The same forces that had emptied the campus resulted in a quiet dining space that Thor and Miriam shared with just a handful of other customers. To the priest's delight, his date was as interested in the wine list as he was, and their conversation cascaded through a variety of topics common to those in their early thirties, who had seen the Berlin Wall fall as children, experienced 9/11 as college students, and watched the evolution of MTV from videos to reality television.

As Thor was washing his hands in the men's room, he looked up to find a rather mentally challenged grin pasted on his face. He uttered an expletive and shook his head, but the sappy boy-crush expression was still there. He knew that alcohol was befuddling his brain, but he lacked the guile to hide his feelings. Forcing the corners of his smile downward, he pitched a paper towel forcefully into the garbage and tried to focus on the bad news about Miriam's father's papers that he was soon to deliver. But when he reappeared, Miriam responded with a wink and raised glass, and his face lit up like a jack-o'-lantern once again. He sat down and tried to dilute his feelings by concentrating on some unattractive feature of her face, but he only managed to convince himself in the end that the thin scar on the side of her throat and the mole just above it on her cheek were the most compelling beauty marks that he had ever seen.

"I have some bad news for you," he blurted out as he picked up his wine glass, "your father's papers have gone missing."

"What do you mean, 'gone missing'?" First confusion, then suspicion.

He flushed and contemplated the baroque pattern on his silverware. "Well, they've sort of been stolen." He felt a sinking feeling as he realized that the most damning part of the story was not the missingness of the boxes, but rather from where they had been taken. He had no good excuse for sharing them with a journalist like James Murphy without her permission.

"Who the hell would steal a bunch of cardboard boxes from a locked closet in a church? Are you sure somebody didn't just move them or something?"

Thor briefly considered blaming the mishap on the church janitor, but a lie was not a good way to start a relationship, especially when his moral compass, as usual, was pointing straight to truthful. "They weren't taken from the church." He frowned and sighed. "I gave them to someone and his house was broken into."

She crossed her arms, leaned back in her chair, and studied him for a long moment. "Why don't you start this story from the beginning?"

He nodded and told her about Murphy's initial visit to his office, his interest in the abduction of Diana Cavendish, and the seemingly benign request to have a look at her father's papers. "In retrospect, I should have asked your permission, but technically they belong to your mother, and when she told me to throw them out, I figured it wouldn't hurt to let Mr. Murphy have a look at them before I gave 'em to you."

He watched her stiffen, and he began damage control. "Of course, I looked through them completely to make sure there was nothing embarrassing in there. It was just a bunch of programs and stuff from conferences and a collection of his sermons . . . no love letters to the church organist or anything like that."

"What?!"

Now panicking, he quickly explained how Murphy had taken the papers home and how they had been stolen, along with the reporter's computer and other documents from his den. He emphasized the journalist's misfortune as a means to distract Miriam from her own sense of loss. Her face was a mask of conflicting emotions. Fortunately, anger did not seem too prominent, but he could read disappointment, sadness, and a disturbing touch of disdain.

"Wait a minute." She cocked her head slightly to the side. "You think that the object of the burglary was my father's papers?"

"Well, they took the computer and a bunch of other stuff, too, but James is convinced that whoever broke into his house doesn't want him looking into the disappearance of Diana Cavendish."

"But what the hell could my father's papers have to do with her disappearance?" She shook her head, deeply distracted by Thor's revelation. Whatever connection they had enjoyed earlier in the evening had come undone.

"I don't know."

"Well, I'm going to find out. I've met Murphy a couple of times, and I bet that he knows more than he's telling you." She began to compose herself. She had a plan of action, and a flash of her former self returned. "I'm going to have a little talk with him tomorrow. He at least owes me an explanation for why he wanted to go through Papa's stuff."

Thor nodded his sympathy and at that moment the bill arrived. He grabbed it and slipped his credit card into the black leather bifold. "Why don't I go with you?" he suggested. He wanted to see her again, but did not want to risk asking for a second date. "I should get a copy of the police report from him in case the vestry wants to make an insurance claim or something."

She nodded and gave him an unsatisfying, formal thanks for the dinner. As they walked to her downtown apartment building, the conversation was desultory and inconsequential. Oddly, her response to the bad news had only magnified his feelings for her. Such passion! Her father wasn't the only strong personality in the Rodgers family.

Although he concluded that she did not bear him a grudge, he did not dare angle for even a peck on the cheek as they parted.

XIV.

RUNAROUNDS

Stanley Hopkins sat in a doughnut shop in Claremont, California, plotting his next move in the increasingly frustrating search for the operator of Mygirlfriendsbikini.com. He polished off a large chocolate muffin and went back to the counter to refresh his coffee and get a couple of custard-filled Bavarian creams. The attorney who had registered the website's trademark had promised to provide the name and address on the cancelled check used to pay for the trademark application. After leaving the Burbank lawyer three unreturned messages, however, the professor now considered that trail a dead end. Instead, he turned his attention to the Internet market for soft-core pornography, something that he knew little about. His previous research and interviews had taken him into the world of hardcore porn stars, not college students in bras and panties taking selfies in dorm rooms.

His searching had revealed several sites that looked like they were competitors to Mygirlfriendsbikini.com, including Sweetiesixteen.com, Myspringbreak.com, Daytonamemories.com, Bykerbabes.com, Carshowhotties.com, and Yourdanceclub.com. Stanley hoped that if he contacted the owners of the competition, he would discover who ran the site that had posted the pictures of the disappeared Diana Cavendish.

Unfortunately, the owners of competing soft-core websites were as difficult to track down as the owner of Mygirlfriendsbikini.com. Almost every one of them used misleading information when registering the websites. What the hell did the IRS do when it wanted to audit one of them? Some of the addresses were outright fraudulent, others were legitimate addresses unconnected to the website, and one led Stanley to a tight-lipped lawyer. Only the address provided by Yourdanceclub.com seemed to be legitimate, but an employee who answered the phone reported that the owner of the site was momentarily away, so Stanley sat in the doughnut shop, fighting the urge to order a couple of crullers while he waited for his call to be returned.

After he finished the morning paper, Stanley denied himself more sweets and quelled his impatience by driving to the physical address associated with the Yourdanceclub website in nearby Rancho Cucamonga. The address listed in the Whois database turned out to be a small store selling dance togs, situated between a dry cleaner's and fabric store in a strip mall. The window in the storefront showed conventional leotards for sale along with more daring outfits. He asked for the owner, and a thin young woman with dyed orange hair emerged from behind a clothes rack and led him through an aisle of tights and shoes to a small office in the back of the store. She rapped her knuckles on the open door, pointed at Stanley without saying a word to her boss, and walked back to attend to a customer.

"Mr. Andrews?" Stanley stuck out his hand to a young man with the most immaculately maintained eyebrows he had ever seen.

"That's me." His hands were small, but the professor felt a firm grip compress his knuckles. "Can I help you?" The store owner took a second look at his visitor, and Stanley brushed some powdered sugar off of his shirt in response.

"I hope so," he replied and handed over one of his business cards. "I'm helping out the FBI with the investigation of a website called Mygirlfriendsbikini.com. I'm contacting owners of other websites with a similar user profile to see if we can find out anything about its owner."

Andrews repeated the name of the website and shook his head. "Never heard of it. Swimsuit shots of girlfriends, I suppose?"

Stanley nodded. "I knew it was a long shot, but your website is pretty similar: pictures of pretty girls in swimwear, pictures of pretty girls in clubwear."

"We've got some video, too," the store owner added enthusiastically. "I make five times more money from the website than I do from the store. And all the content we post is free! The word is out that if you think you look hot on the dance floor, just snap a photo or a video with your phone and we'll post it the next day." He shook his head in amazement. "These girls bump and grind like strippers and they're begging to be seen online. It's the easiest money that I've ever made."

"Do you charge anything?"

"If you want access to the whole archive, yeah, but not to see the latest week of uploads. We make most of our money from the advertisers." He added quickly, "And pay taxes on all of the revenue, too."

Stanley smiled indulgently and made one last stab at getting anything useful out of his visit. "I noticed that both your website and the bikini website have an advertiser in common, an herbal, uh, enhancement pill."

"Yeah, Herbal Wood! It's fabulous. Great product."

The professor gave him a doubtful look and asked whether Andrews would be willing to provide him with contact information for the pill purveyor.

"Sure, but I just deal with them via email. I get paid into my PayPal account, so I've never even talked with them." He wrote down the URL for the Herbal Wood website and its email address on the back of a yellow Post-it. "They might be able to tell you more about your guy."

Stanley thanked him for his help, walked out to his car, and drove back to the doughnut shop. He brought in his laptop and checked out Herbal Wood, which appeared to be a legitimate business taking advantage of the FDA's failure to regulate the market for herbal remedies as stringently as it did the market for pharmaceuticals. Its web page showed a picture of the virile founder of the company and even provided a physical address in Washington State, where unsatisfied customers could apply for a full refund. The general email address was info@herbalwood.com and the address provided by Andrews was busfin@herbalwood.com. He emailed each a carefully worded query about Mygirlfriendsbikini.com, suggesting a cozier relationship with the feds than was technically accurate, and went up to the counter to order a cinnamon roll and a banana smoothie.

There was nothing more to do except wait patiently, a formerly strong talent that had deteriorated steadily since Angela had died.

On the way back home, he passed a home-improvement store and impulsively pulled in. He had been putting off an important project at home for a while and now he decided to finish it. He entered the airy steel-and-concrete edifice and found a waterproof plastic container. To this he added a small bag of concrete and stowed them both in the trunk of his car. As he drove home, his felt his resolve begin to ebb. Nonetheless, as the sun shone high over the San Gabriel Mountains on that clear Tuesday afternoon, he stood in his carport, traced the bottom of the container onto a piece of cardboard, cut carefully along the circle with a utility knife, and laid it as a template on the grass in the corner of his backyard.

If he had been forced to search too hard for his shovel, he might have wavered, but it stood leaning in plain view against the garden shed. He lifted the tool with care and creased the turf around the cardboard outline, leaving a neat pattern in which to dig a hole. He took his time, looking up at the snow-capped peak of Mt. Baldy whenever he doubted the wisdom of his plan, and dropped the soil neatly into a toddler pull-behind for bicycles that served as a makeshift wheelbarrow.

His first attempt at sinking the container into the hole proved that he had dug too shallowly, so he scraped another six inches of dirt from the bottom and saw that the fit was now snug. He wiped a bead of sweat from his forehead and went inside to get a drink of water.

There was not much left to do. He would pour the bag of concrete into the buried container, add water with his garden hose, and create a solid home for the ceramic vase that held the remains of his wife and daughter, cremated together, child on mother's breast. Imbedded in concrete and safe from the elements, the improvised columbarium could be moved when he sold the house or found a more appropriate spot. Prior self-examination had revealed this as a brilliant and eminently sensible plan.

Unfortunately, as he stood on the back porch and surveyed his handiwork, he had to admit that Angela would have hated the idea. She would have no problem with the mountain view or even his selfish desire to keep them close at hand; rather, the unconventionality of it all would have unnerved her. Who buries his wife in the backyard? Usually a husband who's knocked her over the head and rolled her up in a carpet first. The plan might be clever and reasonable, but not a single person out of a hundred would have thought to execute it. Probably not one in ten thousand. But wasn't that why she loved him? That streak of unconventionality? Not really, he had to admit.

When Angela's father died, Stanley took control of the burial arrangements in a successful attempt to keep the two grieving daughters from being ripped off by the only mortuary in their town. He called every funeral director within a fifty-mile radius and was absolutely appalled at the cost of embalming, transportation to a simple graveside service, and the most basic casket. At times, long before his passing, both Angela and her father had decried the expense of funerals and the ridiculous extravagance of planting $15,000 worth of burnished hardwood forever in the ground, so he felt vindicated when he finally found a place that offered a price fifty percent below the closest competition. The two Spanish surnames of the partners who ran the operation gave him pause, but Stanley had gotten a law degree before going to graduate school and he knew that the funeral industry was heavily regulated. There was no reason why he should not honor his father-in-law's parsimony and go with Vásquez & Benitez, Funeraria y Crematorio.

It seemed like a brilliant idea, but Angela and her sister felt uncomfortable in the tiny mortuary, and the crowd of mourners at the cemetery emitted an audible gasp when the hearse emblazoned with the Hispanic trade name pulled into the cemetery. Sr. Vásquez was confused by the simple Episcopal service and kept asking what more he could do (nothing—just leave). Looking back, it was not really a big deal, but the unconventionality of it was remarked upon by many with disapproval. He did not care. He was proud to avoid the traps set by a corrupt industry, no matter how badly society demanded it. But Angela told him afterward that she wished they had spent the extra money. Their subsequent discussion, albeit civil, showed just how far apart they were when it came to satisfying the expectations of their community, at least when it came to the interring of a loved one.

So, he stood next to the hole where he proposed to place the remains of his wife and daughter and looked up again at the mountains. He admitted that burying them himself had never been a good idea. No matter how respectfully and sensibly he laid them down, he would eventually have to tell people about his do-it-yourself columbarium. After all, what if he died suddenly? Someone had to know where his loved ones lay. At a minimum, her sister and mother would need to know what he had constructed in the backyard of his California home. He imagined the conversation and knew that at best they would think him disrespectful, and at worst, some kind of lunatic. His own will mattered little. He threw down the shovel and trudged back into the house.

The despondent grave digger stayed inside only long enough to grab his laptop. Avoiding the urn in the laundry room, he left through the front door, got in his car, and drove north, halfway up the mountain that had been his only companion during the backyard fiasco. His destination was a small coffeehouse in Baldy Village, a tiny outpost at 4,100 feet above sea level, inhabited by ex-hippies, Park Service workers, and the owners of the handful of businesses servicing hikers and skiers on their way up the steep forest road. The converted log cabin had a surprisingly fast wireless connection and a mouthwatering selection of fruit scones. He pulled into the small gravel lot in front of the café with a satisfying crunch of his tires and saw all the chairs under the porch's tin roof were still free. No one was around, and he could sit among the rustic scenery for as long as he wanted, pretending that the weather-beaten cabins and tourist shops were really two thousand miles away, in northern Wisconsin or the Upper Peninsula of Michigan, instead of a short ride from Los Angeles.

Tired of coffee, he ordered a hot chocolate and a scone and sat down on an Adirondack-style wooden chaise on the front porch. Computer in his lap, he lurked on Facebook, sipped his drink, and watched an intermittent stream of battered pick-up trucks drive past. Ever since his wife's death, he had found it too painful to socialize with their old friends, so he instead followed them online. It was nice to know that life was going on without him in a hail of LOLs, LMAOs, and ROFLs. He had posted his own status just once since the accident, and the avalanche of well-meaning comments had been overwhelming. Thereafter, he surfed anonymously.

While reading a heated battle of comments about a friend's left-leaning political post, he felt his phone vibrate in his front pocket a split second before it started playing "Careless Whisper" by Wham! Angela had made the damn song his ringtone and he couldn't figure out how to switch it to something less embarrassing. He fumbled the Android onto the rough-sawn floor and barely managed to reach down and swipe its face before it went to voice mail.

"Hello?" He snuck a quick peak at the number but did not recognize it. The connection was erratic, and it took him a moment to realize that the caller was the trademark lawyer who had registered the Mygirlfriendsbikini.com website. After several frustrating repetitions of his message, the attorney finally managed to communicate that he had an address for the website's owner. As the call began to break up, Stanley shouted for a text and hung up hoping that he would soon have the breakthrough he needed.

Less than a minute later, the address had arrived at his phone and he was mapping the location on his computer. The Google satellite view revealed a large house in Silver Lake, equidistant between Griffith Park and Dodger Stadium. He looked at his watch and saw that any attempt to pay an immediate visit would require a trip across the east-west length of Los Angeles at the beginning of rush hour. Instead of fighting the traffic, he decided to stay put and do some Internet sleuthing on the owner's name, William Simmons, and save a face-to-face confrontation for the next morning.

A Google search for William Simmons returned almost a half-million results, so he tried pairing the name with other search terms. Typing Mygirlfriendsbikini.com yielded nothing new. Searching under the house address plus the name was also fruitless. Entering the address alone elicited the name of a former owner, whose name surfaced in connection with the neighborhood association in Silver Lake and a community choir. When Stanley linked the name Simmons to some words associated with soft-core pornography, like *babe*, he was bombarded with irrelevant hits promising to titillate him, enlarge his penis, or both. On a whim, he also searched William Simmons or W. Simmons in connection with Jacob Granville and Diana Cavendish, but no results surfaced beyond a nineteenth-century genealogical entry showing a long-deceased William Simmons to have been the great-uncle of a long-deceased Diana Cavendish. He then reran all of his prior searches using Bill, Billy, Will, and Willy instead of William, before giving up. He reminded himself that Simmons was not a suspect in the disappearance but rather was probably a hapless purchaser of the photos from a third person who might have knowledge of the crime.

The sun was beginning to set and the air was rapidly cooling when he performed one last search, linking the Simmons name together with Sweaty Palm, the corporate entity that officially owned the bikini website. Nothing. He slapped his laptop shut and drove back down the mountain to Claremont.

★ ★ ★

Stanley waited until mid-morning the next day to drive west to Silver Lake in search of William Simmons. He killed the time waiting for traffic to clear by filling in the empty hole in his backyard, carefully arranging the broken pieces of sod on top and tamping them down until little trace of the disturbance remained. Once on the road, he stopped at a coffee shop a few blocks away from the I-10 interchange and picked up a double latte and two pieces of coffee cake to eat during the ride. Rush hour had mostly subsided, so he made it to Silver Lake in less than an hour. He had never been to the neighborhood before and was surprised by the number of eclectic shops and local eateries dotting the hilly landscape.

He did not expect to find Simmons at home during the day, but he had been unable to find a phone number for the physical address Quintana had provided, so he planned on approaching neighbors until he got better contact information. At worst, he could leave a note and then run some errands and return in the evening. As it turned out, he did not have to work very hard before being disappointed once again.

He walked up dozens of steep steps to the front door of Simmons's house, a multi-tiered brick ranch that crawled halfway up a hill looking down on the small reservoir that gave the area its name. He knocked and after a long minute, a white-haired woman dragging an oxygen tank struggled to open the door. Despite the tubes inserted into her nostrils she managed a friendly smile, but before he could introduce himself, she shouted backward in a surprisingly strong voice to someone unseen who was chiding her for answering the door for herself.

"These nurses don't think I should do anything!" She pulled a face and cast a glance behind her. "What can I do for you, young man?"

Stanley extended his hand and gently shook the delicate fingers proffered by the old woman. "Are you Mrs. Simmons?" When her face registered nothing more than confusion, he added, "I'm looking for Mr. William Simmons . . . He used to live here."

"Oh, Billy!" Her face beamed. "He used to rent the apartment above my garage. Lovely young man!" She pulled her oxygen tank back, opened the door, and invited the professor inside. "Are you a friend of his?"

"No," Stanley confessed, "I don't really know him." He repeated the trademark purchase story he had told Quintana. "I think he might be interested in a business deal that I have to offer him."

"Oh," she nodded knowingly, "you must be in the computer business too, then. I've never seen so many computers in my life! When he moved out, it looked like he was going off to open a Circuit City."

His heart sank. "When was that, ma'am?" When she cupped her ear with her left hand, he leaned forward and rephrased his question. "When did he move out of the apartment? Was it long ago?"

"Oh, about six months. He was here for almost three years and always paid his rent on time." She continued, as if sharing a secret, "There's a lot of money in computers, you know. He never had a regular job, just running those websites of his out of the apartment."

Stanley wondered whether the landlady knew what sort of websites had constituted the livelihood of her tenant and decided that it didn't matter. What he needed was further contact information.

"Ma'am, did he leave you with a forwarding address of some sort?"

"Oh, yes." She turned around and yelled up the stairs from the small foyer. "Cecilia, could you bring me down my address book?"

A voice with a heavy Spanish accent assented, and soon a large woman in nurse's scrubs lumbered down the short flight of stairs. "Here you go, Ms. Cora."

The old woman took a small spiral-bound book from the aide's hand and showed a page to her guest. In neat block letters was William Simmons's name and a postal box number in the main office in downtown Los Angeles. Stanley suppressed a groan. He was back to square one. Unless he wanted to stake out the post office box indefinitely in the hope of seeing Simmons, the trail was a dead end. Even if he asked the woman with the sexy voice in the Atlanta US attorney's office to help identify the box's owner, he bet that the only information on file would be Simmons's name and his old address in Silver Lake.

He wrote down the box number on the back of a business card in his wallet and thanked the old woman for her time. "Ma'am," he paused as he turned to go, "is there anything that you can remember about Mr. Simmons that might help me track him down? Anything at all?"

"Well," she drew out the final consonant with a long exhalation of air, "he was trying very hard to learn Spanish. He would talk with Cora whenever he could, and he left a bunch of Spanish-language magazines in the apartment when he left. All in a neat pile, of course." She gave Stanley a wistful look before he departed. "He really was a lovely boy."

XV.

GENEVA, 2009

Elisa van der Vaart had never seen Brenda so excited. Her English flatmate was usually quite self-possessed about men. They flocked to her, and she either deigned to give them her attention or deftly moved them out of her orbit, but the impending visit of Jacob Granville had her positively babbling. They sat waiting for him in the corner of a brightly lit café, sharing a pot of press coffee and chatting excitedly about his arrival and the latest developments in their respective departments at the WTO. From Brenda's beaming expression Elisa would have thought that George Clooney was about to walk in and take her friend to his house on Lake Como for a long weekend in a hot tub.

"He's so different from English men," she confided. "My last boyfriend in London could not understand why I took this job. He's so chained to his local pub that he thinks *adventure* is a bloody dirty word." She gestured expansively. "Here we are in Geneva working for the World Trade Organization, ninety minutes away from the ski slopes." Brenda didn't ski, but that was clearly beside the point. "This is why I worked so hard at Uni, not to trudge through the rain every day to work for some stuffy upper-class twit in a brokerage house! Jacob totally gets it—he's got big dreams too."

Almost a year had passed since the young American had dropped unexpectedly into their lives, and Brenda had carried on a satisfying Internet romance with him ever since. Although it was mostly a friendly swapping of photos on Facebook, she talked about him frequently, and more than once her laugh burst across their apartment followed by an explanation that Jacob had just posted a funny link or status update. Over time he had become more and more important to Brenda, and no subsequent suitor managed to hold her attention for more than a few weeks. Even though she did not physically spend time with him, she claimed that he was the best boyfriend she had ever had.

Elisa looked across the table with a touch of envy. Even an absent lover was better than the boring parade of technocrats whom she attracted. She felt like someone had tattooed "nerds eat for free" on her forehead, and she meant real nerds, not the heroic kind in movies who really turn out to be handsome and endearing underneath their clunky black glasses.

Brenda and Elisa still shared the same apartment, but it was now better furnished, and a yearly pay raise let them pool their money for a small washer/dryer unit. Elisa had also bought a used car, which enabled her to get back to Amsterdam more often and to spend some time in the Swiss countryside when the weather was fine. All in all, life was good, even if it wasn't raining men.

Elisa had begun to travel a great deal for work, consulting with various developing countries on how to comply with the intellectual property provisions of the massive international treaty system that governed what sort of trade laws member nations could and could not impose on businesses. Even relatively simple issues sometimes justified an exciting trip to a distant locale. Just two weeks earlier, she had attended a conference in Dakar, Senegal, on patent law novelty rules. She learned that in the United States, an inventor had one year to file an application with the US patent office after the invention was revealed publicly. In the European Union, an inventor had to get to the EU patent office *before* any public revelation. The major international treaty was silent on the issue, so developing countries like Senegal had a choice. Which made more sense, the American or the European approach? It was her job to gather up the economic literature on the issue and make recommendations to policy makers in affected countries on behalf of the WTO.

She did not think that Brenda's work was as interesting. Her roommate was involved in complex subsidy cases, analyzing whether nations were providing too much support to their local industries at the expense of worldwide competition. Countries often helped out their own businesses through convoluted exceptions buried deep in their tax codes. Elisa did not envy Brenda the task of plowing through foreign tax regulations, many of which were implemented through obscure administrative rulings. She found her own Dutch tax laws impenetrable; she could not even imagine working through tax issues in a foreign language as Brenda did.

Elisa saw Jacob first, as he strolled down the pedestrian alley looking for the café chosen by Brenda for their rendezvous. He looked the same, still lean and hard, striding toward them with efficiency and grace. She lifted up a hand and he saw her, his tanned face creasing into a warm smile. A large camera hung from his neck, and he stopped to take a picture about twenty feet from their table. Brenda turned and she smiled broadly at the sight of her boyfriend. He snapped the shot and quickly closed the distance between them, planting a quick kiss on Elisa's cheek before giving Brenda's lips a warmer welcome. He then showed them the picture he had captured, an excited English woman and her sphinx-like Dutch friend, shoulders together, sharing a secret that the camera hinted at but did not reveal.

"You must send that to us!" Elisa exclaimed. "It's perfect."

"Oh my God," Brenda objected as she clung to his shoulder, "I look like a stunned cocker spaniel."

"No, you don't," Jacob kissed her again. "You look great."

He sat down and ordered a beer. Brenda peppered him with questions about his trip, while Elisa looked at Jacob's camera. She loved the heft of the full-sized digital SLR. She had only a small pocket camera purchased before mobile phones came routinely equipped with a picture-taking function. The Nikon in her hand looked just like a traditional camera from the front but had all the features she associated with digital photography in the back, including a large view screen that let her scroll through other photos he had taken.

The first thing she noticed was that he had seen them before she had seen him. Right before the lovely shot of Brenda and Elisa came an unposed photo of Elisa raising a cup to her lips. He must have used the telephoto function, since the picture included only a wisp of Brenda's hair. The picture before that one was also of Elisa, smiling and chatting with her friend. She stole a glance at Jacob, remembering their rather creepy walk through the park overlooking Annemasse. He appeared wholly engrossed in Brenda's description of her brother's recent wedding and the ridiculous amount of alcohol the wedding party had consumed before, during, and after the ceremony. She wondered about the two candid shots and concluded that he had not chosen Brenda as his subject because he could only see the back of her head.

She kept scrolling backward through his pictures. He really did have a keen eye for people. He had snapped at least a dozen photos of unsuspecting travelers in the airports he had passed through between Atlanta and Geneva, and each one caught something of the personality of its subject. One particularly striking picture showed an exhausted mother staring into space while her child leaned against her and happily ransacked her purse.

Then came images captured before his travels began, an entire series of pictures of a beautiful woman with long dark hair, photos in a park, on a tree-lined street, in a dance studio, and in a brick-walled apartment. Were they lovers? If not, she was the perfect muse, as each shot was a revealing study of the woman's inner presence and palpable grace. If he did not love her, his camera certainly did.

She slid the Nikon back across the table toward him and cast a glance at Brenda, wondering if her friend was in for a disappointing visit.

That night, the gasps and cries coming from Brenda's bedroom gave no sign of disappointment. Although Elisa had dined with the young couple, she had declined their invitation to join them at a dance club afterward and instead snuggled up with Sophie Kinsella's latest novel and a cup of hot chocolate. She had a presentation to give the next morning and made an early night of it. The boisterous and drunken entrance of her friends in the wee hours of the morning woke her up, and a series of giggles and ineffective shushings ushered the couple from the front door and into Brenda's bedroom. The muse back in Georgia had some serious competition, Elisa decided, as she slipped in her earbuds and switched on her insomnia mix, a multi-hour loop of Haydn symphonies.

Although Jacob was scheduled to stay only a few days, his visit stretched into a week and beyond. Once again, he was on good behavior, cleaning up after himself in the bathroom and offering to help out in the kitchen. Elisa saw little of him. He made it a point to meet Brenda after work and they spent time together in cafés and strolling on the lakeside esplanade. Dining out was so expensive that they mostly ate at home, but Elisa usually gave them space even when they cheerfully invited her to join them. Her roommate was so enthusiastic about Jacob that Elisa tried to like him, too, despite the uncomfortable vibe he had given her during his last visit. She was happy for her friend, who was clearly falling hard for the young photographer.

Usually, Elisa was the first to leave for work, a habit that pre-dated Brenda's desire to steal a few extra minutes every morning wrapped in the arms of her lover, but the Friday morning during the second week of Jacob's stay, a meeting of the Sub-Committee on Subsidies had been called and Brenda had no choice but to drag herself out of bed early to make an eight o'clock presentation. Elisa was left sitting alone at their small kitchen table enjoying a madeleine and a glass of grapefruit juice when Jacob emerged from the bedroom in a pair of boxer shorts, stretching like a languid cat.

He touched her shoulder and wished her good morning as he walked by and filled a kettle with water for his coffee. Elisa watched him warily. A man in his underwear was hardly a scandalous sight for a modern European woman. Indeed, she appreciated the taut stomach that flashed before her when he sat down at the table, but she nonetheless wished her roommate was there with them.

After a few minutes of small talk, he surprised her by mentioning their meeting in the café after he got off of the train. "I noticed you scrolling through the photos on my camera." He casually bit off a corner of a pastry that Brenda had left on the table. "Thanks for not saying anything to Brenda."

"About what?" Elisa remembered the photos of the Georgia muse.

"You saw those pictures of Diana in the camera," he replied, "but you didn't mention them to Brenda."

"Why would I?" Elisa wondered what the point of the conversation was. Failing to pass along her wild guesses about Jacob's love life back in Georgia was hardly something that required a thank-you. "You have a lot of excellent photographs of many different people."

"But Diana's different . . . It shows in the pictures. At least I hope it does." He got up and grabbed his camera from the kitchen counter. He took a moment to find a particularly striking picture of the Georgia girl as she leaned against the side of a large stone building with a pensive expression in her eyes. "She's my girlfriend."

This was not a conversation that Elisa wanted to have. "I thought that Brenda was your girlfriend." She pushed the camera toward him and scooted her chair back.

"She is," he replied with a curious look. "I haven't made promises to either one of them."

"Maybe not," she snorted, "but I'll bet Brenda feels like you've made some kind of commitment."

"After just a week of great sex?" He popped the rest of the madeleine in his mouth and brushed the crumbs off his fingers over the table. "Brenda's a big girl. She knows the score."

Elisa shot him a judgmental look, but he absorbed it easily and smiled as if she were trying to seduce him instead of shame him. He got up, stretched again, and walked around the table behind her. She felt his large warm hands on her shoulders, gently massaging the stiffness he found there.

"You're a big girl, too, Elisa." His fingers found a little knot to the right of her neck and went gently to work. "There's no reason why we couldn't have a little fun together this morning."

She shook her head at the sleazy proposal and reached back awkwardly to push his hands away. She felt his lips brush against the side of her neck as he whispered, "You're an attractive woman, Elisa." She flinched and he moved his mouth to the other side of her head, "I've wanted you for a while now."

He took her earlobe in his mouth and she jerked forward. She hated when anyone played with her ears.

"Sorry, Jacob." She stood and gathered up the breakfast dishes with a hurried clatter. "I can't do this."

"I didn't know you were such a prude." He leaned back against the kitchen counter, blocking her way to the sink with an amused expression on his face. "I thought European girls were more modern than that."

"Modern has nothing to do with it!" Being mocked by a cowboy from the land of George W. Bush was indescribably galling. She pushed past him and dumped the dishes in the sink. "Brenda is my best friend. If you think that I'm going to hurt her in order to fuck an American with a cool camera, then you've got as much shit for brains as your president."

Before she could react, he reached forward and grabbed the belt loops of her jeans, pulling her toward him and pressing his mouth to hers. She put her hands against his chest and tried to push him away.

"You know you want this," he said as he grabbed the back of her head.

Elisa's first instinct, developed after several years of tae kwon do, was to raise her leg and pound down her heel on the arch of his foot. That would teach the smug bastard a quick lesson. Unfortunately for Jacob, her knee rose with the rest of her leg and came into solid contact with his scrotum before she ever stomped. He went down like a tasered thug and lay on the floor moaning. "You bitch," he spit at her, "you fucking bitch."

She did not wait for him to follow through on any of the threats that began to pour from his lips. She grabbed her briefcase and ran out the door without a backward glance.

★ ★ ★

Elisa spent a distracted day at work and returned to the apartment late, hoping that Brenda would be there alone to offer news that Jacob had suddenly left, but instead she was met with the happy scene of the young couple laughing and sharing a bowl of pasta at the dining room table. Elisa almost bolted back out the door, but Jacob saw her before she could react and waved her toward the table with a bottle of Chianti. "Please, eat with us," he insisted. "We have enough for five at least."

She looked at him and, discerning no immediate threat, took a plate and sat down. If her presence were awkward to him, he gave no sign, and the meal passed without incident. She decided to say nothing to Brenda for the time being. She was happy, but her boyfriend was a shit. It was an old problem, but one that would resolve itself soon, as the American announced that he was departing for good. Despite his lack of evident ill will, Elisa made sure that she was never alone in the apartment with him again. He stayed three more days, either closeted with Brenda or typing furiously on his computer, never acknowledging that they had ever clashed.

Elisa doubted that he had said anything to Brenda, since she seemed utterly untroubled in her relationships with either her boyfriend or her flatmate. She did, however, give the impression that she and Jacob were sharing some sort of secret. Elisa caught them talking excitedly in hushed tones on several occasions, as if they were plotting something important. Their intimacy was not merely physical, and this was borne out by the length of their bedtime conversations every night. Once their lovemaking was over, they had a lot to talk about, and by the time Brenda's confidante and coconspirator was gone, Elisa had gotten very tired of listening to Haydn.

Three days after the incident in the kitchen, Jacob left, failing to say good-bye to Elisa, but leaving a broken-hearted Brenda once more sobbing in her bedroom.

"I'm going to America," she said when her roommate knocked softly and entered her room. "He says he doesn't want me to, but I've got to see him again." She sniffed and clutched her pillow tightly to her chest. "He can't stop me from coming."

"Why doesn't he want you to come?" Elisa was sympathetic, but at the same time she rejoiced that the affair seemed to be over and that she would not have to hurt her friend by revealing what kind of a person her lover was.

"He said that I wouldn't like it in the South, that he was really busy, that he'd be traveling, that it was too expensive." She sniffed. "Just a bunch of vague bullshit."

Elisa hesitated. She did not want to play her trump card. What if Brenda did not believe the story of her breakfast encounter with Jacob? What if she were blamed for Jacob's abrupt departure? "Do you think he might have someone else in Georgia? He's a really handsome guy. There's got to be plenty of girls chasing after him," Elisa finally ventured.

Brenda looked down. "Maybe. There was this girl in some of his Facebook posts."

"You know," Elisa said as she sat down next to her friend, "it would look pretty desperate to fly to America and embarrass him, especially if he's trying to choose between you and someone else. Why don't you just let things be for a bit? He doesn't strike me as the kind of guy who would react well to a lot of pressure." She handed over a tissue. "If you play it cool for a while, good things are bound to happen."

Brenda blew her nose and then nodded reluctantly. "Maybe. I get it. Being clingy never works."

Elisa gave her shoulder a reassuring squeeze and breathed a sigh of relief that she did not have to dump even more sorrow on her broken-hearted friend.

XVI

TEAMWORK

Melanie hung up the phone and stared out her office window. A spring rain had washed away Atlanta's usual yellow haze, and in the distance she could see the top of Stone Mountain, the massive pluton that the Klan had once used as a semaphore station for cross burnings. From her vantage point on the twentieth floor, the city looked densely green, apparently covered by a thick canopy of trees, but she knew from her morning commute that asphalt was really the dominant underlayment of the landscape. The vista was just an inviting illusion.

Unfortunately, the owner of the website posting Diana Cavendish's photos appeared to be just as illusive. Professor Hopkins had just informed her of his dead-end attempt to track down the operator of Mygirlfriendsbikini.com, and she was tempted to ask her former FBI boyfriend for a little more help. But if the price for information about the disconnected Arkansas phone number was their upcoming dinner, what would he want in return for tracking down a website owner? She had already mentally taken sex completely off the table, despite the fact that months had passed since she had been with someone. The one and only booty call given to Sammy Goodson after their break-up had been a disaster. An hour in the shower had been insufficient to scour away the memory of a smile that had shown he was getting just what he wanted and giving her nothing she needed.

Nonetheless, a grown-up should be able to ask a favor of another grown-up without offering an excessive quid pro quo. The visit to Vidalia to interview the parents of Jacob Granville had piqued her interest in the Cavendish case, and she really wanted to track down the mysterious pictures of Diana. Granville's parents clearly believed their son was still alive, and the *we* he used in his last email suggested Diana might be with him. Had they staged a crime and run off to Mexico? If so, why? Or had he killed her and was sending bogus messages to cover up his crime? Of course, even that scenario required some evidence of a motive for killing in the first place. She doubted the victim's new haircut had provided adequate provocation, but you never knew.

The other clues offered by the Granvilles were similarly tantalizing. What was Jacob's interest in the Arkansas congressional delegation? Perhaps the reason his name had been entered in the FBI database had nothing to do with the disappearance of Diana Cavendish at all. Online sources had revealed one Arkansas senator and one representative on the committee overseeing the FBI and the CIA, but that didn't necessarily mean anything.

The YouTube evidence was even more opaque. Although the Granvilles had retained all their son's papers, Melanie remembered the uploader as j-gville and easily found his YouTube channel. Jacob had uploaded two videos before his disappearance, and both were confusing. The first video was shot in a trailer, apparently in Georgia, if the Braves T-shirt worn by the primary interviewee was any indication.

"My name is Moussa Ibrahim." A slim African man spoke shyly into the camera in broken English, as if he were somehow embarrassed by his tale. "I farmed the cotton in Mali. I come to America with my son last year."

In fits and starts, he explained that he had worked the family cotton farm for years, barely surviving in good years and nearly starving in bad ones. Eventually, the price paid for his crop was insufficient to satisfy his creditors and feed his family, so he was forced to sell the land and move to the city. The pitiful proceeds of the transaction provided food for a couple of months before he, his wife, and their three children were reduced to begging in the streets and sleeping in a corrugated lean-to on the edge of a brutal shantytown. His large dark eyes glistened as he related how his wife was the first to die, her horrible hacking cough finally silenced in the feverish endgame of tuberculosis. His youngest daughter followed her mother, taken by a bout of dysentery that soon killed her older sister. Only the son remained.

"This is my son, Adama," Moussa managed with a weak smile.

The camera panned across the trailer to a child sitting in a chair and coloring fiercely in a book on the kitchen table. His legs were bent and twisted, encased by a pair of braces rhythmically knocking against the table.

"I carried him on the plane to here. He can walk better now." Moussa explained how a generous émigré uncle had finally responded to their plight. His expression of gratitude to the US for welcoming him and giving his son hope did nothing to lessen the impact of what Melanie had seen.

The second video was equally compelling.

"My name is Marisol Fuentes, and I live in Sabinas, Mexico." A thin young woman choked back a sob even as she started to speak. Her large brown eyes only occasionally glanced up at the camera as she told her tale.

She worked in a textile factory just south of the border, where the maquiladoras took advantage of zero tariffs and near-zero enforcement by the Mexican government of its own labor and environmental laws. She touched a bruise on the side of her face and explained how sickness had forced her to miss a day of work at the factory. Despite the fact that she had worked the previous fifteen days consecutively, her foreman had shown up at her tiny apartment. Without a husband to protect her and her twelve-year-old daughter, he had raped both of them, and when she had told his supervisor, the foreman returned and beat her.

"I have no one here. My village is in the mountains," she explained as she gestured with a hopeless brown hand. "Many miles *fuera* . . . away."

She talked about the futility of complaining to the police about those who ran the factories on which the local economy depended, and she had kept quiet, praying each evening that her tormentor would not return. Her daughter ran out of the room when the camera panned toward her.

"She don't talk no more," was all Marisol could get out before starting to cry again. When she gained a bit of control, she managed to urge the unseen interviewer to talk to other women in the town and hear their stories.

Had Granville himself shot the footage? And why had he posted the interviews? Almost no one had seen them; they had fewer than a hundred views combined. Although both the stories detailed extreme suffering of parents and children, they seemed very distinct in time and place. But these kinds of stories sometimes won Pulitzers, so he might have been trolling for the most compelling subjects, regardless of source. Or maybe he was just a sadistic bastard who thrived on the pain of others.

In any event, she wanted to know more about Granville, and that started with tracking down the source of the Arkansas phone number manned by an unknown woman who seemed just as interested in his case. And that brought her to her impending dinner date with Sammy Goodson.

★ ★ ★

Melanie had taken steps to ensure the meal would be extravagant. Sammy would be anxious to pay, for all the wrong reasons, so she had booked a table at the hottest new restaurant in town, one whose owner had just finished in the top three on *Top Chef*. If she were going to put up with her ex for a long dinner, then she was going to have a pricey bottle of wine and a stunning five-course meal.

She arrived at the restaurant stylishly late and saw the G-man leaning against the bar, drinking something brown out of a glass tumbler.

"Still addicted to the smoke of Scottish turf, I see." Sammy claimed to be an expert on single-malt Highland scotches, and his bookshelves at home contained more than twenty varieties, crowding out all tomes but those relating to gourmet whiskey consumption. The booze tasted like stale cigarette butts to her, and she suspected his appreciation for the drink was entirely feigned.

"You look lovely this evening." He ignored her barb and looked her up and down with an appreciative smile that barely escaped being a leer. "Are you still a gin-and-tonic girl?"

She ordered a glass of a reserve Oregon pinot noir from the bartender in response and sat down on the stool next to him. "Not anymore," she said with a brief glance in his direction.

He was almost six feet three inches tall, distinguished features marred by a crooked nose hinting he'd given as good as he'd got in some barroom brawl. She knew better—his mother had accidently opened a car door into his face when he was eight. His thick brown hair was graying slightly at the temples, which added even more character to an otherwise distinguished countenance. With the exception of those who had slept with him, her girlfriends back in Washington thought her crazy to have dumped him.

"So, what sort of bad guys are you tracking down these days? Still spending ninety percent of your time away from home?" She smiled and settled in for a good listen.

He was appropriately vague about the antiterrorist bit of his agenda but had a good story to tell about an investigation into a major drug-smuggling operation, where a famous defense lawyer had been observed on a yacht full of his client's illicit merchandise, taking full advantage of the prostitutes traveling with the gang's ringleader. The US attorney in the case was planning with great relish to call the lawyer as a surprise witness for the prosecution, and Sammy could hardly wait to hear him attempting to explain how his cocaine-fueled threesome with a pair of teenage Columbian girls was protected by attorney-client privilege.

Melanie was watching him closely and nodding when the maître d' arrived and took them to their seats. The table for two looked down on Centennial Park and the view was extraordinary.

"I had to grease him with an extra twenty," Sammy explained, "but it was worth the wait, don't you think?"

"Absolutely." She studied him carefully as he beamed at her, and she was relieved to discover no leftover romantic feelings for him whatsoever. None. It was a liberating discovery, and her face creased into a smile that he probably misunderstood. She suddenly felt enthusiastic about the prospect of a gourmet meal and found herself totally immune to the pompous and self-aggrandizing monologues that inevitably accompanied dinner with him. She even forgot to ask about the phantom Arkansas phone number until the waiter brought them dessert and coffee.

"Hey, Sammy," she asked between bites of warm salted caramel, "what did you learn about that disconnected phone number listed on the FBI database? You know, the link to the missing couple I was telling you about." She could not decipher the expression on his face. "You know," she insisted, "it's kind of the whole reason why I agreed to meet you for dinner."

"Yeah, yeah," he replied, "I was just hoping you'd forgotten." He reached for her hand, but she pulled it just beyond his fingertips. "We were having such a good time, and now you want to ruin things."

"I don't want to ruin anything." She leaned back in her chair and indulged him with a smile. "And you're right, I've been having a surprisingly good time, but that doesn't mean I'm not curious about an anonymous person who takes my report of an inquiry into a five-year-old kidnapping and then has the phone disconnected before I can follow up." She didn't add that the person she had named in her call, James Murphy, had subsequently been the victim of a mysterious burglary.

"Do you think maybe once you could just put your curiosity to the side and let me take you dancing instead of talking shop?" His eyes sparkled in anticipation of extending the date. He was a good dancer, damn him.

She leaned further back and crossed her arms. "Stop stalling. I love talking shop."

"Okay," he groaned and pulled his hand back to his side of the table. "I made an inquiry higher up—never mind to whom—and got bitch-slapped so fast it made my head spin. I was told to forget I ever heard of that phone number, and I had to promise to make you forget it too."

"What?"

"I'm not kidding, Mel." He leaned forward, his face a study in earnestness. "Forget you ever heard of the case, forget you ever called the number, forget you ever asked me to check it out. Just drop the whole fucking thing."

"Who told you this?" She was livid. No one in the FBI hierarchy, not even the director, had the right to call her off an investigation, no matter how half-assed it was.

"I'm pretty sure it's some politico on the congressional intelligence oversight committee, but I have no idea who." He smiled, confident of having spoken the last word on the matter. She stared at him unblinking. "I'm serious, Mel." He changed the tone of his voice and sounded instantly more professional. "There's nothing there. Just forget that you ever called that number."

"Who told you this?" She repeated her question, a diamond edge to her voice.

"Uh-uh," he grunted with a shake of his head and a staccato emphasis on the following syllables, "No. Fucking. Way."

She was about to jump on his chest and drag the truth out of him when she remembered that he had always, deep down, been a loyal taker of orders. If some superior had told him to shut up, then a dozen terrorists with a crowbar would be unable to make him talk.

She forced herself to relax and took the last sip of her coffee. She'd hit another dead end, but the evening was not a total waste. The food had been fabulous, and she had finally buried the ghost of lovers past.

He interpreted her demeanor as submissive and managed to clasp her hands. He looked into her eyes with a warm smile. "I had a great time tonight, Mel." He really could be charming when he tried. "Wouldn't it be nice to extend it a few more hours?"

She returned his smile with a twinkle in her eyes and gave his hands a squeeze before pulling her own onto her lap and replying with a distinct "No. Fucking. Way."

★ ★ ★

Just before lunchtime, James Murphy noticed Thorsten Carter entering the newsroom with an attractive young woman by his side and saw the receptionist point them to his work space. As the senior reporter at the *Clarkeston Chronicle,* he was the only non-editor to merit his own office. He did not, however, merit a new desk, and so he sat behind a battered oak monster pitted with so many cigarette burns that it looked like the no man's land between World War I trenches. Given that smoking had been banned in the newsroom for over twenty-five years, the textured mosaic of charred wood had achieved a historic status at the paper.

"Hi, Father Carter!" James stood and waved them in, quickly clearing a pile of papers off the only chair he had available for guests. "What brings you to the pulsing news hub of Clarkeston, Georgia?"

Before he could answer, the woman thrust out her hand. "I'm Miriam Rodgers, and we wanted to have a word with you."

"Miriam is the daughter of Ernest Rodgers, my predecessor at St. James," Carter quickly added.

"Oh my God," James said, recognizing her from Jacob Granville's prom picture, discovered on his trip to Vidalia. "I knew your father, but I'm not sure that I've seen you since you were a teenager." He gestured at the open chair but she refused to sit down. "What do you want to talk about?'

"My father's boxes that have gone missing."

Of course. He noticed a sheepish expression on Carter's face. Time to pay the piper. "Why don't we walk down the street and chat over a bite to eat. My treat."

Serious Thai was located on the second floor of a converted cotton warehouse about two blocks from the newspaper and offered authentically spiced Asian food cooked by a Clarkeston native who had lived in Bangkok. The chef's plan was to educate the palate of his town, even if its citizens complained about the heat from the chilies once in a while. James loved the place for its bold approach to the cuisine, the exposed brick and rafters of its dining room, and the fact that it was the only Asian restaurant in town without a greasy buffet line feeding its lunch patrons.

After they ordered, the priest asked James to explain to Miriam exactly what had happened to her father's boxes.

"Well," the reporter said after a quick apology, "I sat down with your father's papers right after Thor gave them to me. I plowed through the first box pretty quickly." He thanked the waiter as his bowl of clear soup arrived. "It was mostly a collection of stuff prepared by other people: conference materials, some old church bulletins, magazines, and the like. Then, I ordered a pizza and sat down with the second box until it got late. I'd say midnight or so."

"What was in the second box?" the young woman asked.

"It was almost entirely sermons. I skimmed through a bunch of them and then went to bed. I intended to finish off the pile the following afternoon when I got back home from work, but they were stolen sometime in the morning when I was away." He shrugged his shoulders and dipped a fresh spring roll in a small dab of chili paste on his plate. "The neighbors say they saw a brown delivery van at the house around ten o'clock or so. The cops think that might be related to the theft. They took my new laptop and a bunch of other papers too."

"May I ask why you wanted to see my father's private papers?" She asked the question without hostility but still implied that his intrusion into her father's work was inappropriate.

The arrival of his basil duck gave him time to think about his answer. He saw no reason not to share his suspicions with the young couple before him. Sometimes the best way to get information was to share it, and one of them might have some insight into the role St. James and its political power brokers might have played in the cover-up of Diana Cavendish's disappearance. He hoped she would talk about her relationship with Granville, although she might not want to bring it up with a potential beau sitting next to her.

"This is kind of a long story," he began, refolding his napkin in his lap and settling back in his chair, "but you'll understand better if I start at the beginning.

"A couple of weeks ago, I saw some pictures of Diana Cavendish online that I had never seen before and that I believe were taken shortly before she was abducted." He could tell from Miriam's expression that she remembered the notorious case. "I believe the photos were taken by Jacob Granville. After all, taking pictures was his main job at the newspaper, so either he posted them himself or someone with access to his camera or his computer uploaded them. In any case, I thought it critical to track down the source of the photos, so I contacted the US attorney's office in Atlanta."

"But not the local police," the priest interjected, with a glance at Miriam.

James turned his attention to Miriam and elaborated. "I've always thought that the sheriff didn't want the case solved, that he was covering up something."

He thought she looked surprised. Was she taken aback by the idea of a cover-up or by the fact that he suspected one? "Anyway, I went to the assistant US attorney, and she's trying to track down the website and find out who uploaded the photos. She also went down with me to Vidalia to talk to Granville's parents." He took a sip of tea and revealed the emails from Mexico bearing Jacob's name.

"So, Jacob is still alive?" Miriam's eyes were wide. She laid her fork down. "They've gotten emails from him? What did they say?"

"Well," the reporter cautioned her, "no one can be sure who sent the emails, and they were very short. The messages basically promised to explain everything later, but except for those three emails received shortly after Jacob's disappearance, his parents haven't heard a thing."

He watched her struggle to process the information. "But what does this have to do with my father's papers?" A puzzled frown creased her face. "Why did you want to see the boxes?"

Now, this was sensitive territory. Surely, she knew her father had been a passionate defender of Jacob Granville, but James had no idea whether she, too, thought he was innocent, or whether she believed her father had been tilting at windmills. He wished he knew when her relationship with Granville had ended and under what circumstances. "You might remember that I was the primary reporter covering the disappearance of Diana Cavendish. Your father was an eloquent advocate for Jacob, and sometimes he hinted about inside information concerning his innocence. He was certainly emphatic that Jacob could not have committed the crime. I've often wondered whether he had any basis for his faith and whether there might be something in his papers to shed light on it." He shrugged his shoulders and resumed picking at his noodles. "You have to admit, the circumstantial evidence points at Granville." He did not speculate on how the sheriff and his priest might have actively conspired to hide evidence relevant to his whereabouts.

She looked unoffended by his explanation and after a moment's reflection offered a cautious reply. "You're right about one thing: Daddy always insisted Jacob could not have done it." Then she unexpectedly waved the waiter over and asked for the wine list. "Would y'all care to join me for a drink?"

James looked at Thor, who nodded cautiously, and Miriam ordered a bottle for them to share. She excused herself to visit the ladies' room and arrived back at the same time as a bottle of chilled sauvignon blanc.

"So," she asked after taking a long sip of the wine, "did you find anything in Papa's papers?"

"Like I said, I only got halfway through the sermons, but I found the one I wanted, where he does everything but come right out and say that all the rumors about Jacob were malicious and untrue." He lifted his glass and took another sip. The wine was crisp and citrusy. It went perfectly with the remnants of his duck. "It's really quite a skillful use of scripture to suggest Jacob was not only innocent until proven guilty, but that he was, in fact, innocent."

He watched her carefully while he spoke, but his story elicited no more than a barely perceptible nod of the head. "The sermon was really well written, but I didn't find anything else related to the case before the boxes were stolen, with one exception." He now looked into her eyes and tried to channel the inquisitorial sympathy that sometimes helped him gather information from reluctant interviewees. "Next to one of the verses about wrongful persecution of the innocent, he wrote in the margin: 'Miriam.'" He speared a red pepper and looked back at her. "Do you have any idea what he could have meant by that? Did he ask you any questions about Jacob around that time?"

Once again, she failed to take offense at his line of inquiry or mention her own relationship with the disappeared photographer. Instead, she put down her wine glass and knitted her brow thoughtfully, as if straining to remember the day almost five years earlier when her father had taken to the pulpit in defense of one of his parishioners. "I have no idea," she finally pronounced. "He knew I thought Jacob was guilty as hell, but he wouldn't have needed to ask me any questions about that." She shook her head. "I'm not the only Miriam in the world."

"True enough," the reporter admitted, "and in the Bible the story of Miriam involves Moses's sister spreading false rumors against her brother and getting punished for it. Maybe that's it." He emptied the bottle of wine with a generous splash in each of their glasses. "You can't remember anything at all?"

She gave another shake of her head and a shimmer of lustrous dark hair momentarily hid her face. "I'd love to help you. I wasn't close to Jacob, and I don't ever remember my father asking my advice on his sermons."

James accepted this without response and the threesome finished their meal in the long pause that followed. He did not know what to make of Miriam's lie. Was she trying to put him off the trail or was she just hesitant to talk about an old flame? If she loved Jacob as much as Jacob's mother loved her, then the subject might be painful. On the other hand, five years had passed, and there was no reason not to help out a hardworking reporter.

James saw the priest looking wistfully at the empty bottle of wine and heard him add his voice to the conversation. "What I don't understand is this: who stole the boxes? I don't believe in coincidences. Why steal only the boxes and your laptop? Didn't you say nothing else was taken?"

"None of my wife's jewelry was taken, nor my coin collection or any other electronics." He shook his head in wonder. "I agree. Why take a box of old sermons?"

"Maybe someone else has the same suspicions as you," Miriam said. "Maybe someone else thought the key to the mystery was somewhere in there."

"Yeah," Thor jumped in, "but who? Only James and I and the church choir director knew who had the boxes!"

Over the course of the next hour and another bottle of wine, the three new acquaintances tried to work out the disappearance of the boxes and how it might be related to the wider mystery of Jacob Granville and Diana Cavendish. James had no trouble convincing the priest that Granville was a murderer on the run, probably trying to cover his trail by emailing his parents. He may have posted the pictures of Diana because he was running out of money or as some sort of sociopathic fuck-you to the police. They all knew stories of criminals who could not keep their mouths shut. None of them, however, believed Jacob had come back to Clarkeston to steal a pile of Ernest Rodgers's sermons. That had to be the work of some third party. Perhaps the choir director had told the sheriff about the boxes? And maybe there had been something deep in the third box, unseen by James and unnoticed by Thor, evidencing a cover-up?

All three speculated enthusiastically about the mystery. James was relieved to share his obsession over Diana Cavendish, and he found himself warming up to the young priest. He found

Miriam harder to read. She was an imaginative theorizer, but whether her energy came from a weirdly renewed connection to her father or other memories of the prime players in the story was unclear. Whatever the reason, she obviously enjoyed the interchange with her companions, and it was she who suggested they meet again in a week. She even proposed an agenda: James was to have another talk with the US attorney who had accompanied him to Vidalia, and on Sunday morning Thor should gently probe the sheriff about the boxes. She volunteered to ask her mother some questions about her father. Perhaps at some point in time he had made connections influential enough to protect Jacob Granville? James added another task for himself. He would track down the parents of Diana Cavendish. He was not aware of anyone who had ever talked to them. As far as he knew, they had never come to Clarkeston.

XVII.

HIJACKED

Stanley Hopkins scratched his head and sat upright in bed. In the hazy fog of images that preceded his waking, a memory from law school had knocked on the door of his consciousness and refused to stop tapping until he answered. A phrase hummed in his brain: *reverse domain name hijacking.* The words came from the intellectual property course that he had taken his third year in law school, but he couldn't remember precisely what they referred to, so he got up, padded into his library, and found his old textbook. The index sent him to the sixth chapter, and he carried the massive treatise with him into the kitchen to read while he warmed a packet of toaster pastries.

He set the book down on the kitchen counter and poured himself a large glass of orange juice. Since his wife's accident, his sweet tooth had contributed twenty pounds to his formerly lean frame, but he lacked the willpower to replace doughnuts and cake with oatmeal and fruit. On his most recent hike he was out of breath when he reached the summit, and he had sworn off sugar for the dozenth time, but that vow had not stuck any better than the previous ones.

When he finally sat down, he placed the book directly in front of him and placed his drink and plate to either side of it. The pages of an entire chapter filled up with crumbs and drops of juice from his moustache as he gradually determined how to smoke out William Simmons, the elusive owner of Mygirlfriendsbikini.com.

Since law school, he had been aware that the Internet domain-name system was a first-come, first-served affair. Whether United.com belonged to United Airlines or United Van Lines depended entirely on which business won the race to file the first application with ICANN, the Internet Corporation for Assigned Names and Numbers, or with one of numerous intermediaries, like GoDaddy.com or Namecheap.com, who could also arrange for registration. Unfortunately, the race-to-file priority rule had encouraged cybersquatters, who registered domain names containing famous trademarks and then sold them to the highest bidder. In fact, Hewlett-Packard, the tech company, had been slow to recognize the potential of the Internet and had seen HP.com registered by a lawyer in California, who offered to sell it back for an exorbitant amount. Congress eventually responded to those sorts of abuses with legislation designed to stop cybersquatting, but the most effective deterrent had come from ICANN itself in the form of a cheap online system of nonbinding arbitration.

A short chapter in the textbook reminded him of the dispute-resolution procedure that governed all ownership fights over domain names. It was regarded as a model for avoiding costly litigation and efficiently transferring URLs to complaining trademark owners. When applying for a domain name, the registrant had to promise to submit all disputes to nonbinding arbitration before a neutral panel of experts. So, if the first person to register Coke.com was a teenage boy in Peoria waiting patiently for an offer from the Coca-Cola Corporation, he was bound to let Coke convene a panel that would cheaply and quickly order the transfer of the domain to the real Coke. Technically, the order was nonbinding, in the sense that the teenager could file a federal suit to protest his imaginary rights, but over ninety percent of panel decisions went unappealed. Because the cases were resolved entirely online and no lawyers were required, most disputes could be decided within a matter of days or weeks for a few hundred dollars.

The low cost and easy access to the dispute-resolution system did pose a hazard. What if someone wrongfully tried to wrest a domain name from a legitimate first registrant? What if Outback Tours, Inc., a small family-run travel agency since the 1920s, were the first to register Outback.com, but the newer, nationwide restaurant chain of the same name pressured the family into giving up its URL? The dispute-resolution system could be used by litigious complainants to wrongfully strong-arm registrants into giving up a name to which they had a proper right. Reverse domain-name hijacking was a real possibility, and arbitrators were on the lookout to stop it.

But an arbitrator could only stop a hijacking if the registrant came forward to defend its rights.

So, Stanley Hopkins popped the last corner of his pastry into his mouth and decided to try his hand at hijacking as a way to smoke out the owner of Mygirlfriendsbikini.com. He was so excited that he called up Melanie Wilkerson in Atlanta to explain his strategy. No one else knew of his fruitless search and no one else would recognize the utter brilliance of his plan. And besides, she had the sexiest voice that he had ever heard over the telephone.

"Okay," he revealed, after waiting fifteen minutes for her to deal with another caller, "here's what I'm gonna do. I know you can't sanction it, but it's just so freakin' cool that I had to tell somebody." He paused dramatically and then laid out his strategy. "I'm going to file a complaint against Mygirlfriendsbikini.com with ICANN, claiming that the registrant is a cybersquatter. I'm going to lie my ass off and claim that I've owned a clothing store by that name for twenty years and have prior rights to it."

"I get it," the velvet voice on the end of the line acknowledged. "This will get the attention of the website owner and when he responds, you'll know who it is."

"Not quite that easy," responded the professor, "because the only address for Simmons on file in the system is the false address we found on Whois. He won't initially know that I've filed the complaint, because he lied when he provided his registration information."

"Then how will this smoke him out?"

He spun out the logical course of events. "My complaint will win by default when Simmons doesn't respond. How can he? The notice will go to the bogus address. The arbitrators will then order the transfer of the website to me as a matter of course. Simmons won't even know he's lost it at that point. Once the domain name is transferred to me, I'll take the whole website offline and shut down all that profitable traffic." He snapped his fingers at the phone. "That will get his attention, and I'll just sit back and wait for him to contact me, the proud new owner of Mygirlfriendsbikini.com."

There was a long silence at the end of the line. "You can't quote me, because I'll deny it, but that's the most fucking awesome thing I've ever heard in my life."

★ ★ ★

Not by his nature a liar or thief, Stanley struggled somewhat with the morality of his strategy, but he managed to overcome his qualms by emphasizing the reason why he had to adopt such devious means. Simmons, as owner of the website, had provided false information to ICANN in violation of the express rules that all domain-name owners promised to abide by. He had deliberately and wrongfully hidden himself from view, and now that he was needed to provide information in a murder investigation, he was unavailable. It was his fault. Besides, Stanley would transfer the domain name back to him just as soon as he obtained the name of the person who had submitted the photos of Diana Cavendish.

At the end of their conversation, Melanie had expressed the worry that the elusive website owner might start up another site rather than respond to the hijacking, but Stanley wasn't worried. The goodwill established in any successful website was tremendously valuable, and the upset owner would not be able to attract the same number of customers merely by adopting another name and starting up another site with the same content. Of course, if the owner were the murderer, then he would likely stay hidden, but Stanley thought that scenario doubtful. Simmons's website looked like he collected free uploads from amateurs and maybe bought some professional soft-core images to augment his content offerings.

The first half of the plan went easily. The hijacking worked as predicted, and with the help of a colleague in the computer science department at Belle Meade College, he found himself in control of the website in less than three weeks. His friend explained how easy it was to disable the website so that those searching for it would get nothing but an error message.

It took less than twenty-four hours to hear from William Simmons. Stanley received a panicked email and then a hostile phone message on his machine at Belle Meade. Simmons had evidently checked the Whois database and tracked him down. Stanley had registered his work address and hoped his home address in Los Angeles would be obscured among the seven other men with his name in the phone book. The professor responded immediately to the email, with a suggestion that they meet and discuss the terms of the retransfer of the website. Stanley chose a café in Silver Lake that had caught his eye when he had visited Simmons's last-known residence there, and he asked the bikini czar to bring his laptop and all of his business records. Stanley made it clear that he needed information, something other than money, in return for the domain name. Simmons agreed via email within minutes.

Stanley arrived at Café Intermezzo an hour before the scheduled meeting. He wanted to make sure that the Wi-Fi connection was adequate for his purposes, and he wanted to run through the instructions provided by his friend for putting Mygirlfriendsbikini.com back online if Simmons cooperated. When he was satisfied with his preparations, he ordered a large slice of blueberry coffee cake and a latte with a shot of caramel syrup. He then sat down behind his laptop watching the door for the "nice young man" who used to rent a garage apartment a short walk away.

Stanley hoped to intimidate Simmons by signaling that he had done his research thoroughly, right down to choosing a meeting spot close to his old home.

About five minutes after the appointed time, a well-dressed young man with a Patagonia computer case and a perfectly groomed soul patch burst into the café and immediately trained his glare on its half-dozen patrons. When his eyes met Stanley's, the professor invited him over to his table with a solemn nod. Simmons stormed across the café and unceremoniously slapped his briefcase down and jolted Stanley's laptop six inches closer to his chest.

"Do you realize that you're costing me $1,000 a day?" Despite his scowl, the soft-core mini-mogul sounded more peevish than threatening. A phone rang from the interior of his brushed-corduroy jacket, but he silenced it with a squeeze of his hand through the fabric.

"Sorry to inconvenience you, Mr. Simmons," the professor responded with the inevitable shrug of a French kiosk owner announcing that he had just run out of Gauloises, "but it couldn't be helped."

"What the fuck?" the confused entrepreneur inquired. "What's that supposed to mean?"

"I've been trying to find you for weeks, but you registered your website with a false address, some hotel in Beverly Hills." Stanley sipped his coffee. "This was the only way to get your attention."

"Well, you've got it now," Simmons said. He leaned forward and whispered in a voice that was as agitated as a shout. "What the hell do you want, anyway, and when are you giving me my site back?"

"You can have everything you want this afternoon by giving me a single address." He flipped open his computer as if to ready the website for activation.

"That's all you want?" The young man straightened up and scooted his chair back a few inches. "Are you kidding me?"

"Nope." He then handed the webmaster a series of pictures of Diana Cavendish with the URL of each image highlighted at the top of each printout. "I need you to look at your records and tell me who sold these pictures to you."

"My records are confidential." He pushed the pictures across the table and one of them fell to the floor. Stanley calmly picked it up before replying.

"Too bad. Then I guess we won't be doing business." Stanley shut his laptop and started to put it back in his satchel. With losses at $1,000 per day, he doubted Simmons would call his bluff.

"Just wait a minute!" Simmons made an unconvincing attempt to add some menace to his tone. "I've talked to my lawyers . . . We can sue you and get the site back. If you'll just transfer it to me now, you'll save yourself a lot of trouble."

Stanley laughed: this little turd had no idea what trouble really was. "Yeah?" he responded scornfully. "And at $1,000 a day, how much are you going to lose while you fire up the lawyers? And how much do they cost a day? Just give me the contact information for those photos and you can have your domain name back right now for free." He opened up his computer. "Is the photographer your friend or something? You trying to hide him?"

The young man picked up the pictures again and scrutinized them more closely. He shook his head. "I have no idea who sent these to me."

"But you could find out, right?"

Simmons did not immediately answer, but he opened up his briefcase and pulled out his computer, setting it on the table directly across from Stanley, like an electronic gunfighter facing off at the O.K. Corral Café. The professor noticed that the webmaster had a brand-new Apache Pro laptop; the soft-core porn business must indeed be profitable. After a couple of minutes punctuated by staccato keystrokes, the entrepreneur announced that he had found the address of the person who had sold him the photos. "You promise that you'll transfer the domain to me if I give this to you?"

"Absolutely, I'm all ready to go, and I'll fix you up as soon as I have the address, but first I want to make sure you're not fucking with me. Show me how you traced the address from the picture."

Simmons flushed but he mastered himself and tapped his mouse a couple of times, before spinning his device around and moving his chair next to Stanley's. "Okay, here are the pictures." Diana Cavendish looked like she was ready to walk right out of the high-definition monitor.

"In the web page meta tags," he continued, clicking on View and then Source to reveal the HTML version of the web page they were looking at, "I bury an alphanumeric that identifies who sent me the picture." He pointed at a number that appeared on the bottom of the page. "All I need to do is query that number in my payment records." He minimized the screen and brought up his accounting software. "Voilà. I paid twenty-five dollars two months ago to expatsoller@ocea.es."

"That's it?" Stanley cried out in despair. "Just an email address?"

"What did you expect?" The businessman frowned. "You think that I cut these people checks? Everything gets done through PayPal. All I need is the email address of someone with an account and I can pay them instantly anywhere around the world."

"Yeah, yeah," Stanley said bitterly, "I see how it works." He looked hard at the webmaster but could see no trace of a lie. The email address was most likely the only relevant information Simmons maintained. If he were running an X-rated porn site, he would have to keep records of the ages of the girls depicted there, but he avoided that regulatory requirement by accepting swimsuit photos only. Unless the professor got really lucky when he googled the email address, he had hit another dead end.

In theory, if they could prove reasonable suspicion, the feds could get a court order forcing PayPal to reveal the photographer's bank account information, but that wasn't going to happen. He slumped back in his chair. He had wanted to be the one to bring the identity of the photographer back to US attorney Melanie Wilkerson in Atlanta. He had even fantasized about flying to the Southeast to personally deliver the good news. He briefly questioned whether his impulse to fly across the country to meet an unknown woman was consistent with his intense mourning for his wife. But those two parts of his brain were on tracks that had not yet intersected.

"Are you still there, dude?" The impatient blackmail victim waved his hand in front of Stanley's face. "Are you gonna transfer my property back to me or not?"

Stanley nodded and maximized a screen that had been waiting patiently at the bottom of his computer desktop. "Here's the transfer request with everything filled out except your real address, which I still don't know." After the information was reluctantly provided, he clicked on the Submit button and initiated the reregistration in Simmons's name.

The professor then pulled up another screen and followed the instructions on how to bring the domain name back online. "That's it," he said without much enthusiasm.

Simmons typed the web address into his computer and the home page of Mygirlfriendsbikini.com instantly appeared on his screen. He flipped his laptop shut and returned it to his briefcase. "I could say that it was a pleasure doing business with you, but it wasn't. I'm still out a couple thousand bucks." He gave Stanley a disgusted look. "And for what? A single fucking email address?"

"Well," the professor replied as he packed up his own bag, "if it makes you feel better, I'm getting this information for the Justice Department." He decided to tie up a final loose end with a thinly veiled threat. "So don't even think about alerting this guy. Just keep quiet and consider yourself a patriot in the war on terror."

XVIII

ROADTRIP

Melanie got on the road by six thirty Saturday morning, and in less than three hours she was driving past a sign proudly declaring Highlands, North Carolina, at 4,118 feet, to be the city with the highest elevation east of the Mississippi. The dashboard thermometer confirmed that she was now far above the muggy Georgia Piedmont; it was almost fifteen degrees cooler than when she started, and some of the elderly women toddling down the sidewalk of the resort town were clutching knitwear they had stopped wearing in Atlanta two months earlier. The elevation made the village a popular summer getaway, and Melanie was glad to see that James Murphy had arrived early and grabbed a table at the Pioneer Inn before the gray-haired mob snapped up the remaining seats. She slid into a booth across from him and ordered a coffee from the waitress.

"Thanks for coming up to help me with Diana's parents," he said, shoving a newspaper to the corner of the table. "By the way, the hash browns here are awesome."

"Better than Waffle House?" she asked doubtfully.

He responded with a surprised laugh. "I said awesome, not transcendent." He pushed the bowl of creamers over to her as she got her coffee. "The blueberry pancakes are great too."

"Do you come up here a lot?"

"Not so much." He handed the menus back to the waitress. "I grew up about ten miles from here, and even though

Highlands has only got a couple thousand people and one grocery store, this used to be the big city to me."

She was surprised. The village was isolated and the mountains contained mostly small cabins and trailers. Perhaps his parents had retired early and bought a home nearby. "What brought
your family here?"

He layered a bit more mountain twang to his voice. "They
always lived in one holler or another up here." He poured some
sugar into his coffee and added, "My dad was a pulpwooder in
the summer and a drinker in the winter. My mom had us kids,
tried to keep a tidy house, and defended us with a big iron skillet
when she had to."

Melanie couldn't tell whether he was serious or not. He
seemed awfully sophisticated to have grown up in the hardscrabble tangle of the Carolina mountains. "Are they still here?"

"Mom's dead. My dad and brother live together. The
old place is falling apart, so it's not really a very fun visit." He
shrugged and gave her a warm smile. "I wouldn't mind having
one of those vacation homes on the edge of town, though."

She imagined him in a flannel shirt, sitting on his porch and
banging out stories about his childhood on his laptop. He was
relaxed in his native element, and she figured his wife must be a
complete idiot to let him go. "I left home as soon as I could, too.
It was great to escape, but I took awhile to get used to the east
coast. And now it's been pretty weird coming back."

He gave her a pensive look that tossed a little butterfly into
her stomach when it turned mischievous. "I hear you, but the
journey down the mountain to Clarkeston was plenty strange,
too, maybe even more eye-opening than the trek from Atlanta
to Yale. And I'll tell you what: there's zero chance of a return
move back to Walnut Gap."

She studied him while he went back to work on his pancakes. He made a nice contrast to the cookie-cutter lawyers and
bureaucrats that filled her life whether she was in Atlanta or
Washington, DC.

"Did you ever track down the Arkansas number?"

"Not yet. My friend in the FBI did some digging but was warned off before he found out. He thought the source of the interference might be someone on the congressional intelligence oversight committee, but he wouldn't say who." She frowned and speared a pancake. "You remember that list of Arkansas politicians Jacob Granville's parents gave us? I did a little checking online and found that two members of the delegation are on the committee that oversees the FBI: senator Elbert Randolph and representative Rebecca Kesan. Maybe one of them is keeping tabs on Granville."

"I think I've seen Randolph on television," he shrugged, "but that's not much to go on."

"Nope. And the number I called is not listed on either one of their websites." She took a sip of her coffee and poured in a bit more cream. "Did you have time to look at the links I sent you to the two videos?"

"Yeah." He shook his head. "God, that was depressing. An African farmer struggling unsuccessfully to keep his family alive and a woman raped along with her daughter. I had to watch about ten episodes of *The Daily Show* to wash that out of my head. I can't figure out what Granville was up to."

"Was he working on any stories that might be relevant?"

"He was just a photographer. The paper would tell him to go out and shoot a car accident or a PTA fund-raiser. I think the editor in chief might have given him some graphic-design work to do, too, but he wasn't a reporter."

"Was he just some sort of sick voyeur?"

"I don't know," James said. "He was really ambitious and maybe he was trying to come up with his own stories, but I don't know what to make of the videos ... except that they punched me in the gut. I keep seeing the eyes of the African guy just staring at me from the screen."

She nodded and then noticed their waitress approaching with the check. "So how far away are the Cavendishes?"

"Not too far. Maybe five minutes. I did a little checking. Dr. Cavendish used to be a urologist in Nashville, but he retired shortly after the disappearances."

★ ★ ★

The short drive from the village shops to the Cavendish home was a steep and windy foray through the temperate rain forest that blankets western North Carolina. Murphy explained that many locales averaged more than eighty inches of rain per year and the result was vast expanses of fir and cedar, ash and maple, rhododendron and dogwood that stretched as far as the eye could see, once one broke above the arboreal canopy. And the Cavendish residence did exactly that, jutting out from a rocky outcrop over the first valley north of the town. As they got out of the car, they were treated to a magnificent leafy vista, complete with patches of the wraith-like fog that gave the Smoky Mountains their name.

A young woman opened the door and introduced herself as Jessica Cavendish. At first, Melanie thought she was looking at Diana's sister. The thin woman looked barely older than the pictures of Diana, and the attorney wondered whether she was a second or third (or fourth?) wife, for she could not possibly be Diana's birth mother. The woman led her guests to a richly paneled library off the foyer, where she introduced them to her husband, who sat on a sofa with a computer in his lap. He stood up, shook their hands, and invited them to sit down in a pair of wingback chairs separated from the sofa by a massive coffee table crafted from the polished slice of a tree trunk, the only rustic element in a room that was otherwise quite modern.

Julius Cavendish looked like he was working hard to keep up with his pretty young wife. His clothes were Patagonia and North Face, meant to suggest that mounting a hiking expedition was the next thing on his agenda. The impression of youthful vigor was, however, belied by a face a little too stretched and hair a little too dark not to be the result of discreet visits to the plastic surgeon and color salon. He looked at them suspiciously before asking them why they had come.

"Mr. Cavendish," the reporter ran his fingers through his hair as he cautiously broached the subject of Diana's disappearance, "I recently became aware of some pictures of your daughter that were posted on the Internet. I have reason to believe that they were taken shortly before her abduction, so I immediately called Ms. Wilkerson of the Justice Department for some help in tracking down who posted them." He talked straight to Cavendish, his voice serious and concerned, as if it pained him to bring up the subject. Melanie would have taken the same considerate tone with the retired doctor, but Murphy sounded as though he really felt the father's pain. He wasn't just acting; he really empathized. As a prosecutor, Melanie had cauterized most of those nerve endings years ago. Her version of compassion was more circumscribed and distant.

She nodded. "We're tracing the photos, but we haven't yet found the individual who posted them."

James continued. "I'm revisiting my stories and have started to interview folks, some of whom were never fully questioned by the police." He waved his hand, as if to caution Cavendish not to overreact to his next statement. "I must say that we've found quite a few loose ends, and I was hoping that you might be able to shed some additional light on your daughter's disappearance."

His eyes narrowed. "I've already told the police everything that I know."

Melanie shot a glance at the reporter. He had told her that the authorities had never formally interrogated the Cavendishes, who had been on vacation in California at the time of the disappearance of their daughter.

"Could I see the pictures?"

Melanie could not tell whether the father's expression was one of curiosity or trepidation. She watched her partner reach into his jacket pocket and pull out several pages of photocopies. She wondered whether the doctor would question why his daughter was standing in front of a white sheet in a bikini. Instead, one look at his daughter aged him fifteen years and he was overcome with emotion, lifting a hand to his face and fighting back tears. He forced himself to look at all the photos and clutched them while he spoke.

"Such a beautiful girl," he explained in a hoarse whisper. "She looks just like her mother at that age." He tried to say more but instead apologized, stood up, and left the room. Jessica, who had been standing in the corner listening intently to the conversation, gestured awkwardly and followed her husband.

The two investigators sat in embarrassed silence until the couple returned, bearing a large bottle of mineral water and several glasses.

"I'm sorry." The doctor sat down and poured himself a glass. His wife poured for their guests. He drank and seemed to get himself under control. "I can't help but get emotional when I think that I might never see my daughter again."

The attorney thought the phrasing odd and inquired gently. "Are you hopeful she might reappear?"

Cavendish looked over at his wife, who frowned from the corner, arms crossed over her chest. "I know her apartment looked pretty bad, but she was never found and we got a couple of emails after she and Granville disappeared. It seemed like they could be from Diana, but it wasn't from her regular address."

"Could we see them?" Melanie wondered if they, like Jacob Granville's parents, had been told not to divulge the existence of the tantalizing communications.

Cavendish picked up his laptop and a few moments later spun it around. Murphy hunched down next to Melanie by the coffee table, and they both read two emails purportedly sent by the abducted girl within a week after her disappearance. The first merely stated that she was okay and out of the country. The second was slightly longer:

J and I in a little trouble and had to bail out. Business gone bad; more later.

"Do you have any idea what 'business' she might have been referring too?" Melanie spoke first. "That is, assuming the message is really from her." She leaned back away from the computer screen and studied the grim-faced father.

"I always figured this had something to do with drugs. I think that worthless boyfriend of hers was selling something. Diana got busted for possession of pot when she was in high school. That's why she ended up at Clarkeston College instead of the University of Georgia. Her boyfriends were usually mixed up in something stupid." He shook his head in disgust. "Probably got her bad judgment from her drunk of a mother."

"Could you forward those emails to me so that I could analyze them?" She handed him a business card that contained her contact information. She badly wanted to see if the messages came from the same ISP address as those sent to Jacob Granville's parents.

Cavendish gave her a puzzled look and then started tapping the keys on his computer. A minute later, he clicked his mouse with finality and met Melanie's gaze. "You realize that I sent all this to you all years ago." He leaned back in his seat with an expression that questioned the efficiency of the federal bureaucracy.

"Us all?" Melanie asked.

"Yeah," he said impatiently, "you, the FBI. We were interrogated by two agents when we got back from California, and we passed these along to them right away." He looked at his guests as if he were seeing them for the first time. "What's going on here, anyway?"

Murphy looked a little panicked so Melanie jumped in. "I know we get confused with the FBI quite a bit, but I'm an attorney with the Justice Department, not the bureau."

Cavendish looked at Melanie with widening eyes but pointed at her partner. "But he told me that he was an investigator." Suddenly becoming red in the face, he blustered, "I assumed that he was with the FBI. We're not supposed to talk to anyone else."

She looked at James. "What did you tell him?"

"I told him my name and that I was updating my investigation of his daughter's disappearance. He told me to come up right away, so I assumed he recognized my name from the bylines of the stories about the case." The reporter looked like he had made an honest mistake, but she doubted that Julius Cavendish would be very forgiving. Time for some damage control.

She sat up straight in her chair, put her hands in her lap, and looked searchingly in the retired doctor's eyes. She shook her head apologetically and added an extra layer of sweetness to her cultured southern lilt.

"Mr. Cavendish, I am so sorry if we gave the impression we were from the FBI." She put her hand over her heart. "I'm afraid that my colleagues there are not actively investigating the case, so when Mr. Murphy—who's been covering the case for the *Clarkeston Chronicle*—brought these pictures to me," she gestured reverently to the photos on the table, "I thought it best to pursue the lead myself. We never meant to mislead you."

She finished her explanation with a little fishing expedition. "And if the FBI has sworn you to secrecy, then we're especially sorry."

Cavendish leaned back in the sofa, partially mollified by the pretty face offering the polite apologies. He took a sip of water and shook his head. "You're all the federal government, right? I don't see that it matters, but the agents were pretty insistent that we tell no one about the emails, or anything else, for that matter." He set his glass down on the table and finally cracked a smile. "Right arrogant bastards they were, too. We call every six months or so but never get through to anyone who knows anything."

"Is there anything else that you can think to tell us about Diana or Jacob?"

He thought for a moment and looked at his wife. "Jessica and I have been over this a thousand times and it always comes down to two possibilities." She shook her head, but he continued. "I mentioned the first already: maybe they got mixed up with some drug dealers and had to leave the country. But if that's the case, why just the two short emails? There's no reason why she couldn't get in touch with us again."

"Were you close?"

Given his emotional response earlier, she expected a profession of parental devotion, but he surprised her.

"No," he admitted. "She was sixteen when her mother and I divorced, and she blamed me." He avoided his wife's gaze, sighing deeply. "She didn't cut me off completely, but she was pretty frosty. I thought things were getting better right before she disappeared."

"You mentioned a second possibility," Melanie pressed him.

"That Granville killed her and tried to throw everyone off the scent by sending us emails pretending to be her." His expression soured and he walked over to the wall of glass that looked over the valley. There wasn't a single smudge on the window and it looked like he could reach out and touch the mountaintops on the other side of the valley. "That's what Jessie thinks."

Melanie turned her attention to the young woman for the first time. She was standing by the bookshelves a couple of paces away from her husband, trying to blend in to the woodwork. "What makes you think that?"

Jessica answered reticently. "It's been five years now. We should have heard something." She appeared not to care much one way or the other, and Melanie wondered whether the missing woman cared enough about her father to stay in touch.

"What about Diana's biological mother?" James jumped in. "Has she heard anything?"

"I don't know." Julius Cavendish walked away from the window and stood by his wife. "The divorce was pretty acrimonious and we haven't really spoken in the last fifteen years."

"Not even after Diana disappeared?" Melanie found it hard to believe that two upset parents would not contact each other when their daughter was clearly in danger. If they had been in touch, she doubted he would admit it with his current wife in the room.

"I didn't know where Diana's mother was until weeks later. I'd lost track of her and the FBI took a while to find her."

"But they did locate her? Do you know where?"

"They said Chicago, but I don't know the address," he explained. "She was using her maiden name—Carolyn Williams—and that made it harder to find her, I suppose."

"What does she do?" She saw a wave of suspicion cross his face. "I'd like to find her, and if I learn that Diana has been in contact, I'll let you know."

He thought for a moment. "She was trained as a graphic artist, but she stopped working after Diana was born. I don't know what she's doing now." He gave a disapproving look. "She always talked about opening up a fancy cake shop once Diana went off to college. She got a big enough settlement, so maybe she did."

"Could I ask one final question? And could I see your computer for a second?" When he nodded, she took his laptop, went to YouTube, and opened up the two videos posted by j-gville. She clicked Play and handed the device back to Cavendish. "This is a video uploaded by Granville less than a month before he disappeared. Have you ever seen it before? Do you have any idea why he might have uploaded it?"

He watched for a minute with increasing discomfort. Melanie could hear the young Mexican woman telling her horrifying tale in broken English. He snapped the laptop shut abruptly when the video was half-over. "What's all this about? Are you implying that Granville did something like that to my daughter?"

"No, not at all," Melanie exclaimed, although the thought had crossed her mind. "We're just looking very hard at every aspect of Granville's life. I take it that he didn't share this link with you?"

"Absolutely not," Cavendish barked. "Like I said, I couldn't stand the guy. And he didn't make any effort to befriend me, that's for sure. So, no, we weren't email buddies."

Given the strength of his response, Melanie doubted whether showing him the African video would be very productive. Then she saw Jessica walk over to her husband, take his arm and whisper pointedly in his ear. He replied, but she could not hear the short conversation. Guessing that their presence was becoming tiresome, and not wanting to destroy the goodwill that she had rebuilt, she stood up and declared that they had no more questions.

★ ★ ★

"What do you think?" James looked over at Melanie as she drove them back to Highlands. She had not said a word since Julius Cavendish had closed the door behind them, and her expression was inscrutable. He watched her concentrate as she took the curves on the windy road. Her face looked as dangerous as the scenic highway.

"What do I think?" She glanced over while negotiating a hair pin curve that threatened to sling the car into the valley below. "I think you should do a better job explaining who we are before we start an interview."

"Sorry." He felt like an idiot and acknowledged that her cool head had saved the day.

"Don't worry about it." She tapped the steering wheel with her fingers. "You heard old Julius—we wouldn't have gotten any information at all if he had known you were a reporter."

He thought he saw a trace of a smile in the corner of her full lips.

"But what did we really learn?" James found the emails intriguing, whether they were from Diana or a Diana imposter, but he felt no closer to finding her missing boyfriend. "They basically gave us the same stuff as the Granvilles: mysterious messages and warnings from the FBI."

"Yeah, but hearing the same story twice means something." She pulled onto the main road into Highlands. "But I doubt it means anything good."

She found a parking spot close to James's rusty Honda and turned off the car. He was surprised how bad he felt for letting her down in the interview. Why did he care so much what she thought of him? He normally didn't feel the need to impress every beautiful woman that he met, but Melanie was different. She was so smart and sophisticated and yet unexpectedly earthy. He felt a momentary pang of guilt for the depth of his appreciation of her—he was still a married man, after all. Oddly, the appreciation of her personality prompted shame, while his admiration for her legs had not.

"What I don't get," she said, "is why we don't see a connection between the FBI and the Clarkeston cops, when they are both restricting information about a case that should have instantly started a huge public manhunt."

"I've got an idea," he said, trying to draw out their time together as long as possible. "Why don't we walk and talk about this at the same time? Those pancakes have shaved about fifty points off my IQ, and I need to get my blood flowing. About fifteen minutes from here is a Forest Service road that leads to an unmarked trailhead and then to a nice waterfall. Only the locals know it's there. It'll take about an hour round-trip, and we can walk off breakfast and try to figure out what to do next."

In response, she looked down at her feet. "Lead on, James. You're lucky I wore my flats."

This time they took his car, as the Forest Service road was rutted and muddy from a recent rainstorm and Murphy trusted only himself to pick the proper path between root and rock. After twenty minutes that severely tested the springs and shocks of the old Honda, the dirt road finally leveled off into a small glade surrounded by a thicket of rhododendrons and privet, with just enough room to turn the car around. A bullet hole–ridden No Trespassing sign bent over the entrance to a narrow trail at the end of the cramped parking area.

"No worries," the Western Carolina native declared. "We're in the Nantahala National Forest. I have no idea who put that sign up, but nobody who loves Secret Falls is about to pull it down."

The trail broadened quickly, so the pair walked side by side under a dark green ceiling of hickory, maple, ash, and mountain laurel. Occasionally a rhododendron hell would force them to stoop and proceed single file, and James wished the sun were shining more brightly as they made their way toward the roar of falling water. The path was shrouded, and it reminded him of the shortcut through the woods he used to take home from school. He would pop out in his backyard, surprising his mother as she took in the laundry. At the time, he hadn't understood the sadness in her eyes when she smiled at him. Now he knew how much she had feared his leaving, even when the fateful day was still years away. Sometimes he wished she had been as tyrannical as his father; then he wouldn't feel the guilt of his escape so acutely.

"The more I think about this case," Melanie said as they hopped over a small but swiftly flowing stream, "the more careful I think we have to be. You're already pretty paranoid about the local cops, but there's some things about the feds that I haven't told you."

James nodded and offered his hand as she climbed over a log blocking the trail. She grasped it firmly and he felt an instant jolt of intimacy. He wished they could walk hand in hand the whole way.

"First, I found a mention of Jacob in the FBI database," she said, "but there was no information except a notation to call a number in Arkansas if anyone made any inquiries. As a loyal and stupid public servant, I gave them your name when they asked for information, and lo and behold, your house is broken into a couple of days later. Now, that could have been a coincidence, but I'm starting to doubt it."

"What do you mean?" Her story put him on full alert. He did not like the idea that the FBI was aware of his renewed investigation. Moreover, he was pissed that Melanie had given him up so easily. He would never reveal any of his own anonymous sources. He stopped and faced her. "Who answered the phone? What did they say?"

"They didn't say anything." She grimaced and then looked down. "I got nothing from them, and when I called back, the line was disconnected, so I asked a friend at the FBI to track the number down for me. He asked around and then warned me off the case."

"And now we hear from both the Granvilles and the Cavendishes that the FBI has told them to shut up too," he added quietly, still trying to determine whether Melanie's slipup was merely negligent or a deliberate throwing him under the bus to protect her career.

She turned to him, paused a moment, and then nodded her head gravely. "Someone's got friends in high places who don't like you poking around in their business."

The roar of the falls was getting louder, and they had to raise their voices as they made their way down the steep path to the base of the cascade. They moved slowly, grabbing and bending branches to keep from slipping on the mossy trail.

"Are you dropping the case, then?" he asked when they reached the level bottom of the path, a broad pool of roiling water just visible through the brush. "Am I on my own now?"

She moved past him toward the base of the falls. A small sandbar, the size of a child's sandbox, jutted out into the pool, offering an unobstructed view of a muscled cord of ice-cold water cresting a precipice fifty feet over their heads. The far end of the pool churned and plunged down a further desfile, but their little beach was fairly still. She picked a stick off the sand and tossed it into the water. It moved slowly into the current and then dropped down into the next set of cataracts.

"I've been thinking about this," she said. "As far as the FBI and the Justice Department are concerned, I'm done. I'm a smart girl who plays by the rules and by all appearances will have no more to do with Diana Cavendish or Jacob Granville. So, whatever you do, don't call me at work, and most certainly don't pay me a visit there."

Melanie now faced him with her back to the torrent, wispy strands of water at the edge of the falls waving around the edge of her thick brown hair. Despite his misgivings, he did not want her to cut him loose. He wanted more of the look she was giving him right now.

"But," she continued, "I've got someone in California that no one knows about, tracking down those pictures on the web, and I know a small-town reporter who's like a bulldog with a piece of raw meat in his jaws." She put one hand on her hip and smiled brightly at him, issuing an irresistible invitation to accept her plan. "If I'm discreet, I can help track down Diana's mother. You can keep interviewing people, and hopefully we'll finally get a firm lead on the website photos."

James nodded his head. "And I've got some resources that you don't know about," he added. "I've gotten to know the new priest at St. James and have already asked him to press the sheriff. And the former priest's daughter is going to see if she can uncover any links between her father, the sheriff, and maybe even the feds."

"That's a good start," she agreed. "Just tell them to be careful."

He wondered how far they could get without the formal apparatus of justice on their side, but he had confidence in his own ability to ferret out a story, and having an experienced prosecutor helping from the sidelines was a huge plus. If nothing else, it was a joy to bounce ideas off her, but he deflated somewhat when he realized that they should not be seen together talking to potential witnesses.

"I guess today is our last interviewing roadtrip," he said reluctantly.

She nodded. "That's probably a good idea." She took one last look up at the falls. "It's dangerous, but beautiful, too," she said with another glittering smile. "Thanks for bringing me here."

He told her briefly how he had learned of the place, and then they ducked under a tree branch and headed back up the trail. When they got to the top of the slope that led down to the falls, he turned and helped her up the last slippery bit. Her hand was firm and dry and it lingered in his for a moment as she stepped up onto the trail.

"I've got an idea," he said as they started back to the car. "Would you like to come to Clarkeston next Saturday and go through Jacob's stuff at the newspaper with me? When he disappeared, we just threw everything in his desk in a couple of boxes. I went through it five years ago, but it would be really nice to put a fresh set of eyes on it."

She leaned against him for a long moment, maybe because the path narrowed suddenly. "Sure," she replied, "it's a date."

XIX.

Escape

Stanley laughed for the first time in months. He stared at the computer screen and howled until tears splashed down his face.

After his meeting with William Simmons, the operator of Mygirlfriendsbikini.com, he had delayed conducting an Internet search for the person who uploaded the photos, identifiable only as expatsoller@ocea.es. On the drive home from Silver Lake, he felt something indefinably sweet about having the address and not knowing yet whether it would reveal a treasure trove of information or whether it was just the empty finale to a frustrating search. In either case, he wanted to be lounging in his recliner when he learned the answer. He stopped at the grocery store on the way back to Claremont and bought a frozen burrito and a bottle of pinot noir. He had drunk almost no alcohol since the accident that took his family, partly because he didn't feel like drinking when he was depressed, but also because voluntary self-denial helped him cope with the absence of those things that had been denied him involuntarily and permanently. The burrito? Well, that was the consolation prize if he turned up nothing in the search.

Once the frozen snack was in the oven, he sat down at his computer and picked around the edges of the email address until he heard the ding of the timer. The name Pat Soller generated over a thousand hits with links to both men and women. Maybe one of them had divorced and was now ex-Pat Soller, now Pat Somebody-Else. Then again, the person could be an expatriate of the United States with the last name of Soller and with any first name at all. Or maybe it was someone running a solar-energy firm who had flunked spelling class, or a foreign businessman with a loose grip on English who provided solar power to American expatriates.

Once he had the steaming burrito on a plate next to his chair and a wine glass in his hand, he got serious and ran a search on just the email address. The result was a single hit. This prompted a yelp and a small spray of pinot. No searches ever returned a single hit, especially email addresses, which either multiplied across the web like horny bunnies or were held like precious secrets close to the breast of their owners.

He clicked on the link and found a single PDF page consisting of a league competition schedule, all matches taking place on Wednesday nights in Pub Wellington. At the bottom of the page, questions about the schedule were directed to Reggie at expatsoller@ocea.es. That was the sum of the web presence. Stanley studied the page carefully, discerning little more than the list of team names and dates of matches. There was no updated list of rankings, nor any indication of the sort of competition other than the notation that a particular match was "cricket" or "301." The mysterious nomenclature, however, was resolved quickly enough by opening a new web page and conducting a search pairing the two words. Darts.

He pumped his fist and pitched backward in the recliner. His quarry helped to run a dart league in a pub called the Wellington. At worst, he could generate a list of pubs with that name and contact them to ask whether they hosted dart-throwing leagues. That would give him a place to start tracking down Reggie without his knowledge. Of course, he could try emailing directly to expatsoller@ocea.es and pretend to be interested in joining the league. There was no reason why a generic query would prompt any suspicion on Reggie's part, and his response might provide a surname or a clue to the whereabouts of the pub.

Then, another giggle erupted and soon turned into laughter so uncontrolled that it hindered the typing for his last bit of searching. What an idiot! Look at the fucking email address! It's not ".com" or ".edu" or ".org" . . . it's ".es." A Spanish email address for an *expat* dart thrower. And the name of the venue was not The Wellington Pub or Wellington's Pub, but rather Pub Wellington, as the Spaniards would order it. And his history was good enough to remember the popularity of the good old duke who had driven Napoleon out of the Iberian Peninsula at the beginning of the nineteenth century. A final search limited to Spain revealed three Pub Wellingtons, but when he clicked on each link, he saw only one was located in Port de Sóller, where expatsoller had presumably gone to live. He had his man and there was no need to risk a direct email. He poured another glass and toasted the image of the quaint village pub that appeared on his computer screen. To Mallorca!

★ ★ ★

"Say that again: you're going where?"

Stanley enjoyed hearing surprise and confusion from Melanie Wilkerson on the other end of the telephone line.

"Mallorca," he repeated, "Port de Sóller. According to Wikipedia: *The village consists of shops, restaurants, and bars, but is quiet and away from the major tourist areas such as Magaluf on the south of the island.* Sounds to me like a nice place to track down our photographer and celebrate the end of the semester."

He was rewarded with a burst of laughter that warmed his heart all the way from Atlanta.

"You realize that the Justice Department can't pay for your trip? Not that I'm not totally grateful, but there's no way to fund this at all."

"Don't worry about it," he said graciously. "I need to get out of Los Angeles, and I'll figure out some way to deduct it from my taxes. I just wanted to let you know that I've got his name, well, his first name, and a pretty good idea exactly where he is going to be next Wednesday night. If I leave tomorrow, I'll have a couple of days to sightsee and get over my jet lag before I track him down."

"What are you going to do when you find him?"

"That's the other reason I called," the sociologist admitted, "I'm not entirely sure what you want me to do."

There was a moment's pause and Stanley imagined a gorgeous yet hard-bitten caricature of a film noir heroine pursing her lips and pondering the question. "Well, first of all, I'm going to have a friend email you a picture of the photographer who disappeared with Diana Cavendish. If your dart player turns out to be Jacob Granville, then you really shouldn't approach him at all. He's probably dangerous, and we don't want him running off. Things are going to get super complicated if we have to deal with an international-fugitive situation."

"What if it's just some slightly kinky English photographer who likes sitting on the beach and playing darts?" It had been a long time since Stanley had this kind of fun on a research project. He had already checked on early summer temperatures in Mallorca and mentally packed his suitcase.

"Well, in that case, I'd really like to know how the hell he got a-hold of those pictures." She paused. "So, I don't see any reason why you couldn't chat the guy up and find out what he knows." She thanked him once again before she hung up, a genuine gratitude ringing in her voice, an affirmation that sent him directly to his favorite travel website to purchase his tickets.

★ ★ ★

When he saw that he had to connect through Boston and Madrid, Stanley cashed in a pile of frequent-flyer miles to upgrade to business class and arrived in the air terminal in Palma de Mallorca tired but not exhausted. He had felt a thrill of release from the moment his flight took off from LAX. Why hadn't he left Los Angeles earlier? He had had plenty of free time in the last nine months, but even during the long Christmas break he stayed home, watching television and depleting the inventory of the local doughnut shop. On Christmas Day, he walked far up into the foothills of the San Gabriels, ignoring the calls of friends and family seeking to console him. Before going to bed, he paid a visit to the urn in the laundry room and stared at it expressionless for a long time, empty of grief, empty of sorrow, empty of joy, just stuck in the tar pit of Southern California waiting for some sign that it was okay to move on.

He rented a car at the Palma airport and drove straight to the "villa" he had found online. Nigel, the British estate agent, met him in the driveway, and for once, the website photos had undersold the property. The view down over the marina was expansive, and he could trace every inch of the harbor from the blue of the Mediterranean to the shops along the wharf. The house itself was immaculately clean, a calming and cheerful mix of terra-cotta tile and varnished timber, with a small covered porch that would allow him to take in the views while he surfed the Internet and sipped on a beer.

He thanked Nigel for the tour and paid him the amount owing on the rental. "By the way," he queried idly before his landlord left, "do you know a pub called the Wellington down in the port? A friend told me I should check it out."

"Well," the overly-tanned Brit replied doubtfully, "I suppose it's all right if you're craving a Guinness, but it's not exactly a taste of the local color, if you get my meaning."

"I understand. My friend is a dart thrower, and I think he must like the board there or something." The same talents he had developed as an interviewer in his academic research served him well when he needed to dissemble. The years in law school didn't hurt either. "He said there's actually an expat dart league there."

"I think I heard something about that." Nigel ran his fingers through the sparse wisps of ginger on his head. "You can take the Englishman out of England, but . . . well, you know the rest. Me, I married a Spanish woman twenty years ago, and you wouldn't catch me dead in the Wellington talking about cricket and pining for a sausage roll." He shook Stanley's hand and prepared to leave. "If you want the real thing, try El Langustino down by the wharf. María's English isn't very good, but the menu's got pictures and she serves up an amazing plate of *boquerones!*"

Stanley thanked Nigel for the recommendation, followed him out to the driveway, and walked down the hill in the direction of the village. Before he had taken a dozen steps, he encountered a striking brunet in a crisp white blouse walking up the hill to the other side of his duplex.

"Hola!" He offered as she passed, expending twenty-five percent of his Spanish phrases in a single word.

"And hello to you," she replied in a cultured English accent.

He stepped aside as she turned into the tiled entryway of her villa. "How did you know I spoke English?" Normally, he wouldn't ask such a sophomoric question to a stranger, but he wanted to prolong the encounter.

She took off her sunglasses and opened her door. "Your shoes," she said as she gestured to his feet with the glasses. "Plainly American." She smiled, as if to make clear that her critique was not unfriendly, and surveyed him further with a slight tilt of her head. "And they don't match your belt. Number one fashion sin in Spain, I'm afraid." And then she was gone.

He laughed. Here he was in an exotic locale on a spying mission, and an imperious foreign beauty had just deigned to look him up and down.

It took him thirty minutes to make his way to the bottom of the hill and find a small grocery just before it closed for the two o'clock siesta. He bought a few beers and a bag of thick local potato chips. By the time he returned to the villa, he, too, was ready for a nap, and it was nearly five before he awoke. The sun was still shining brightly, and he spent the rest of the afternoon and evening drinking on his porch, checking his email, cruising Facebook, and catching up on a backlog of academic reading.

His guidebook told him that it was senseless to arrive at a local restaurant much before nine in the evening, so it was almost dusk when he went back down to the village in search of El Langustino and María's delicious *boquerones*, whatever they were. When he got to the tiny village square, he walked up to a friendly old man with a wooden cane and stammered, "*Por favor . . .* El Langustino?" in his best accent, managing the terminal inflection that made it clear he was asking a question. A directional wave of the battered cane and two blocks later he found a small stone building that housed the restaurant. When he walked in, he could see that its back end opened up to the harbor and offered plenty of space for eating outside. He could see no one about as he walked onto the flagstone patio, except for the middle-aged Englishwoman whom he had met at the villa. He nodded at her, strolled nonchalantly past her table, and looked out over the water.

"You can sit wherever you like." Her voice was friendly, but reserved. "María's helping out her husband in the kitchen."

He looked back at her and nodded as if he understood that this was the way things worked around here.

"But I'm being silly," she continued with a frown, "surely you must sit at my table if you'd like to. We're likely to be the only ones in here tonight."

"Are you sure you wouldn't mind?" He put his hand on the top of the chair. "It would be nice to have some company. I've only just arrived."

"Please." She gestured again and he sat down. "I'm Vanessa." She extended a ringless hand, and he introduced himself. To his right was a worn stone wall and to the left was the sea, a safe place to rest his eyes should they linger too long on the space that would have been covered by the open third button on her blouse. Where his gaze was already resting.

"I changed my belt." He blurted out, raising his eyes and eager to show he had not ignored her fashion advice.

She raised an eyebrow in response. "But not the shoes?" She lifted a glass of wine to her lips.

He was sure he saw a smile behind her drink. "I packed in a hurry, I'm afraid. Not to mention this is my first time in Spain."

"Well, then," she said firmly, "what you need is a solid pair of leather sandals. Good for all occasions around here." She wrinkled her nose. "Unless, of course, you intend to wear them with black socks. You wouldn't do that, would you?"

He laughed. "No, I'm not a barbarian!"

Stanley was thankful that he had spent a semester in Cambridge during college and had learned a little bit about the English. One admonition that stuck with him was that Americans talk about themselves far too much, so he began their conversation with some polite questions. He even managed to impress her with the knowledge, gained on a cross-country hike, that her home near Abergavenny must be close to the English-Welsh border.

She was divorced, probably in her late thirties, given the ages of the children she mentioned who would be joining her once the school term ended. Is there a stereotypical English woman? Stanley supposed there were many radically different versions: the prim schoolmarm, the Cockney flower girl, the flirtatious Moneypenny, Spice Girls, dowager countesses, Princess Di, Bridget and her diary, and girls bending it like Beckham. But Vanessa Wilcox fit no mold that he knew. She was serious but not humorless, well educated but without an Oxbridge pedigree. Her beauty was displayed in the soft brown of her hair, the sparkle in her hazel eyes, and the generous curves that her expensively tailored clothes tastefully did not hide. Her nose might have been too large to ever grace the pages of *Vogue*, but her skin was flawless and fairly glowed in the soft outdoor light of the café. He found it hard to keep his eyes off her.

When María finally emerged from the kitchen, Stanley pointed at Vanessa's wine glass, smiled, and haltingly mispronounced *boquerones*. She nonetheless got his meaning and disappeared once again.

"What did I just order, by the way?" He confessed his ignorance of the local cuisine. "I'm just following my landlord's instructions."

"*Boquerones* are unsalted anchovies, fileted and marinated in olive oil, garlic, and a bit of lemon juice." She seemed to approve. "They make a nice little appetizer."

"Well," he replied, "so far, so good! But maybe you could recommend something for a main course? I'm afraid my Spanish is virtually nonexistent."

She opened the menu and described the seafood dishes in a way that showed she knew the local cuisine inside and out. He decided to let her order for the both of them and avoid the embarrassment of pointing at the attractive pictures on the menu with a hungry grunt. María approved of whatever Vanessa ordered, and so began a lovely meal that extended almost three leisurely hours through several courses, dessert, brandy, and coffee.

The conversation flowed easily, and when Vanessa finally asked Stanley what he did for a living, she seemed genuinely intrigued by his career and the strange turn of events that had taken him to Los Angeles. He described his trip to Mallorca as a much-needed vacation. She herself had been a primary school teacher until her marriage to a banker brought two children, now teenagers in a boarding school.

"They're just over in Herefordshire, though, home on weekends and all that." She took a sip of her wine. "It's quite a nice place, boys and girls together, none of the discipline nonsense that you read about in politicians' memoirs." Then her eyes dropped to the gold ring on his left hand. "Do you have any children?"

He paused. He could tell a long sad story and turn the meal into the sort of pity party that he had avoided for months, or he could lie and push the evening in a different direction. Was there no middle ground?

"A daughter," he responded, his voice strong and inviting no expression of condolence. "I lost her and my wife a while ago." He managed a stoic grimace. "Not a great topic of conversation, I'm afraid."

Thank God for the English, he thought when she immediately changed the subject and described in detail how she had come to choose Port de Sóller and to buy the villa where she was staying. No other nationality is so capable of ignoring emotion and sailing on to calmer waters without a glance behind them. And by the end of the evening, he realized he had even scored points with her by sparing her the details of his loss. After a friendly tussle over the bill, she let him pay, and they headed back through the narrow streets of the village and up the hill to their twin villas.

The conversation petered out in the dark of the lampless path, but silence seemed an appropriate companion for chirping crickets and the occasional echo of the surf from the harbor below. About halfway up, Vanessa stumbled on a cobblestone and grabbed Stanley's shoulder for support. Her hand lingered, and then slid down his arm and took a firm grip on his hand where it remained comfortably for the rest of their walk. She really was lovely, and he had to fight the impulse to tell her so.

The path to Vanessa's door came first, barely visible in the moonlight as they crested the hill.

"Would you like to come in for a drink?" she asked.

He could barely see the expression on her face, but in his mind's eye it was confident and inviting. Her hand was still touching his, and her fingers pressed his palm as she adjusted her hand and turned toward him.

He had wondered during the lovely stroll what he would do when they arrived. The connection between them at dinner had been genuine, and they were both free to spend the night wherever they wanted. When he remembered her later, it would be with undeniable lust, but there in the darkness he just wanted the night to end perfectly, with no fumbling over birth control or worries about his lack of recent experience. He was almost ready, but not quite.

"I'm completely wiped out," he replied in an exhausted voice. "Could I see you tomorrow?"

"Of course," she said as she planted a moist kiss on his cheek and then headed to her door, "and we'll see to those sandals."

He heard the door click shut and stood quietly for a moment looking over the village. It was enough to have been seen and heard and felt.

XX.

CONVERSATION

Father Thorsten Carter felt like he was making definite progress with Miriam Rodgers. In theory, he should not be wooing a parishioner, but she hadn't set foot inside St. James for more than a year, and surely there was some sort of statute of limitations working in his favor. And even if his bishop might prefer that he bring her back into the fold instead of dating her, his own theology had never held that attending St. James, or any other church, for that matter, was a prerequisite for salvation. Thankfully, the theft of Miriam's father's papers had turned out to be a blessing, as she had plunged herself into the mystery and had even been poking around her childhood home and questioning her mother.

"I know that my dad was a chaplain during Vietnam." She sat with Thor outside a downtown Clarkeston café, sipping a cappuccino. "I don't remember him saying much. I got the impression that he found his time in the service to be pretty boring. On the mantel there's a picture of him in uniform in the middle of a bunch of officers, but that's about all I know."

Thor wasn't sure where she was headed with the story, but she suggested some governmental conspiracy might be at work. Who else but the feds, she had asked, would drive around a fake UPS van and steal her father's stuff? She thought that James Murphy's renewed interest in the disappearance of Diana Cavendish and Jacob Granville was logically connected to the theft.

"Anyway, my father spent most of his life in Clarkeston, so I figure that if he made any influential friends or enemies, it would have to have been when he was away at school or during the war." She flipped the top off her coffee and sprinkled in a no-cal sweetener. "My dad went to Clarkeston College under-grad but left to go to Harvard Divinity School after. My mom didn't go to Boston with him, but they got married after he graduated and got drafted. She was with him in Washington, DC, where he was posted to the chaplain's office in the Pentagon. I suppose the Harvard degree or someone he met there got him the job."

"And he never talked about his years there?"

"Neither of them did," she replied with a shake of her head. "But my mom was happy to talk about it now. Apparently, she found it pretty exciting. The war was far away and no one he worked with was personally heading off to shoot at the Viet Cong. He ministered to a group of young officers during his time there and apparently made some good friends. I don't remember ever meeting any of them, but Clarkeston is the back of beyond and I doubt they were holding reunions here."

"That's not a whole lot to go on," Thor said.

"That's not all, though. When I asked my mom for some names, she took down that photo I mentioned, and written on the back of the picture were the names of about half the officers in it. I was able to track down quite a few of them on the Internet. Most are retired, but a couple of them are still working in the federal government. Almost all of them, even the retired ones, seem to be really well connected. This was an ambitious little group that my dad was hanging out with."

"So, he could have met someone there who still has some influence." Thor did not want to come right out and accuse Miriam's father of pulling strings, but the implication could not be avoided. "Someone who could have helped him protect Jacob Granville."

"Look," she explained unapologetically, "my dad was absolutely convinced of Jacob's innocence. He would have had no qualms whatsoever about enlisting an old friend to help him."

"All right," replied Thor, "I get that. It's not too much of a stretch to imagine a connection, but your dad's been dead for a couple years. Why would anyone suddenly be interested in his stuff?"

"Well, if someone used their influence to help my dad with Jacob, they might be worried that his papers could expose them."

"I suppose," the young priest said doubtfully, "but how did the thief learn about the papers in the first place or find out who had them?" He shook his head. "I don't like coincidences any more than you do, but even if your father had an anonymous friend helping Granville escape, I can't see this person suddenly materializing in Clarkeston five years later and ripping off James Murphy."

She seemed loathe to concede the point, and he wondered whether her paranoia was getting the best of her. "I don't know, but my father was one crafty son of a bitch and if his friends are half as tenacious as he was, then anything is possible."

She smiled and took a sip from her drink. "When I was a kid, the vestry was considering withdrawing its support for a community soup kitchen that was serving lunch every day to a lot of illegal immigrants. About half of the budget came from St. James, so it was a pretty big deal. My dad went along with the conservatives until the very end, when he announced that when the soup kitchen closed down, it would be reopened at St. James so that the church could better monitor who was receiving food." She gave a delighted laugh. "The thought of having a crowd of poor people eating in their church every day got them rethinking their position pretty quick, and that's how Papa saved the day." She sighed and looked at Thor wistfully. "God, I really miss him sometimes."

Thor appreciated her tale and what it said about his predecessor, but he couldn't help thinking that Miriam might not be so forthcoming if she learned anything that put her father in a bad light. And if the old priest had helped cover the tracks of a murderer, then the glare of that light might get pretty harsh indeed.

★ ★ ★

The following Sunday, Thor's own level of suspicion ratcheted up after a short conversation with Porter Johnson, Clarkeston's sheriff and one of his least spiritual parishioners. Before the service, he had seen Johnson emerging from a Bible-study group and decided to ask about the stolen papers. Although the primary victim of the theft had been James Murphy, the papers had been entrusted to the priest and it would hardly be remarkable for him to show some concern as to their whereabouts. Johnson, however, made little effort to hide his annoyance with the question.

"I don't comment about ongoing investigations with anyone outside the department," he explained as he walked toward the coffee stand in the fellowship hall.

"Of course not," Thor swung in beside him, "but Ms. Rodgers has been asking me about them and since it's my fault they ended up in Murphy's house, I wanted to ask when you thought they might be returned."

"Are you kidding me?" The police officer's contempt was barely concealed. "It's just a bunch of papers. Believe it or not, we actually get some serious crime around here. Between the crackheads in the projects and the meth-heads in the trailer parks, we've got real policing to do. I can't put a man on a few missing boxes of paper." He offered a patronizing smile. "Even if they were owned by a priest."

"But have you discovered anything at all? Murphy's a reporter—maybe he could use the newspaper to try and flush out whoever broke in? You admitted that you're short handed."

"Look," the sheriff lowered his voice and put a hand on Thor's shoulder. "We don't need any help from nosy priests or journalists." He gave a little squeeze. "Take my advice and just drop it. Forget you ever heard about those boxes, okay?"

At that moment, a young woman with a bulletin in her hand timidly approached with a question. Johnson greeted her by name, offered Thor a dismissive pat on the back, and turned to get his coffee. The priest watched him carefully as he walked away, struck by the power of his rolling, proprietary stride.

★ ★ ★

Stanley Hopkins wore his new sandals to spy on Pub Wellington's Wednesday night English expat darts league. He and Vanessa had spent a relaxing morning poking through the shops and open-air market in Port de Sóller, ostensibly looking for sandals, but mostly enjoying each other's company and the balmy perfection of the coastal climate. He insisted on buying her lunch in return for her help with both language issues and questions of style, and he was quite certain that she would have consented to join him again for dinner, too, if he had not needed to make contact with Reggie, a.k.a. expatsoller@ocea.es, and ask him how he had come about certain pictures of Diana Cavendish. He had dated no one in California since Angela's accident, but somehow the distance and exotic locale had prompted a good bit of flirting with the attractive divorcée.

He had several photocopied images of Jacob Granville in his pocket as he entered the cave-like bar, and if Reggie were really the Georgian hiding after murdering his girlfriend, then the professor would withdraw discreetly and call Melanie Wilkerson in Atlanta. He was no action hero, and he would be happy just to identify the missing person and then spend some time exploring the island.

Stanley ordered a beer at the bar and sat down in the corner waiting for the dart teams to arrive. He had no idea how many people to expect. There were four boards tucked into a far corner of the bar, so he guessed that all eight teams in the league would be in action, but whether the Dartyrs of Doom or the Flights of Fancy consisted of two or ten people, he had no clue. It was also unclear to which particular team Reggie belonged, so he intended to wait for all the matches to begin before asking anyone any questions. Before his drink was half-empty, a small group of English speakers had found their way to the bar to order drinks before pulling their dart cases out of their pockets and making a few practice throws at the bristle boards. Apparently, the sport required only minimal warming up, because the competition was in full force by the time Stanley had bought his second beer.

He adopted the guise of a fellow darter who wanted more information about the league and had discovered Reggie on the schedule web page. He found a website on his phone devoted to darts and learned enough to avoid detection as a novice, as long as he didn't have to actually throw. He watched the group unobtrusively as he educated himself. If Reggie were there, then he was definitely not an alter ego of Jacob Granville, as no one in the pub resembled the picture of the young American.

After thirty minutes, a middle-aged man shook hands with his opponents and his partner, put his darts in a small leather case, and approached the bar. While the man waited for his drink, Stanley came over and introduced himself.

"Excuse me," he said, "is Reggie here? I was hoping he could tell me a little about the darts league."

"Not tonight, or I would have won the first round. We usually play together."

"So, you're his partner?"

"Not partners, per se." A wisp of a smile curled around the lips of the tan, sandy-haired Englishman. "But we do throw darts together a good bit."

"That's what I meant!" Stanley blurted out. "I found the league online and it listed Reggie as the contact person."

"Reggie Wilkins is the organizer, for sure, but I might be able to help you out. Reg lives way up on the Alfabia Ridge and only comes down about once a week to go shopping and play some darts." He leaned against the bar and took a sip of his

Spanish whiskey with a grimace. "Reg couldn't make it today. What do you want to know?"

Stanley longed to show him the pictures of Jacob Granville but settled for a short conversation on the logistics of finding a teammate and joining the league. He quickly exhausted his slim knowledge of the sport. He was about to excuse himself, and hoped that an Internet search of *Reggie Wilkins* and *Port de Sóller* would generate a business or home address, when something clicked in his memory.

"You said that Reggie lives on the Alfabia Ridge. Isn't there a hiking trail up there?"

"A famous one, in fact." He nodded, and Stanley mentally thanked the editors of his Lonely Planet *Mallorca*. "There's a road that runs right along the old pilgrim's way and Reg's house is toward the end. Amazing view up there. It's a wonder he ever comes down to the village at all."

When the darter turned down the offer of another drink, Stanley finished his beer, thanked his new acquaintance, and started the long walk back to his villa, eager to see what the Internet might reveal about Reggie Wilkins, darting czar of eastern Mallorca.

On the way home, he stuck his head in at El Langustino, hoping that Vanessa might be dining there again. He did not find her, but the smells wafting out of the kitchen seduced him on their own and led him to the back patio, where he decided the inconvenience of surfing on his phone was more than offset by the chance for more *boquerones* and a plate of marinated cuttlefish.

Combining Reggie's full name with the village and island revealed that he ran a data-storage-and-retrieval business that seemed to extend well beyond Mallorca. His business web page was vague, repeatedly referring to "solving the server space problems of data-intensive businesses" without spelling out precisely how one took advantage of his service. Stanley then turned his attention to the Alfabia Ridge, where Reggie lived. Here, he had more luck, finding several hiking websites that provided detailed descriptions of the route, which wound its way up and over the ridge of mountains on the east coast of the island. The trail started in Sóller, a small sister village of Port de Sóller in the foothills, and ended at a monastery in the interior of the island, about thirty miles away. The stony trail had been a pilgrim path for centuries.

One of the hiking sites included images from the official Spanish survey map of the island, and Stanley could see a thin road that paralleled the trail about three-quarters of the way to the top before it spurred to the south and dead-ended. He magnified the image on the screen with a deft parting of his fingers and could visualize where the house would be. Google Maps showed no concentration of residences on the ridge, just a reference to a single *finca*. Stanley put down his phone, looked out over the harbor, and popped a tangy little anchovy in his mouth. He could see no reason not to pay the elusive Reggie and his stacks of porn-clogged servers a visit the next day.

XXI.

PAPER

James Murphy sat down slowly at the kitchen table and tossed a manila envelope down on the chipped Formica surface. Later, he would read the lawyer's letter again, carefully parsing each phrase and trying to feel some essence of Sondra in the formal legal language, but for now it sat like a bomb on the table, partially exploded, a concussive wallop to his gut and the promise of more frightful devastation still to come. His wife had taken the steps necessary to obtain a legal separation, requesting a division of their assets, with or without his cooperation. His first reflex was to toss the papers—he'd give her everything and show who the magnanimous, loving spouse really was. His next impulse was to pound the table in anger, but without someone in front of him to push against he stalled, slumped in his chair, and stared out the window.

How could she not understand what she meant to him? Despite her mood swings, Sondra held everything together. Meeting her had changed his life as much as coming down to Clarkeston from the mountains. She was an integral part of what he loved about the place. He was certain that if she understood, she wouldn't leave. But she was not returning his calls, and her sister would not tell him where she was staying.

Thank God his week was full of attention-diverting tasks. The zoning commission was meeting to discuss a site that Walmart wanted to develop, and a Clarkeston college student had brought sexual-harassment charges against one of her professors. The police blotter was especially lively, with a string of burglaries in an affluent neighborhood, and a Peeping Tom, naked and covered in Vaseline, caught peering in the windows of an assisted-living center. Between the stories that needed covering and existing prose that needed editing, James had little time during the day to dwell on the cold and sterile communication his wife had sent through her attorney. But when he got home to the empty house, the full measure of his failure as a human being was set before him on a platter of self-pity and Budweiser.

On Friday morning, James was out at a local elementary school covering the dedication of an organic-gardening project, when the phone buzzed in his pocket and he ended a tedious interview by waving the device importantly at a young student teacher. To his surprise, the caller was Melanie Wilkerson in Atlanta, wondering if he still wanted her to help look through Jacob Granville's old stuff at the newspaper office. They arranged to meet at the newspaper mid-morning Saturday, and James went back to his computer to write a mixed review of the organic initiative at an elementary school that still offered Coke and Mountain Dew to its students at lunch.

★ ★ ★

Melanie was beginning to appreciate the benefits of leaving Atlanta every Saturday morning and driving out into the country. The air was cleaner, the traffic less chaotic, and the number of young professionals roller-skating with their designer dogs dramatically reduced. When had the population of Southern California beach towns displaced true southerners in midtown Atlanta? Elton John even had a condo in Buckhead, for chrissakes. Melanie was no cheerleader for the old South, but there was no reason to banish good thick accents and greasy fried chicken along with segregation and cross burning. In any event, her tolerance level for her new-old hometown was significantly higher after a bit of decompression in the countryside, tilting at windmills with the increasingly intriguing James Murphy.

She found the newspaper office with little problem. The *Clarkeston Chronicle* occupied a surprisingly large red-brick building along the river on the northern end of the downtown business district. The front door was locked, so she called James, who soon appeared to let her in.

"Sorry!" he apologized through the glass, as he pulled his keys out of his blue jeans. She felt a warm hand on her back as he ushered her into the building. "We used to keep the front entrance unlocked on the weekends, but a couple of computers walked off and now we've got a key-card system." He tugged the door behind her until the lock caught with a soft click. "Let's head down to the basement and see if we can find Granville's boxes. Do you need a coffee first?"

She declined his offer and walked beside him down the central hallway of the building, heels tapping loudly against the cold marble floors. She wished he had kept his strong hand on her back, but he looked tired and preoccupied.

"Are you okay?"

He looked surprised, as if she had guessed some sort of secret.

"I'm fine. Just a long night, that's all."

When they reached the far side of the building, he took a plastic card out of his pocket and ran it through an electronic reader along the side of an unmarked metal door.

"This is the back way into the archives. The last time I checked, Granville's stuff was just jammed in the back of a closet. The cops told my boss to hold on to his things for a while and nobody's ever gotten around to tossing 'em out." He led her down a concrete stairwell into the bright fluorescent basement light and stopped in front of another metal door. He tossed her a weary smile. "At least I hope they haven't thrown 'em out yet."

If that were the case, he was going to be taking her out for a very nice lunch to repay her for a wasted trip.

"They're still here. Let's take them over to a reading area." He picked up the bigger of the two boxes and she, the other.

"There's a big oak table we can use—my office is a disaster area right now."

The newspaper archive room was a few steps farther down the hall and contained a row of battered metal file cabinets labeled "Photographs" and an old-fashioned microfilm reader placed next to a case containing reduced versions of the *Chronicle* going back over a hundred years. In the middle of the room sat two wooden conference tables, pushed together to form a large work space.

James set his box down on the table. "We usually put our summer interns down here, but they won't arrive for another week or so."

"What exactly are we looking for?" She put her box down and flipped open the top. "You said you already went through this stuff right after Diana disappeared."

He shrugged his shoulders and sat down next to her. "I'm not sure. Five years ago, I was looking for stuff directly related to Granville's relationship with Diana or some sign that he was planning something. Nothing jumped out at me at the time." He opened his container and pulled out a folder full of photographs. "That's why you're here. Fresh eyes and all that."

She turned to her box while James flipped through the glossy images, occasionally muttering to himself when he recognized a picture. Only a couple of blocks—and twenty years—away she had sat around a similar table with her co-clerks as they worked on their bench memos for the Judge. Sitting with James felt much the same, a quiet camaraderie, a shared purpose, and a hint of magnetic attraction.

She sorted through a pile of office supplies that seemed irrelevant and pulled out the manila file folders at the bottom of the box. She set to the side a broken stapler, a pair of scissors, an old-fashioned rolodex with no names or addresses on any of the cards, a box of Kleenex, and a phone book, making a mental note to flip through the directory to search for marginal scribblings.

The first folder contained information related to Granville's employment with the newspaper: a memo about the newspaper's copyright policy, several blank expense-reimbursement forms, and a thin handbook describing insurance and retirement options for new employees. She tried to imagine some way any of the documents might be relevant to the disappearance of Diana Cavendish.

"I thought you said Granville was part-time." She passed the handbook to James. "Why would he have retirement decisions to make?"

James looked at it briefly and then turned his attention back to his photos. "Part-timers can contribute to a supplemental retirement account if they want. The paper doesn't make any contributions for them, so anyone can participate." He smiled. "Good thinking, though."

Turning her attention to the next file folder, she found two dozen pages of printed text, bits and pieces of prose that looked like partially completed stories for the newspaper. She read the first piece, an almost finished narrative about the proposed demolition of a local historic building. Granville had interviewed several local preservationists and the developer, who wanted to put in a new block of apartments. She slid closer to James and showed him the draft.

"Was Granville a reporter too? It looks like he was writing stories for the paper."

"He wanted to be. He said he was going to be a famous photojournalist." James did not sound overly impressed by Granville's career goals. "He talked with me a couple times about how to break into the print side of things, but he wasn't very good at taking advice."

She put a hand on his shoulder and leaned closer to show him the text. He smelled nice, and she could feel his muscle flex as he turned. "You didn't like him much, did you?"

"Not really." He shook his head but did not elaborate.

"Did he write about anything controversial?" She flicked the corner of the demolition story with her finger. "He's taking on a developer in this one."

James looked at the headline. "Oh, I remember this . . . yeah . . . the story never ran. The developer won, and down came the old Tate Mansion."

"Did he ever get anything published?"

"Yeah," he nodded, "a couple of fluff pieces here and there."

"Could we find them and see if he ever said anything interesting in a published piece?"

James frowned and leaned back. Melanie's hand slipped from his shoulder but he didn't seem to notice. "Not if they were credited as having been written by 'staff,' but the online archive goes back almost ten years, so you could run a search for his name and see if anything comes up."

She nodded and promised to take a look at the corpus of Granville's published work when she was through with the box. The rest of the stories in the file all seemed innocuous. He seemed to have taken an interest in business-related stories, an odd choice, given the lack of opportunities for exciting action photos. She read about the opening of a new Italian restaurant in downtown Clarkeston, the dim prospects for a light-rail line between the college town and Atlanta, a scandal with the kitchen sanitation rating at a local nursing home, and violent protests by demonstrators at the latest World Trade Organization ministerial meeting. There seemed to be a consistent skepticism about corporations in his work, but nothing seemed connected to Diana Cavendish or any other incendiary topics. As unpublished works, they seemed especially unrelated to any potential friend or foe of Jacob Granville.

"Here's something . . ." James pushed a photo across the table to her. He had already gone through everything in his box except a slim folder of photos. "Look at the back, too."

She held in her hand a large photograph of a striking woman with thick dark hair, rosy cheeks, and a captivating smile, standing with her arm around a subdued and pensive friend with thin pale hair and blue eyes. "Neither is Diana Cavendish."

"Turn it over."

On the back were written two names, Brenda and Elisa, and a date, March 15, 2009. If the order of the names matched the picture, then the brunet was Brenda, and the other woman, Elisa. They both dressed formally, in dark wool skirts and blazers, each with a satchel draped over her shoulder. The image captured something intrinsically interesting about the personalities of both girls. Whatever he was, Granville had talent with a camera. Looking at the photo was like meeting the two women, not merely looking at them.

"Nice," she said. "Now, tell me why it's interesting."

"Two reasons," the reporter replied as he took the picture and flipped it over. For the first time that day he seemed energized. "First, the date is less than ten days before Diana Cavendish disappeared." He paused a moment and looked at her briefly over his glasses. "Second is the location." He put his finger on a sign visible in the background of the photo. "Correct me if I'm wrong, but isn't the World Trade Organization in Geneva, Switzerland?"

She took back the picture and studied it more closely. He was right about the sign, and the architecture of the building looked vaguely European. "What the hell was he doing in Geneva just before Diana disappeared?"

"Good question." He took off his glasses and polished them with a white handkerchief. For a moment he was as animated and flirtatious as he had been during their visit to North Carolina. "Hold that thought and let's keep looking."

It took them another thirty minutes to finish with the remaining items in the boxes. Nothing appeared worth taking, except for the picture of the two girls, which James slid into a folder and tucked under his arm as they returned the containers to the closet.

The reporter looked at his watch and suggested bringing back some food from a nearby sub shop for lunch. He slipped out to pick up their order before Melanie remembered to ask for the access password to the newspaper's Wi-Fi system. Sure enough, when she tried to log on, even the "guest" option required a password. While she waited for Murphy's return, she retrieved the phone directory from the closet, took it back to the archive room, and leafed through it. As she feared, she found no scrawled notations next to any interesting numbers, although one partially torn page contained an underlined name: Miriam Rodgers.

After twenty minutes, James returned, and although the food was aimed at the unsophisticated palate of the college students just across the river, the sandwich was surprisingly tasty. He let out a deep sigh as he took a bite out of his Reuben.

"You seem really preoccupied," she said as she caught his eye and gave him her most winning smile. "Out partying all night?"

"Hardly." He paused as if he were considering whether to elaborate. "I got legal-separation papers served on me yesterday. Not very conducive to a good's night sleep, I'm afraid."

"Shit. I'm sorry." That explained the glum mood, she thought. His wife must be a real piece of work. "Do you want to talk about it?"

"Not really." He gave her a sad smile. "Just hanging out down here and working through this stuff with you helps as much as anything."

Nice.

They finished their food in silence, and she turned her attention back to her computer. Her first search on the newspaper website returned dozens of hits mentioning Granville in connection with the disappearance of Diana Cavendish. She then limited her search to the time period before the disappearance and found two articles authored by the young photographer. One, entitled "Bars Protest Smoking Ban," was a short piece filled with predictions about the dire effect Clarkeston's new antismoking ordinance would have on local drinking establishments. The other headline read, "Congress Carefully Watches WTO Case." She remembered the unpublished fragment in her file and the picture that James had found, and read the story carefully.

Granville's article reported that Brazil had filed a case before the dispute-settlement body of the World Trade Organization complaining about Washington's support for US cotton growers. India, Pakistan, Chad, and other major cotton-growing countries had joined the complaint, which alleged an astounding and undisputed fact: Congress subsidized US cotton growers over $18 billion per year to produce a crop that was worth only around $11 billion. Although American taxpayers were apparently unaware of or untroubled by the huge subsidy, other cotton-growing countries around the world were incensed. As the largest exporter of cotton in the world, the US, with its subsidized low price, shrank cotton profits worldwide. The massive influx of artificially cheap cotton from the US suppressed prices and cost some of the poorest farmers in the world billions of dollars per year. Since several of the top cotton producers in the world were in sub-Saharan Africa, the story emphasized the potential human-rights dimension of the case. Wealthy corporate farmers raked in piles of cash from Congress while impoverished growers in Mali starved. The case had been briefed, but the WTO decision had not been rendered, at the time Granville wrote the article.

She reread the story and tapped her thumb impatiently just below the space bar on her laptop. "Read this." She handed the computer to him over the remnants of his sandwich.

He read the article quickly and then scrolled back to the top of the screen. "This came out about four weeks before that picture was taken in Geneva."

She caught his eye and saw a familiar intensity. "A photo of two girls posing right in front of the WTO." She took back her laptop and bookmarked the page. "At least we can guess what he was doing in Geneva right before Diana disappeared: researching the cotton case."

James looked puzzled. "Trust me, the newspaper did not spring for a trip to Europe for him to work on this story."

"So he paid his own way." She shrugged and offered a quick theory. "You said he was ambitious."

"Yeah, ambitious but not rich."

"Maybe his parents paid for the trip." Melanie tried to come up with a reason why Granville might travel to Geneva for the story. Surely, the details of the case were public, and expert commentary could be solicited by phone.

"His parents didn't mention any foreign travel when we talked to them."

"Why would they?" she argued. "Why would they think it was relevant?"

He sighed. "I don't know that it is relevant." He took a sip from his Coke. "I mean, it's super unusual. Photographers squeezing by on a part-time salary do not self-finance trips to Switzerland to cover international trade stories for small-town Georgia newspapers. It's definite weirdness."

"Agreed." She clicked her computer shut and slipped it into her shoulder bag. She hated coincidences, and the timing of this "weirdness" with Diana Cavendish's disappearance was as unlikely as the timing of her own phone call to Arkansas with the theft at Murphy's house.

"Oh, shit," she said suddenly. She took her computer back out, moved around the table next to him and reconnected to the Internet. "You remember the farmer in the YouTube video?"

She found j-gville on the website and clicked Play on the first upload. Once again, the stoic face of the Malian farmer who had lost his wife and two daughters appeared on the screen. Thankfully, Melanie's question was answered before they were forced to see the twisted legs of his son once again. She turned and grabbed his shoulder. "That's what I thought! He was a cotton farmer."

James looked up at her with piercing blue eyes. Why didn't he just lean over and kiss her, anyway? He was separated now, after all.

"I'm going to talk with my editor tomorrow and see if he knows anything about this. After all, he approved the first little story on the cotton case, and he might have talked with Jacob about a follow-up. Maybe he even saw the video."

"And I'm going to track down Diana Cavendish's mother." Melanie shut the laptop and put it back in her carryall. "If she was as close to her daughter as her ex-husband says, then she might know something about Diana's boyfriend."

Their joint declarations seemed a natural end to the morning's investigation. They speculated briefly about the girls in the Geneva photo and Granville's possible motivations for killing Diana, but they still had too few pieces of the puzzle, even assuming what they had collected belonged to the same picture. To avoid communicating by email or telephone, Melanie agreed to return to Clarkeston the following weekend so they could share whatever new information they had gathered.

James walked her to her car and held the door open for her. "Thanks for taking my mind off my personal bullshit." He nodded back to the building. "That was good work in there."

"Yeah," she replied as she gave him a moist kiss on the cheek and slid into the car, "we make a pretty good team."

XXII.

TABLES

Thorsten Carter put his feet up on his desk and tried to concentrate on writing Sunday's sermon, but thoughts of Miriam Rodgers kept interfering with his attempt to put some fresh spin on the appointed gospel reading, the venerable parable comparing rich men to camels trying to pass through the eye of the needle. He imagined himself preaching for her, despite the fact that she would not be in the congregation. What a change that would be: seeing a friendly face in the crowd instead of a sea of encrusted privilege squinting their doubt of his worthiness to occupy the pulpit. No, he would be left preaching to the frozen chosen, who would be expecting him to explain how Jesus's disapproval of the rich man did not bar their own entitlement to salvation. He was tempted to teach the parable literally and demand that they give up all their possessions or burn in hell for eternity. That might shake them up.

Unfortunately, Thor did not believe in hell and had no real desire to threaten anyone with devils, pitchforks, and lakes of burning fire. Nonetheless, he did want to rattle them a bit. More than a bit, truth be told, and he stood up to search his bookshelves for a source that might provide him with the proper sort of theological dynamite. Although he had been ordained for less than five years, he had amassed a decent collection of scholarly commentaries on the Bible, many of them gifts from friends and relatives upon his graduation from seminary or his ordination. They were occasionally helpful, usually because the writer had tackled the scripture in its original language and had some insight to offer based on the inadequacy of the English translation, but he wanted more than just insight into language this time.

His scanned his collection and leafed through a couple of reliable sources, but none added anything earthshaking to his own understanding about the interrelationship of wealth, charity, and salvation. Beside his own books were several dozen volumes belonging to Father Rodgers that he had appropriated as his own. On occasion he had found something useful among his predecessor's tomes, and after studying the titles he found one that held some promise. It was written by John Shelby Spong, the outspoken former Anglican bishop of Newark, New Jersey. Spong was famous for rethinking almost every major position in traditional Christianity, from the virgin birth to the resurrection of Jesus to the marriage sacrament. If anyone had anything radical to say about the parable, it would likely be him.

As he pulled the book out and flipped to the index, he noticed a letter marking the start of a chapter entitled "Miracles in a Post-Newtonian World." It was postmarked Washington, DC, and was handwritten on generic Department of Justice stationery. The letter was authored by someone named Giles Keefe, who promised to recommend Miriam Rodgers for undergraduate admission to Harvard. Given the text of the letter, Keefe was clearly responding to an earlier request by her father to use his influence to help Miriam in the application process. The letter was very personal and invited a response updating Keefe on how Ernest and his wife Caroline were doing. The tone was informal and demonstrated a friendship of significant vintage. Thor smiled and immediately picked up the phone to call Miriam.

"You never told me you went to Harvard!" The priest's voice conveyed how impressed he was.

"I didn't." Miriam sounded confused. "You know that I went to Georgia."

"I thought that was just grad school."

"What makes you think I went to Harvard?"

"Well, I was flipping through one of your dad's old books and out pops a letter from someone who's supposed to be helping you get in." He held the letter in his hand and fingered it in the sunlight. The postmark was ten years old, just about the time she would have been applying for colleges.

"Harvard was Dad's thing. He always wanted me to go there, even when I was a little kid, but there was no way you were getting me that far from home. Even being in Athens made me homesick sometimes. I didn't apply anywhere outside the state."

This surprised him. Miriam struck him as extremely independent and cosmopolitan. He liked Clarkeston, but he could not conceive of what might keep an ambitious young woman so tied to the town.

"Well, whether you wanted it or not, some guy named Giles Keefe went to bat for you with the admissions committee."

"Who?" Her voice was emphatic.

"The letter was from Giles Keefe. Why? Do you know him?"

"No, but I think that was one of the names on the back of that Washington, DC, photo of my dad's." She paused for a moment. "Let me check it out tonight and I'll give you a ring. Maybe this guy was my dad's connection."

Once she had hung up, Thor had to wonder whether his girlfriend (dare he call her that?) was getting a little obsessed with events far in the past. Well, if wanting to play Nancy Drew was her biggest fault, then he would count himself a lucky man indeed. In fact, when she called back, he planned to ask her to Chez Pierre, the best (or at least the most expensive) restaurant in Clarkeston, and see if he could turn the heat up in their relationship. Her last goodbye kiss seemed to be pointing to something tantalizingly steamier.

When she called, she had learned nothing new about Giles Keefe but insisted that her mother's reaction to the name had been interesting. Caroline Rodgers denied any memory of him, even after her daughter took down the picture of their group of Washington friends and pointed out Keefe as an attractive and unusually tall man standing next to her husband.

"She flat out denied knowing the guy and was pretty combative when I pressed her."

"Isn't your mother always pretty combative?"

"You know what I mean! She was really interested in telling me stories about their time in Washington when we talked before. Now she seems to have amnesia."

Thor thought about the contents of the letter. "I don't want to feed your paranoia, but this guy specifically referred to your mother by name. As of ten years ago, he certainly had not forgotten her."

"I'm telling you: something is really fishy here. I'm going to track this guy down."

Thor suggested that she tell him the result of her snooping over dinner the following evening and was rewarded by a spontaneous acceptance. Now, if Sunday's sermon would just write itself, the week would be perfect.

★ ★ ★

Melanie sat at her desk looking at the address and phone number of Carolyn Williams, Diana Cavendish's mother. It had taken less than forty-eight hours for one of her investigative staff to track down Julius Cavendish's ex-wife. His speculation about her profession had made the job easier, as her business address was listed as Cakes By Carolyn on the north side of Chicago, not too far from Wrigley Field, if Melanie remembered her geography correctly. As requested, the investigator had supplied basic background information on the woman, including her credit rating (quite good), her arrest record (a ten-year-old drunk-driving charge), and a glowing review of her cakes from a *Chicago Tribune* article. She had apparently become one of the most popular supplier of fancy pastries to well-to-do residents in Lincoln Park.

As a precaution, Melanie had the report sent to her private Gmail account rather than her official Department of Justice address. Her investigator had used government search tools, but

Melanie doubted that the name Carolyn Williams would set off any alarm bells, and she had not mentioned to anyone the connection to Diana Cavendish or Jacob Granville. To make her tracks even harder to trace, she decided to call Williams from an empty conference room several floors below her office.

Melanie was surprised when the businesswoman picked up on the second ring. She was preparing for a wedding the following day, but found time to talk when she learned that the investigation into her daughter's death had been reopened.

"I know this may seem a strange way to start a conversation," Melanie apologized, "but I wonder if you've heard anything from your daughter since she disappeared."

"No." She sounded confused and then a note of suspicion entered her voice. "Why? Have you found her?"

"No," Melanie hesitated. "I haven't." She was taken aback by the mother's response. She had expected a flurry of optimistic questions or an outburst of tears or a fearful readiness for bad news. She wished she could see the woman's face and read her body language. "Your ex and Granville's parents have both shown me emails that may have come from Diana."

"What do you mean, *may* have come from Diana?"

More suspicion. Melanie did not want to lose her. "They bear her name but there's no way to tell if they're authentic."

"I don't know about any emails," Williams finally replied, "but then again I don't think that Julius or Jacob's parents even know where I am. It's not like we're trading Christmas cards." Her voice trailed off. "I accepted long ago that Diana was dead. It's easier that way."

"It's unclear what's going on," Melanie said in a soothing voice. "There were only a couple of very short messages, both of them received right after the disappearance. No one's heard anything for almost five years, but we just found out about this and are trying to follow up."

"Shit." A long exhalation of breath. "So, they could just be Jacob's idea of a sick joke."

"Why do you say that?"

"He kills her, runs off, and taunts the parents." She paused. "And then gets bored with taunting. Maybe I should be happy that he didn't contact me." Another pause. "What did the messages say, anyway?"

"They indicated that Jacob and Diana had run into some trouble in Clarkeston and had to leave. Neither message was more than two lines. Apparently they were sent from a new email account set up in Mexico." Melanie thought back a moment. "Did Jacob even have your email address?"

"Oh yes. Definitely. He and Diana visited me in Chicago about a month before they disappeared. The three of us emailed back and forth, what time they were arriving at the airport, that kind of thing. Afterward we shared some stuff we found on the Internet. I sent him links to a couple of stupid cat videos as a joke. His links were usually political."

Melanie mentally kicked herself for not previously considering a now obvious line of inquiry. "Were you Facebook friends?"

"Yeah, it was just starting up back then. Diana made me sign up. I didn't post much stuff then, but it's been really great for the cake business recently."

Melanie took a deep breath and crossed her fingers. "Could you log on when you get back home and copy everything off of his home page? Everything that he ever posted? You'd be surprised what might be helpful to us. It's not like I can friend him now and see it myself."

Carolyn took a moment to respond. "If you've got a website where I can verify who you are, I'll forward what I can find, but he hasn't posted since the disappearance. I've checked a couple of times."

Melanie gave her the URL of her Justice Department online profile and then continued. "You said earlier that you think Granville kidnapped Diana . . . Is that just a logical assumption or are you thinking of something more concrete?"

"Well, I'm not sure what you mean by *concrete*." She was thoughtful and unruffled. No sign of the drinking problem with which her ex-husband had branded her. "It's more an informed instinct, I suppose." She gathered her thoughts. "I'm an alcoholic. I haven't had a drink in years, but I'm still sensitive to addiction. When Jacob and Diana were visiting, I could tell that they were getting high, so when they went out, I took a look through their bags and found a huge amount of pot. Way more than you'd just use yourself. If Jacob was dealing and stringing Diana along, something could have gone wrong."

"I see," Melanie replied. "Was there anything else?"

"It's hard to say . . . I got along pretty well with Jacob. He was funny, intelligent, and handsome, but there was also a hardness about him. He had a way of nodding while you were talking, like he was listening closely but really thinking you were an idiot. Diana adored him, but I never thought that he was Prince Charming and they would live happily ever after."

"Do you think he was capable of murder?"

Her response was immediate. "I think everyone is capable of murder."

"But he more capable than most?"

"Maybe." She sighed. "I don't know. Like I said, I didn't trust him."

Melanie liked the woman on the other end of the line. She was no-nonsense, analytical, and tried to keep emotion separate from reason. Melanie had seen this before in other former alcoholics, a thoughtful tentativeness about judgment.

"Carolyn," she continued, "thank you so much for speaking with me. This is extremely helpful, and I only have a couple more questions. Most important is whether you know anything about Granville's trip to Geneva, Switzerland, the week before he and Diana disappeared."

"A little," she answered and then interrupted herself, "wait." She gave instructions to someone in her kitchen about the spelling of a name on the cake. "Sorry about that. I knew that Jacob was going. He claimed that he had a source within the World Trade Organization and was going to break a huge story. He didn't say what it was about, but he claimed that the *New York Times* and the *Washington Post* would be fighting to hire him once he published it."

"Did he mention his source or say anything about the research?"

"No. He let slip the pronoun *she* a couple of times, so I figured that his source was a woman, but he was pretty tight lipped about the story itself."

"But he never mentioned a name?"

"No."

★ ★ ★

The same afternoon that Melanie was on the telephone to Chicago, James was talking to his editor at the *Clarkeston Chronicle*. Stewart Mitford had inherited the paper from his father, but not before he had acquired an MBA from the University of Georgia and spent several years working in almost every one of its departments. After he sold the paper to a large regional news conglomerate, he stayed on as editor in chief and managed to prevent the quality of the *Chronicle's* content from plummeting too precipitously. He had a light-handed management style with his reporters, preferring to pay more attention to the advertising department, which funded the local stories that kept his readers from switching to the *Atlanta-Journal Constitution* or *The New York Times*.

James found Mitford sitting behind his desk, frowning at a pile of resumés. "Jesus!" the editor exclaimed. "We've got almost a hundred applicants for two unpaid summer internships." He shook his head. "Talk about proof that the economy really is in the toilet."

"Not a good time to be launching a career in print media."

James liked his commercially savvy boss. He was a bit risk averse when running stories critical of local figures, but as long as a reporter had all of his facts double-checked, the editor would sigh and let it run.

"No kidding. We haven't hired a new full-time reporter in over three years. I don't know how the hell anybody can even get started these days."

James figured that at least some of the talent that used to go to newspapers now found something to do on the web, but he hadn't come to discuss the pressure the digital age was putting on the *Chronicle*. Mitford had, at least, started an online version of the paper. "Speaking of failing to get a career started, I was wondering if I could ask you a question about Jacob Granville."

"What do you want to know about Jake?"

"It's almost five years since he and Diana Cavendish disappeared, and I'm doing a retrospective on the story." He watched the editor's face closely for any sign of disapproval. "I went one more time through the stuff Jacob left here and found a possible lead that I never pursued. Right before he and Diana vanished, he went to Geneva, Switzerland, to research a story. I checked online and saw that he had published an article on a World Trade Organization case. I was wondering whether his trip was following up on his article."

Mitford drummed his fingers on his desk. James had never determined whether the editor was a supporter of Granville or had come to the logical conclusion that the paper's former photographer had committed kidnapping and murder. He had never quashed any of James's stories about the case, but he had demanded extra verification of facts on several occasions.

"Yeah," Mitford finally replied, "he asked me for money to go to Geneva to talk to some super-source." He shook his head. "Are you fucking kidding me? We barely have enough money to pay people gas money to Atlanta!"

James suppressed a smile. Unlike the stereotypical newsman, Mitford almost never swore.

"And to make matters worse," he continued, "the kid wouldn't give me any details of his plan. He acted like I might steal his story if he told me too much. He just kept going on about international scandals and corrupt politicians."

"Were you aware that he went?"

"Yeah, he needed to ask for the time off, but I sure as hell didn't pay him. If he had been full-time, he would have had to choose between his trip and his job."

"Did you tell the cops any of this?"

"I don't remember." Mitford shrugged. "It was a long time ago, and it didn't seem relevant. Still doesn't."

"Did you ever see any videos he posted on YouTube?"

"No."

"Did Jacob ever mention a different story, having to do with violence against women in Mexico?"

"Not that I remember." The editor shrugged.

James thanked his boss and promised rather disingenuously not to waste too much time on the Diana Cavendish retrospective, but Mitford had warmed to the idea and suggested that he recycle some of the material from his old stories. When James got home and found Melanie's message, he emailed back a quick response, suggesting a meeting on Sunday afternoon, since his youngest son was making a trip home from college on Saturday to pick up some things from his room. He sent a message to Thorsten Carter too. It was about time to get everyone together who was poking around the case.

XXIII.

CLIFFS

Stanley Hopkins piloted his rental car slowly through the narrow streets of Sóller, Mallorca. The little village at the foot of the eastern coastal range was connected by a streetcar to the port that bore its name, but the professor drove his rental on the assumption that he could drive through the village to the dirt road indicated on his map and wind his way up the mountains to Reggie's spectacularly located house. Once past the far edge of the ancient town, he began to doubt his plan, as the road began to resemble a cow path more than a proper street. About a kilometer past the city limits, he encountered a locked gate crossing the gravel trail, and he was almost relieved that he had no choice but to park the car halfway in a grassy ditch and proceed on foot.

The day was warm and sunny, but a row of Spanish chestnut trees shaded the lane and kept the glare off the laminated map that sketched his route. Across a pasture, an old pilgrim's trail climbed up the mountainside almost to the crest of the Alfabia Ridge before a spur veered south to the landholding marked *finca* at the end of the dirt road, which started where he stood. *The Hiker's Guide to Mallorca* advised that a fit walker could make the ridge in two and a half hours. Although Stanley's doughnut consumption had abated since his arrival in Spain, months of sugar addiction had left him somewhat short of the fitness level he had attained the previous year on his frequent treks up into the San Gabriels. Nonetheless, he had remembered his hiking boots and had little doubt that he could follow the pilgrim path up to the *finca* that he assumed was Reggie's lair.

He walked across the pasture and was surprised to see that the trail was laid with stone and that for the most part it was in the shade. The route followed a broad desfile along a stream, passing the occasional hardscrabble farm serviceable only by donkey, as it steadily gained in elevation. After ninety minutes of continuous slogging, Stanley found the air was noticeably cooler, and he reviewed his plan for the upcoming encounter. He needed to be prepared if Reggie turned out to be Jacob Granville in hiding. If so, he intended to adopt the guise of a lost hiker looking for directions and leave any confrontation to the authorities. Hopefully, Granville would not be too suspicious of an American magically showing up on his doorstep. If Reggie were a stranger, then Stanley might finally get an answer to the question of who posted the pictures of Diana Cavendish on Mygirlfriendsbikini.com.

He had mixed feelings about being at the end of his search. The trail had been full of frustrating dead ends, but it had nudged him off the center of his grief, gotten him out of Los Angeles, and led him to Vanessa, El Langustino, and the most beautiful hike he had taken in a long time. Two hours of walking brought him far above the elevation of his own villa several miles down the ridge, and unfamiliar contours of the coastline tumbled spectacularly south in an unending serpentine of rock and inlet. He sat for a long time on a rock, looking down on the water and feeling the terrible events of the last year lurch slightly further into the past.

He turned and saw a whitewashed house beckoning far above him, but the main trail wound to the left and proceeded along a series of switchbacks until it disappeared, presumably to snake its way back to the right and toward the villa before making its way into the valley beyond. A fainter footpath aimed directly at the house and offered a substitute route. His meditation had put him in the mood for a further climb, so he trudged up the steep incline, pausing every couple of dozen steps to appreciate the view and catch his breath.

After fifteen minutes, the trail steepened yet further, to the point where the rocks jutting out of the mountainside became necessary handholds. Finally, the path petered out altogether, leaving the choice of a slow retreat or a rough scramble to the top. *Shit*, he thought as he looked up and then down. The villa was no longer in sight, and the view below him was as terrifying as it was glorious. The route had edged increasingly close to the point where the Alfabia Ridge plunged straight down to the ocean. The pilgrim path, far below on the left, had veered away from the cliff and proceeded to the ridge along more gradually sloping ground. Where he was headed, the landscape tilted toward the ocean. A quick look up, however, showed that the rock was volcanic, with plenty of handholds. Perhaps ten minutes of work until the top of the ridge?

The thought of trying to crabwalk down the steep slope and rejoin the main path was as dispiriting as continuing upward was daunting. Unwilling to backtrack, he ignored the urgent voice in his head counseling caution, retied the loosened laces of his boots, and climbed.

Stanley scrambled, hand, foot, hand, never fully secure and steadily veering slightly farther south, imperceptibly around the shoulder of the ridge that separated steep from vertical. His heart began to pound, and he clenched a stone spur and jammed the toe of one foot into a crevice before looking up: the rock face rose at least another hundred feet to the top. He was out of breath and the pulsing rhythm of blood in his ear told him to get the hell out of there. Time to rethink the plan. The handgrips were getting smaller and a nearly vertical rock climb without rope or helmet or companion awaited him. Proceeding, in other words, was really stupid. This was precisely the sort of climb that he had promised Angela he would never attempt.

Time to retreat. Life was a gift not to be squandered on shortcuts or endorphin rushes.

Then, he looked down and tightened his grip in panic, pushing his left cheek hard against the rock face. It was straight down. Not steep. Straight. He studied the lines on the rock in front of him. He tried to focus on the colorful little veins, some of which were filled with lichen or moss. But the calming effect of the geology lesson quickly ran its course. The shock of his quick look down nearly three thousand feet had rendered his legs jelly-like, and his hands were cramping from his tight grasp on the stone. Angela would really be pissed, but Angela was dead, and there was no choice but to make the top or join her. Trying to move blindly down would be suicidal.

He swallowed hard and reached up to a rocky knob. It crumbled away in his hand and he slipped, foot dislodged, life now suspended by a single handhold. He reached again, found a barely usable indentation for his fingers, and then moved his right foot to the ledge immediately below where his stomach had been. Carefully testing each grip and foot plant before proceeding, he moved finger by finger, toe by toe, ignoring the sparkling blue sea far below him, concentrating on every motion, clutching the rock face in a desperate embrace that sent several buttons plunging to the sea.

The last three feet of stone were nearly smooth, as if the cliff edge had been mortared together, conspiring to defeat his attempts to find a purchase. After a pause, during which he willed himself not to look down at the surf pounding more than a half mile below, he spotted a crack in which to wedge his right hand and with a convulsive effort managed to hook his left arm over the top of the last row of rock. His feet dangled in space for a moment, but a burst of adrenaline powered his shoulders over the top, and he flipped down onto his back, flat on a surface of stone. The sound of the ocean was lost and replaced by a quiet hum and curious slurping sound.

"Ahem."

Stanley rolled to his side, away from the wall at the top of the cliff, and immediately encountered the figure of a very tanned and very leathery old man sitting completely naked on a plastic lounge chair and sipping a tall drink through a straw.

"Nice climbing, old pip!" He offered a toast with his glass. "Would you like a gin and tonic?"

Stanley could only blink. His heart was still pounding with the effort of the climb, and his overwhelming sense of relief at being alive forestalled a coherent response, if one could be made at such a sight.

"Reggie?" he croaked.

"That's right!" The man got up, sagging belly obscuring his manhood. "Have a seat and I'll get you that drink."

When he returned, Reggie was wearing a pair of faded Bermuda shorts and a Mallorca F.C. T-shirt. He brought a small pitcher of water and a glass along with the promised gin and tonic. "Thought you might be a bit thirsty," he added, as he placed the drinks on a small table next to the chair where Stanley had seated himself.

He sat back down and took a long sip from his glass. "Now," he said in a posh accent that would be the envy of a BBC One presenter, "I'm at a bit of a disadvantage in that you know my name, but I don't know yours."

"Stanley," he replied. "Stanley Hopkins." He drained the glass of water. "And I've come all the way from California to talk to you."

The revelation elicited no more than a slight raising of the Englishman's left eyebrow. "Really? Well, in that case, I'll break out the Tanqueray No. 10."

The professor dropped the complicated fabrication he had planned for the meeting and decided to cut straight to the heart of the matter. The Englishman surely had not personally taken the photos of Diana Cavendish. He must have bought them from a photographer, and he didn't seem like the kind of person who would hesitate to reveal a potential murderer. Stanley started at the beginning, with his first encounter with Diana's picture, and traced his own search through William Simmons, the cryptic expatsoller email address, the dart league, and finally the unplanned ascent of the Alfabia Ridge.

"Anyway," Stanley concluded, "I really need to know who sold you those pictures, along with any other relevant information you might have about them."

Reggie shook his head slowly. "You're on a wild-goose chase, old man, but let's go inside and you can show me your pictures."

The villa was spacious and covered in the same ochre tile that kept Stanley's rental so light and cool. The back patio opened into a living room and eating area next to a true chef's kitchen complete with a massive butcher block and hanging copper-bottomed pots and pans. The Englishman led him to the back of the house and opened a door that contained a large room filled with computer servers. A small desk with a work station was tucked underneath the only window in the room. An air conditioner hummed, cooling the room to a constant temperature, presumably to prevent the servers from overheating.

"Have a seat and show me what you're looking for."

Stanley pulled a photocopied picture of Diana Cavendish out of his pocket and typed in the URL. Up popped the Clarkeston dance major, eternally smiling and twirling her hair. He leaned to the side so his companion could get a better view.

"Pretty, that one. And you say that I sold it to this website?"

"The owner said he paid the expatsoller email address via PayPal."

"Right. Do you mind if I sit down and show you something?" The Englishman switched places with his guest. "I'm going to run a neat bit of software for you." Using his mouse, he drew a box around Diana's face, saved just that image, and then opened up another program. "This is image-searching software that will crawl through the net for pictures that match the one I just snipped. Sort of like what the cops use for CATV facial searches. It's especially efficient if I can combine the search with a word I expect to find in a web page meta tag, like *porn* or *softcore*." He hit the Enter key. "It will search for this young woman's face and return web addresses wherever it's found."

Stanley watched the screen and within minutes the program had identified 237 websites. Reggie clicked on several of the URLs at random and they each immediately displayed the same familiar set of photos of Diana Cavendish.

"You see," Reggie explained, "I'm just a middleman who buys from about a half-dozen different consolidators. I pay the consolidators, who pay the photographers, who often buy from amateurs rather than taking pictures themselves. Everything is done in bulk, terabytes of content for a price, not picture by picture. I couldn't even tell you which consolidator I initially got the pictures from. There's utterly no point in my keeping any records beyond how much I pay or receive and how many terabytes I buy or sell."

Stanley knew suddenly that this was truly the end of his search. Weeks of work and a clever trick to smoke out a website owner had brought him no closer to the identity of Diana Cavendish's photographer. He had been defeated by a porn industry where pictures of a pretty girl in a swimsuit were divvied up around the world like real estate derivatives in the financial market. One desperate hope remained. "And you're not the source of all 237 hits?"

"Maybe a couple of them, but there's many other middlemen like me who would be the source for the others." He gestured to the computer. "Your girl is all over the web and has been for quite a while. No one will be able to tell you exactly where she came from." He looked up curiously at Stanley. "You didn't really think that you had stumbled on the only web presence of a girl you happen to know, did you? Wouldn't that be a hell of a coincidence!"

Stanley had seldom felt so stupid, but as he contemplated the top of the Englishman's nut-brown head, despair gave way to a sense of relief. He had done his best and pushed the search as far as any could have taken it. He'd managed to get out of California and have the climb of his life. He'd met a naked Englishman and gotten a peek into the colossal netherworld of Internet porn. Worse things could have happened.

He gave a sigh of submission and offered his wrinkled host a crooked smile. "Thanks, Reggie. How about another G&T?"

★ ★ ★

Stanley spent the rest of the afternoon on Reggie's patio, sipping a drink and marveling at the expanse of blue water over which he had recently been dangling his life. The rush of his climb took hours to fade and mingled merrily with alcohol being administered through a thin plastic straw. Reggie kept him amused with stories of local politics and subtle character assassinations of the other participants in the dart league. As the sun lowered to the point where looking westward became a painful squint, the Englishman offered to give him a ride back down to his Land Rover. He had some shopping to do in the village and was happy for an excuse to drive down the ridge.

Stanley was relieved to find the car where he had left it and drove carefully through Sóller and back to the coast. As he made his way back up to his villa, he saw a lone woman, Vanessa, swaying slowly up the hill, plastic shopping bags clutched in both hands. He stopped and offered her a ride, which she accepted with a grateful smile.

"Are you interested in having dinner tonight?" he asked, after stowing her bags in the back seat.

"How about a cocktail right now on my patio?" She pushed her sunglasses deep into her thick auburn hair, smiled, and gestured to her bags. "I've just bought a bottle of top-notch gin."

Stanley laughed and explained how he had already gotten off to an early start on the cocktail hour. Fascinated by his encounter with her fellow countryman, she kicked off her sandals, mixed a pair of gin and tonics, and led him to a shady corner of her back patio.

"Naked, you say." She shook her head in approval.

"Not a stitch on."

"Remarkable."

She put her feet up on a stool and Stanley was treated to a long length of fit and tanned leg, quite unlike the barnacled undercarriage of his new dart-throwing friend. He shook the image of Reggie out of his head and finally told her the purpose of his visit to Mallorca. She was interested in and impressed by his quest, and her questions assumed he was some sort of daring international crime fighter rather than a conventional academic. It had been a long time since he felt so comfortable with himself or with other people, and he could not help but smile and tell her that if he were James Bond, then she was lovely enough to be the perfect Bond girl. The gin made him bold, and the look on her face told him that it might have been a while since someone had dared look at her so frankly.

Later, while she made another round of drinks, the professor suggested going to El Langustino, but they never made it to dinner that night and instead shared a delightful breakfast the next morning under the approving eye of the gentle island sun.

XXIV.

CONFLUENCE

Melanie was glad that Carolyn had sent her screenshots of all of Jacob Granville's Facebook content before getting the bad news from Mallorca about the impossibility of sourcing the Cavendish photos. The tantalizing information on Granville's page had softened the blow that no killer would magically be revealed by the images that kicked off the investigation. Oddly, Professor Hopkins did not sound too disappointed, despite his wasted efforts. He seemed to have enjoyed the search and was planning on spending a few more weeks on the island.

"I owe you at least a fancy dinner if you ever to come to Atlanta or if I make it to Los Angeles."

"I may take you up on that sooner than you think," he said before he rang off. "My in-laws live in Roswell, Georgia, and I'm thinking about visiting them on the way back from Europe."

She put her cell phone down next to the papers on her dining room table. She had read twice all the Facebook entries made by Granville and was very interested to hear what James Murphy would have to say about her discovery. He had arranged a meeting in the priest's office of St. James church in Clarkeston after the late Sunday-morning service and claimed that the priest and his girlfriend had also uncovered some valuable information.

She was comfortable including Murphy's two friends. The content of Granville's Facebook page, after all, was not top secret. He had over two hundred friends at the time of his disappearance and presumably all of them still had access to his page.

The photographer had been online less than a year and most of his posts were routine status updates, but he had uploaded dozens of photos taken in both Clarkeston and Europe. Most everything seemed irrelevant, except for a couple of long rants about the cotton case and a picture of the same two women featured in the WTO photo found in the newspaper basement. This time the two girls were linking arms and smiling in front of Lake Geneva. The portrait was subtitled "Brenda Harvey, WTO Cotton Queen."

"Hello, Brenda," she murmured to herself, "could you please tell me everything you know about Jacob Granville?"

The posts about the cotton litigation revealed how obsessed Granville had become with the WTO case. He described Congress's subsidies of cotton growers in Texas and the Mississippi Delta as nothing less than acts of murder. The evidence showed that even though the subsidy was a disaster for US taxpayers ($18 billion handed out to farmers who created a crop worth $11 billion), it had succeeded in making US growers the number one exporters of cheap cotton in the world, driving down the world price for cotton and ruining poor farmers in sub-Saharan Africa. It was impossible to calculate the number of deaths caused by US agricultural policy, but it was clear that poor African farming families suffered and starved as a direct result. To make matters worse, according to a later post, the beneficiaries of the subsidies were not small US cotton farmers, themselves barely scraping by, but rather, huge industrial farms owned by a small number of incredibly wealthy landowners. The icing on the cake was that much of the US cotton crop was sold cheaply to garment-manufacturing maquiladoras in Mexico that exploited their laborers and reaped a huge profit themselves.

The connection to Granville's Mexican YouTube video was not lost on her.

He repeated these facts over several posts, becoming increasingly strident when his friends seemed uninterested or took issue with his characterization of Congress and wealthy growers as intentional murderers.

Melanie got up from the table and walked into the kitchen. Sunlight was streaming through the skylight onto her green quartz countertops, and she put on a kettle for some tea. Although Atlanta as a whole failed to charm her, she loved her tidy townhouse in Buckhead, especially the bright kitchen space that looked over her backyard. She really should have a dinner party, but socializing with her subordinates seemed like a bad idea, and the small peer group at the top of the office hierarchy was too busy hauling kids to soccer practice and school plays. She flicked the spent tea bag into the trash with a sigh. She really needed to get a life.

After a quick check of her mail, she sat back down and reconsidered Jacob Granville. What had he hoped to learn on a trip to Geneva that he could not glean from the myriad of online and in-print sources? The directory portion of the WTO website provided names and pictures of only a select number of figures running the Secretariat, which did not include Brenda. Melanie did learn to her astonishment, however, that the entire World Trade Organization employed fewer than six hundred people. *Brenda Harvey,* entered into the WTO website search function, returned two hits, both listing her tersely as a collaborator in the Subsidies and Countervailing Duties working group.

She knew from the Justice Department website that many search engines were not designed to crawl through documents that were scanned and uploaded as PDFs, and sometimes searches refused to generate results from PDFs at all. To test the WTO site, she found archived PDF reports related to subsidies and clicked on the first one retrieved. It was written by a researcher identified as Gert Hydriks and included his email address and phone number. She then ran a general search on the site using his name and got several hits, none of which were the document she had opened. *Bingo.* She would not be wasting her time if she trolled manually through the PDF archives of the Subsidies working group. And since the department had only fifteen employees, she figured it would not take too much time to find something authored or coauthored by Brenda Harvey.

Sure enough, an hour later, she had found five reports coauthored by Harvey, each listing the same contact information and all dated 2009 or before.

She emailed Harvey from her Gmail account and leaned back in her chair wondering if she should also call the contact number. She looked at her watch. It was three o'clock in Atlanta and eight o'clock in Geneva, well after working hours. She would call in the morning if she received no response to her message.

* * *

The central operator at the WTO spoke perfect English, and probably a dozen other languages, and she took a moment to check the WTO directory and records.

"I'm sorry, but Ms. Harvey no longer works here."

Melanie put her coffee down. "Do you have current contact information?"

"I'm sorry," the woman said, "but there's no further information listed."

Melanie thanked her and yelled *Shit*, and then resorted to conventional Internet searching, but Brenda Harvey was too common a name and generated too many disparate hits. She was in no mood for needle searching in digital haystacks.

It was six o'clock in the morning, and she had time to follow one more lead before heading into work. Brenda's companion, named Elisa in both photos she had seen, had dressed similarly and even carried the same sort of business satchel. It was possible that they both worked at the WTO, so she searched for the name on the website and learned that seven Elisas worked there, none of whom seemed to be associated with the division of Subsidies and Countervailing Duties. She wrote down all the last names and decided to take a shot in the dark. She signed on to Facebook and searched for each of the seven. Six of the WTO Elisas were on the social network, and three of those six had multiple pages, because their last names were fairly common. All told, she had almost two dozen potential Elisas. Six of those completely blocked the public from accessing any information from their profile. The rest allowed limited access to basic information, including their photo avatar. In less than fifteen minutes, she was staring at the small photo of a young blond woman named Elisa van der Vaart, employed by the Intellectual Property Division of the World Trade Organization. Brenda's friend.

She called the WTO once again and was cheerfully connected to a voice mailbox, where a pleasantly accented voice explained in English that Elisa was taking a short vacation and would be back on Monday. Melanie smiled as she imagined the look on James Murphy's chiseled face when she revealed the identities of the Cotton Queen and her IP sidekick.

★ ★ ★

James awoke on Sunday morning with hot asphalt for a brain and the sour taste of bile in his mouth. He might have survived the dozen beers if he had not topped them off with two stiff tumblers of Four Roses bourbon. He tried to remember the last time he had drunk himself sick—talking to God on the big white telephone, his son called it. Maybe at his brother's wedding, fifteen years earlier? He crawled out of bed, made his way unsteadily to the kitchen, and shook two extra-strength ibuprofen into his hand. A glass of milk seemed safest, so he chased down the pills with some two-percent and then mixed a second glass with some Hershey's syrup to sip on the living room couch. Two hours, a shower, and a bowl of oatmeal later, and James could walk about without dizziness, but he still felt nauseous and crusty around the edges.

The previous day had started well. His son, Robert, had arrived back from the University of Georgia in the late morning, and after loading his car up with a number of items deemed essential to his college career, they had tried a new seafood place on the edge of town. As James was wiping a spot of drawn butter from his chin, he heard his son whisper in a tentative voice, "Is that Mom by the door?"

James looked up and saw his wife, looking very sharp in a new skirt, being escorted into the restaurant by Pastor Neville Armstrong, youth minister and slugging first baseman for the First Baptist softball team. Sondra had cut and dyed her hair in a way that accentuated her high cheekbones and lovely complexion. She looked achingly beautiful. The restaurant was large enough, and the father and son far enough away in the corner, for them to remain undetected by the smiling pair. James and Robert watched without speaking as the newcomers sat down across the room and studied the menu together, holding hands and talking animatedly.

"What's she doing with Pastor Dumbass?" Robert asked in a voice that suggested he guessed the answer. "You guys are just separated, not divorced."

James had no answer for that; long habit had suppressed his ability to criticize Sondra in front of their children. He just stared in horror as each brush of the hand, touch of the shoulder, and guilt-free burst of laughter told him that his wife would not be coming back home. Ever.

A wave of anger surged through him. Had Pastor Armstrong told her the whole story behind his resignation as a deacon and his abandonment of First Baptist? What if she thought he was some sort of pedophile, and she had found a solid rock of the church to cling to in the stormy seas of his perversion? He stood up and took a step toward the couple but found his son blocking the way.

"It's not worth it." Robert's grip was as firm as his whisper, and James looked with surprise into his son's eyes. For the first time he saw a man.

"Let's just pay the bill and get out of here, Dad."

He barely remembered being led out to the car, but he did recall the odd comfort Robert had provided as James began pounding down the first of the beers back at the house while his son sipped on a Coke. If Robert were to be believed, neither of his two children understood why their parents had stayed married for so long. Events James had dismissed, as the occasional round of bickering and subsequent sulk, were seen from the outside as evidence of profound incompatibility. He was stunned to learn that the kids had expected a divorce long ago and wondered how their intellectual and rather quiet father had ever married their mercurial, materialistic mother. Robert was kind enough to add that he loved his mom. She was vibrant and funny, but she was so unhappy, so unable to enjoy to life in Clarkeston. Then he dropped the biggest bombshell of all. During at least one of her prior "vacations" from the marriage, she had an affair with the divorced father of one of his friends.

"Why didn't you tell me?"

"I talked with Sis about it, but we figured you guys were getting divorced anyway and then it would all come out." Robert looked apologetically at his father, who was sinking ever deeper into the chair in the corner of his study. "Then, you guys got back together and it seemed like a really bad idea to bring it up. I'm sorry if we did the wrong thing."

"No," James conceded, still trying to process the inevitability of the end of his marriage, "you did the right thing."

"Are you going to be okay? I've got to head back."

"Maybe." James got up and shrugged. "Eventually. Yeah."

He embraced his son as he stood by the car.

"Are you sure you don't want me to stay?"

The offer was generous, but James knew the last thing his son needed was to see his father drink himself shit-faced in despair. "No," he replied grimly, "but thanks for asking. Kiss your sister for me." Then, he returned to his study, turned up his stereo, drank, turned off his stereo, drank, watched *Love Actually* twice, and then finished the entire supply of Budweiser in his refrigerator.

★ ★ ★

The reporter looked at his watch and saw that it was still two and a half hours until the planned meeting with Melanie, Thor, and Miriam at St. James church. He had not attended any services since his abrupt departure from First Baptist and had felt the disruption in his weekly routine. His wife's church had never satisfied him spiritually, but he had plenty of friends there and he had found the Sunday morning routine pleasant, especially when the hymns were familiar and they went to the local pancake house for lunch immediately after the service.

He checked on the St. James website and saw that he had time to shave and still make the ten thirty service there. The last twenty-four hours had given him plenty of reason to seek divine intervention, so he splashed some cold water on his mottled face and put on a suit that might satisfy the sartorial norms of the famously formal crowd at the downtown Episcopal church.

The last bit of throbbing in his head faded soon after he entered the cool stone sanctuary of the church. The light coming through the stained glass windows was muted, and the organ played a Bach prelude quietly as the rather elderly congregation filed in. Rather than process into the sanctuary, the choir arranged itself on either side of the altar and offered an exquisitely delicate version of the Duruflé *Ubi Caritas* before Father Carter stood up and gave the opening prayer.

Until the sermon, James did not carefully attend to the liturgy, happy to float along with the prayers, Bible readings, and beautifully chanted psalm. His brain was not prepared to do any work, but when Thor took the pulpit, he caught the attention of the fallen-away Baptist, if only because the priest seemed so anxious about the message he was about to deliver. He cleared his throat, took a quick sip from a glass of water, and began.

"I was on a plane last year and found myself sitting next to one of our Pentecostal brethren, one of the kind who enjoys talking about religion on long plane flights." This elicited a chuckle from a couple of congregants, and the priest seemed to take heart as he continued. "We talked about our backgrounds and he eventually asked me if I were saved." He paused. "I said yes, and he smiled broadly at me and asked me when. He wanted my story and probably wanted to tell me his too. Well, as you might imagine, I told him the truth: 'I was saved the exact same day that you were,' I said. 'When Jesus died on the cross.'"

He took another sip of water. "Now, this is not what he wanted to hear, because in his mind, salvation is something earned through right belief and tithing, perhaps by good deeds or through a charismatic revelation. For some reason, as wonderful as the story of the cross should be, he did not want to hear it, possibly because any notion of universal salvation would necessarily include Muslims, Hindus, Jews, atheists, and inveterate Christian sinners. That's not the kind of crowd that he wanted to hang out with for eternity."

James listened carefully as the priest summarized various arguments over the nature of salvation that he had had with friends, family, spiritual advisors, and fellow seminarians. His delivery was awkward on occasion but his sincerity was compelling as he mixed theological history and personal anecdote. It had been a long time since James had heard a sermon where the specter of hell, by implication or assertion, did not pervade the message from the pulpit.

"In the end," Thor concluded, "the only argument that ever made complete sense to me was that God does not fail. And he wants to save and redeem the world. He cannot fail . . . by definition. Everyone agrees with that, and quite frankly, I find it very difficult to talk to people who imply that God is a failure. That he wants to save people but cannot. That his will to save can be thwarted by mere mortals."

He leaned forward over the pulpit and surveyed his congregation. "So, this is the key to the parable of the rich man and the difficulty of passing a heavily laden camel through the eye of the needle. The rich man is getting through, his camel is getting through, and so are his servant, his enemies, and the band of lepers dogging his steps asking him for alms. Everyone is getting through, and it is so fantastically difficult to comprehend that we tend to sit outside, waiting for an invitation that we fear will never come."

A long pause as he prepared to drop one final bomb on the congregation. "I'll finish with something one of my teachers once told me long ago, and I hope that you don't take it the wrong way: You're all saved . . . now start acting like it."

James felt an absurd impulse to give the brave young priest a standing ovation or at least a loud amen, but nothing could have been more out of place among the sober audience that sat as if it had not heard the sermon at all, a message that at First Baptist would have caused a riot. It was a relief, therefore, when everyone stood to sing and he could offer his appreciation in a rich, but sadly under-pitch, baritone voice.

★ ★ ★

Melanie was the last to enter the priest's study after the service, and James introduced her to Father Thorsten Carter and Miriam Rodgers. The earnest, ginger-haired priest took her hand warmly and offered her a seat on the sofa next to James. Melanie took a second look at Miriam and tried to remember where she had seen the face before. Maybe on a prior trip to Clarkeston? Then, with a lurch, she remembered the interview in Vidalia and the wistful sentiments of Jacob Granville's mother. Miriam had been dating Jacob before he met Diana Cavendish, and Jacob's mother had lamented the substitution of the young dancer for the pretty, immaculately groomed woman sitting in front of Melanie.

"Let me start," James began, after everyone had turned down Thor's offer to bring in some coffee. "As you already know, I came across new pictures of Diana Cavendish on the Internet a while ago and contacted the Justice Department with the information." He nodded to the federal prosecutor. "Since then, Melanie's been trying to track down the source of the photos, and together we've been reinterviewing people like Jacob's and Diana's parents."

He smiled at Thor and Miriam. "You two got dragged into this when I brought Father Rodgers's papers back to my house and they were stolen shortly thereafter. I've mentioned already to Melanie that you two have been trying to determine whether Miriam's father and his friends may have obstructed the initial search for Jacob and whether anyone might still be interested in doing so.

"I thought," he continued, "it would be a good idea for all of us to get together and talk about what we've found."

From long experience, Melanie knew the power of speaking last, so she sat back in her chair and waited for someone else to pipe up. She needed to gauge the trustworthiness of her two new companions before she revealed what she knew about Granville's trip to Geneva.

"Well," Miriam broke the short silence, "I've been trying to track down anyone that my father might have known who would have had the power to influence the FBI's investigation—"

"Or failure to investigate," James broke in.

"Or failure . . . yes . . . and I think I may have found a link. An old friend of my father's named Giles Keefe occupied a high position in the State Department at the time of Jacob's flight." She paused. "I got a phone number for him in northern Virginia yesterday, but I've only talked to his wife so far."

Miriam looked around the room and Thor nodded at her to continue.

"I didn't ask her any questions about Jacob or Diana, but she asked me to say hello to my mother. Apparently, they were fast friends during my father's years in Washington, but my mom denies knowing either Keefe or his wife and has clammed up totally about the time she spent with my father in DC. She's definitely covering something up."

She reached over and touched the priest's hand. "We wouldn't know any of this if Thor hadn't found an old letter from Keefe in his office."

Melanie had the resources to do further fact finding on Keefe, if necessary, but what intrigued her the most was Miriam's motivation for making her father look bad. Surely she could see that implicating him in a cover-up would damage his reputation.

Unless, of course, she thought Granville was innocent and her father merely a Good Samaritan. But if that were the case, why join this Hardy Boys amateur crime-stoppers unit dedicated to uncovering his whereabouts?

"Could you say a little bit about your own relationship with Jacob?" Melanie spoke sweetly, sounding idly curious, as if the fact of their romance were already known to everyone in the room. Miriam reddened and dodged Thor's interested gaze.

"What do you mean?" She mechanically smoothed the top of her skirt.

"I mean, when did you and Jacob stop dating?" Melanie smiled. "Mrs. Granville was quite sad that you never became her daughter-in-law. She showed us pictures of you and Jacob together."

The look of confusion on Thor's face made it clear that he was hearing this for the first time. James looked merely curious, as if he had been considering bringing up the subject and was pleased with how the attorney had slid it into the conversation.

"I don't think my personal life is relevant." She tried to wave away the subject with a flick of her right hand. "That was a long time ago."

"Maybe, but Mrs. Granville said that Jacob broke up with you." Melanie was extrapolating from the mother's remarks, but she hit home nonetheless. "Whether you're still carrying a torch for Jacob or you hate him for dumping you, I imagine that it's hard to be objective about him."

Miriam's eyes flashed and she leaned forward in a combative stance but did not answer the question.

"Miriam," the attorney prodded, "do you believe that Jacob killed Diana?"

"Never," she replied emphatically as she stood. "He would never hurt anyone!" She tried to stare down Melanie, a slight quaver in her voice. "Why are you here, anyway? Are you looking for evidence to convict him or are you trying to clear his name?"

"We're just looking for the truth."

"I just told you the truth." Miriam shook her head furiously and walked out the door.

Melanie saw the distress in the priest's face and thought that he might follow her, but he stayed put.

"Was that really necessary?" He sighed.

"All I did was ask her questions . . ." Melanie's response was right out of the lawyer playbook, but it sufficed to silence the rattled priest. "I take it this was news to you?"

"Yeah." He shook his head. "I don't know why she didn't tell me. I guess she thought that if she could track down her dad's contacts, we could track down Jacob." He groaned when he realized the implication of what he had said.

Melanie took pity and turned her attention from the priest to James. "How did the conversation with your boss go?"

"He said that Jacob asked permission to go to Geneva but wouldn't say much about the story. Jacob thought it was a huge scoop. He was convinced it would make his reputation."

"Geneva?" the priest interrupted. "As in Switzerland?"

James started to explain but Melanie held up her hand. "Father Carter, we're happy to share what we know. After all, you're in the middle of the church that supposedly shielded Jacob, but you need to promise not to speak to Miriam about anything we tell you. We can keep you in the loop, but only on that condition."

He ran his hand through his hair and frowned, then he got up and shut the door that Miriam had left open. "You know," he said slowly, "I'd just as soon forget about the whole thing, but I'd like to help if I can. Last week I asked Sheriff Johnson about the investigation and he came this close to threatening me." He pinched his right thumb and forefinger together. "I don't think that James is paranoid about a cover-up, and I don't believe that the theft of Father Rodgers's papers was some kind of crazy coincidence." He sat back down. "You can count me in."

"And no word to Miriam?" Melanie insisted.

He thought for a moment and nodded. "For now, but I think you're overreacting."

"Maybe," James interjected. "But remember the sermon that I found, the one Ernest Rodgers preached about Granville's innocence? Written in the margin next to his conclusion was 'Miriam.' I thought the reference might be to Moses's sister, but now I think he might have been relying on information about Jacob from his daughter." He made a deferential gesture to the priest, "I don't think she's done anything wrong, but I really wonder if she can be objective."

Thor nodded. Melanie watched him carefully, and he seemed to understand the need for discretion.

"Right," she turned her attention to the reporter, "what else did your boss have to say?"

"Not much . . . He just emphasized how hot Jacob was for this story."

Melanie looked back to Thor. "To fill you in: The week before Jacob and Diana disappeared, he flew to Geneva to meet someone about a story involving a World Trade Organization investigation of US cotton subsidies. We found a picture he took there of two girls in front of the WTO building. We thought the timing was interesting, so we've been following up."

She smiled broadly and took a folder out of her satchel. "And now let me show you both what I've been up to." She sorted through the folder while she spoke, first detailing her conversation with Diana's mother and then her exploration of Granville's Facebook page. She passed out two copies of his most comprehensive posts about the cotton case and waited for them to read before passing around the new picture of Brenda, "The Cotton Queen," alongside her friend Elisa.

She handed a paper to Thor. "And here's a copy of the photo of them we found in the newspaper archive."

Thor studied both photos and then Granville's posts on the cotton case. "Murder is a strong word to use to describe US agricultural policy."

"Maybe," James answered, "but it's kind of shocking that Congress wants to give $18 billion to corporate farmers so that they can produce a crop that's only worth $11 billion.

Jacob was onto a good story, for sure, but everything about the subsidies and the case itself is out in the public. It's hard to see why he needed to go to Geneva to talk to Brenda." He turned and smiled at Melanie. "Do you know how the case came out?"

Her face must have shown her embarrassment because his smile broadened in response, the little crinkles around the corner of his eyes teasing her failure to check. "No," she confessed, "I never bothered to look."

"Well," he explained in a more serious voice, "we lost. The developing world took on the US at the WTO and beat us soundly."

"That's a surprise," Thor interjected.

"Maybe, but the summary of the panel report makes the decision sound like a no-brainer, like Congress must have known it was violating the subsidy rules. But here's the big thing: We've never complied with the ruling. Congress refuses to stop writing the checks."

"What?" Melanie was stunned. The US actively promoted the WTO and had been essential to its formation. In order to convince other member states to play by the international economic rules that it often wrote, the US government had to set a good example. Failing to comply was a dangerous strategy.

"Yup, someone's got some serious clout. Congress keeps the money flowing, while the WTO is set to allow the winners in the case to hit several US industries with serious trade sanctions in retaliation." He shook his head and for a moment lost his journalistic detachment. Melanie thought the sudden burst of passion suited him. "It's a lose-lose for us. We keep pissing away our taxes on the subsidies while our manufacturing sector will get slammed with a round of new tariffs."

"Someone's got some clout," Melanie repeated.

"And no conscience," added the priest quietly.

The three sat in silence. Sunshine streamed through the windows of the study, making the room a little stuffy, so Thor cracked open the leaded-glass casement to let in some air. The breeze that blew in was warmer than the room. Summer had finally arrived in Clarkeston.

"I'd love to have a word with Brenda," James said contemplatively. "Just to have some clue what was driving Jacob. He wasn't stupid. He wouldn't have gone to Geneva without a good reason."

"Well," Melanie replied, to the reporter's surprise, "I tried to call her yesterday, but she apparently no longer works at the WTO." She detailed her search through the organization's website and her successful discovery of Elisa van der Vaart. She also disclosed to the reporter for the first time that the search for the origin of the photos had officially gone nowhere. "But Brenda's friend will be back in her office tomorrow."

"Are you going to call her?" James asked, with a glance at the photo in his lap.

"I'm not sure. If there is something hush-hush going on, then I don't want her to warn Brenda." She laughed. "God, I sound like an international spy." Mostly, she hated interviewing people over the phone. Any sort of delicate communication was always better conducted face to face. She didn't want to ask the wrong question and be punished with the click of disconnection on the other end of the line.

"As a former colleague of Jacob's, I could call and say that I'm following up on his story or something."

"No." Suddenly, she had the answer. "Not yet, anyway. I've got a better idea."

XXV

PRINCIPALITIES

"Geneva?" Stanley was surprised by Melanie's request that he go to Switzerland and pay a visit to the World Trade Organization, but the more he thought about it, the more he warmed to the idea. He loved the thought of mountains, and his brief affair with Vanessa was winding down. Her ex-husband had arrived with their kids, and the chance to spend time together had seriously diminished. And although under Reggie's tutelage his darting skills were rapidly improving, the sport was a poor reason to turn down a persuasive voice asking for an exotic favor.

Melanie explained her desire to make contact with Elisa van der Vaart and trace the whereabouts of her friend Brenda Harvey. "I checked on Travelocity, and it looks like there are some cheap flights from Palma to Geneva. From what you've told me about your sociological work, interviewing people is a big part of your job, right?"

Almost all of Stanley's academic research had been conducted in the field. In fact, his role in solving the murder of the infamous porn star Jade Delilah had been a direct outgrowth of his professional interrogations. Flying to Geneva to ask a few questions and then heading up into the Alps for some hiking sounded like a good excuse to prolong his European vacation and work off the remainder of his doughnut flab. "Sure," he replied, "tell me what you want."

The attorney filled him in on the details of the cotton case and on Jacob Granville's trip to Geneva five years earlier. She sent him links to the WTO panel report in the case, scanned the two pictures of Brenda and Elisa, and provided him with Van Der Vaart's contact information at the WTO. He booked a flight for the next day.

Although he asked Vanessa out for a final meal at El Langustino, her ex-husband had left the children with her for the evening, and Stanley had to be satisfied with drinks on the patio while her teenage boys roamed around complaining about the intermittent Wi-Fi access. After an hour or so, she walked him to the door, and they had a moment to themselves.

"Vanessa, I can't possibly tell you what a wonderful time I've had." Knowing that an emotional acknowledgment of the healing nature of her affection would be awkward, he hoped a broad smile and warm, lingering kiss would convey his depth of feeling.

"Me, too," she said, standing close and stroking his cheek briefly. "I know you've got no plans to come to England, but I'd love to see you again whenever you do. Please come by." She pressed his hand tightly and then turned back into the villa.

The brief affirmation sufficed. He departed feeling appreciated and desired and all without the pang of guilt that often comes with the final parting from a lover.

★ ★ ★

Stanley sat in the Palma de Mallorca airport and studied the documents that Melanie had sent him, working on a plan to elicit the information she needed. He eventually decided to pay Elisa a visit in person rather than make initial contact by phone or email. His main objective was to find her friend, and she might well hesitate to provide contact information to an unknown man over the phone.

He arrived in Geneva on a Tuesday morning and took the train from the airport to the city center. The area around the train station was a weird combination of middle-class and seedy. The buildings were modern and clean, consistent with anyone's assumptions about Swiss orderliness, but the human element muddied the scene. Prostitutes in impossibly high heels made no attempt to disguise their business plans as they swished past clumps of well-dressed men (Eastern European? Middle Eastern?) who hung around the doors of darkened clubs. Stanley felt no danger as he crossed through the neighborhood, down toward the lake and his hotel, but it was an uncomfortable stroll as he deflected the glances of people who thought he might have come looking for women or dope.

He eventually found his hotel, at a busy intersection close to the lakeside path that would take him to the headquarters of the World Trade Organization. His room was a bit noisy, but the lively bustle beneath his window was energizing and spurred him to take a quick shower and then head directly to the WTO to find Elisa.

After a quick detour to a patisserie across the street from his hotel, he strode contentedly to the lakeshore, croissant and coffee in hand. Realizing he had no reason to hurry, he sat down on a shaded park bench and alternated flakey bites of pastry and strong, perfectly bitter espresso. The famous water jet danced merrily in the steady breeze, and to its right he could just make out where the old city lay. He had been to Geneva once before and planned to make a visit to the small medieval center of town that stood in such stark contrast to the shiny towers of inter-governmental bureaucracy that dominated the skyline. He knew of a tiny wooden tavern where he could buy Calvinus beer on tap, a memorable and tasty slap in the face of the dour Protestant leader, who would no doubt be horrified by the commerce being done under his name.

When he finished, he took a tree-lined route along the shore to a walkway that curved away from the lake and around to the front of the four-story stone headquarters of the WTO. As he wandered up a flagstone path past beds of recently planted flowers, he was surprised by the informality of the place and the lack of security. No guards holding Uzis patrolled the grounds, no checkpoint with scowling soldiers barred his path. It didn't look like the secret headquarters from which the Trilateral Commission controlled world governments.

Stanley approached a smiling staff member at the reception desk and asked for Elisa van der Vaart of the Intellectual Property Division. The woman nodded, rang a number, spoke briefly for a moment, and then asked his name. In response, he handed her his business card, identifying himself as a professor at Belle Meade College in California. This seemed to satisfy her, and she asked the sociologist to sit down while he waited for Ms. van der Vaart.

He recognized the young woman immediately as she popped through a pair of glass doors on the right side of the lobby. She looked to be in her late twenties, and the blond hair that had hung in her face in both of Melanie's pictures was tied back in a neat bun. She was not conventionally pretty, but she had a slim, athletic build and striking blue eyes. The look on her face when she spotted him was hard to pin down. Friendly, but not quite smiling, and clearly intelligent. Maybe talking over dinner would be a good idea.

He stood up and held out his hand. Her grip was firm and dry. "Hi. I'm Stan Hopkins. I teach sociology at Belle Meade College in Claremont, California, and I was hoping that you might have a few moments to talk to me."

She gave him a curious look and led him to a modern cube-like couch in a corner of the lobby. "Are you doing research on intellectual property?" she asked. "I've been talking to an anthropologist for over a year now about protection for traditional medicine, so I suppose it was only a matter of time before the sociologists showed up too."

Her playful introduction was as surprising as the flowers in the building's front lawn and the congenial receptionist. He wondered whether there was an international angle worth pursuing in his research on labor unions. "No, I don't have any academic interest in the WTO right now, although I have to say that this place is really interesting."

He pulled out a folded photo from the vest pocket of his jacket and handed it to her. "I was hoping that you could help put me in contact with Brenda Harvey. She used to work in the Subsidies and Countervailing Duties Working Group."

Stanley watched her face turn as white as the paper. "You seem to be friends in the picture."

Her eyes welled up with tears and her voice thickened. "She was my friend and my roommate." She pushed the paper back to the professor. "She died five years ago." Her eyes narrowed. "You did not know this?"

Stanley did not have to fake surprise or empathy. The date of her death set off alarm bells, and the young woman before him was clearly in pain. "I'm so sorry. I had no idea." He folded up the paper and gestured weakly with it. "I never would have shoved this in your face if I knew."

She nodded. "Where did you get the picture?"

He wondered where to begin and settled on an abbreviated version of the facts that would be most likely to keep her engaged. "I'm helping the US Department of Justice investigate the abduction and possible murder of a woman in Clarkeston, Georgia. We think that a man named Jacob Granville might have killed her and gone into hiding. We found two pictures of you and Brenda among his things: one in some old files and the other on his Facebook page."

Elisa looked around the lobby. Several groups of people were waiting for appointments or chatting in the bright, open space. She nodded her head and eyed him fiercely, as if she were scrutinizing his DNA with the intensity of her gaze. "Let's talk someplace else," she said. "I think that Jacob might have killed Brenda."

★ ★ ★

When Stanley had suggested that they meet for dinner and encouraged her to think big, since he was picking up the check, she had chosen a quiet restaurant tucked down an alley on the edge of the old city. Their table was snug and private, and it was no surprise when she revealed that they were in the oldest timbered building in Geneva. The pair talked easily as they sipped their wine and waited for appetizers to arrive. Stanley began with small talk, not wanting to jump straight to what might be a traumatic conversation about Elisa's dead friend. They had enough in common that it was almost an hour before Stanley filled her glass with a crisp Côtes du Rhone and finally asked her about Brenda and why she was suspicious of Jacob Granville.

"Jacob came here to visit Brenda, and the day after he left, I found her in her bedroom." She was in firm control of her emotions now, her voice calm and analytical. "It looked like a drug overdose, but I knew that Brenda never did anything other than smoke some marijuana, and the police agreed that the circumstances of her death were troubling. The case is still open, as far as I know, but it's labeled something that would translate as 'suspicious misadventure' or something like that."

"What made you suspect Granville?" He refilled his own glass and took a sip. "And did you say anything about him to the police?"

"For sure! I always thought he was a creep. I knew he had a girlfriend in Georgia that he never told Brenda about, and he propositioned me twice." She spoke emphatically and with the merest trace of an accent that he heard most clearly and charmingly when she tried to wrap her mouth around the word *Georgia*. "He was a dog. I think that's the right word."

"That doesn't make him a killer."

"No," she conceded, "but you must understand, Brenda was gorgeous and she was his lover, yet when she leaves for work he tries to seduce me?" She shook her head and held her palms upward. "Come on! Why would he come at me?"

He began his protest before finding appropriate words. "Well, I'd certainly make a pass at you!"

Her eyes widened and eyebrows rose.

"Wait! That didn't come out right!" He waved his hand and then saw that she was enjoying the misunderstanding. "I mean: don't be so modest. It just means he's a shit and not necessarily a murderer."

"Did you ever meet him?"

"No."

"Unless you're a woman," she sighed, "it's hard to understand how some guys have this negative aura. He was too sure of himself. He felt entitled to anything he wanted. He liked to be in control." She smoothed the napkin on her lap and put her hand over her glass when the waiter tried to refill it. "I don't know. He just lacked sympathy for women. He broke Brenda's heart when he left, but she was determined to follow him to America."

Stanley nodded. "And that would have caused problems with the other girlfriend."

"It gave him a motive," she explained, punching the air with her words. "Get rid of the clinging girl who makes your life so complicated. It wouldn't be the first time. Men have killed for much less."

"They have," Stanley was forced to admit. He could see no doubt in her eyes; she really believed that Granville had killed her friend. "What did the police say when you told them your theory?"

She shrugged. "They are Swiss. They wrote it all down and promised to investigate. I heard several weeks later that he had disappeared and the trail was cold."

Stanley had no problem imagining a hypothetical world where Jacob Granville solved his problems with women by killing them, but the manner of death—a fake drug overdose—didn't seem violent enough for someone who was supposedly so misogynistic. The professor had also read Granville's posts about the cotton case. The reporter's commitment to a serious human-rights issue also seemed inconsistent with his being a serial killer.

"Did Brenda tell you why he made his last visit to Geneva?"

For the first time, Elisa looked reticent. "She was helping him with a story that he was writing."

"About the cotton case?"

She looked surprised. "Yes. She was helping the panel with research into the economics of the world cotton market." She frowned. "That was how she got him to come. She was heartsick, and she told him that she had secret information that she could only reveal in person. Phone and email were too dangerous, she said." She paused while the waiter finished pouring more water. "She was really in love with him."

"That would provide another motive," Stanley reasoned. "He finds out he's been duped by her into coming and gets really angry."

She nodded her head and concentrated on the filet of sole that had just been placed before her. He encouraged her to start and grabbed a piece of bread. He had interviewed enough people to know when he was not getting the whole story, and he sensed that she was holding something back. He also knew that pushing too hard sometimes drove valuable information down a deep hole from which it never emerged, so he changed the subject and asked her about her job in the IP Division.

She turned out to be a talker. Single well-worded questions elicited long, thoughtful, and enthusiastic responses on a variety of different topics, from the geopolitics of patent law to the best place for a single woman to live in Geneva. She had one thing in common with Granville. She saw the work of the WTO through a human-rights lens. Even obscure topics like international patent treaties were imbued with humanitarian considerations, and she had a passionate commitment to introducing rules that would reduce the price of patented pharmaceuticals in developing countries. Stanley liked women with strong opinions, but not every guy did. He wondered about her personal life. Was she alone with her commitments or was she adored by some nice young liberal man?

The evening passed quickly and pleasantly. When she finally slowed down, rather embarrassed that she had spoken so much, she managed to draw him out about his family and seemed genuinely fascinated by the long trail of evidence that had dead-ended in Mallorca. She seemed especially amused by his encounter with Reggie, the mad dart-throwing nudist. He finished his tale with Melanie's request that he come to Geneva.

"So, you came all this way because of a picture of Brenda and me?" She shook her head in amazement.

"Not every bit of evidence we have points to Granville. We really wanted to know what was so important about Brenda's story that he had to come to Geneva. The timing of the trip in relation to his disappearance is striking." He finished the bottle of wine with equal pours into their glasses. "I still don't understand what she must have said to him."

Elisa bit her lower lip and frowned. She reached out and touched the top of his right hand as it rested on the table. "Please forgive me for not saying anything before, but I wasn't sure if I should trust you." She looked embarrassed and spoke with her head slightly bowed. "I do know what Brenda said. She desperately wanted to see Jacob, but she also did have a big story for him. Someone tried to bribe the panel of arbitrators in the cotton case. She wouldn't give me all the details, but someone offered her a lot of money to approach one of the panelists with a bribe."

"Did she say who?"

"No, but she said it was a North American, that he wanted the panel to rule in favor of the US."

Stanley tried to digest her story. Here was a compelling reason for Granville to travel to Europe. Corporate farmers had convinced Congress to hand out billions in cash, and one of the beneficiaries wanted to bribe the WTO to maintain the status quo. Who had the most to lose if the WTO ruled against the US and threatened the stream of cotton subsidies? It would not be hard to write a sensational story starring corrupt businessmen willing to go to any length to fleece American taxpayers and screw poor African farmers. The story had *Pulitzer* written all over it.

He muttered *shit* and felt a sudden chill. And what would the bad guys do if they learned that Brenda was talking to the press?

"Do you know anything else?" he asked. "Did she report the bribe to her boss or anything like that?"

"I told her to," Elisa said in frustration, "I told her to go right away, but she wanted to get some proof to give to Jacob. Get a picture of the guy or a recording or an email, something she could give to him for his story. If she told her boss right away, he would just take her off the case and that would be it. If Jacob had not decided to come, I'm sure she would have reported the attempted bribe."

"Do you know whether she eventually did?"

"No. I think she was going to, but then Jacob broke up with her and she was so upset that all she wanted to talk about was him and how to get to the States to see him. He was all she talked about the day before she died." She shook her head angrily. "What a waste."

"Did you ever tell anyone about the bribe?"

"I was really upset, but before I said anything, the panel ruled against the US, so there didn't seem to be any point. I certainly had no proof either."

"And you never saw any connection between the bribe and her death?"

She leaned forward in her chair. "No. Why?" She crossed her arms and leaned back. "Jacob killed her."

"Maybe," he spoke slowly, "but if you had Congress writing you checks for billions of dollars every year and if you were willing to starve African peasants to keep the money rolling in, wouldn't you go to extreme lengths to prevent the world from knowing that you were trying to bribe the World Trade Organization?"

"Oh my God." She put her hand to her mouth and her eyes widened. "But you said Jacob killed his girlfriend in Georgia, too."

"What if he were murdered to kill the cotton-bribe story? What if his girlfriend was just collateral damage? Neither of them has ever been found."

"But we can't know," she said in a voice that was almost a whisper. "We don't know what happened."

He took her hand. "No, but we can try to find out."

* * *

The next day Elisa met him at her apartment in Annemasse. She had moved to a smaller flat than the one she shared with Brenda, but even with a raise she could not afford to move into Geneva proper. She made some tea and they sat on the sofa in front of the only window in the apartment. She felt a cool breeze and heard the faint hum of traffic drift over their conversation.

"I sat up all night trying to think of anything that Brenda might have told me about the cotton case or the bribe." She tucked a lock of hair behind her reading glasses. "It's been five years, and the only thing that I didn't tell you was that the bribery guy had an accent. She thought it might be Spanish. But that's all I remember. She really didn't want to get me involved."

He nodded and then smiled. "I don't suppose you have any of her passwords so that we could check old emails or anything like that? Any pictures of the bribery guy on her Facebook page?"

She liked this American. He had a sense of humor and a light touch with everything, unlike most of his fellow countrymen, who loudly bullied their way to what they wanted. She was glad that she had a surprise for him, an answer to some of his questions, maybe.

"Once when she was out of town her laptop crashed, and she called me to check her email on my computer. She had to tell me her password, which was Brenda, with an *8* instead of a *B*. Unfortunately, I made fun of her because I thought the password was too easy, and she must have changed it. When I tried to log on to her account last night, it failed."

"Nice try, though."

"Then I went through her stuff. After she died her parents came and collected most of her things. They left behind some books and papers and other little stuff. I went through it last night, but there is nothing interesting. I even flipped through the books to look for notes, but there was nothing."

"Crap." He leaned back on the sofa and stole a look out the window. He was six or seven years older than her, mid-thirties or so, darkly handsome and intelligent face, and like most Americans, a bit overweight. His best feature was, for lack of a better word, his karma. He wasn't trying; he was just doing, just being. The contrast to the humorless gray suits bustling around Geneva could not have been more pronounced.

She poured him some more tea. "I do have one thing. When I was cleaning up to move out of our old apartment, I found Brenda's cell phone wedged way down in the sofa."

"Didn't the police find it when they searched the apartment? Given how she died, they must have searched the place thoroughly for drugs."

"They did. They brought in the super-sniffing dogs and went all over the apartment, but the dogs found nothing, except the stuff left next to her." She put some milk in her tea and stirred. "This is why they believed me about Brenda. A real addict would leave traces all over the place."

"Do you still have the phone?"

She reached into her purse and pulled out a nondescript cell phone. "Take a look at the messaging history. I topped up the battery with my old charger and already read through it." She got up and looked for some cookies in the kitchen while he scrolled through the messages sent and received. She knew what he would find, evidence of a stupid plan inspired by watching too many spy movies.

A series of short messages between Jacob and Brenda revealed that she had set up a meeting in a café with "Gomez." Jacob was to discreetly snap pictures of the meeting and Brenda would carry a small recording device. The scheme was not spelled out plainly in their short bursts of communication, but Elisa thought that the plan was fairly clear and wanted to know if Stanley would come to the same conclusion without her prompting him. Most disturbing was Brenda's final text to Jacob, following a succession of pleas for him to return. It read simply, "They know!" There were no messages that were sent to Gomez or received from him.

When she heard Stanley set the phone down on the glass coffee table, she sat next to him and placed some shortbread next to the teapot.

"Your friend was very foolish," the professor said soberly.

"What do you think she did?" She listened to his interpretation of the messages and was not surprised to hear that he had the same idea: Brenda had set up a meeting and somehow she and Jacob were discovered. The mysterious Gomez was the person initiating the bribe and possibly the person who arranged for them to be killed.

"You and I are not going to be so foolish." He held up the phone. "Can I take this with me back to the States? I want to bring it to the US attorney in Atlanta who's running the investigation and tell her what we think happened. She'll know what to do, and she'll understand that we need to keep your name completely out of it. Right now, no one knows that you know anything. I think you're pretty safe, but she may have some ideas about how to track down Gomez or at least figure out who he works for."

She nodded. If anyone suspected her, she would have met Brenda's fate long ago, but it was nice to see the concern in his eyes. He wanted both to protect her and to find out who killed her friend. "You can keep the phone," she said.

"Thank you," he said. Then, for the first time, a hint of awkwardness entered his voice. "And would you mind if I come back to visit you when this is over?"

She blushed and poured him another cup of tea.

XXVI

NUMBERS

Melanie offered to pick up the Professor Hopkins at the new international terminal of Hartsfield Airport in Atlanta. He was due to arrive in the early evening, and she had time to finish the day's work and then grab a cup of coffee while she waited for him to clear customs. She had considered inviting James Murphy to meet with them, but Stanley Hopkins had been her agent, and given the fact that she had never even met the man, she wanted to question him first in private. The sociologist had been rather cagey on the phone when he called from Geneva, hinting that he had a long and complicated story to tell. Although she had come to trust James implicitly, her genes themselves protested at the thought of inviting a journalist to a debriefing that could head in any number of sensitive directions. So, she stood alone by the baggage carousel, looking for a traveler whose face matched the darkly handsome picture of Hopkins she had found on the Belle Meade College website.

After a fifteen-minute wait, she saw him round the corner into the baggage-claim area, just as the first suitcases spewed from the bowels of the carousel. She studied him for a second, forgetting to wave and mark her presence. His hair had a bit more curl than the picture showed, and his face was more boyish. He carried a bit more weight than he needed to, but he still moved like an athlete. After a quick scan of the room, he began walking toward her.

"Ms. Wilkerson?"

"How did you know?"

He extended his hand with a cryptic smile. "Your suit matches your voice."

What the hell did a $500 Armani voice sound like? She didn't exactly know but figured it had to be a compliment. "Okay. Why don't I take you to the hotel and let you get settled while I wait in the bar?"

She dropped Hopkins off in front of the downtown Sheraton and then circled back to park in the hotel garage. She was finishing a large but undistinguished margarita when he appeared, clean shaven and hair wet, eyes sparkling despite the travel fatigue he must have felt. He flagged down the first waiter who passed by, ordered a Sierra Nevada, and immediately jumped into the story of his extraordinary trips to Mallorca and Geneva. She sat in fascinated silence, unwilling to interrupt until he ended his tale with speculation that Granville and the English girl in Geneva had been discovered in their attempt to document the cotton-case bribery plot.

"So, you don't think that Jacob murdered Diana?" She resisted reconceiving the prime suspect as possible victim.

"No, I don't." He licked a bit of foam off of his upper lip. "It's possible that he's some kind of super crafty serial killer, but I doubt it. He doesn't really fit the profile. He was a serial cheater, for sure, but I think he and Brenda just got in over their heads. I'd say they got burned and that Diana Cavendish was just collateral damage."

Melanie nodded, still struggling to fit all the facts to his theory. "Okay, but the reporter who brought the story to me in the first place says that the local police or the FBI or both tried to cover Granville's tracks." She filled the professor in on the history of obstruction Murphy had encountered investigating the disappearance. "Why have a conspiracy to protect someone that's dead?"

The prosecutor watched as Stanley processed the information. He leaned back in his chair and bit his lip. "How would the cops or the FBI know that he was dead?"

It was a simple question, but a good one. If Ernest Rodgers and Sheriff Johnson knew that Jacob was dead, they would not have wasted their time slowing down the pursuit of him.

"Granville's friends," he continued, "may well have thought him alive and falsely accused. If they were sure he wasn't the murderous type—and he probably wasn't—then they might have thought they were helping him, not knowing that he was beyond their aid."

"Of course, we don't know for sure that he's dead."

"Fair enough," the professor conceded as he signaled for another drink.

"But what you say makes sense. If he wasn't a killer, then their willingness to obstruct the investigation fits a little better."

"If they obstructed at all," Stanley replied.

"The locals all knew him from childhood."

He shrugged, "I suppose." He put a big dent in his beer and yawned. "So, what next? We've identified a mysterious bribery guy who may have killed Brenda, Jacob, and Diana, or had them killed to protect some cotton-rich client, but that trail is stone cold." He pulled Brenda's cell phone out of his pocket and handed it to Melanie. "I brought you Brenda's phone so that you can read the text messages between her and Jacob. I think you'll agree with me about what likely happened to them."

"Could you hang around for a day or so?" She swiped her smart phone and checked her calendar. "I'm gonna want to talk to you again after I have the techies look at the phone." She put it in her purse. "They might be able to pull some more data up. And it'd also be nice if you could give me something written, sort of an official narrative of your travels."

"Sure," he said, "but I wonder if Lonely Planet would approve of my porn-and-murder itinerary." He stood up with a broad smile and helped her out of her chair.

She felt a sudden urge to give him a hug. "Thank you for everything," she said as she took his hand. "I can't believe you've done all this for nothing. It must have cost a fortune!"

"It wasn't for nothing, and I've got more money than I know what to do with. Trust me, I really needed to get out of California, and this is the most fun I've had in a long time." He gave her hand a squeeze. "And hanging around is no problem. I'm going to visit my late wife's folks in Roswell and then go over to Athens for a few days to hang out with a former colleague of mine. I'll write your report and spend a day in the University of Georgia library satisfying my curiosity about the cotton case. Some researcher must have written something intelligent about it by now."

★ ★ ★

That night, Melanie read and reread the text messages between Jacob and Brenda, and although they were cryptic and fragmentary, she agreed with Stanley's analysis of the situation. The next day at work, she brought the device down to the basement lair of the Department of Justice tech department, but they found nothing more of interest in the phone, apart from a list of calls made and received, all of which were to numbers in the EU or Switzerland. When she asked whether they could be traced, Hans shook his head. Privacy rules were stronger there, he explained, and from his own bitter experience, he was sure that only Interpol would have any hope of getting the cooperation of the phone companies.

Melanie mulled the situation over as she made her way back to her office. She sat down and put her feet on the window ledge. The early summer heat was rising off the parking lot and an office block in the distance shimmered in the sodden air. She would not be tempted to open her windows again until late September. So, what now? As the professor had concluded, the trail was five years old and maybe it was time to move on.

But not all the crimes were five years old. The past had reached out at least once during the investigation, and maybe it was time to coax it out again and whack it with a ruler. When she gave James's name to the woman in Arkansas, his home was burglarized the very next day. And when she queried the FBI through Sammy Goodson, he refused to provide any information and warned her strongly off the case. The trail from these incidents was not five years old, and considering what she had learned in the last several weeks, she decided to give Sammy another call. She left a message on his voice mail and told him to call her back in the evening.

★ ★ ★

She was sitting at home watching *The Voice* and checking her email when she heard wind chimes tinkling on her cell phone.

"Hey, babe," Sammy whispered in his best seductive voice, "are you in town?" Only Sammy Goodson could interpret her picking up the phone and saying hello as some sort of intricate come-on.

"No," she said firmly, "I've just called to confess that I've been bad."

"Ooh!" he exclaimed, "then tell me what you're wearing."

"No, you idiot. Do you remember our dinner in Atlanta?"

"How could I forget? You had those new black boots on—"

She interrupted his fantasy before he asked her to start talking dirty. "I asked you about an Arkansas phone number and some nameless drone over your head warned me to back off."

"Yeah," he replied guardedly. The reminder had the desired cold-water effect on his libido. "I remember."

"Well, I didn't take his advice or yours." She could hear him breathe out heavily on the other end of the line. "To make a very long story short, I called that number because a notation in an FBI file stated that all inquiries about a guy named Jacob Granville should be directed there. I told the woman who answered about the reporter who had come to me asking about Granville, and two days later his house was broken into and some important papers stolen. Now, I've dug up quite a bit of shit on

Granville, and I need to know who else is still so interested in his case."

"You think that the bureau broke into this reporter's house?" he sputtered. "Are you a lunatic?"

"No! I've worked with the FBI long enough to know you're not thugs. I'm not attacking the bureau." It was true. The break-in at Murphy's house did not smell like the FBI. "But you guys do share information with people outside the bureau. In fact, on occasion the law requires you to do it, and who knows how that information might be used or by whom."

"So what's you point, Mel?"

"I need the source of that number."

"Are you on crack? As it is, I'm going to have to report you just for asking." He could barely contain his exasperation.

"Come on, Sammy! Grow a fucking pair! You don't have to tell anybody anything. Just do a little routine snooping around in your databases and find out for me who owned that number."

Silence. She could hear the wheels turning even though her former lover was almost a thousand miles away. "What do I get in return?"

"What do you get? You get the assurance that you're not a dick." She tempered her approach. "You get to be on the side of justice and help out the good guys."

"No, no, no . . ." He paused a moment more and then she heard a sound that closely approximated a cackle. "I want to fuck you one more time."

"What?"

"You heard me."

"You're serious!"

"Absolutely. Dead serious." He laughed. "No nookie, no number."

She considered his repulsive offer. She'd rather sleep with a urine-soaked bum in a New York alley, but there was no other choice, not if she really wanted to know what was behind the death of Diana Cavendish. She sighed and tried to remember a younger, more attractive version of her blackmailer. "Yeah, I'll fuck you."

★ ★ ★

Stanley had fun in Athens. His friend Kirk had moved there from Illinois at the same time as his own move to California, but whereas Stanley had been fleeing a denial of tenure, his friend had moved away to take a prestigious endowed chair. Stanley closeted himself deep in the University of Georgia library, using his friend's password to access electronic resources during the day and then sampling his home-brewed IPA in the evenings. Kirk insisted on putting him up in his large and comfortable spare bedroom. He and his wife, Erica, had known Angela well, and for the first time since the accident Stanley found himself able to have a prolonged conversation about her. It hurt, but it wasn't paralyzing.

Until Erica asked where he had laid her to rest.

He couldn't very well answer, "The laundry room," could he? So he changed the subject and then went back to the bedroom to think, but no solution to the problem magically appeared.

The next day, his reading in the library diverted him from his personal situation. He looked first in law journals for an explanation of the legal rationale for the WTO decision that US cotton subsidies were illegal. Interestingly, the WTO panel held that the US had violated its own express commitments to reduce a certain sort of agricultural payment. The US had simply not lived up to its own promises. The articles did a good job of translating the technical aspects of the panel's decision into plain English, and he was left with the sense that the case had been pretty straightforward, but for its political implications. Several articles had been written after Congress had refused to comply with the decision. These were more interesting and focused on the huge risks the US was taking by refusing to bend. Not only was it undermining an international institution that the US frequently relied upon, but the threat of

WTO-approved economic retaliation against US industry was very real, if not inevitable.

The law articles sent him scurrying to the political science and international relations literature. These were the folks who thought hard about the realpolitik behind the decisions of international actors, at least so his colleagues in those departments at BFU and Belle Meade claimed. After skimming a couple of theoretical pieces that opined about noncompliance generally, he found two long articles arguing that cotton subsidies were a key to understanding US foreign policy. He found the conclusions about US trade doctrine to be facile, but he was fascinated by the in-depth factual analysis of how the cotton subsidies came to be and why they were sustained.

Just as Bill Clinton's sheep-herding friend, senator Max Baucus of Montana, seemed to dictate US policy on lamb production, senator Elbert Randolph of Arkansas seemed to play the same role for cotton. The son of a wealthy cotton grower, he had pushed for higher subsidies from the moment he was elected, and now, as the head of the powerful Senate Agriculture Committee, he controlled regulation of the commodity. Senate rules allowed him to single-handedly block any legislation related to cotton that he disapproved of. He was supported, of course, by any number of industry lobbying groups, all of which heavily funded his Senate campaigns. Interestingly, he had come under fire as frequently from environmental groups as from human-rights groups. Cotton was by far the most pesticide- and fertilizer-intensive crop grown in the US, and the environmental damage caused by cotton farming was apparently enormous. Randolph shrugged off all criticism.

The senator had divested all his farm holdings shortly after being named to the Senate Agriculture Committee, but his connections, both familial and social, to the small coterie of Texas and Arkansas cotton millionaires were incestuously tight.

What the popular press had to say about the senator was also illuminating. Apart from the occasional environmental rant, newspaper stories were generally positive. The American people cared little about issues surrounding subsidies. In fact, the Farm Aid movement had even glorified them as necessary to save the family farm. No one seemed to have noticed that the vast majority of cotton benefits went to wealthy corporate farmers. Liberals cared more about issues like civil rights, and the senator's positions on race and literacy were admired by many in the press, as was his support of a recent campaign to address childhood obesity in Arkansas. He had been one of Ted Kennedy's best friends before the senator from Massachusetts passed away.

He seemed like a nice guy. Unless you were a struggling cotton farmer in Mali watching your family starve.

Although there was no reason to believe that Randolph himself was behind the attempt to bribe the WTO, the stories painted a vivid picture of an industry that could not survive without massive injections of money from Congress. Granville had accused the millionaire supplicants of killing African farmers. Might not one of them have been willing to kill more locally to maintain his status? Certainly the environmental press accused them of killing the sensitive ecology of various river deltas.

Stanley spent the rest of the afternoon delving into the environmental literature that demonized Randolph. He had never responded directly to criticism, but organic farmers had made claims of harassment against two of Randolph's best friends, massive cotton growers Howard Stewart and Jamie "Weevil" Bulmer. News stories described allegations that Stewart and Bulmer had engineered successful counter-demonstrations against environmentalists who "wanted to destroy the family farm." When an office was set up in Little Rock by a green activist group, it was firebombed. Statements from an Arkansas cotton trade group about the bombing bordered on cheerleading.

Stanley delved yet deeper and found no shortage of farmers and lobbyists willing to go to extremes to keep cotton alive and well in Arkansas. The most incongruous player of all was the Mexican government, which strongly supported all of Senator Randolph's initiatives. A large percentage of the US cotton crop went straight to maquiladoras on the Mexico-US border that manufactured clothing to sell back to the US market. Without the cheap US cotton, Mexico had little chance of competing with Asian fabric dynamos. The senator was photographed smiling broadly with factory owners and the Mexican ambassador to the US after they all had testified before Congress about the win-win situation cotton subsidies presented for the two neighboring countries. Here, labor groups, rather than environmentalists, took aim at the senator for implicitly approving of the horrific working conditions in the factories just south of the border.

After the dozenth article, Stanley had had enough. He was depressed and his curiosity was satisfied. He blinked and sneezed hard as he emerged from the library into the bright sunshine of the campus's main quadrangle. He sighed. Education was clearly not the answer to all human problems. His research expedition had just provided an excuse to ignore Erica's question about Angela. God, he dreaded going back to California.

★ ★ ★

While Stanley read in the library, Melanie conducted a review of all cases currently heading for trial under her direction. She had been distracted for several weeks now, and she called a parade of attorneys into her office, demanded memos, and generally terrorized the young prosecutors while she waited for Sammy to call her back. With the exception of a botched response to an evidentiary request made by a counterfeiter of DVDs, she expressed satisfaction with the efficiency of her department. She was scanning her case log when her cell phone rang.

"Hey, Gorgeous!" The enthusiastic chirp of Sammy Goodson's voice was unmistakable. What had she ever seen in this guy? He was handsome, quite intelligent in his own way, and a surprisingly attentive lover, given his other shortcomings, but he really was as shallow as a kiddie plastic wading pool. Their jobs in Washington had kept them so busy and their lives so separate that his character flaws never seemed too horribly relevant until her thirties were a thing of the past. "I've just bought tickets to come to Atlanta!"

"Lucky me." She didn't even try to hide her lack of enthusiasm.

"Hey," he replied, an edge to his voice, "you're not having second thoughts about our deal, are you?"

"Well," she said, "it depends on what you have for me. Who did that Arkansas number belong to?"

He hesitated for a moment. "You've got to promise me first that you're not going to do anything stupid with the information . . . you need to just let things be."

"Just spit it out, Sammy."

"All right," he sighed, "it belonged to someone in the federal building in Little Rock that houses members of Congress and their staffs. I can't tell you any more than that, because there's been dozens of numbers associated with that building over the years. They are all landlines and they all move around. The records only provide the building address, not any particular office."

Melanie digested the information and regretted the bargain that she had struck with her ex-lover. "Thanks, Sammy. I appreciate the information. You're right, there's not a whole lot that I can do with that."

"Now," he replied in the smokiest voice that he could muster, "please tell me that you'll be around next weekend."

"Oh, I'll be around," she said cooly, "but you don't need to bother coming."

"What! You promised you'd fuck me!"

"Yeah, that's true," she said before she hung up. "Consider yourself fucked."

XXVII.

FLIGHT

Stanley drove past Melanie's townhouse and admired the perfectly manicured landscaping and the wisteria-covered arbor that connected the garage to her home. She had asked him to come over for a final debriefing around seven o'clock in the evening, and he was surprised that she was paranoid enough to avoid her office or any other downtown venue where they might be recognized. He regretted not seeing her in action in her office. His favorite part of law school had been the criminal law clinic, and he had often wondered what life would have been like if he had chosen her path rather than bailing out and going to graduate school. Nonetheless, the law kept coaxing him out of the ivory tower. His role in solving Jade Delilah's murder two years earlier had led to a number of productive collaborations with various police departments, and now he was considering turning his scholarly attention to the complex sociology of law enforcement.

The traffic coming into Atlanta from Athens had been mercifully light, and he arrived in Melanie's neighborhood forty-five minutes early. He found a parking space across from her townhouse and pulled out his smart phone to check his email and kill some time until the appropriate moment to knock on her door.

The street was a quiet cul-de-sac, and as he finished with his messages and looked up, he noticed a large red Chrysler driving very slowly past and then parking a hundred feet away on the far side of Melanie's residence. After waiting for another car to pass, a bald man in an ill-fitting blue suit and running shoes walked up to her door and rang the bell.

The man stood, shifting his weight impatiently from foot to foot and eventually turning his back to the door to survey the empty street in the late afternoon haze. But for the sun's reflection on the professor's windshield, the visitor might have spotted him. As it was, oblivious to Stanley's presence, he walked slowly away from the entrance to her house and along the sidewalk before ducking into the narrow alleyway between home and garage. Stanley watched the gap closely for a moment but the thuggish caller failed to reappear. Something was definitely wrong. This guy was no meter reader or delivery man. The professor was getting out of his car and dialing Melanie when the garage door suddenly began to open. He sprinted to his right and looked for the intruder in the garage, but his view was almost immediately blocked by a dark BMW pulling into the driveway. The prosecutor was arriving home.

"Shit," he murmured, intuition telling him that she needed to flee, "answer your phone."

On the fourth ring, she picked up.

"This is Stanley," he said quickly. "Is that you in your car?"

"What?" She sounded confused. "Uh, yeah, I'm in my car."

"Then you need to back out of the driveway and get the fuck out of the neighborhood."

"Why?"

"Just do it!" he shouted. "I'll be right behind you. Stay on the phone and get out of there now."

She backed out of the driveway without further protest and accelerated down the street. He followed close behind as she exited the subdivision and headed toward a shopping center several blocks down the main artery that ran past her neighborhood.

"What's going on, Stanley?" Her voice was tinny in the cell connection. She shifted in her seat and glanced at him through her back window.

"Maybe nothing," he said, "if you were expecting a skeezy guy in a blue suit to ring the doorbell and then disappear behind your house."

He saw her wave to the left.

"Crap. Follow me into the parking lot."

They switched off their phones and stopped a moment later on the edge of a busy lot servicing a gigantic mall. Melanie slid into his car and thanked him for the warning. "Are we just being paranoid?"

"Maybe," he shrugged, "but are you in the mood to take a chance?"

She shook her head, pulled out her cell phone and called the police. She placed an anonymous report of a break-in currently in progress at the address of her townhouse. "Maybe it's the same guy who broke in to James's place." She thought for a moment and then continued. "I did just really piss off someone at the FBI."

She explained how the gambit with her ex-lover had gotten her the location of the elusive Arkansas phone number. He could not help but laugh at her brush-off of the horny FBI agent, but the seriousness of her predicament quickly sobered him up.

"You know, it could be worse than someone just ransacking your house." Stanley filled her in on what he had learned in the library. "You've been messing with some very powerful and well-connected people, and it's not just about money anymore. There's a string of bodies for somebody to worry about."

"I'm a US attorney." She frowned in disbelief. "Nobody's stupid enough to fuck with me."

"Are you sure about that?" He watched her closely. He could tell that she was not the type to scare easily, but events were escalating. "Tell me about the Arkansas number."

"It belonged to a phone somewhere in a congressional office building in Little Rock—no surprise, given what you've just told me about the politics of cotton. I'm guessing that the initial notation in the FBI file was just a courtesy to some politician.

The FBI is probably just an information conduit to people it doesn't suspect are the real bad guys." She shook her head and frowned. "Sammy probably ratted me out to his boss just to get me in trouble. He was pretty pissed, but given your description, it doesn't sound like the prowler back at my house is some FBI agent. We need to find the real bad guy in the information chain."

"Well," he said grimly, "I think he's currently lurking around in your backyard."

"Shit," she said suddenly. "James is on the radar screen too. I better give him a heads-up." She grabbed her phone, managed to get ahold of the reporter before the call went to voice mail, and explained the situation as quickly as she could. "We need to meet. Stanley's here, and we've got a lot to talk about." She nodded her head several times before finally swiping her finger across the face of her phone.

Stanley looked at her expectantly and was rewarded with a cryptic expression that approximated a smile. "My newspaper dude has seen too many spy movies, but I agree with him that there's no sense taking chances." She opened up the back of her phone and took out the battery. "He's worried about someone picking up our conversations or tracking us using the GPS on our phones. He said to meet at Secret Falls and to go silent before we left." She held up her disassembled device and Stanley pulled his apart in solidarity.

"I assume you know where Secret Falls is?"

"Yeah," she nodded with satisfaction, "and I guarantee you that no one else does."

★ ★ ★

James Murphy was working late, and after Melanie's call he decided not to find out what might be waiting for him at his house. He bolted from his office as soon as he had disabled his phone and walked quickly to his car, grateful that he had parked on a busy street in front of a popular diner. Remembering a story that his father had told him about escaping a carful of angry moonshiners he had surprised in the mountains, James drove through Clarkeston constantly checking for a tail in his rearview mirror as he covered the five miles to a police substation on the bypass. He drove deliberately, almost inviting pursuit, knowing that he could duck into the station and get help if necessary. By the time he passed the red-brick building surrounded by police cruisers, he was certain that no one had followed him to the edge of town.

He decided to drive immediately to the North Carolina mountains and the hidden waterfall that he had visited with Melanie the weekend they interviewed Diana's father. He hoped she remembered how to get there, for on the spur of the moment he had been unable to think of another place he could reference that would mean something to her but not to anyone else who might be listening. If he drove straight to the Forest Service road, he would arrive at the little parking area before her and wait there without actually having to navigate the trail to the falls in the dark.

James drove in silence and speculated about how much danger they might be in. He knew that Melanie's friend had arrived from Geneva, and he wondered whether that trip had somehow set back in action the dark forces behind the disappearance of Jacob and Diana. In any event, whoever was stalking Melanie had the advantage of knowing far more about them than they knew about her pursuer. He made no apologies for his skittishness and momentarily wished that Sondra were with him. His wife had always been contemptuous of his quiet career and his apparent lack of adventure, but now here he was on his way to a perilous midnight rendezvous with an elegant and powerful woman who looked like Heidi Klum's hot American sister. Imagining Sondra's eyes bugging out in astonishment almost merited the trouble he might be in.

So, he pushed the Honda through the twilight, frightened and vaguely excited, knowing that some of the best journalism he had ever read had been produced by those two intertwined emotions.

It was dark when he approached Highlands, and he almost missed the small brown-and-yellow sign that provided the only marker for the Forest Service road. When he entered the woods, he rolled down his window and felt the coolness of the air with his hand as he picked his way slowly through the ruts and pot-holes and finally splashed through a small stream into the grassy parking area. When he cut the car's engine and turned off the lights, he was instantly plunged into the heart of the forest night: chirping crickets, croaking tree frogs, rustling leaves, and the faint rumble of the falls in the distance. He got out of the car, and as he urinated against the trunk of a softly fragrant hemlock, he listened carefully for any pursuit. If anyone had managed to escape his detection, the crunch of gravel far up the road would alert him, and he would take off down the trail to the falls. Not even a native would be able to find him in the tangle of moun-tain laurel and rock along the streambed.

He sat on one of the stumps that marked the transition from the level glade to the steep slope where the trail began and let his eyes adjust to the darkness. He felt relatively safe. The woods at night had never been a scary place to him. People were scary, not trees and animals, and with a nearly full moon rising slowly over the foliage, his seat felt as familiar as the stool in his darkened study. Nonetheless, when he heard a car moving along the road, he scampered down the trail a hundred feet to watch its approach from behind a bush, ready to sprint farther if anyone other than Melanie and her friend emerged. The car stopped and the glare of the headlights prevented him from identifying its driver.

★ ★ ★

The last person that Thor expected to see at his door was Miriam. She had ignored all of his recent calls and his texts, and he had concluded that either she was still upset over Melanie's mistrusting questions or, even worse, maybe she was still in love with the dashing and ill-fated photographer, Jacob Granville, and therefore had no time for a bumbling young priest.

Yet there she stood, looking vaguely apologetic and holding a bottle of wine.

"Come in!" He did little to hide his excitement at her surprise appearance. "I'll get a corkscrew." He motioned at the futon couch in his small living room. "Have a seat."

Thor lived in a small two-bedroom apartment in a warehouse converted to lofts close to downtown Clarkeston. He liked the brick walls and the high ceilings, but his neighbors tended to be well-off students rather than fellow young professionals, and he had finally concluded that the hipness of the space did not offset the annoying party noise that started late on Thursday night and lasted until early Sunday morning. He also lacked the funds to furnish the place properly, and his battered coffee table and mismatched garage-sale couch and easy chair declared that he was not too far removed from his own student years.

"Here you go." He handed her a generous portion of the pinot noir that she had brought and sat next to her. At least he had two good wine glasses.

"I want to apologize for my behavior the other day." She took a sip of the wine and then frowned. "That bitchy attorney pissed me off, but I shouldn't have just run. Probably just confirmed her suspicions about me, whatever they are."

Thor was so happy to see her that he would have forgiven far worse transgressions. "There's nothing to apologize for! She was being pretty confrontational. She is a lawyer, after all."

"The thing is," she paused and frowned again, "she was right. I have been sort of carrying a torch for Jacob. I know it's stupid. He's either dead or long gone and not coming back." She finished her glass in one long swallow. "You know what they say: you never forget your first love until the next one comes along."

"Ouch," the priest blurted out.

Her face initially read curious but soon blushed as she backpedaled. "No, I didn't mean . . ." She looked down and kept her eyes on the wine bottle as she topped off her glass. She swished the fluid around for a moment and then gave Thor a skeptical look. "Are you really interested in me?"

"Well, of course!" God, how bad was he at this! How could she not have noticed the way he looked at her? The longing and soul-searching expression? Maybe her failure to read him meant that he came off suave and aloof? Doubtful. And anyway, the hell with subtlety. "You're totally awesome. Any guy would be lucky to be with you!"

"That's debatable," she murmured, before her face brightened and she raised her glass. "Well, let's consider this our first date, then."

"First for you," he smiled. "The fifth for me."

This turned out to be the right thing to say, because she laughed and kissed him on the cheek. "Now, I've got even more interesting stuff to tell you."

"Well, that was pretty interesting."

"No," she laughed again, "I mean it. I've been talking with my mother about Giles Keefe. When I left you all, I was so pissed that when I got home I told my mom that I knew she was lying about Washington and that Keefe's wife had told me to say hello to her."

Thor had no trouble imagining fireworks between the two strong-willed women. "What did she say?"

"Pretend this is the confessional, because you cannot tell anyone. Ever. But Giles Keefe was her lover! She had an affair with him while they lived in Washington, and my dad never found out."

"Holy crap."

"You bet." She filled his now empty glass. "And Keefe was my dad's connection in the government. Dad told her that he called Keefe about Jacob."

"Have you contacted Keefe yet?" He wondered whether Miriam's desire to find her former lover still compelled her curiosity. He could see why it might, given the circumstances under which Granville disappeared.

"Not yet," she sighed. "I'm thinking that maybe I just need to let some of this stuff go."

★ ★ ★

"James?" Melanie's voice was unmistakable, and the reporter emerged from his hiding place and strode into the car's lights with a little wave of his hand.

"Sorry to be so dramatic," he apologized as he approached her, "but I couldn't think of a less obvious place to meet."

His heart leaped as she gave him a quick and unexpected hug before responding. "You've definitely achieved not-obvious. Kinda creepy, but definitely private." She stood aside and made room for her traveling companion. "This is Stanley Hopkins, sociology professor and globe-trotting cyber-sleuth."

James gave the man's hand a firm shake and asked Melanie to switch off the lights. "Even if you weren't followed, this road technically closes at dark, and there's no sense getting the attention of a forest ranger." He gestured to the line of stumps in front of the vehicles. "Why don't you guys sit down and tell me what you know."

The professor began by revealing what he had learned in Mallorca and Geneva, and as he explained his theory of how a plan to expose an attempted bribe had gone horribly wrong, James's mind wandered back to the mysterious picture of the two girls taken by Jacob Granville. So, one of them was gone, too, brushed aside as easily as Diana Cavendish. The African farmer and the Mexican textile worker in Jacob's YouTube library came into focus, too, their suffering no longer so disconnected and mysterious.

Stanley then outlined his research at the University of Georgia library and explained how billions of dollars provided plenty of motivation for the violent silencing of the English girl and later Jacob and Diana.

"Shit," James murmured, "I wish we could prove some of this." The moon had risen overhead, and he could easily see his companions nodding in agreement. "What I don't understand is why Melanie's getting suspicious visitors now. There's nothing to tie you two together."

He heard the attorney sigh. "I asked my friend in the FBI to track down that Arkansas number again last week. I think he got pissed and told somebody that I was digging around in the case."

"Fuck," James replied. He almost never swore, but, according to the professor, either the FBI or some politician or some cotton planter or some Mexican factory owner was coming after Melanie, and he was the next most likely target since his name was already on the books. "You got a plan?"

"Sort of." She pulled a rubber band out of her pocket, ran her hands through her hair, and gathered a small ponytail behind her head. "I need cover, so I'm going to tell my boss everything. As the head US attorney in Atlanta, he's got a great working relationship with the FBI, and getting everything out in the open should make us pretty untouchable. There's no sense silencing people who've already talked."

James had been keeping half an ear on the conversation and half on the road behind them, and now he heard the faint crunch of gravel in the distance. He reached out and grabbed Melanie's hand. "Someone's coming. It's probably just a ranger or some kids, but let's get down the trail a bit. It takes a hard turn to the right, and we can look through the leaves and see who shows up. Given what you guys have just said, I'm not in the mood to take any chances."

Keeping hold of her hand, he hustled them down the path. The moon was bright enough that no flashlight was necessary to keep them on the well-worn track, and James realized as the sound of the car got louder and louder that its headlights were off. None were necessary to navigate the Forest Service road in moonshine. All he could see was a large shadow moving through the woods, until a sedan emerged into the clearing and its ignition was switched off.

A stocky man got out, closed his door quietly, and walked warily over to the two parked cars. He put his hand on both of the hoods while he peered into the woods. James thought he could see a bald pate glint in the moonlight.

"That's the guy from your house, Mel," Stanley whispered urgently. "He's checking to see how long the cars have been here."

That was all James needed to hear about the muscular intruder stalking around the parking lot. "Follow me." He led them swiftly down the path and then stumbled as he kicked a large root with an audible thump. "Be quiet," he whispered to himself as much as to his companions as they plunged deeper and deeper into the forest.

★ ★ ★

When Stanley looked back up the trail, he could see a bobbing light following them, probably their pursuer using his cell phone to help him scan the path. James seemed to know exactly where he was going, and the professor wondered whether the moonlight alone would have been enough of a guide. It was hard to tell how far back the man in the suit trailed them. Maybe a minute or two? James claimed that he had a plan, and Stanley hoped it was a good one.

James stopped as they reached a twist in the path, where it dipped steeply downward toward the roar of the falls. "We're going to go down about twenty feet and then take a hard left off the trail into a bunch of mountain laurel. I'll lead us up a steep couloir that will take us to the top of the falls. We can wait there until this dude gives up and goes back home."

He took several swift steps down the path and Melanie followed closely behind but then gave a yelp and fell to the ground. She grabbed her right ankle and writhed in agony. Stanley hopped down to her and tried to pull her up. He looked back and saw the light bobbing steadily closer.

"I've twisted it." She tried to get up and collapsed with a curse. "Motherfucking shoes."

Stanley looked down and saw that she was wearing a pair of black leather pumps with a low chunky heel, but a heel none-theless. James sent Stanley into the mountain laurel to the beginning of the side trail and then crouched down at Melanie's side. "Get on my back."

She crawled jerkily to her knees and slipped her arms around his neck. With a low grunt, he got to his feet, reached backward until he caught the crook of her knees with his arms, and ducked in front of Stanley into the dark.

They moved as quickly as possible, the noise of their foot-falls covered by the growing cacophony of the falls. After a minute, they began a steep ascent up a narrow passageway, hand-holds of root and rock making it possible to climb nearly straight up. James soon began to struggle with Melanie on his back. He asked her to reach up and use a branch to pull herself over his ducking shoulders, and Stanley saw with relief that she could climb steadily with one good leg and two strong arms propelling her. She might not be able to walk, but on the ascent she was almost as quick as her companions.

As they neared the plateau at the top of the falls, James paused and whispered, "Here's the tricky part. You need to keep your hand on this root and follow it to the top. You squeeze between those two boulders." He pointed five feet straight up. "It's the only thing you'll have to hold on to. I'll go first, and Stanley, you stay behind Melanie and push her up and over if you have to."

James quickly disappeared over the ledge between the two large rocks and then reappeared with his arm outstretched to the hobbled woman. He pulled her up and Stanley followed, easily managing the last several feet onto a narrow escarpment next to the falls. There was barely enough space for the three of them to stand next to the rushing water, which plummeted eighty feet into a surging pool. Stanley leaned back on one of the boulders to create more space, but he felt it tip slightly, and he inched closer to James. The huge rock probably just had a pebble under its pivot point, but he was not in the mood to chance falling down the rock face they just ascended.

"James," Melanie said, with more than a hint of panic in her voice, "I've got to sit down." She was standing on one foot, balancing herself with a hand on the rock face that penned them next to the torrent. Stanley backed up as far as he could and looked on doubtfully as Melanie slowly slid into a sitting position, threatening to push James either into the water or over the ledge to the sand spit at the base of the falls. The journalist deftly placed his feet on either side of her legs and straddled her while she slipped. As her legs extended, they kicked a small pile of rocks and twigs over the ledge.

"Shit," Melanie cursed her clumsiness and looked up in alarm.

Stanley grabbed a boulder and leaned out over the empty space, trying to see if the noise had alerted their pursuer. Backlit by the moon, he was rewarded with a flash of light from the beach and the ping of a bullet ricocheting off the stone behind his head. He pulled himself back and another shot rang out a moment later.

"Fuck! That was meant for me! The stones must have landed right in front of him." He looked at James. "Is there another way out of here?"

Their guide shook his head. "Not with Melanie." He pointed to the river. "It looks crazy, but if you've got good balance and strong legs, you can walk across the top of the falls pretty easily, but there's no way she's doing that in the dark."

"Why don't you cross and go for help?" Stanley offered. "I'll stay here with her."

James looked doubtful and squeezed past his companions to the ledge over the couloir. Pressing his head against one of the two boulders at the top, he snuck a peek downward. "Forget it. He's coming up. It'd take me two hours to get to civilization from here and he's going to be up in two minutes."

Melanie grabbed Stanley by the wrist and James by the calf. "Think of something quick! At least give me a rock or something!"

Stanley's eyes met James's and saw they both had resolved to share the fate of their hobbled companion. "You got another plan?"

He was surprised to see James offer a grim smile, nod, and sneak a quick peek down the narrow chimney.

"He's almost up," the journalist said. "Sit down next to me and put your back against the rock face and your feet against the tippy boulder." Stanley squeezed tightly next to him. He could feel his new friend's leg tense against the stone. His whole body was rigid. James turned his head and their foreheads briefly met. He whispered, "When we hear him right below us, we're going to push about five hundred pounds of granite down on this fucker's head."

Stanley could hear the scuffling of their pursuer's ascent right beneath them and saw James nod.

"Push!" The journalist grunted, and they both strained against the weight of the boulder. For a moment, nothing happened, then suddenly it tipped forward and rolled through the cleft at the top of the ledge. It disappeared and they heard a sickening thud and then a series of crashes as it careened off stone and branches down to the base of the falls.

"I've wanted to do that since I was a little kid," James said solemnly.

Stanley gave him a shocked look. "What? Crush somebody?"

"No!" James shook his head. "Roll that rock off the cliff!"

James scrambled back up to a standing position and looked down at their handiwork. "I don't see him, so I don't know if we just knocked him down a bit or squashed him like a bug." He looked at his companions. "Should I go down and take a look?"

"No!" Melanie said firmly. "Even if he's badly injured, he could still get off a round and kill you. Stay here. You keep a lookout down the chute, and we can wait until morning to see what's happened."

"I think she's right, James." He smiled at his new friend and gave an appreciative nod. "Nice plan, by the way: rock and roll."

The night grew cooler as they settled in on the ledge, James positioned on the side closest to their morning descent and Melanie sheltered between them, shielded from the mist of the river's rushing current. No one slept much, but they stayed warm enough as they watched the moon set and the stars take over the job of lighting the night sky, until the yellow glow of dawn revealed the comfort and the horror of the men's handiwork.

XXVIII.

SANCTUARY

Melanie opened her eyes to find James and Stanley hanging over the ledge and looking down at the base of the falls. From their conversation, she entertained little doubt that the man who had pursued them now lay dead far below. She tried to stand and see for herself, but an electric jolt from her left ankle knocked her back into a sitting position. At her yelp, both men turned.

"Let me take a look at that leg." James crouched down and gently took off her shoe. The ankle was swollen and discolored, but not twisted at any sort of unnatural angle. "It's probably just sprained. If you'll trust me, we can get the swelling down a bit and make it back to the car."

He pointed to the water flowing rapidly past her perch. "Slide over to the edge."

She nodded warily, and James helped her scoot to the stream, where he nudged her injured foot in an eddy of freezing water. "Goddamn, that's cold!" Her foot felt as if it were stuck in a pail of jellyfish ice cubes.

He smiled. "That's why it works. In about fifteen minutes, the swelling will be a lot better and you'll feel good enough to climb down."

"After fifteen minutes, I won't feel anything at all," she snorted, but she forced herself to keep the foot in the icy whirlpool. "I can kind of move it around a bit," she added with a wince. "You're right. It's probably just a sprain." After a few minutes of frigid agony her foot went completely numb and the sensation of the moving water felt almost therapeutic.

When James was satisfied with the condition of her ankle, he slipped over the rock ledge down into the couloir and told her to follow him, sliding feetfirst on her belly. Stanley guarded her from above, and she maneuvered between them as she slowly picked her way down the rock chimney. Descending was far harder than going up had been, and several times she had to trust James to place her good foot in a solid notch before daring to proceed. The handholds were easier to manage, except for a slippery knob about a third of the way down, which left her fingers bloody with a remnant of their pursuer's rapid and involuntary descent.

When they got to the bottom, Stanley found her a stout walking stick, and she was able to hobble without help, as long as she did not try to move laterally on her bad ankle. She followed the men out of the rhododendrons at the base of the couloir and out onto the sand spit, where she saw the body of a large man in a dark suit, his bloody head cocked at an impossible angle on the edge of the water. The boulder that had knocked him there lay three feet into the pool.

"If I were a better law-enforcement official," she proclaimed, "I'd tell you not to disturb the crime scene, but you need to go through this guy's pockets."

The men checked the back of his pants, and then flipped the body over to check the front. When they moved his torso, his head remained grotesquely in place, embedded in the sand and fraying at the neck. Melanie felt her gorge rise. She vomited over the side of a mossy log and sent an iridescent-green beetle scuttling under a rock. She sat down and waited for the professor and the journalist to return with the dead man's belongings.

"We found a money clip with plenty of cash and a Mexican driver's license for a Jose Morales." James's expression was grim. "The picture looks like him . . . as far as we can tell."

"We've also got his cell phone and the keys to the car," Stanley added. "There could be more stuff in the sedan."

She reached for the phone and he handed it to her. The small, conventional handset still held a charge. She quickly clicked through the call history and the address book. "It's just a burner. It's only ever been used to call two numbers, one of which has a foreign prefix." She handed it back to Stanley. "Take good care of that. I've got an idea about what to do with it, but let's get back to the cars and get the hell out of here first." She looked at her watch. It was a little after six o'clock, enough time to search their assailant's car and get out of the forest before someone visited the falls and discovered the body.

The pain in Melanie's ankle faded to a dull throb as they walked back, and as long as she strode straight ahead, she found she could maintain a relatively normal pace. A tightly wrapped Ace bandage, and she'd be as good as new. When they arrived at the small parking area, they found the three vehicles still alone in the glade. As they approached the Mexican's rental, Stanley clicked the keyless entry and Melanie cautioned them before they searched. "Eventually, someone is going to find Jose back there and put two and two together, so don't leave any finger-prints and don't disturb anything more than you have to. James, why don't you take a look inside while Stanley and I check out the trunk."

The trunk was pristine and completely empty. Stanley used his elbow to snap it shut, and the pair turned their attention to James's careful inspection of the interior. Using a wad of Kleenex, he searched the glove compartment and other interior storage areas, finding nothing except a pair of sunglasses and a black metal device sitting in the passenger seat.

"Boy, this guy traveled light," the reporter commented. "The only thing here is the obvious—the electronic thingy." He took out another Kleenex, pulled the oblong device out with two hands, and set it on the hood of the vehicle. All three took turns looking at it and shaking their heads.

"Any ideas?" Melanie asked.

"No," replied Stanley, "but let's turn it on. There's a little switch on the side." Before anyone could object, he flipped the toggle with his wrist through the cuff of his shirt and a GPS screen appeared, covered with terrain contours and snaky black lines.

James leaned over it closely and used his hands to cut the glare shining on the screen. "That's here," he pointed. "It's a digital map of where we are right now."

Stanley took a peak. "That doesn't look like any GPS that I've ever seen."

"Oh, fuck me," Melanie exclaimed, as she pushed them aside and squeezed in for a closer look. "I know what it is. It's a professional-model LoJack. I wondered how the hell that guy knew we were meeting here! If you crawl under my car, I'll bet you a million bucks that you find a tracking sensor."

Both men flopped on the ground beside her car and in less than five minutes Stanley emerged holding up a small black disk like a trophy.

"Check under James's car, too, just in case, and then let's get out of here."

★ ★ ★

Thor had not shared a bed with anyone for several years, and as he leaned on the crook of his arm studying the peaceful form of Miriam Rodgers, he was not sure whether he ever wanted to go back to sleeping alone. Her face was completely relaxed, no sign of the lines that appeared sometimes when she was excited or worried. He marveled at how beautiful she was and hoped that he might be able to hang on to her for a while. All the more reason to wow her with a stack of blueberry pancakes, fresh fruit salad, and a pot of his tastiest organic, fair-trade, song-bird-friendly, shade-grown, Jamaica Blue Mountain coffee. He slipped out of bed without waking her and went to work in the kitchen.

He didn't know if he had impressed her in the bedroom, but she was clearly appreciative of his work in the kitchen, and breakfast progressed lazily from carbohydrates in his little dining nook to the *New York Times* and coffee in the living room. Miriam seemed in no hurry to go home as long as Thor topped off her cup, and they were both still lounging on his sofa when a buzz from the intercom announced they had company. Miriam retreated to the bedroom while the priest checked to see who had come calling.

He was surprised to hear James Murphy asking in a semiserious voice for "sanctuary" for himself and two friends. The priest buzzed them in and shouted a warning to Miriam. When he opened the door, he was confronted by James, accompanied by the woman from the US attorney's office in Atlanta, and a man in his mid-thirties whom he didn't recognize. All three looked exhausted. The men's jeans were creased and dirty, and Melanie's smartly tailored blouse and slacks were torn in several places.

"You weren't kidding," he said as he waved them in. "You look like you do need sanctuary!"

"Thanks, Father," James said. "We need to avoid my house and Melanie's place in Atlanta for a while." He motioned to his companion and offered a non sequitur. "And Stanley's from Los Angeles."

"What the heck is going on?" The priest said, as he waved them to the kitchen table and began to brew another pot of coffee. "Do you want something to eat?"

All three nodded vigorously, and while he mixed a new batch of pancake batter, they took turns explaining the events of the last twenty-four hours, filling in the relevant background details of Stanley's trip to Geneva and the professor's research into the cotton case. Thor interrupted repeatedly as the trio of friends connected the dots from the attempt to bribe the WTO in Geneva to the murderous fallout of Brenda and Jacob's plan to expose it. He was dumbfounded by the tale of their pursuit into the mountains.

"So, who is after you?" Thor asked.

"We'll know a lot more after I track down the numbers in the Mexican cell phone." Melanie speared the last piece of pancake off her plate and turned down the priest's offer to make her another stack.

"How are you going to do that?"

"I'm going to be bad," she said with a dangerous smile. "I've got a pending request to trace about a hundred different numbers in a huge drug case that we're prosecuting. I'm just going to bury the cell's numbers in with the latest affidavit and see what pops up." She sighed and accepted a refill of her coffee. "But first I need to find out whether it's even safe to go in to work."

Thor nodded and wondered whether he himself might be in danger. "So, you think that Diana and Jacob were killed by the same person who killed the girl in Geneva."

"I'm certain of it at this point," James replied. "Those emails to their parents came from Mexico, probably sent as red herrings by whoever abducted them." His face was grim. "I think that Diana and Jacob are both dead."

Thor heard a loud moan, and everyone around the breakfast table turned to see Miriam, ashen faced, stumble into the room. "Jacob's dead?" Her body sagged against the kitchen counter and her eyes flitted from person to person, looking in vain for someone to contradict her. She repeated her cry in a weakened voice and, obtaining no comfort from the surprised group at the table, staggered back into the bedroom, followed immediately by Thor.

★ ★ ★

While the priest was consoling his lover, Stanley was trying to decide what to do next. No one except for James, Melanie, and Elisa had any idea of his involvement in the investigation, and he could put all danger behind him by just catching a plane back to California. The longer he stayed, the more likely that someone would observe him with James and Melanie and add him to the shit list. Fleeing was the safest option, but he hesitated. Seeing the mystery through would be substantially more interesting than working on his lesson plans for the upcoming semester and, moreover, the night spent on the rocky ledge had intertwined his life with James and Melanie's. He couldn't leave them to their own devices now.

The three companions debated whether it would be safe for either Melanie or James to visit their offices and whether it would be wise to tell the whole story to their bosses, now that it included a dead body lying in the North Carolina forest. They were far from consensus when Thor emerged from his bedroom with an arm wound tightly around Miriam's shoulders.

"We'd like to help if we can," the priest said, "especially now that we're after Jacob's murderer." The young woman next to him nodded, her eyes still wet with tears.

The young couple sat down on the sofa together, and Melanie took the easy chair next to it. James and Stanley dragged two bar stools in from the kitchen nook.

"Until you get things sorted out, one or two of you can stay with me," Thor explained, "and Miriam's mom has some room in her house. No one will have any idea where you are."

"That's great," Stanley said. "I'd like to hang around and help sort this mess out."

"Thanks. That buys us time to plan," Melanie added, "but we can't just camp out in Clarkeston forever." She frowned and tapped her fingers on her knee. "If we knew for certain that the FBI wasn't interested in us, then I could go in to work and do some digging on the numbers in that cell phone. Hell, if I were able to tell the US marshal's office that I've been threatened, then they'd even send someone to watch my house for a while."

Thor looked at Miriam. "We might be able to help you out there. Miriam knows who her father contacted in Washington about Jacob. He's apparently superconnected, and Miriam's found his number. If her father thought that this Keefe guy had influence with the FBI, then he might have the clout to learn whether you're in trouble with the feds or you're just being chased by a bunch of cotton thugs."

Stanley thought he could see the wheels spinning in Melanie's head.

"Could I use your laptop?" She pointed to the device on the coffee table. "What's this guy's name again?" Miriam gave her the full name, and the attorney tapped and clicked and nodded her head. "Sweet. Giles Keefe is pretty high up in Homeland Security. If he's willing, he could contact the FBI with our names and see whether we're on their radar screen or we're just the victims of information leaked to some other source."

She pulled her phone out of her handbag and saw that it was still separated from the battery. She looked at Miriam. "I don't want to take a chance that someone might track my phone's GPS. You could do us a huge favor if you'd make a call on your phone and tell a little white lie for us."

Miriam fished for her phone. "Just tell me what you want me to do."

"First, call Keefe and tell him that you're his old friend Ernest's daughter. Tell him you know that he was contacted by your father about five years ago, and that it turns out that your dad was right about Jacob. He was innocent, and a local reporter claims to have evidence of him and Diana being murdered. That'll make him feel better, if he actually intervened for Jacob. You might even suggest that he was your fiancé."

Stanley saw Thor wince.

"Tell him," Melanie continued, "that you've been contacted by two people who are asking you about the case, but you don't trust them: Melanie Wilkerson from Atlanta and James Murphy from Clarkeston. They seem a little sketchy. Could he check the FBI and Homeland Security databases? There's no way that he'll share any confidential information, but if he really was a good friend of your father, then he should be willing to warn you off us if he sees any red flags. If he tells you to stay away from us, then we'll know that we're currently under suspicion."

"Why don't you just call him?" Miriam asked.

"Why would a US attorney call him instead of contacting the FBI directly?" Melanie explained. "And why would a US attorney be wondering whether the FBI was on her tail? Red flags would go up all over the place."

"I see," she said slowly. "Do you want me to try now?"

When Melanie nodded, Miriam disappeared into the bedroom to make the call in private. The attorney shrugged and offered a doubtful look to her friends, as if to indicate that it was a shot in the dark. While they waited for Miriam to return, the three visitors helped Thor clear off the breakfast dishes and wipe down the table. Stanley thanked him for the hospitality and offer to help. Thor laughed when Stanley assured him that the humorless pastor in his childhood Presbyterian church would never have allowed himself to get mixed up in abduction and murder. Thor had a brand of evangelism that he could get behind.

When Miriam returned, she sat down on the sofa and waited for the others to gather round. "That was interesting," she said softly.

"You were right," Miriam continued. "Keefe wasn't willing to give me any specific information about anyone, but he said he'd check out your names and give me a general thumbs-up or down. He's not even supposed to do that, but he feels obligated to my dad. He said he'd get back to me in an hour or so." She shook her head. "I think there's still a whole bunch of stuff that my mom's not telling me."

"Did he say anything about intervening for Jacob five years ago?"

"Yeah, he made it really clear that he didn't do much of anything." She took a deep breath and retained her composure. "My dad wanted the FBI to stay out of Jacob's case, but Keefe had no power to prevent that and he wasn't willing, anyway. All he could do was promise to let the FBI know that Jacob should be treated with care, that he wasn't some maniac on the loose . . ."

Melanie spoke as the young woman's voice trailed off. "Sort of the opposite of 'shoot first, ask questions later.'"

"That was all he could do." She slumped against Thor, who had once again taken the seat beside her. "Not that it mattered in the end."

When the call from Keefe came two hours later, Melanie was resting in the bedroom, James was furiously tapping on a computer, and Stanley, at the urging of his host, had stretched out for a nap on the sofa. Almost as soon as his head hit the cushion, a wave of exhaustion washed over him and he fell fast asleep. The buzz of Miriam's phone woke him with a start, and it took a moment to process where he was and why he was there.

Miriam answered the call and listened intently, occasionally murmuring her understanding of the brief message from her father's old friend in Washington. A wisp of a smile crossed her face as she said good-bye and swiped the screen of her phone. "He was very careful about what he said." She cocked her head and spoke in thoughtful recognition of how the communication had been packaged. "He said that he'd done a Google search and had discovered that Melanie Wilkerson was a highly regarded federal prosecutor and that James Murphy was a well-respected journalist from Clarkeston."

"That was it?" Stanley asked, nonplussed. "No mention of the FBI?"

"That was it."

Melanie smiled and clapped her hands together. "We're cool! He's not supposed to make Homeland queries to the FBI for personal reasons. I'll bet people do it all the time, checking out their daughter's new boyfriend and stuff like that, but Keefe wanted to send the message without revealing he'd made the official query. He wanted to let you know that we're okay, without admitting that he had broken any rules. If the FBI were hunting us down, he never would have given you the green light like that. I like this guy!"

"What next, then?" James asked. "Can we go back home? Can we start using our cell phones again?"

Melanie paused for a moment. "Until word of the our attacker's death gets back to his boss--whoever he is--we've got some breathing room, but I still think that you and Stanley should avoid your house and spend the nights at Mrs. Rodgers's." She looked at Miriam. "As long as that's still okay with you?"

Miriam nodded and the attorney continued. "I'll go into Atlanta today and start tracking down the two numbers we found in the cell phone. I'm going to be very surprised if they go anywhere other than Arkansas or Mexico. In the meantime, I want you guys to do some more research for me." She looked in Stanley's direction. "I want to know, apart from Senator Randolph, what other politicos in Arkansas are part of the cotton mafia? What about the other senator? Which Arkansans in the House of Representatives are owned by the cotton lobby?"

She turned her attention to James. "And you could track down landowners in Arkansas who benefit the most from the subsidies. Who has so much at risk that they might be willing to kill? And most importantly, which of them sell directly to the Mexican clothing maquiladoras? Scour the Internet and drive over to UGA library in Athens if you have to, but I want as complete a picture as possible of the connections between these folks. When we know more, we'll meet back here." She looked at Thor. "As long as the priest is still willing to offer sanctuary."

"Absolutely," he replied with a grin. "I'll keep the coffee on."

XXIX.

BURROWS

When she walked into the federal building in Atlanta, Melanie felt like she had been gone for twenty days instead of twenty hours, and despite the assurance of Giles Keefe's phone call, a paranoid corner of her mind expected an FBI SWAT team to rappel down the walls of the atrium and bundle her into custody. Instead, she got friendly banter from the marshals as she walked through the metal detector and a broad smile from the lobby receptionist, who used to work on her floor. When she arrived at her office, her assistant expressed surprise that she had missed a bond hearing that morning, but assured her that the judge had delayed the motion until someone else filled in.

"You should always call when you can't come in!"

"Sorry, Vonda," Melanie lied, "but I was sick as a dog and couldn't drag myself out of the bathroom." She patted her stomach. "Must have been some bad chicken, 'cuz I'm feeling fine now."

"I told you before not to go to Paschal's." The Atlanta native shook her head. "If you want fried food, then you stick to Mary Mac's Kitchen."

"Amen," agreed the attorney, her accent making an especially sweet appearance as she stretched out each syllable.

Melanie asked Vonda to hold her calls, walked into her office, and looked around with a keen eye. Everything seemed in its proper place. She never really thought that the FBI had sent an assassin from south of the border to stop the investigation of the Cavendish case, but you never knew if someone had been corrupted by a slice, even a small slice, of the billions of dollars at stake over cotton. She would take no chances and decided to request a US marshal to watch her townhouse until she felt safer.

But when would that be? And just what was the endgame? She had gotten sucked into Murphy's obsession with a cold case and managed to increase spectacularly the excitement level of her job, but the next move was unclear. So far, she hadn't broken any major rules. She had pursued a case on her own, to be sure, but apart from asking Sammy to check on a phone number and convincing Miriam to bend the truth a bit in her conversation with Keefe, she had not abused her official position. She hadn't yet put her career in jeopardy.

Well, there was the matter of the broken man sprawled at the bottom of the falls. He had been killed in self-defense, of course, but she and her friends had failed to report the death, failed to report their own attempted murder, in fact. A regular citizen would have no obligation to inform the authorities about the incident, but she was a federal law-enforcement official. Not to mention that she had taken his money clip, cell phone, and driver's license. And she still had his keys in her purse.

With the incident less than twenty-four hours old, she still had time to come clean to her boss. She'd get a dressing-down, but she'd been shot at and spent the night on a rocky ledge next to a waterfall in the-middle-of-nowhere North Carolina. That kind of shock affects people's judgment, and she would be excused. On the other hand, no one in the world was going to connect her to the body unless she was stupid enough to identify herself when she made her upcoming inquiry to the dead man's rental-car agency.

She sat down in her chair and laid the dead man's effects in front of her. It was all the hard evidence that she had, not enough to put anyone in jail or even start a prosecution. Stanley had made some convincing guesses about who was behind the deaths of Diana and Jacob—not to mention the poor girl in Geneva—but they had no hard evidence that the man chasing them had been some henchman of a cotton magnate or textile-factory owner with Arkansas political connections. She couldn't even produce the bodies of Diana or Jacob. If she told her story and turned over the cell phone and keys, someone else would decide whether the leads were worth pursuing. As an interested party, a victim, in fact, she would be put on the sidelines and the case might even be dropped. She wasn't paranoid about the FBI, but given the ephemeral and speculative nature of the evidence, politics might influence the intensity of the investigation. Hell, she'd already been warned off the case by Sammy and his unnamed superior.

She picked up her phone and asked Vonda to bring a list of all telephone-record subpoenas to be filed that afternoon with the federal magistrate. She wasn't going to give up the Cavendish case to someone who might view it as a wild-goose chase, at least not until she knew more about the numbers in the cell phone. If they went straight to some politician's office, then she would tell her story to the US attorney and let nature take its course. But if the hard evidence led nowhere, then she couldn't trust anyone else to keep up the pursuit. She would be relegated to serving as a witness with a crazy story to tell about a cold case, a globe-trotting sociology professor, and a bikini-trolling journalist. And her relationship with James was especially damning: federal prosecutors never worked hand in hand with journalists, even nice-looking ones with eye-crinkley smiles.

Vonda brought in the day's stack of motions, and Melanie soon found one that suited her purposes nicely. An ongoing investigation into a Colombian drug cartel smuggling brown heroin into remote Georgia airstrips required Magistrate Durbin to consider several dozen requests for search warrants and telephone records. She could easily alter the motion to include the two numbers in the cell phone, and if the magistrate moved with his usual speed, she'd be able to contact the cell phone service provider by the afternoon. The result of that call would determine her next move.

She accessed the relevant document on the office shared drive, added the two numbers, printed it out, and then substituted it for the original motion. Buried in the midst of dozens of other numbers, her minor alteration would escape detection, and even if someone noticed, her signature as overall supervising attorney was already on all the motions in the stack anyway. No one would see a special connection to her.

While she waited for the requests to be processed and the magistrate's order to issue, she took out the keys to the dead man's rental car, which was presumably still parked on the Forest Service road leading to the hidden falls. She didn't dare request a court order for the records of the car-rental company. The cops who found the car would undoubtedly ask for a subpoena, and they would wonder why she had made the same query to the rental agency first. No one could know that she had any interest in the car, or questions would be asked that she did not want to answer. Nonetheless, she could make a call to the rental-car number on the key chain and ask some careful and anonymous questions.

Using the phone in an empty conference room above her office, she dialed the number and pretended to be the wife of Jose Morales, the name on the driver's license found on the body. Sure enough, the car was rented under that name.

"Hi," the prosecutor said brightly, "my idiot husband has lost all the rental documentation on our car and can't remember which day we're supposed to bring it back."

"Next Friday," replied a man with a strong Asian accent. "It must be into the Atlanta Airport office by six o'clock in the evening."

"Hmm . . . ," she murmured contemplatively into the phone, "we might want to extend the rental, then. What credit card did we put it on, anyway? I told him to put it on the Amex so we'd get our SkyMiles."

"No, madam," the man answered, "it's on a Visa card."

"I knew he'd screw up!" she exclaimed. "Which Visa, anyway? Hopefully not the Chase card! We're at our limit on that one."

"Let me check." She heard a flurry of keystrokes and then a struggle to pronounce the issuer's name. "No, the deposit record says it's a Visa issued by the . . . Banco de Sabines."

She asked him to spell the bank name and turned down his offer to formally extend the rental period. A Google search for *Banco de Sabines* revealed a regional bank with several offices all close to the Mexican town of Sabines, about a three-hour drive from Laredo, Texas. It wasn't much, but it was something to share with James and Stanley when they finished their homework.

Melanie spent the rest of the day catching up on a stack of motions and interviewing several young law graduates for a position in her expanding immigration unit. Late in the afternoon, Vonda knocked on her door and dumped the results of the morning's warrant motions on her desk. All had been granted by the magistrate, with the exception of a request to conduct an unannounced search of a Walmart warehouse in a trademark-counterfeiting case.

She pulled out the motion that included the cell numbers she wanted and asked Vonda to fax a copy of the order to the cell phone's service provider. She waited thirty minutes and then called the corporate attorney charged with responding to court-ordered records requests. His name was Jerry, and she had dealt with him on several prior occasions, because not all of his company's five million cellular customers were innocent citizens planning the next backyard barbeque. After some friendly small talk, he confirmed receipt of the faxed order and agreed to expedite the request on both numbers. He would get back to her the following morning.

★ ★ ★

Stanley and James sat in the main reading room of the University of Georgia library, alternately tapping away at their computers and searching for hard copies of books and journals in a large reference room serviced by a small but knowledgeable group of research librarians. Stanley dove into the entire Arkansas congressional delegation, surfing the senators' and representatives' websites and reading articles attacking and praising each member's work on Capitol Hill. He had little trouble finding lobbying disclosures and other tax-related documents coughed up like hair balls in the course of the most recent campaign. Every congressman had an enemy, and a clear picture of the Arkansas congressional delegation slowly began to emerge.

For his part, James charted the location and ownership of the major clothing maquiladoras, all of which were fairly close to the US-Mexico border. Accessing several business databases, he created a spreadsheet identifying the firms that purchased the most cotton directly from the US and noted any interlocking corporate relationships. His Spanish was good enough to peruse foreign-language websites, and he found several key databases created by labor groups documenting the abuse of workers and by human-rights groups documenting who benefited from the multi-billion-dollar subsidies that enriched not only Arkansas cotton growers but also the buyers of their cheap commodity in Mexico.

The two compared notes over a quick lunch in leafy downtown Athens and then worked through the afternoon and into the early evening, each feeding off of the other's energy until empty stomachs and the shared need for a beer put an end to the day's operations. As the sun began to set, the two researchers sat outdoors in front of a faux-English pub with a wide variety of American microbrews and European ales on tap and a decent selection of food on order at the burnished-oak bar. Rather than drive back to Clarkeston, Stanley had arranged for both of them to spend the night with his former colleague, Kirk, who was happy to hear that he was back in town so soon.

"I've got a couple dozen documents in a file folder on my computer," the journalist explained, "everything that I could find on the textile maquiladoras, including data that I got from the SEC's EDGAR database and Hoover's, which is Dun & Bradstreet's business-data arm." He explained how corporate annual reports and other disclosures mandated by the Securities and Exchange Commission were available through the newspaper's subscription service. "And I asked the library to scan a couple hard-copy sources, which should be ready by tomorrow morning. I've also downloaded a bunch of news articles off of LexisNexis."

"Excellent," Stanley replied, "I still need to see which Arkansas farmers I can pair with which politicians."

"If you can do that by lunch, then you can give me Arkansas names to run through my data folder. I can just do a simple word search in the folder and see who crops up where in the stories and business records. We'll see if we can trace factory owners to cotton sellers to sleazy politicians."

Stanley took a long and satisfying draught of his Terrapin Rye Pale Ale. "Let's keep our fingers crossed. It'd be nice to impress The Boss."

James and Stanley had settled on The Boss as a descriptor for Melanie. Having successfully defended the life of the beautiful prosecutor, they only needed a couple of pints to share their admiration for her fierce intelligence, no-nonsense attitude, and shapely legs. The premature end of both of their marriages provided even more common ground for discussion as they sipped the tasty local brew and watched the college students traipse by. Stanley did not take long to figure out that James's interest in The Boss was becoming more than just professional.

The next morning went as planned and by early afternoon they had identified three major pipelines of Congress's billions. Three of the largest corporate farmers in Arkansas consistently sold their crops to three major Mexican textile firms. Those planters in turn made large donations to all members of the Arkansas delegation, but no one received even close to the feudal dues collected by senior senator Elbert Randolph. They also identified several smaller players in the subsidies game by comparing the data in the journalist's digital source folder and the professor's spreadsheets. If Melanie had any luck tracking down either number in the Mexican hit man's cell phone, they could fire into nerd hyperdrive, flip open their laptops, and burrow into action.

★ ★ ★

Melanie arrived at the office two hours early the following morning and caught up on her work before any of the staff arrived. By the time she heard from the phone company about the owners of the two phone numbers that had been called by her deceased assailant, she was back up to speed on the most important cases her subordinates were arguing that day and was ready to make a personal appearance in a bond hearing on a meth dealer whom she considered a serious flight risk.

"What do you have for me, Jerry?" she asked the phone company corporate counsel when he finally called.

"Not much, I'm afraid," he said in a genuinely apologetic voice. Unlike some private attorneys, Swanson always seemed eager to rat out his criminal customers to the feds. "Both of the numbers are associated with pay-as-you-go phones, bought and topped up with cash, so we don't have the same information we'd collect if they were on a two-year plan or something."

Her heart sank. She had been hoping for landline connections. "Do you have names, at least?"

"Yeah," he replied, "but it's what you'd expect. One was bought by a John Smith and the other by a Juan Cruz, which is pretty much John Smith in Spanish, as far as I can tell."

She sighed. Cell phone records were helpful in charting patterns of communication between bad guys, but criminals were seldom stupid enough to buy a phone or purchase air time in their own names. Any sophisticated perpetrator—and even the unsophisticated ones—used aliases in establishing their networks.

"Can you tell me where the phones were bought?"

"It's the SIM cards that matter," he corrected her and then read aloud two addresses, one in Little Rock, Arkansas, and one in Sabines, Mexico. He apologized that he had so little information to share and promised to send her his company's records related to the other phone numbers in the drug case she was investigating.

As soon as he hung up, she sat down at her computer and googled the Little Rock address, which turned out to be a Magic Market on South Arch Street, a couple of blocks away from the federal building in downtown Little Rock. The address in Sabines was also a convenience store.

So that was it. More inferences, more suspicions of connections, but no smoking-gun trail leading directly to a corrupt politician or a murderous businessman. She closed her browser with an angry click that sent the mouse scurrying across her desk. She was not going to let go of the investigation until there was some obvious suspect to prosecute, and right now the only person who had clearly committed a crime was lying dead in the North Carolina woods.

She retrieved her mouse and reopened her browser to check whether the body by the falls had been discovered. Given the remoteness of the site and the rain that had begun to fall soon after they made their escape to Clarkeston, she was not surprised to learn that no news of an accident or foul play in the area had been reported.

A few minutes later, Melanie took the elevator down to the third floor of the building and vented her frustration on opposing counsel in the bail hearing, asking for, and getting, bond set at a level so high that the scrawny meth cooker would rot in jail until his trial. Maybe the forced meditation time would do him some good, although his crazed Charley Manson stare did not suggest an introspective spirit. When she got back to her office, the phone rang almost immediately. James wanted an update on the phone numbers.

"I didn't get much," she admitted, "but you can tell Stanley that the Arkansas connection is still strong. One of the numbers our dead friend was calling was purchased from a convenience store in downtown Little Rock. The other number comes from a Mexican town called Sabines. It's about three hours from

Laredo. There's no wiki page on it, so I don't know anything about the place."

"Hang on a minute," the journalist replied and then passed on the name of the town to his partner. She heard the faint clicking of a computer keyboard and the sound of the two men conferring excitedly. She was about to ask what was going on when James's voice returned to the phone.

"We need to meet," he said. "When are you free?"

"I've got a couple of hearings tomorrow," she said, with a glance at her calendar, "but I could get away by the late afternoon."

"Perfect." James muttered something inaudible to Stanley. "We'll need a little time to prepare."

"When and where do you want to meet?" She felt safer after an undisturbed day in the office but was still worried that this might change when the body was discovered. "Where are you, anyway?"

She heard something oddly gleeful in the journalist's response. "Are we still paranoid?"

"Maybe a little," she conceded. "I think we should keep playing it safe for a while."

"Okay. Then let's meet in the lair of the Norse hammer god at six tomorrow. We'll bring pizza."

"The which god?" Then her memory kicked in. "Yeah, yeah. I get it. Cool. I'll see you there at six tomorrow." She paused. "I'll bring beer."

XXX

PLANS

Father Thor sat at his kitchen table and excitedly grabbed a third slice of pepperoni pizza. His parents had told him tales of attending clandestine meetings in homes and church basements when they had worked in the mid-1980s' sanctuary movement, helping to shelter refugees from Guatemala, El Salvador, and Nicaragua from right-wing death squads. Their stories had helped fuel his desire to become a priest, and he was thrilled that his loft was now serving as a safe haven for his new friends as they schemed against the perpetrators of an insidious new kind of human-rights abuse—subsidies worth killing for. Brenda Harvey, Diana Cavendish, and Jacob Granville had all died so that no one would question the morality or wisdom of paying large corporate farmers to grow artificially cheap cotton to sell to sweatshop owners. And the price of corruption went beyond the lives of the three martyrs; thousands more in Africa starved as their cotton crop was sold for depressed prices.

After a brief summary of the research trip to Athens, Stanley flipped open his laptop and spun it around so that Melanie, Thor, and James could all see. He smiled and shrugged, "I'm a professor. I can't really explain anything without a PowerPoint presentation."

James motioned to his colleague to begin. The reporter and the sociologist had spent the afternoon comparing and distilling data, drinking beer, and pasting photos into a slide-show presentation that they hoped would impress the woman they called

The Boss. Thor knew much of what was coming, but he stared with fascination nonetheless at the fruits of their labor.

"All right, let's start with senator Elbert Randolph, head of the Senate Agriculture Committee." Up popped a picture of the senator smiling into the camera during a campaign speech. "He's not a bad guy, apparently." A picture of the senator sitting in earnest conversation with a class of African-American elementary school students. "He's authored several pieces of key education legislation and is considered to be the foremost proponent of school reading programs in the Senate.

"But," the professor continued, "he is also a Son of the Land." Black-and-white photo of an unsmiling man. "His father was a cotton farmer." Sepia-toned picture of slaves picking cotton in the antebellum South and an amused rumble from James. "And his closest buddies from school and church and politics are some of the wealthiest landowners in the state." Several photos of the senator attending functions held by an Arkansas cotton-growers association. "Here is one of his longtime friends, Cameron M. Swinton, chairman of the board of CotCo, Inc., which farms tens of thousands of acres of land and sells seed to those farming hundreds of thousands more."

James interrupted, "Since CotCo is publicly traded, we've pulled a shitload of data on the company and its officers from the EDGAR system and Hoover's. This guy is one rich son of a bitch."

"What's most interesting is Swinton's connection to a particular Mexican maquiladora. CotCo sells most of its cotton to a textile company located in"—both Stanley and James gave the kitchen table a brief drumroll with their hands—"Sabines, Mexico." They waited for Melanie to respond.

She nodded her head in appreciation and added, "Where someone bought a phone to talk to our Mexican stalker and where a bank issued a credit card to pay for his car rental."

"Exactly," Stanley nodded, "and Swinton's connection with the Sabines textile mill is not just business." A picture of two smiling men at a Randolph fund-raiser. "Swinton's got a personal connection to Moro Zingales, the owner of the mill. Unfortunately, the maquiladora is not a corporation, so we don't have access to many records, but Zingales himself is well known." The cover of a report flashed on the screen. "Several human-rights groups have filed complaints about the working conditions in his plants, and he's testified before Congress on the mutually beneficial relationship between Arkansas growers and Mexican mills.

"He's got a cute wife," Stanley continued, with a click on a new photo, "three kids, and a big Newfoundland dog named Chupacabra." Kids and adorable dog playing on a beach. "But in 1985, when he was in college in Monterrey, he was accused of beating a classmate nearly to death." Headline from a Mexican newspaper. "The charges were dropped when the main witness recanted his testimony."

James continued the presentation. "We think this guy Zingales or someone close to him sent our Mexican friend to keep an eye on me and Melanie."

"But why?" Thor interjected. "How could he know that you were a threat?"

This time Melanie answered. "Some Arkansas politician, perhaps Randolph, must have told Swinton or Zingales that James was poking around in the Cavendish case. When I called that number in the Little Rock federal building, I put someone on red alert. That call got his house broken into and his computer stolen, and then my queries to the FBI put me on the radar screen. And, of course, my darling ex told someone that I had refused to drop the case. Somehow that got back to the wrong ears."

"You did get some valuable information, though," James consoled the prosecutor. "The Sabines connection makes the money trail and the surveillance trail clearer, and the Little Rock cell number confirms that someone there was also communicating with the Mexican dude, and I'll be surprised if it's not someone from Randolph's office, maybe even the senator himself."

"That's the problem, though," Melanie added thoughtfully, "we have no proof who in Little Rock is calling the shots."

The group fell silent for a moment and Thor felt the vibrating of his cell phone in his pocket. It was a text from Miriam containing a link to an article on the *Clarkeston Chronicle* website. He tapped on his phone and a story appeared a moment later, a short piece on the death of an unidentified hiker near a Highlands, North Carolina, waterfall.

"Someone found the body in the mountains, guys." He waved his smart phone and slid it across the table. "Late-breaking news from Miriam."

James and Melanie leaned together and read the story off the phone's screen while Stanley did a quick search on the computer. "They haven't identified him yet," the professor declared, "but it won't take too long to track down the car."

Melanie nodded. "It's just a matter of time before Zingales, or whoever, figures out his man is dead and we're still alive."

"Well," Stanley added quietly, "they know you and James are alive. They don't know about me and Father Thor."

The priest's phone buzzed again, and he saw that Miriam had sent a link to another story about the body in a regional newspaper.

"What the hell should we do?" James asked the question, but he clearly didn't expect a quick and easy answer. He tossed an empty beer can in the garbage and cracked open a fresh one from the refrigerator.

Stanley spoke first. "We could confront Randolph. Tell him what we know and ask him to call off the dogs."

"He'll never admit to knowing anything about this," Melanie replied with a shake of her head. "We'd be better off just telling the whole story to the FBI and coming clean. I'm sure they'd be willing to protect us, even if they charge us with messing up a crime scene."

"Screw that!" James exclaimed. "That threatens your career and my career and leaves Diana and Jacob rotting in their graves for nothing. I say we go for the throat. I say we bring these cocksuckers down!"

"But how?" Melanie looked sympathetic. "How do we smoke out the bad guys? I'm sure not everybody in Arkansas is crooked. Hell, Senator Randolph might not even know what's going on."

Thor's phone, now on the table, vibrated again.

Stanley pointed to it and smiled. He caught the eye of everyone in the room before speaking.

"Let's text the Arkansas cell number. Let's go to Little Rock, sit down in a café close to the federal building, and text the number in cell phone." He pantomimed tapping a message: "Urgent. At Fred's Café with documents for you. Come now."

The room fell silent.

"So, we just sit, drink coffee, and wait for the Mexican connection to show up?"

"Why not? That way, we know we've got the right person." Stanley grabbed a pepperoni off the last remaining slice of pizza and popped it in his mouth. "We've just been assuming it's Randolph. It could be some other congressman. All we've found is the trail of reported donations. Maybe some Arkansas congressman or woman has taken a bunch of money under the table from Swinton or Zingales or both."

Thor sat and listened as his three companions excitedly discussed how to best smoke out the owner of the Arkansas phone number. The near-death experience in North Carolina had created a bond between them, and they talked as if they were old friends who had known each other for years. He admired their willingness to take on the combined forces of government, farm, and factory, and he ached to take part in their plan.

He took advantage of a pause in the conversation and cleared his throat. "The texting idea is brilliant, guys, but it will work only as long as the bad guys think your Mexican hit man is still alive and his phone is uncompromised." The priest let the realization sink in. "If you're going to do this, you need to move very quickly."

He was gratified to see Melanie nod her head vigorously.

"Father Thor is right. We've got to get moving." She grabbed the laptop and opened up Google Maps. "Nine hours from here to Little Rock. That will give us some time to think. You guys took Stanley's rental car here, right? We'll use it, since my car is known."

She saw the surprised looks on the faces of the reporter and the professor. "You guys are in, aren't you?"

They looked at each other and smiled broadly.

"Roadtrip," James said.

"Roadtrip," Stanley replied.

As the three got up from the table, Thor blurted out, "What about me? Should I come too?"

Melanie thought for a moment. Her bearing was erect, almost regal. No wonder James and Stanley called her The Boss. He had a sudden understanding why she had never married. It would be hard to find someone who was not intimidated by her.

"No," she said. "We need someone to stay totally off of the radar screen."

She thought for a moment. "I want you and Miriam to be our backup plan. If things go badly in Little Rock, I want you to contact Miriam's source in Homeland Security. You know pretty much the whole story. Write it all down and be ready to email it to him, and to James's editor, if we give you the word or if we disappear."

"Make a video, too," the professor added. "Use my slides and tell everything you know on camera, and have something ready to post on YouTube if something happens to us." Melanie and James nodded enthusiastically. "If we go down, we're taking everyone with us."

In less than fifteen minutes, the three were gone and Thor had summoned Miriam to start on the multimedia nuclear option suggested by Melanie and Stanley. He felt better now that he had an official role to play, but he wanted to do more. Realizing that the success of the venture turned on delaying the identification of the body in North Carolina, he decided to open a new Gmail account at the public library and start sending emails to the media and the authorities investigating the case. A couple of calls from a new pay-as-you-go cell phone would not be a bad idea either. Soon, an anonymous informant would be telling the story of the Arab visitor who had been asking suspicious questions about the lake dammed outside of Highlands. To a southern sheriff, a dead Mexican might well be confused with a dead Arab terrorist, and the confusion might buy the others additional time to crash the party in Little Rock.

★ ★ ★

The following morning found Melanie, James, and Stanley sitting in different corners of a coffee shop in downtown Little Rock, lattes in hand and laptops open on the small tables in front of them. Café Libris had formerly been a used-bookstore and the walls were still lined with an eclectic mix of fiction and nonfiction titles. Any displayed book could be swapped for a newly donated volume or taken home for a dollar, but none of the titles distracted James's attention as he instant-messaged with his companions. Melanie had sent a text from the captured cell phone ten minutes earlier, and there was still no sign of an answer.

During the long drive to Arkansas, the three had explored several different strategies for approaching the Little Rock contact. The text needed to require movement on the part of their prey, and they struggled to craft a message that would draw its recipient out without creating undue suspicion. They settled on the following: *Trouble in Georgia. Envelope in Café Libris. Find Goya Sketches in art section. Contact later with instructions.*

They had worried that the unexpected text would raise alarm bells, but they couldn't come up with a better approach. If all went well and someone arrived to fetch the nonexistent envelope, Melanie would head directly to the federal building, pass through security, and wait for the person to enter. Whoever responded might be worried about someone following but would likely not anticipate that a pursuer lay ahead. James would also leave early and sit in the car outside, ready to track elsewhere if the federal building was not the respondent's destination.

Stanley would stay behind in the coffee house, watching the disappointed envelope hunter and taking discreet pictures with his cell phone.

Fifteen minutes after the text was sent, a middle-aged woman in an expensive gray skirt and white cotton blouse walked into the café and slowly approached the counter. While she ordered her drink, she looked carefully around, first at the handful of occupants of the tables and then at the wall of art books to her right.

I'll bet that's her. Melanie messaged her companions and kept her head down. *I'm going to the courthouse. If she doesn't look for the envelope, text me and I'll come back.*

The attorney was two blocks down the street and three blocks from the federal building when she got a text from James. *It's her.*

Melanie walked quickly to the federal building and passed through security. She meant to follow the woman to her office, and that could be accomplished most discreetly if she were the first through the line and was studying the elevator directory when her quarry finally appeared. Melanie could step into the elevator with the woman and act pleasantly surprised when it turned out they were going to the same floor. If the woman left the café and walked elsewhere, then James would tail her and text the location.

Melanie sat on a low couch in the foyer of the building and held her phone in her hand. The cool marble and high ceilings reminded her of the courthouse in Clarkeston, where she had spent a tumultuous year clerking for one of the most famous judges in US history. She would forever associate the unforgiving stone of old federal buildings with her first murder case.

On her way to you, James texted.

She smiled at the message and looked up at the smartly dressed woman entering the building with a look of consternation on her face. She was maybe forty, striking dark hair framing a face where the glamour of high cheekbones was offset by an almost juvenile choice of makeup. Melanie had seen this before in the South: the sight of that first wrinkle triggering an overreaction that everyone noticed except the cover girl. It was a pity, because she had a killer figure.

Melanie turned to study the building directory and a few moments later slipped easily into the elevator with the unsuspecting object of her pursuit. They both got off on the third floor, and the prosecutor paused to sip from a stained ceramic water fountain to let the woman pass her and head down the long hallway. At the end of the corridor was the office of senator Elbert Randolph. The woman disappeared past a pair of heavy walnut doors into his chambers.

Ten steps later, Melanie entered and greeted the senator's receptionist with a broad smile. "I'm sorry," she said, "but was that Senator Randolph's wife who just came in?"

The young man's eyes widened, and he shrieked. "Oh God, no! That was Sharon Williams, the chief of staff." He started to explain why Melanie's apparent confusion was so humorous, but then he repositioned the black-frame hipster glasses on his face and asked in a rather singsong voice how he could help.

"Well," she explained, "that's quite a coincidence, because I'm here to see Ms. Williams." When he looked at her funny, she added, "Obviously, for the first time."

"Do you have an appointment?" He pushed his spectacles down and studied the computer screen.

"No," she confessed, "I don't, but I'm quite certain that she'll want to talk to me."

"What's your name?" He put his hand tentatively on the phone.

She smiled sweetly. "Just tell her that I sent a text about twenty minutes ago, and I just missed meeting her at Café Libris."

He looked doubtful but placed the call anyway. He looked up in surprise and nodded his head after he passed along Melanie's verbal calling card. "She'll see you right away. Just follow me."

He led the prosecutor down a short hall to the left of his desk. Just past a beveled wooden door embossed with the senator's name, the receptionist turned and ushered her into a spacious office dominated by a large glass desk and conference table. The woman with the thick foundation and unnaturally red lips stood in the corner, arms across her chest, eyes flashing in confusion as Melanie sat down on a small sofa without invitation and suggested to the receptionist that he was now free to leave.

Williams glared but nodded her dismissal of the young man and waited to speak until the door was shut. Her voice lacked any trace of a southern accent, any trace of an accent at all. Despite her deep Georgia roots, Melanie could do this, too, wipe away childhood and present a generic front to an adversary.

"Who the fuck are you?" Randolph's aide-de-camp slipped behind her desk and sat with her arms crossed, rocking nervously back in her chair.

"Let's talk about that with the senator." Melanie smiled and flicked a piece of lint off the top of a pant leg. "All you need to know right now is that I have a phone that used to belong to a rather violent Mexican friend of yours."

"I don't know what you're talking about," she said.

"Oh, I think you do." Melanie leaned slightly forward. "You see, your guy has been following me and a friend of mine. He has two numbers on his speed dial, yours and his boss's in Sabines, Mexico. And neither he nor his boss are people that you really want to be associated with, Ms. Williams." She paused. "And these are certainly people that the senator does not want to be associated with." She paused again. "That's why we all need to sit down together and have a little talk about the cotton and textile markets. Me and my friends, and you and the senator."

More than a hint of panic seeped into the chief of staff's eyes. "I'm sorry, but he's down in Texarkana checking out flood damage."

Melanie had read about a storm that had troubled the region the previous week. "Well, he'll need to come back, then. We can wait until tomorrow afternoon for our meeting."

"I'm afraid that's impossible." She shook her head decisively. "He's scheduled to leave straight from there to Washington."

"Oh," Melanie laughed, "it's very possible."

She stood up and prepared to leave. Years of practicing before some of the toughest federal judges in the country had made impromptu responses second nature.

"You *really* do not want me taking my story to the media or to the Justice Department, do you?" Melanie said. "Think just for a moment about what your Mexican buddies have done. If you want to keep this all under wraps, you'll get the senator back here by tomorrow. Let's say we all get together around two?" The prosecutor put on what her colleagues called her "bad-news happy face," the deceptively cheery expression she adopted when informing a defense attorney that the best deal the government could offer was life without hope of parole.

She stared sweetly at Williams until she saw a tiny nod of assent.

"Excellent!" Melanie said enthusiastically. "See you tomorrow!"

XXXI.

KNOTS

Stanley shook his head in amazement as Melanie recounted her meeting with Senator Randolph's chief of staff. She had been supposed to follow the woman, identify her office and her name, then retreat to discuss the next logical move with James and him. Instead, she had freestyled her way into a meeting with the senator himself. A meeting that would take place in less than twenty-four hours.

"I saw an opportunity," she explained with a shrug. "We need to act quickly, because once the body in North Carolina is identified, our options start shrinking."

"Okay," the professor asked, "just what are our options?"

The three companions sat in the corner of a steak house with a coach lantern and rough-sawn wood motif on the outskirts of Little Rock. Stanley and James had had the rental car ready and waiting outside the federal building when Melanie emerged, and they had driven quickly away from the downtown area to a commercial cluster on the bypass that housed their anonymous chain hotel and a number of mediocre restaurants. No one had followed them, and they had little fear of being recognized so far away from the scene of their covert downtown operation.

"Well," she sipped a frosty mug of beer and pitched a peanut shell on the floor, "a lot depends on how we read the senator tomorrow. If he's smack in the middle of a conspiracy to bribe the WTO and kill off everyone who knows about it, then we have no choice but to run to the Justice Department and duck for cover."

"I thought you said that we don't have enough to prosecute him," James asked.

"We don't." Melanie shook her head. "We've got nothing on him except his voting record on the subsidies and an old friendship with Swinton, who happens to sell his cotton to Zingales, who we suspect is behind the Mexican gunman. Even if we had subpoena power, I doubt these people are sloppy enough to have left any significant paper trail. I've got nothing to bring a case with, but that's not the point."

She took another sip and continued. "If the senator is the real bad guy and he knows that we've told everything we know to Justice, then he won't dare touch us. It would be an admission that we were onto something. My career might be in the shitter if we tell the story of our little adventures, but I don't think that he'd take out a contract on any of us. It'd just be too dangerous and really wouldn't get him anything."

"What if the senator is clueless, and it's Williams who's calling the shots?" Stanley still had not decided whether he was going to attend the meeting with the senator the next day. At this point, he was still anonymous. If he stayed in the rental car while Melanie and James confronted the senator and his chief of staff, then he could skip back to California unnoticed and unthreatened by any physical or political retaliation. On the other hand, he'd flown to Spain and Switzerland, been shot at, and spent the night on a ledge overlooking a roaring waterfall. He had some skin in the game, as Warren Buffett was fond of saying, and he wanted to see the story through to the end. Most of all, he found it hard to imagine letting Melanie and James walk alone into Randolph's office with only their wits to protect them.

"And Williams might not have ordered the deaths of Diana, Jacob, and Brenda," James interjected. "That could have been Zingales acting on his own."

"Maybe," Melanie replied, "but think about it: why does she need to be on the dead man's speed dial?"

The waiter laid down a plate in front of each of them, well-scored cuts of beef sizzling on stainless-steel platters, and James ordered another round of beer. All three cut into their steaks and were surprised to find that the chef had managed to achieve the proper level of pink in each portion.

"I've been thinking," James said after taking a bite of his porterhouse, "about what we want from the meeting. Number one, we don't want to be looking over our shoulders for the rest of our lives. We're on the radar screen of some really bad people, and I think Melanie is right in thinking that we've got to get the story out in such a way that killing us makes no sense."

He speared a piece of meat and marinated it in the juices collecting in the corner of his plate. "I also agree that unless the senator or his aide wants to confess, we're never going to have enough hard evidence to convict anyone. And if we pushed Justice for a full-blown investigation, then all of the lizards are going to crawl back under their rocks and we'll never get the whole story."

"So, what do we do?" Stanley asked. "We've got the phone. Don't we sort of have them by the balls?"

"We got them by *a* ball," the journalist responded cautiously, "and I think that we should give it a good hard squeeze." He sat back and focused his attention on his co-conspirators. "What if we make a deal with Williams and the senator? What if we offered to say nothing to the FBI or Justice in return for some kind of an affidavit spelling out what happened to Diana, Jacob, and Brenda? We've pretty much pieced together the rest of the story. We've got motives for the killings, but we've got no details. We don't even know where Diana and Jacob are buried. If we knew the location of their bodies and knew how they died, then I could publish one hell of a story."

Stanley, whose academic work had familiarized him with the need to authenticate data, understood immediately. "If we have an affidavit that correctly identifies the location of the bodies, then it's self-validating. It becomes the spine of the whole story, and you could lay out everything we know about the bribe, the WTO, the subsidies, and the Mexican textile connection. The whole thing will hang together, and your editor will let you publish."

James nodded and smiled at his friend. "We'll have to promise not to name the senator and Williams or they won't cooperate, but I could make it clear in my story that the source of the information is 'a senior legislative staffer.' Williams might be willing to cooperate as long as the story that gets told is untraceable to her."

"It's a nice trade," Stanley said thoughtfully. "You get your story, and that story essentially immunizes us because it reveals the crux of what we know. Any action against us would blow up in the bad guys' faces. And Randolph and Williams get a sort of immunity, too, if they believe that in return for an affidavit you won't implicate them.

"You know," the professor continued, "as nice as it would be to hammer the senator, it's almost better that the corrupt legislator in your story is anonymous. Most of Congress voted for the goddamn subsidy, even after the WTO declared it illegal. Anonymity lets us tar all of Congress with the same brush. Williams might be the only one with actual knowledge of Mexican hit men, but all these fuckers were willing to sell out the whole African continent so smug bastards like Swinton can send their kids to college in new Hummers." At that moment he decided that he would accompany them the next day. He wanted in all the way.

Melanie had been sitting quietly, pressed into the corner of their booth. When Stanley finished his diatribe, she nodded and spoke. "Does the assistant US attorney get to be anonymous too?"

James smiled. "Does she want to be?"

"I have to be." She finished her beer. "A journalist can hide behind the confidentiality of his sources. I can't. If you name me in your story, then I'll be called and questioned. The senator and Williams will know that. You'll have to promise them that I won't be named in your story, if you want to convince them to give you an affidavit with details of the deaths of Diana and Jacob."

"Well," the journalist opened a pretend laptop on the table and began to air-type, "an incredibly beautiful and fearless federal prosecutor defied all odds to identify the killers."

Stanley had never seen Melanie blush before. "Too obvious," he added with a wink. "Everyone will know who it is." The color in her face deepened from cheek to cheek. "You better go with a disheveled, yet determined, former-football-player-turned-prosecutor."

"Ugh," said James. "Sounds like a bad novel."

"But safe," said Melanie with a smile.

★ ★ ★

Thor and Miriam pulled an all-nighter preparing a YouTube exposé of Elbert Randolph, Cameron Swinton, Moro Zingales, Jose Morales, and their roles (as best they could guess) in the corrupt maintenance of congressional cotton subsidies, the attempted bribery of the WTO, and the deaths of Diana Cavendish, Jacob Granville, and Brenda Harvey. They felt no need to verify sources or feign journalistic integrity. The video was an indictment, a nuclear deterrent fit for intimidating powerful and dangerous people, even if much of it was rank speculation.

The video began with Thor, deadly serious and sporting his clerical collar, introducing himself and warning the audience that they were about to see proof of a wide-ranging conspiracy to divert taxpayer money into the pockets of US and Mexican corporations at the expense of some of the poorest farmers on earth. Even more shocking, he continued, was the willingness of the beneficiaries to bribe and to kill to keep the gravy train rolling. The live-action introduction was shot by Miriam on her new iPhone and uploaded onto Thor's MacBook. The rest of the video was a mashup of photos and graphs from Stanley's PowerPoint presentation, plus other material found on the web. The capstone pieces were the stark interviews with the

Malian farmer and the Mexican factory worker. Miriam had not seen the videos before and she was still crying long after they finished playing.

By mid-morning, the finished product looked professionally polished and was ready to upload whenever necessary. Miriam had extensive experience in her job making presentations for the state insurance commissioner's office, and she was intimately familiar with the media software Thor's computer ran. The style and tone of their work was reminiscent of the "Stop Kony" YouTube videos that had been so effective in drawing attention to the plight of child soldiers in Africa. If all went well in Arkansas, then the world might never get to see their compelling mix of hard facts, intelligent guesswork, and acidic vitriol, but it was ready to deploy if their friends found their backs against the wall. They watched the eighteen-minute video one final time before uploading it to Google Docs.

"Holy shit," Thor muttered to himself, "this is a defamation suit waiting to happen."

"I don't know," Miriam leaned over and put her arm on the young priest's shoulder, "you don't actually call Senator Randolph a murderer. You just say his associates told a bunch of Mexicans to kill a US attorney, a journalist, and a professor who were investigating the prior murder of a young American couple and an English girl."

He smiled. "Maybe we should add some speculation about the senator's presence at Dealey Plaza in Dallas in November of 1963."

"Now, you're talking." She thumped him on the back. "And his secret funding of Area 51 in Nevada!"

He sighed. "You don't think we've gone too far, do you? I mean, if we have to release this, we want to be as accurate as possible."

"We've synthesized the collective wisdom of some of the smartest and bravest people I know," she replied. "If we made any mistakes, we made them in good faith."

"And we made them to save their asses."

"Amen." The video file was too large to send via email, so Miriam sent a link to the Google Docs file to Melanie, James, and Stanley. Then she downloaded it to two thumb drives. "I'll drop this one off with the editor in chief at the *Chronicle* and ask him to open it in case anything happens to James, and I'll keep one myself."

Thor thanked her and kissed her without making too big a deal of it. In the course of the night, their work had knitted them into an "us" in a way that sex, no matter how satisfying, could never accomplish. There was no doubt that making the video with Miriam had been worth missing several meetings at St. James. They were taking a chance together. They were both helping the good guys. Screw the altar guild.

After Miriam left, Thor brewed another pot of coffee and planned the rest of his day. He had resolved not to sleep until he had executed his plan to obfuscate the identity of the body now in the hands of the North Carolina authorities. If his anonymous phone calls and emails to the media and law-enforcement authorities did the trick, then rumors of a mysterious plot by Middle Eastern extremists to blow up western North Carolina dams or to poison local drinking water would soon be on the evening news. The dark-skinned man with the smashed face found in the mountains had obviously been plotting against America's most treasured freedoms.

★ ★ ★

"I still see a couple of problems," Stanley said, a nasal midwestern twang making an unexpected appearance.

James and Melanie had left the steak house with him and were walking through several acres of asphalt parking lot back to their hotel. It was a clear night, but light from the expressway, hotels, and restaurants obscured all heavenly bodies except a thin sliver of moon hanging low and yellow in the sky. The two men walked protectively on either side of her.

"First," the professor continued, "what if Williams doesn't know where the bodies are? Even if she ordered Jacob killed, that doesn't mean that she knows where they're buried. I doubt she did the dirty work herself, not with Zingales probably having a ready supply of thugs at his disposal."

James thought for a moment. "She's going to have to ask, I suppose."

"But what excuse does she have for asking? Why would she need to know? Just asking the question will probably raise all kinds of alarm bells with the Mexican connection." Stanley held out his arm as Melanie teetered on a narrow grassy area separating two parking lots. She grabbed his wrist and cursed as her heels sunk into the soft soil.

"Even if she's willing to tell what she knows," Stanley added, "she might not be willing to ask where Diana and Jacob were taken."

"We've got to have that information." James stopped as they approached the hotel lobby.

A minivan pulled up, and a family emptied out and trouped into their hotel. A little girl in a baseball cap and a superhero backpack trailed behind her siblings, struggling to pull a small plastic suitcase.

"We need to give her a plausible lie to tell," Melanie suggested. "What she needs to say to Zingales or whomever is that the feds captured the guy who was following us and he's ready to sing like a bird. That's why he's dropped off the face of the earth and he's not returning anyone's phone calls. Williams needs the location of the bodies right away so that they can be moved before he confesses and rats out everyone in the chain of command."

"That's not bad," James said.

"People are always happier to share information when they think you're trying to solve their problems."

"She'll have everyone shitting pickles," Stanley said, "if they think the Mexican dude who was chasing us is in custody."

They entered the lobby and took the elevators to their two rooms on the eighth floor.

"One other problem," Stanley said as the doors parted and they started walking down the hallway. "What if Randolph and Williams just deny everything? They are politicians, after all. The Big Lie will come naturally to them."

Melanie stopped in front of her door. "Don't worry about that." She gave them both a broad smile. "I've got a plan so clever you could pin a tale on it and call it a weasel."

The two men looked confused.

"*Black Adder*? Rowan Atkinson? No?" She shook her head and stepped forward, kissing Stanley on one cheek and James on the other before zipping her key card into the lock and disappearing with a wave over her shoulder.

The men shrugged and headed into their room, each wondering whether her lips had lingered just a little longer on the face of the other man.

XXXII

WEEVILS

Melanie, James, and Stanley arrived at Senator Randolph's office at precisely two o'clock. An hour before the meeting, Stanley had passed through security and walked around the building, carefully looking for any sign that a trap had been laid. He spent time in the lobby of each of the four floors, sitting and reading a book, listening to conversations, and watching for any unusual influx of US marshals or trim gray-suited men who might be FBI. He even entered Randolph's office and asked the intern sitting behind the reception desk for campaign literature. While the young man briefly disappeared to fetch the requested materials, Stanley took a quick look around but saw nothing unusual. He wasn't surprised. Sharon Williams really had no clear idea what they were up to. Any conspiratorial reaction from her or the senator would likely come after the meeting, not before.

The intern was expecting them and led the three down the hall to Williams's office, not the senator's inner sanctum. James shot a questioning glance at Melanie, but she looked unconcerned as they entered and found the senator and his chief of staff sitting at a coffee table. Both of them seemed surprised to see three people ushered into the room, and Williams told the intern to drag an extra chair from the corner and set it by the table. James and Stanley sat on a small sofa facing the senator and his aide, while Melanie stood by the new chair. Neither of their hosts got up or offered any of the usual politicking and hand-clasping pleasantries. Williams was overtly hostile and suspicious, the senator a mixture of curious and annoyed.

Melanie ignored Williams, glided over to the senator and extended her hand. "I'm Melanie Wilkerson, assistant US attorney for the Northern District of Georgia, and let me introduce my companions: James Murphy, investigative reporter for the *Clarkeston Chronicle*, and Stanley Hopkins, associate professor of sociology at Belle Meade College, Los Angeles, California."

He stood up cautiously and shook her hand before motioning for her to sit down. He scrutinized the two men on the sofa but offered no formal greeting. "Are you here on official business?" Randolph's eyes narrowed. "If so, I'd like to get Hank Woodard over from the US attorney's office here in Little Rock."

"That won't be necessary," she replied with a shake of her head. "At present," she explained, "but only at present, my superiors have no clue that I'm here."

"I see." He paused. "Or rather, I don't quite see." Randolph was tall and slim, still athletic despite his sixty-five years, with thinning salt-and-pepper hair. His accent was broad and palpable, but distinct from Melanie's cultured Georgia lilt, with hints of Missouri and southern Illinois rather than the deepest South. He waited for Melanie to clarify her intentions.

"If you and Ms. Williams are willing to answer a few questions for us and perhaps do us a little favor, none of my colleagues in the Justice Department need ever know that we paid you a visit."

The senator took a moment to respond. He appeared to struggle briefly with his self-control before adopting a genteel and polite tone. "Ms. Wilkerson, you're going to have to provide a few more details before we can help you. Sharon indicated to me that this was an emergency." He looked at his watch. "I'm supposed to be on a plane to Washington right now."

"Oh, I think you'll find this worth your time." Melanie stood up and walked behind her chair, putting two hands on the top and using it as a makeshift podium. "I think the best place to start is four nights ago, when the three of us were assaulted by a young Mexican man with a gun. To make a long story short, he tried to kill us but failed.

"You might wonder," she gestured to James and Stanley with her left hand, "why someone would attempt to shoot three upstanding citizens, and you might wonder why we want to talk to you about it."

Stanley watched the senator carefully as she spoke. They had decided that during Melanie's disquisition he would watch Randolph and James would watch Williams, on the theory that their reactions might provide some clue of their complicity in the conspiracy to cover up the murders of Diana and Jacob. So far, the senator appeared intensely curious, interested but not personally threatened by her story.

"We believe," she continued, "that this Mexican fellow had orders to shut us up because we've been investigating the disappearance and presumed murder of two young Americans: Diana Cavendish and Jacob Granville." Randolph held a poker face. "They were killed because they uncovered an attempt to bribe a WTO judge to rule for the United States in a case involving billions of dollars of congressional cotton subsidies paid to people like your friend Cameron Swinton."

Randolph started to object, but Melanie cut him off. "You are familiar with the cotton case, aren't you, Senator?"

"I certainly am," he roared. "It's one of the most egregious attacks on this nation's sovereignty that I've ever seen." His face reddened. "Congress helps out ailing American farmers, and then some communists in Geneva try to tell us we can't do it. No goddamn bureaucrat in Switzerland is going to tell the American government what to do."

Stanley's instinct was to cut in and argue the merits of the case and point out that the US generally benefited greatly from WTO positions, but Melanie remained calm and serene, her message on track.

"Then you can easily understand why some cotton grower in the US, or some Mexican textile firm buying cheap American cotton, might want to influence the decision."

"Maybe in the land of total theory," he conceded brusquely, "but I don't know anything about any bribe."

"And we have no proof that you do, Senator," Melanie replied, with a tight smile and a nod at his chief of staff, "but someone in your office certainly knows about it."

"What?" Williams said.

"I'll not stand for you slandering my aides," Randolph interjected and started to stand up.

"Senator, give me a moment before you decide whether I'm off base." Melanie, still poised and focused, motioned down and continued. Years of manipulating judges and juries had prepared her to deal with this small, but important, audience.

"We do have substantial evidence that an attempt to buy a WTO panelist was made, and we have substantial evidence that a photographer named Granville discovered the bribe."

Stanley suddenly thought of Elisa, alone and vulnerable in Geneva, unaware that her story was being discussed half a world away.

"Unfortunately," Melanie continued, "the people behind the bribe discovered that he was a journalist preparing to write up the whole story. He and his girlfriend, Diana Cavendish, were then kidnapped and killed in Clarkeston, Georgia, shortly after Granville arrived back from Switzerland. The killers also eliminated his connection at the WTO, an English woman who initially leaked the bribery story to Granville." She nodded at James. "Mr. Murphy here covered the Cavendish case for his newspaper and has been working on it for five years. He knows more than anyone else about her disappearance."

This was James's cue to take over. "I discovered new evidence in the case a couple of weeks ago and took it to Ms. Wilkerson. We started asking questions, following up leads and making some serious headway, when all hell broke loose. My house was burglarized, a tracking device was planted in Melanie's car, and three days ago, an attempt was made on our lives."

"This is all quite disturbing," the senator cut in and scowled, "assuming it's true. But I'm afraid I still don't understand why you're all here." He looked directly at Stanley and furrowed his brow. "Especially this fellow who's trying to stare a hole through me. What's his story?"

"I'm a sociologist," Stanley said with a grin. "I'm just here to watch you all interact."

"Good question!" James ignored the comment and addressed Randolph. "We're here to get an explanation why our investigation of the disappearance of Diana Cavendish put us on someone's hit list."

The senator's patience finally ran out. "Well, you can get the hell out of here, then, because I have no goddamn clue." Stanley found him hard to read. If Randolph was being disingenuous, then his anger effectively masked it.

"Perhaps you don't," James conceded, "but we're quite sure that Ms. Williams does."

The senator turned to his aide and gave her a dangerous look.

"They're lying," she spit out. "I have no idea what they're talking about."

"Senator," Melanie's firm and commanding voice drew all attention to her, "we have in our possession the cell phone owned by the man who tried to kill us. It is a cheap burner that's been used to call only two numbers. The first connects to a phone bought in Sabines, Mexico, the home of a massive textile factory run by a particularly nasty fellow named Moro Zingales, who turns out to be very close to your buddy Cameron Swinton."

"He's not my *buddy*," Randolph responded with a snort. "We might belong to the same country club and, hell yeah, I see the bastard all the time, but he's been a pain in my ass ever since he struck out with the bases loaded and lost us the conference baseball championship our junior year in high school!"

Melanie acknowledged his tirade with a polite nod and pulled the cell phone out of her pocket. When the senator's eyes finally fixed on it, she continued in deliberate fashion. "The second number in his phone goes to Sharon Williams." She pressed her thumb down on the phone pad and a moment later a muffled ring could be heard coming from a purse on the floor next to the chief of staff.

The senator's aide turned white. "It's a trick," she exclaimed, "they've gotten my number and programmed it into that phone. We don't even know where that phone came from!"

Stanley watched Randolph closely out of the corner of his eye. The senator got up from the sofa and made his way over to his desk. He sat on it with a casual air but made sure that his right hand was resting on its edge. The longest finger on his hand snaked around to the underside of the overhang and appeared to caress something textured. A panic button? Was he preparing to summon security?

"Sharon," Randolph eventually said in an even voice, "why would a prosecutor, a journalist, and a professor band together to appropriate your cell number and try to frame you?"

Williams had a wild look in her eye, like a child cornered by a large and unfriendly dog. Her lower lip quivered, but no sound passed over it.

"And, by the way," he added with a malevolent nonchalance, "did you start dating Cameron before or after he divorced Sally?"

"How did . . . ?" Williams's voice trailed off.

"Darlin'," the senator responded with a shake of his head, "you know how small this state is." He dipped his head toward Melanie. "I think you need to tell the nice prosecutor lady what you know and assure her that I'm not part of whatever you and Cameron have been cooking up."

Stanley watched Williams give her boss a panicked look while he continued to finger the button under his desk. If the aide threw Randolph under the bus, then Stanley had no doubt that a squad of security guards would be rushing in to carry her away. The look on his face was an undisguised threat.

"Yes, Senator," she said in a small defeated voice. "I'll explain to them."

Over the next hour, Melanie and James peppered Williams with questions, and slowly a story emerged, although it was clear that the aide was obfuscating her role in any violence.

She admitted to knowing about the WTO bribe, claiming that Swinton had bragged to her about the plan and his ability to distance himself from the attempt by calling on Zingales, the sole buyer of his cotton and a tough guy who knew how to make things happen. The plot had spun out of control when Zingales told Swinton that one of his men had killed a girl in Geneva and also a photographer and his girlfriend in Georgia. Apart from requesting a price renegotiation for his efforts, Zingales's thug claimed that there was nothing to worry about, but Swinton panicked and asked Williams to contact the FBI to check on the events in Clarkeston. Pretending to act on the senator's authority, she requested a note be put in the FBI file to keep the legislator's office in the loop on any developments. It was Williams who answered the phone when Melanie made her initial call to Arkansas six weeks earlier. Williams had been getting updates from the FBI, but denied authorizing the burglary at James's house or putting the tracker on Melanie's car.

"If you had no clue what was going on," the prosecutor asked, "then why was your number on his speed dial? And how did Zingales know we were investigating the Cavendish case? The FBI sure as hell didn't call up Zingales and tell him."

The room was silent. The beleaguered chief of staff was so obviously scrambling that Stanley doubted the truth of what she said next. "Cameron got really paranoid when I told him that I got a call from a prosecutor in Georgia, one who was talking to a journalist. He must have given the names to Zingales."

"That still doesn't explain your phone number in the cell."

"I already told you! Cam was paranoid and made me be the go-between. He didn't want anything traceable back to him. He gave me the phone and said that someone would be watching you guys and keeping me informed of anything that happened." She reached into her purse and pulled out her phone. "Here, take it! Check the call history—I've never used the thing."

Melanie took the phone and scrolled to the outgoing-call memory. Such histories were easily erased, but Stanley didn't want to blurt it out and put Williams on the defensive. The prosecutor handed the phone back without comment and gathered herself to make a closing argument. First, she caught Stanley's eye and then nodded her head subtly at the senator. Once Williams had begun her story, and it was clear that she was not going to implicate the senator, he had relaxed and moved his hand to a more natural position on his desk. Stanley concluded that the senator knew something, but Williams's loyalty, whether earned by fear or respect, had given them no evidence of his guilt. Melanie had predicted precisely this the evening before, when they had sketched out their strategy.

"Senator Randolph," she now turned her full attention to her host, "I'm sure that you're deeply disturbed by everything that you've heard here today, most of all your colleague's admitted knowledge of wrongdoing, even murder, and her participation in a shameful attempt to cover it up." She waited for him to acknowledge the seriousness of her statement. "I'm also sure that you understand our personal dilemma. Swinton's friend Zingales has already tried to kill us, and we currently see no reason why he won't try again to shut us up."

The senator nodded slowly in response.

"There is no point, however, in shutting us up if the story is already out," Melanie explained. "So, that presents us with two choices. First, we could go to the Justice Department with everything that we know and let nature take its course. Once we've talked to the FBI, there'd be no further point in anyone threatening us."

The senator sat very still, unable to move his eyes away from the force of nature sitting across from him.

"Or," she continued, "Mr. Murphy could write a story for his paper instead, a story that omits your name and even the names of Ms. Williams and Mr. Swinton, not to mention avoiding my name and Mr. Hopkins's too. His story would describe the bribery attempt and how Zingales's thugs killed three innocent people and tried to kill three more to cover it up.

"This is probably better treatment than your chief of staff deserves, but we are willing to proceed in this fashion if you will encourage her to sign an affidavit swearing to what she has told us here today."

Williams started to protest, but James interrupted her. "This is not an affidavit for the purposes of starting a prosecution. You can sign it Jane Doe, and then I can append my own affidavit swearing that Jane Doe is personally known to me and has sworn to the truthfulness of its contents in my presence. It can't be used in court, but it's more than sufficient for my editor to run the story. The risk to you is minimal."

Williams seemed to shrink in her chair, but her boss had no mercy as his voice drilled into her. This was a good deal, and he knew it. "Of course, she'll sign it. In fact, it will be her last official act in my office before I kick her ass out the door." His aide now looked both miserable and frightened. "She'll never work again, anywhere, if she doesn't cooperate with you."

"Are you on board, Ms. Williams?" Melanie asked.

The aide's shoulders sagged and she nodded her head.

"Good!" The senator said as he suddenly stood up. "I don't know about you, but I could use a drink." Everyone declined except Melanie. He walked to the credenza behind his desk, poured two generous tumblers of whiskey, and handed one to the prosecutor. "I greatly admire your discretion in this case, ma'am. I won't forget it."

Melanie nodded and took a sip. "There is one more thing. It's critically important to both James's story and the peace of mind of the parents of Diana Cavendish and Jacob Granville that we know where their bodies are buried. We were hoping, Senator, that Ms. Williams could make a discreet inquiry in that direction and include the answer in her affidavit."

"I don't know anything about that!" she protested. "I found out way after it happened!"

Melanie turned and faced her. "I really hope for your sake that's true, but you do know who to ask. You must find out the location of the bodies, and as soon as we know, we'll confirm their location." The prosecutor then suggested that Williams contact Zingales and tell the story she had fabricated the night before, that the Mexican assassin was in custody and ready to sing. Williams could claim that an anxious Swinton was willing to move the bodies in a hurry before Zingales's assassin confessed and they were discovered.

"Is he really in custody?" the senator asked anxiously. One talkative thug could destroy the delicate compromise he had reached with the prosecutor.

"No," Melanie replied, "that's a convenient lie, I'm afraid."

"But what happens when he finally shows up?" Williams looked first to the senator and then to Melanie for help. For the first time, she looked almost pitiable.

Melanie stood up and motioned to James and Stanley. The two men joined her by the office door. "One of us will come back tomorrow morning and pick up your affidavit. And as for our Mexican friend, you don't have to worry about him showing up again." She smiled sweetly before she opened the door. "Ever."

XXXIII.

GRAVES

By noon the next day, Melanie, Stanley, and James were streaking over the Mississippi border and into Alabama on the way back to Georgia. Earlier in the morning, Stanley had returned to the federal building to fetch Williams's Jane Doe affidavit. The receptionist had been expecting him and handed over a sealed envelope as soon as he announced himself. Neither the senator nor his aide were present, and Stanley spent ten minutes in the foyer of the office reading the document and assuring himself that Williams had kept her promises. The affidavit told a decently complete story of the attempted WTO bribe and the deaths of Cavendish and Granville without mentioning the senator or his chief of staff or Cameron Swinton by name. When Stanley finally walked out of the building, he gave a thumbs-up to his friends waiting in the rental car while he walked across the street to a Kinko's, made a copy of the affidavit, and mailed it to Thorsten Carter in Clarkeston. Ten minutes later, the trio was cruising out of town at seventy miles an hour, laughing and carrying on like bank robbers who had just pulled off the heist of the century.

Once the relief of their escape from Little Rock began to subside, Melanie looked over her companions. James was driving, and Stanley rode shotgun, trying in vain to find something other than country or Christian on the radio. They made an interesting pair. Each was good-looking in his own way: The handsome professor carried some extra pounds he could do without, but he looked fit enough to climb the nearest mountain and burn them off. The journalist was wiry and ruddy, with a kind and expressive face. The two men seemed to get along well together, and that added to their attractiveness, as did the absence of huge sprays of testosterone marking their respective territories. If she were asked to choose between the two, she had to lean toward James. They shared something that she could not quite put her finger on.

"I hate to remind you guys, but we have to make a stop on the way back to Clarkeston." Stanley turned in his seat and James glanced in the rearview mirror as she spoke. "We need to make sure that Williams isn't lying to us about where to find Diana and Jacob."

Stanley groaned. "You don't mean that we should open . . . ?" He turned down the radio and shifted uncomfortably in his seat.

"No," she said, equally disturbed by the image of five years of decomposition, "but we should check and see if the container is there."

The affidavit described the location of the bodies with some precision and revealed the cold-blooded efficiency of the hit men who had killed Diana Cavendish and Jacob Granville. The two killers had followed Jacob to Diana's apartment and shot her in the process of abducting them. Melanie guessed that one man forced Jacob to drive them in his own car away from town on the narrow road to Toccoa and then back behind an abandoned textile mill on the Oconee River. His partner must have followed in the killers' vehicle.

Melanie could imagine the two men coaxing the young couple out into the secluded parking lot and executing them in the quiet of the Georgia countryside. In a dilapidated shed built against the river side of the old mill, she would find a large oil barrel. The killers had lined it with a plastic bag and squeezed both bodies into the cylindrical metal coffin before sealing the bag and the barrel top.

Melanie had seen dozens of abandoned mills in Georgia, and she was not surprised that the bodies had gone undetected for five years. Around Atlanta, such buildings were turned into condominiums, but out in the country they lined old waterways, unused and crumbling after American textile jobs had moved to Asia. Having taken precautions to prevent the odor of decay from alerting the occasional trespasser, the killers had ensured that discovery of their victims would likely take years. Once the task was completed, they could have driven eighteen hours straight through the night and reached the Mexican border. She bet that Granville's car was being chopped for parts before Cavendish's barking dog alerted her landlord that something was wrong in her apartment.

"I think it's a good idea to check it out," James agreed. "Once I get a draft of the story ready to go, I can tell the cops that I've got a tip where the bodies are. The publicity generated by the discovery will be the perfect moment to publish the whole story. I'm going to look pretty stupid if I publish and there's nothing there! And quite frankly, if she's lied about this, how can we trust anything else that's in the affidavit? I need to be able to tell my publisher she's accurately identified the location of the bodies. Only someone with truly inside knowledge could know that, so he'll green-light me."

"Makes sense," Stanley said, "but we need to be careful when we get to the mill. I wouldn't put it past those douche bags to organize a welcoming committee."

The men were silent for a while once the decision was made, and Melanie watched as each contemplated visiting the site of the murder that had propelled one from California to Europe to Georgia while offering the other a chance to write the story of his life.

"The affidavit is silent about a couple of things that I wish we knew," the professor added thoughtfully. "How did the pictures get on the Internet and who sent the emails to Diana and Jacob's parents?"

"I've been thinking about that too," James replied as Melanie eavesdropped from the backseat. "Jacob obviously took the pictures sometime during the week before the murder. He must have had the camera with him the night they were abducted, and I'll bet you a million bucks that the killer couldn't bring himself to toss it away. Jacob bragged about that Nikon to me a couple of times, and it cost $2,000 if it cost a dime. Why not take it across the border and sell it? Collect a little bonus for the job? Who the hell in Nuevo Laredo or Sabines is going to connect the camera to two deaths in Georgia?"

"But what about the pictures?"

"Either the guy sold them on the Internet or whoever bought the camera sold them. Didn't your nudist friend in Mallorca say that they had probably been floating around for years?" Stanley seemed satisfied with the explanation and nodded while his friend continued. "And I think that we can put the emails down to Zingales trying to divert the investigation, even though it didn't turn out to be necessary."

Stanley puzzled this out for himself. "Yeah, it wouldn't be too hard to find the parents' names in the media reports of the crime, and you can usually track down email addresses if you're patient enough." He laughed. "I once found the email of a famous porn director buried in an online church committee mailing list."

Melanie and James had never heard the full story of the professor's role in apprehending the killer of the world's most famous porn star, and they were almost in Georgia before he got to the end of his tale. When he finished, Melanie told him that most public radio stations were located at the bottom end of the dial in Georgia, and he finally found a news broadcast without too much fizz and crackle.

"They might be interviewing you next week, James," Stanley teased the reporter. "I hope you won't forget the little people when you're a star."

"Shhh!" Melanie hissed, as the host of an hourly news show detailed an aborted terrorist attack in the mountains of western North Carolina.

A man, in his early thirties and likely of Middle Eastern origin, was found dead last Wednesday at the base of a waterfall outside of Highlands, North Carolina. One source indicates that he was in the area plotting to destroy a local dam or poison its reservoir. He apparently died in a climbing accident, possibly as he surveyed upstream sources of the town's water supply. A cell of Al-Qaeda operating out of Mexico has been implicated in the alleged plot. Federal authorities have opened a full investigation.

James took his eye off the road long enough to look at both Melanie and Stanley, who returned his look with a simultaneous shake of their heads.

"What the fuck?" Stanley blurted out. Then he paused and thought for a moment. "I guess the guy's face was pretty much caved in."

"He was really dark," James added, "but someone out there is really letting their imagination fly."

"And thank God for that," Melanie exclaimed, as she reached forward and grabbed their shoulders. "It bought us the time we needed in Little Rock." She leaned back in her seat and pulled out her cell phone. "I'm going to call Thor and let him know when we should be getting in. Maybe he knows more about the North Carolina story."

The priest did not answer his phone, so she sent him a text with an approximate time of arrival in Clarkeston and a link to the story she had just heard on the radio. Fifteen minutes later she received back a text that filled the car with shrieks of laughter: *Your arrival time is fine. You're welcome for the story. Yours truly, Mohammed Akbar Sanchez.*

★ ★ ★

It was almost midnight when the trio pulled onto a rocky path off a country road west of Clarkeston. The driveway to the abandoned mill ran parallel to the river, and years of erosion and disuse had rendered the entryway nearly impassable for the low-slung sedan. James crept the car slowly over the ruts until they were stopped by a cedar tree that had fallen where the driveway connected to the parking area behind the crumbling building. They had driven past the old mill twice, shining the car's headlights into the parking lot from the high ground of the road and assuring themselves that no carload of assassins awaited them. Even so, their senses were on full alert as they surveyed the scene.

As the engine cut off and they opened the doors, they were assailed by the roar of water rushing over the rock-choked mill race and the piercing whine of thousands of tree frogs and cicadas. The massive red-brick structure leaned over them to their left, the peak of its roof silhouetted against a nearly full moon. James switched the car lights off, and after a moment of adjustment to the darkness, they were able to see a way to squeeze around the foliage to the back of the building. Stanley carried a flashlight purchased twenty minutes earlier at a Walmart off the Clarkeston bypass.

Shattered glass crunched under their feet as they skirted the edge of the building and emerged on the other side of the fallen tree. The side of the mill had dozens of windows, all in rectangular series of fist-sized panes, almost all broken by storms and stone throwers over the years. Stanley went first, shining the light onto the parking lot and then scanning the far edge of the mill, looking for the exterior shed described in the affidavit. He wanted to locate their goal and get out as quickly as possible before anyone could pull in behind their car and block them in. Any sign of trouble, and he was ready to run for the river and lose himself in the woods.

"That must be it," he said, bouncing the beam of light on a corrugated-tin roof jutting from the far side of the building. He moved ahead and improved his angle. "Yeah, I think that I can even see a barrel."

He waited for the others to catch up, and together they made their way across the weed-choked pavement toward the shed. When they reached the center of the open space, Melanie heard a pane of glass break on the asphalt behind her and then a man's voice cut through the buzzing of the north Georgia woods.

"Stay right there and don't move."

Melanie instinctively put her hands on her head even though the voice had not asked her to do so. The men seemed to contemplate fleeing but then followed suit and turned around with their hands held high. Hoping to see a night watchman or a curious county sheriff, she instead encountered the rigid form of a man holding a semiautomatic assault rifle. Sharon Williams stood at his side, arms crossed over her chest and looking anxiously from her companion to the three people who had disrupted her life in Little Rock.

"Mr. Swinton, I presume—"

"Shut the fuck up, bitch!" Swinton yelled. "I'm doing the talking here, not you goddamn left-wing pieces of shit." He raised the rifle and sighted it in the middle of Melanie's forehead. When James took a step forward, he swung the weapon toward the journalist. "Do it," Swinton said in an even voice, redirecting his aim but keeping an eye on Melanie. "Be a hero."

James stepped back and Melanie thought that she could see Swinton smile. "That's what I thought. You're more comfortable in front of a computer than a gun, aren't you?"

Swinton lowered the heavy firearm, but kept it pointed at his three captives. A self-satisfied grin pasted on his face, he tilted his head toward his girlfriend. "Put the duct tape on 'em. Arms behind. Start with the newspaper prick."

A moment later, Melanie felt her wrists being tightly bound behind her back. When Williams finished with their arms, Swinton ordered her to wrap the tape several times around their ankles. There was nowhere to run. The parking lot was large and offered no cover. Swinton's attention never wavered from his prey. Trying to escape would be suicidal.

When they were finally bound, Swinton swaggered behind them and gave each a vicious kick behind the knees, dropping them to the ground. Stanley fell awkwardly and cut his face on a piece of glass. Melanie entertained a fantasy of him secretly grabbing a shard and freeing himself, but Swinton hovered closely overhead and yanked the professor up to a kneeling position as his face bled profusely from a long gash in his forehead.

"Any last words before I send you all to hell?" Swinton said, the tone of his voice suggesting, strangely, that he expected a response.

She considered asking how the Arkansas couple knew that they would be coming directly to the mill, when she remembered her own promise made in the senator's office to Sharon Williams: *You must find out the location of the bodies, and as soon as we know, we'll confirm their location.*

James made the first effort at distraction. "Cameron, are you a Baptist?"

Melanie could see the cotton planter lay the barrel of his rifle against the former deacon's temple and smile. Williams stood behind him, eyes wide open, fascinated by her lover's exhibition of power. "Good guess, comrade, although it doesn't take a rocket scientist to guess that about a farmer from Arkansas."

The reporter spoke quietly. "What would your pastor think about this?"

Swinton gouged the gun sight slowly into James's cheek, leaving a jagged and bloody line running across the right side of his face. The reporter took the punishment silently and managed to look up into his antagonist's eyes. "And what would Jesus do? Isn't that what we're always supposed to ask ourselves?"

Swinton grabbed the rifle barrel, pivoted and brought the stock down, striking a glancing blow on the head of the speculative theologian. "Jesus would fuckin' kill your ass! All three of you! You think he's on your side? Trying to rip down the United States and hand it over to the World-Fucking Trade Organization? You'd like to see every one of our freedoms handed over to those left-wing pinheads in Geneva, wouldn't you? Cheer while they fuck the American farmer right in the ass, wouldn't you?" He raised the rifle butt again and smashed it down on the journalist's right cheekbone. If James had been conscious for Swinton's tirade, he wasn't any longer.

The cotton planter brought the weapon quickly to his shoulder and pointed it at James's head. "And you can be the first to go."

"Wait!" Melanie shouted and ripped her knees up as she scuffled across the asphalt toward Swinton. "I don't give a fuck what Jesus would do, but I do care what a rational Cameron Swinton would do, and you need some more information before you fuck yourself in the ass."

He turned to her and gave her a curious look. "What you got, sweetie? Do you think your begging is going to save him?"

"No." She kneeled as straight as she could and looked him unflinchingly in the eye. "But it might save you." She paused to make sure that she had his full attention. "Reach into my back pocket and pull out my smart phone. There's something you need to see before you do anything stupid."

He trained the rifle on her chest. "Is this some kind of trick?"

"Yeah," she managed an impressive level of sarcasm, despite the shards of glass chewing at her kneecaps, "I'm about to leap up and drop-kick your balls." She rolled her eyes at him and spat. "Just pull out my fucking phone and watch a little video that you star in."

Swinton looked first at his companion. Williams shrugged and accepted the gun from him as he reached behind the attorney and grabbed her phone. He swiped the screen. Melanie told him her access password and directed him to the email she had received two days earlier from Thorsten Carter.

"Click on the link in the message and watch the video. If anything happens to us, what you see will be immediately posted on YouTube, with an alert to every major media outlet in the country. We're not idiots." For a wild moment, she thought that she had overplayed her hand. If Carter's email address made his identity obvious, then all four of them might soon be dead. As Swinton accessed the video and started watching, her shoulders slumped with relief as she remembered his account name, an obscure homage to ancient *Saturday Night Live* episodes that would not identify him: joeepiscopo@gmail.com.

After a minute of watching, Swinton turned and wandered away, eyes glued to the phone, muttering under his breath. She could barely see him in the corner of the parking lot, but she imagined that Thorsten and Miriam's go-for-the-throat exposé was engendering both dread and rage. The young couple had named the senator, Swinton, and Zingales as deliberate coconspirators in bribery and murder plots, laying out the inexorable logic of their findings. The priest hadn't labeled it the nuclear option for nothing.

When the clip was done, Cameron walked to the far edge of the parking lot, threw the phone in the river and took the gun from Williams. He walked purposefully to Melanie.

"Getting rid of the phone won't make the video go away," she said as calmly as she could manage into the barrel of the gun.

"No, but it makes me feel better." And with that, he backhanded the attorney across the face and kicked Stanley in the stomach, leaving both of them prostrate on the pavement. He pulled his leg back to kick the professor in the face, but he restrained himself with an effort and swore loudly. He kicked a broken bottle and cursed again as it skittered across the parking lot. "Fuck me!" he yelled as his foot lashed out at a clot of crumbled asphalt. "Fuck me!"

He suddenly turned and took three quick steps away from his inert antagonists and then stopped with an abrupt crunch of gravel and glass. He breathed audibly, controlling himself with an effort. "Remember to keep your side of the bargain in the reporter's story. He doesn't identify me or Sharon. If he does, then we've got absolutely nothing to lose and I swear to God this won't be the last time you see me. You got it?"

Both Melanie and Stanley grunted their assent and Swinton once again began walking away. Sharon Williams stood staring at the three people lying unmoving on the pavement, until her lover called without a glance backward: "Are you comin' or not?"

XXXIV

COLUMN-BARIUMS

S tanley sat at his kitchen table, checking his email and wondering what to do for supper. The refrigerator hummed noisily in the corner, and he saw that its vibrations had rotated the vase containing the remains of Angela and Carrie slightly to the right. Since his return from Georgia, he had moved them from the laundry room to the top of the fridge, where they oversaw his evening's activities: cooking, drinking wine, and listening to random French songs from the forties and fifties on YouTube. A ping drew his attention back to his laptop, and he saw that James Murphy had sent him an email with an attachment. Five days after the attack at the old mill, the reporter had finally finished his story.

James had remained unconscious while his two companions managed to scrape away the duct-tape bindings that held their hands behind their backs. Once free, they lifted the journalist by the armpits, dragged him back to the rental car, and drove directly to the hospital. By the time he was admitted, he had regained consciousness and was complaining of a massive headache. They had all been treated for cuts and bruises, but James's concussion and fractured cheekbone had proven to be the only serious injuries. The next morning, he convinced a skeptical doctor to discharge him, and he was ready to write. Thor and Miriam picked him up at the hospital entrance, and Stanley, exhausted from sleeping in a chair in the journalist's room, gave his friend and the priest each a warm hug, kissed Melanie Spanish-style on both cheeks, and headed to Hartsfield Airport for a flight back to Los Angeles.

The professor clicked on the attachment without paying much attention to the contents of the email itself. He read the draft of the newspaper article slowly, savoring every twist and turn of the story, marveling at how James managed to indict the entire US legislature without mentioning Senator Randolph specifically or implying that he was part of the plot to bribe the WTO in the cotton case. An anonymous cotton planter and legislative aide were clearly implicated in the bribery plot and the murderous cover-up, but no member of the reading public would be able to guess the identities of Swinton and Williams. Stanley was glad. He had little doubt about the sincerity of the Arkansan's final threat in the mill parking lot. Swinton truly would have nothing to lose if he were exposed. In an ideal world, he and the senator's former chief of staff would be spending the rest of their lives in prison, but Melanie, aware of the ridiculous liberties she had taken in the investigation, was not willing to chance a prosecution based only on the encounter in the parking lot. Williams's affidavit was inadmissible in court, and although the cell phone was hard evidence, the numbers contained in it were merely circumstantial proof of unrecorded conversations.

Nonetheless, Melanie seemed confident that justice would be done, although she was short on details.

Stanley smiled when he saw that he was mentioned by name and laughed when James described his exploits in Europe and the North Carolina mountains as if he were some kind of megaspy. Melanie was written up as daring, brilliant, and innovative, but her identity was cloaked in the guise of an overweight, middle-aged male prosecutor from an unnamed midwestern state. James would have been happy to turn her into a media sensation, but she had no interest in returning to the spotlight. Her star turn as runner-up Miss Georgia twenty-five years earlier had satisfied her desire for fame, not to mention that no one in the Justice Department would be very happy with her creative approach to criminal problem solving. She preferred to keep her job rather than become the next cookie-cutter blond "expert" on Fox News.

After a moment's thought, he realized that he shared her desire to avoid publicity. He had no classes to teach until August, still two months away, and California still felt weird. He clicked off the story and returned to James's email. After reading it carefully and clicking on the link his friend had included, a plan began to form in his head. By the time he closed his laptop and looked back up at the vase, he knew what he was going to do.

★ ★ ★

Timing is everything, James thought to himself with a shake of his head. Sondra had just left his office, having explained tearfully that her relationship with Brother Armstrong was over and she no longer had any desire to be parted from her husband. She claimed that the revelation of her renewed affection had come suddenly, romantically, like a love bomb dropped by the enormous hand of God out of a clear blue sky. Unfortunately for her, the revelation arrived two days after his story of the cotton case had gone viral in the national media and two weeks after she had not-so-tearfully announced that her lawyer had drawn up divorce papers. Had she arrived before the story had broken, he might well have taken her back. As it was, he had seldom seen a more transparently insincere conversion. Oddly, the encounter left him feeling cheered. He realized that at some point during the last few weeks, he had ceased noticing the dull ache of her absence and betrayal. With a pleasant sense of surprise, he found himself looking forward to signing whatever papers her lawyer had prepared.

Since the story had been published and the media firestorm had begun, he had also gotten a call from Melanie. She announced that she was paying a visit to Clarkeston and wanted to introduce him to an old friend. She would be arriving within the hour. He looked at his watch and turned off his cell phone. Interviews were occupying nearly all his free time, and the next request could wait for a while. He walked to the coffee shop where he was to meet her, ordered a latte, and graciously accepted the congratulations of the occasional customer who had seen him on television answering questions about the sensational murders of Diana Cavendish and Jacob Granville.

The attorney arrived fifteen minutes later, elegant as ever, a slightly nervous smile tracing her generous red lips.

"Hiya." She kissed him on the cheek as he stood up. "How does it feel to be a media darling?"

He tossed his cup into the garbage, and he put his arm lightly on her back as they walked out of the café and into the bright June sunlight. "I don't know. It's pretty weird. Have you seen any of the interviews?"

She nodded as they got into her car. "Yeah. A couple."

"I feel more like a professor than a reporter. No one seems to understand the importance of the subsidies part of the story. They want to hear about the details of the murders and attempted murders, mountain adventures, and all that stuff. I have to force the conversation back to US cotton planters, congressional subsidies, and the downward pressure on international cotton prices. Two dead bodies in an abandoned mill seem to be way more important to CNBC than millions of impoverished farmers in Chad and Mali. I end up sounding like an econ professor, not an investigative reporter."

"You sound great," she said seriously. "This is exactly what they need to hear."

"I suppose, but it's really frustrating." He shook his head and they drove in silence for a minute. "The CNN interview was the worst. For them, the big story was a legislator trying to bribe a WTO panel. Sure, that's huge. I get it! But what's behind the bribe? The whole fucking Congress giving away billions of dollars a year and still defying the decision of an organization it begged the world to create."

"NPR did a little better." She smiled and straightened his crooked shirt collar. "Don't get frustrated! It's an amazing story, and you're doing a great job. Having all this come out of

Clarkeston is unreal, and you should be really proud of yourself.
You've got your own voice. You don't sound like some slick New
Yorker expecting the world to be bedazzled by his scoop. You're
really authentic and thoughtful." She laughed as they slowed in
front of a large wood-frame house in the oldest neighborhood
in Clarkeston. "And that little North Carolina mountain lilt in
your voice doesn't hurt one bit."

He laughed. "I admit that it does feel good to have written
at least one big story in my life."

"There'll be others," she said with a curious certainty as
they pulled into the driveway.

James knew the neighborhood well but not the particular
dwelling where Melanie had brought him. In years past, all of
the town's wealthiest citizens lived along these streets just west of
downtown Clarkeston, but now the population was mixed, some
living in expensively refurbished antebellum mansions complete
with shining pillars and porticoes. Others, unable to modernize,
did the best they could in shabbier circumstances. The house of
Melanie's friend was somewhere in between. It was large, with
an inviting wraparound porch, but it needed a paint job and the
driveway was so overgrown with grass that James could not tell
whether it had originally been gravel or asphalt.

Melanie knocked on the door, and it was opened by a
middle-aged woman with a beautiful face and a riot of thick
dark hair, streaked lightly with gray. She enveloped Melanie in a
warm embrace and then reached her hand out to James. "I was so
glad when Arthur said the two of you were coming to visit!" She
introduced herself as Suzanne and then cried out to her husband
to bring some tea as she led them to a comfortable, but mismatched, collection of furniture on the side porch of the house.

A lean and attractive man arrived moments later bearing
a tray with a pitcher and four glasses of sweet tea. Upon seeing
Melanie, he set the tray down on the coffee table and hugged her
awkwardly before she could fully stand up.

"I couldn't believe it when you told me you were in Atlanta!"
he said. "You should have come to visit before now." His voice

was light and carefree, but his expression spoke volumes. He was connected to Melanie in some intimate way. He loved her but was not romantically drawn to her. And Melanie seemed weird and a little tentative, as if she were exorcizing some sort of ghost.

"Well, I've been crazy busy getting the office running the way I want it," she said in a sheepish voice that James had not heard before. "Arthur, I think you might have met James, whom you've recently been seeing on television." His smile broadened as his hand enveloped James's in a firm grip. "And James, I think I told you that Arthur and I clerked together for the Judge twenty years ago, but instead of running off to Washington like me, he stayed here with Suzanne and her daughter and teaches history at the college."

A look passed between the two former colleagues that James could not interpret, but there was something both ginger and comfortable in it. Suzanne noticed, too, and offered the reporter a cryptic smile as she handed him a glass from the tray. He suddenly recognized her from a story he had written on the volunteer efforts of women working at the local homeless shelter, and he asked her about her role there, while James and Melanie caught up on twenty years in an excited flurry of questions.

When they finally paused to take a breath, Melanie's expression became more serious. She looked first at James and then at Arthur. "Apart from the fact that you three are wonderful and all live in the same town and really should know each other better, I have an ulterior motive for getting you together today."

Her three friends refreshed their tea and leaned back on the sofa and the porch rocker as she began to speak. "On the way over here," she continued, "James said that this cotton business was the only big story that he'd ever write." She glanced at Arthur. "I'm thinking that he might be interested in something that you worked on when we were clerking for the Judge."

Arthur's face darkened momentarily, and he took a deep breath. "Albert Gottlieb."

James recognized the name of the notorious serial killer from the late seventies and early eighties, executed in the Georgia electric chair.

She nodded. "We had a pretty interesting year."

"That's one word for it."

"Maybe you could tell James sometime about Gottlieb's last appeal and maybe something about Averill Lee Jefferson too."

Arthur looked at her with something that could have been relief or resignation, and then glanced at Suzanne, who nodded her head gravely. "Maybe. Yeah, maybe that's a good idea." He brightened. "You do seem to understand how to tell a story."

★ ★ ★

Melanie's job involved prosecuting and punishing people who did bad things. As best she could, she tried to compartmentalize her public and private lives, tried to not be hardened by the inevitable result of a job well done—the incarceration of people who most decidedly did not want to be locked up. This was easier in the typical case, where she merely prosecuted, and juries and judges decided guilt and sanction.

As she sat in her office, two weeks after the story of the cotton case had broken wide open, she stared at a *New York Times* article and worked through her feelings about informal punishment, about just desserts delivered off the books. The story detailed the sensational murder of a prominent cotton farmer named Cameron Swinton and his partner, a former legislative aide, Sharon Williams, as they vacationed together in Aruba. In what appeared to be a gangland-style execution, both had been shot in the head while they slept in a luxury suite in the most expensive hotel on the island.

Melanie shook her head. As soon as she had read the first draft of James's story, she knew Swinton and Williams were as good as dead. She had said nothing to James, not wanting to burden him with her foreknowledge, but she had dealt with violent criminals for two decades, and there was no way that

Moro Zingales was going to let them live. He had been named in James's article, and although the journalist had cleverly hidden the identities of his informants, she knew that Zingales would realize who was leaking information. After all, Williams had contacted him in order to discover the location of the bodies, and that request had surely signed her death warrant. Melanie knew it at the time, and the feeling was reaffirmed as soon as she saw the published article. Did that make her judge, jury, and executioner? Did it matter that Williams and Swinton themselves had been eager to put a bullet in her head? All to protect a corrupt farm subsidy?

She sighed, closed her laptop, and looked out the window. She'd survive her misgivings, just as she survived the idiotic cases where frat boys snorting lines of cocaine got six months in the federal pen and homeboys smoking the same amount of crack got six years. She had no misgivings, however, about the email she had just sent the attorney general in Washington, DC. It contained a link to the data entry next to the name of Jacob Granville in the FBI database and enough information about the appended phone number to lead the Justice Department straight into the chambers of senator Elbert Randolph. Sharon Williams's affidavit, the Mexican cell phone, and an annotated version of James's news story would arrive under separate cover, and she had little doubt that the ensuing investigation would be enough to topple the senator from his snug Beltway perch.

She felt good, but it was not enough. For the first time in years she craved a life outside her job. She wanted something more than law, and she had an idea where to look for it.

★ ★ ★

Father Thorsten Carter smiled as he saw Stanley Hopkins walking up the sidewalk to St. James Church carrying a blue Oriental vase in his hands. The sociology professor had called several days earlier and asked whether one needed to be a parishioner at St. James in order to inter a loved one in the columbarium in the western churchyard. Technically, the answer was yes, but the vestry had been showing Thor a bit of deference lately, and an exception had been made. James's story had mentioned the priest by name several times and assigned an essential, albeit somewhat vague, role to him. The parish's view of him was not quite heroic, but there was a real appreciation that he had helped clear the name of Jacob Granville and removed the whiff of scandal that had hung over the church for the last five years.

Thor got up and greeted Stanley in the vestibule in front of his office, gave his friend's hand a firm shake, and led him around the church and into a secluded garden separated from the neighborhood elementary school by a tall brick wall. Ten years earlier, the vestry had voted to set aside a large portion of the back churchyard for parishioners who wished to be cremated and make St. James their final resting place. Plenty of spots still remained among the azaleas, phlox, redbuds, and maple trees that shaded and colored the space. It was late afternoon and the sound of children playing floated over the wall, filling the place with life.

Thor waved Stanley around a large tree, and they found James standing next to a small hole in the ground. Stanley smiled and gave his friend a bear hug.

"This is beyond lovely," James said, "much better than my idea."

"Yeah," Stanley replied, "but you got me thinking on the right track."

Thor gave the two men a puzzled look and James explained. "I went online and found this website that lists temporary resting places for urns. Basically, you can be about anywhere in the US—well, anywhere pretty urban—and have ashes transported from columbarium to columbarium as you move around. I forwarded the link to Stanley, figuring that might be better than what he was doing."

"It wasn't quite what I wanted," the professor said to Thor, lifting the vase slightly. "They need a permanent space. I should be the one doing the moving, so I got to thinking where I would like to visit. Where would I enjoy going to? Why not Clarkeston? I'm not sure that I have a much better friend now than James, and he's not going anywhere. And you literally saved my life. I know you won't be here forever, but the town is lovely and it's always going to hold great memories for me."

Stanley gestured to the garden and turned to James. "And Angela's mother is in Atlanta. What a beautiful place for her to come and visit her daughter and granddaughter. She's out of the country now, but Thor is going to show her when she gets back."

He handed the vase to the priest.

The service of committal of remains in the Book of Common Prayer is brief and to the point, and when Thor was done reading, he slipped the vase into the small hole and covered it with a shovelful of dirt. The two other men took their turns, and then the priest marked the spot temporarily with a small wooden cross. James and Thor walked back to wait in his office while Stanley stood quietly over the freshly turned soil.

The professor knocked on the door later and offered a smile to let them know that he was okay. Thor led them several blocks away to a small pub with a shady back patio, for lunch.

The weather was warm, the beer was sweet, and eventually the conversation turned to Thor and Miriam. The priest blushed as the two older men pushed him for details and accused him of making the attractive and intelligent young woman his concubine. "What about you two?" he stammered at James, trying to deflect attention away from his own love life. "Has Sondra seen the error of her ways?"

James laughed. "Sort of." He took a large draught from his third beer. "It's as over as it could be, and that's fine. It really is." He centered the glass precisely on the cardboard coaster and paused. "In fact, I'm going into Atlanta on Friday to have dinner with Melanie and see a play."

"We could see that coming a mile away." Stanley grinned at Thor, who nodded his head vigorously. "The Boss had the hots for you from day one."

"Uh, I doubt that," the reporter blushed and struggled to find a response to the laughter. "She's easy to talk to. We have good conversations."

"Oh, God," Stanley grinned. "Are you serious? You crack me up!"

More beer and burgeoning thoughts of food. The heat of the day starting to fade. Thor felt fuzzy, a bit sloppy, in the nicest way imaginable. "How long are you going to stay, Stanley? When do you head back to California?"

The professor took a moment to reply. "I'm not going back for a while. Unlike you guys, I don't like talking to television reporters about my astounding exploits. I'm heading off to Europe again. I'm going to go to Geneva and tell Elisa the whole story. She deserves to hear it all in person, I think." He smiled wistfully and raised his glass one more time. "She deserves a nice dinner, too."

POSTSCRIPT

After the US lost the cotton case in 2009, the WTO approved massive trade sanctions against the US in favor of Brazil, the main complainant. Instead of changing its cotton-subsidy program to comply with the WTO decision, the US government chose to pay $147 million a year to Brazil, a legal bribe that allowed Congress to keep billions of dollars of cotton subsidies in place from 2010 to 2013. Tired of making the payments to Brazil, but unwilling to drop its support for cotton growers, Congress in 2014 adopted an insurance scheme in the yearly farm bill, called the Stacked Income Protection Plan, to ensure profits for American cotton growers. Brazil and impoverished cotton-producing African countries vow to fight on.